MY BROTHER'S ENEMY

A GRAYS HOCKEY NOVEL

TIJAN

Copyright © 2025 by Tijan

All rights reserved.
No part of this book may be reproduced in any form or by any electronic or mechanical means, including information storage and retrieval systems, without written permission from the author, except for the use of brief quotations in a book review.
Without in any way limiting the author's exclusive rights under copyright, any use of this publication to "train" generative artificial intelligence (AI) technologies to generate text is expressly prohibited. The author reserves all rights to license uses of this work for generative AI training and development of machine learning language models.

Edited by: Jessica Royer Ocken
Developmental Editor: Becca Mysoor
Proofread by: Amy Briggs, Paige Smith, Amy English, and Michele Ficht, and Kimberly Holm
Cover model by Paperback Model (regular paperback)
Special edition illustration by Milena Rives Illustrations
(hockey player illustration on front cover)

For those who grew up feeling invisible.

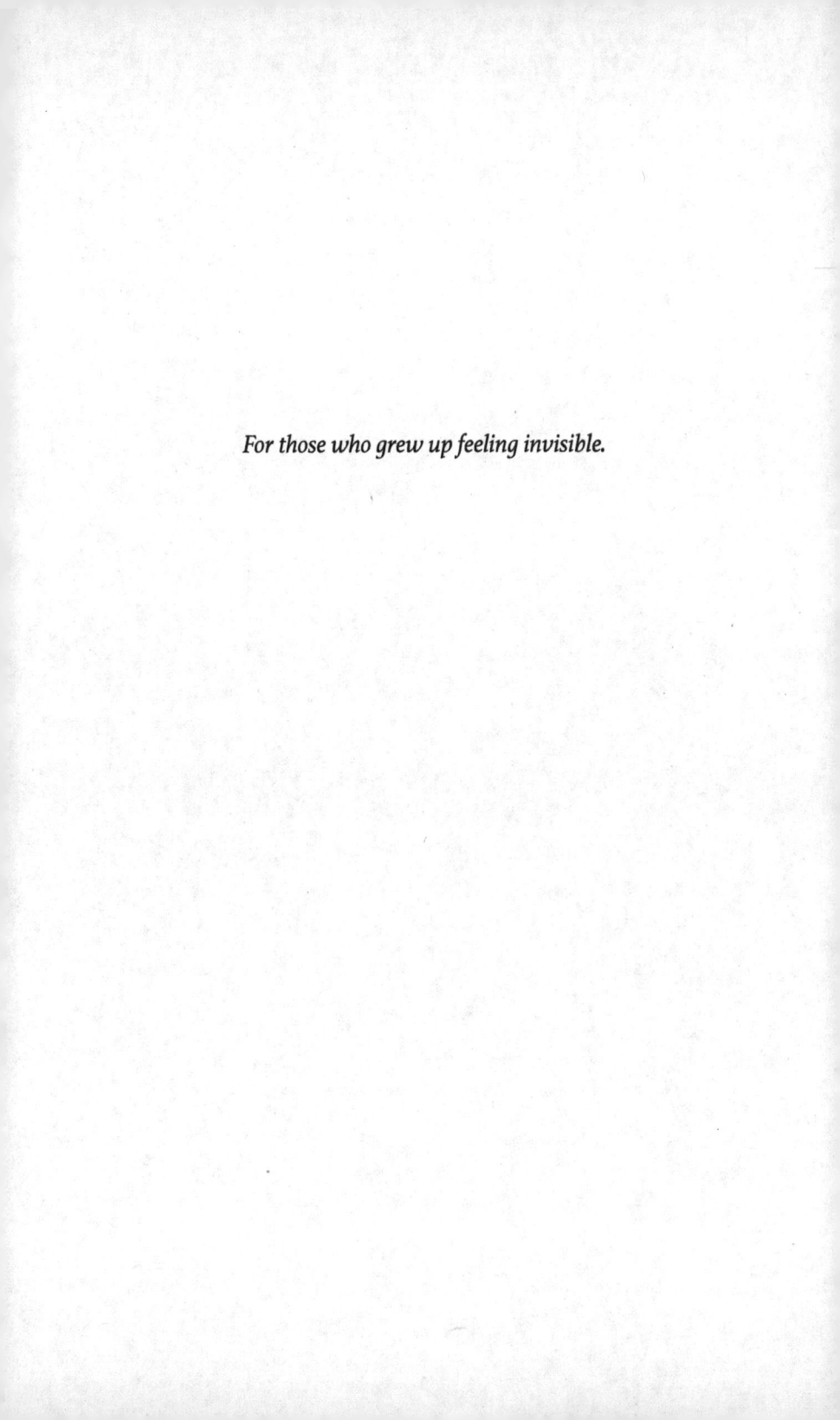

NOTE TO THE READER

No other book needs to be read before reading My Brother's Enemy.
This is a standalone with all new characters.
Also, this story does talk about suicide and suicidal ideation.

1

RAIN

Kansas City

I shouldn't have bought the gun.

What was I thinking?

I mean, I knew what I was thinking, but... *What was I thinking?*

A cold dose of reality slapped me in the face, and I slumped down.

Stupid. I was so stupid...

I sat in my kitchen, staring at the handgun on my table. Just staring at it. As soon as I got home after buying it, I'd put it there as if it might burn me.

I couldn't bring myself to touch it again—not to move it, put it away, or *fuck*, use it for the reason I bought it. I couldn't even think about that.

Shit. Shit. Shiiiiit.

My phone buzzed, and I jumped, cursing. This was ridiculous. All of it. I reached for my phone and shoved up from my seat, needing space from the gun as I answered the call.

"Hello?" That came out garbled. I cleared my throat and tried again, stronger this time. "Hello! Sorry. This is Rain." Powerful. *Attagirl.*

My name was Dylan Rain Connors. I was the third kid, following Daniel and Dane, and since my dad was already hooked on Dylan, the fact that I was a girl had no impact on his decision. He still named me Dylan, so my mom chose my middle name.

"Is this Dylan Connors?" asked the man's voice on the phone. "Sports psychologist consultant?"

"Yes, but you can refer to me as a behavioral or mindset consultant. And it's Rain, please."

I had degrees in sports psychology, but my doctorate had focused on professional athletics. These days I helped professional athletes do better. Entire teams had hired me, as well as individuals, but what nearly all of my clients had in common was discretion. They didn't want it out there that they needed a "doc" or "shrink" to help unravel whatever was stopping them from performing to their potential. It didn't matter that I wasn't either of those things. I was not their doctor, nor their shrink for their personal life.

"Can I help you with something?" I asked.

"Yes. Or so I'm hoping. You were recommended to me by a colleague, Gathaway."

Oh. Justin had helped set me on my career path. I owed a lot of good things to him. "Of course. Justin. He's a good person."

"He is, and before I tell you my name or why I'm calling, I'm hoping you'll meet with me. Dinner. I'd like to pitch something to you."

I frowned, but a call like this wasn't that unusual in my line of work.

His area code was 612, Minnesota—where I'd lived for half of my life. And he'd used Justin's name on purpose.

I already knew I was going to hear him out because of Justin, but it just so happened that I'd be in Minneapolis over the weekend for a client.

I moved to the island, picking up a pen. "Okay. Tell me when and where."

2

TYLER

New York

I woke up to my phone ringing and a hand stroking my dick. I was awake real fast after that. It was my sister's ringtone, and she would never call at five in the morning unless it was an emergency. I shoved the girl's hand off my dick—I'd stupidly neglected to call her an Uber last night—and swung my legs over the side of the bed as I reached for the phone.

"Yeah?" I grunted in greeting, knowing—goddamn *knowing*—but trying to tell myself that eerie fucking twin-vibe thing wasn't happening. There'd been another call like this, at a similar time in the morning, and Skylar and I had never been the same. That call had let us know our parents had died in a car accident.

My sister's sobs were the only thing I could hear at first.

Jesus. My heart sank.

I rose from the bed and snapped my fingers at the girl next to me.

"Ski? What happened?" My voice grew hoarse as her childhood nickname slipped out.

I hadn't been able to pronounce her name when we were little, but I'd loved to play in the snow, so I came up with Ski. Everyone else shortened her name to Sky, but I got to call her Ski. I'd once overheard her telling a boyfriend that name was reserved for her twin and only her twin.

Fuck, I loved my sister.

I covered the phone and hissed at...I couldn't remember her name. "You need to go." I turned around, starting for the closet. "Ski?" Still only sobbing on the other end. "Ski!"

Pulling open my drawer, I grabbed some clothes, but when I turned, I realized the girl from last night wasn't leaving.

She'd leaned forward, and hunger flared in her eyes. She chewed her lip, her focus on my phone. *Christ.* She wanted to overhear some gossip. And her phone was in her hand. She had it angled awkwardly, the camera lens pointing my way. She was filming me.

I growled, starting for her. "You need to go."

The girl's eyes were wide but defiant. She clutched the bedsheet, pulling it to her chin, but she sat up straighter as I closed the distance between us.

I'd been riding a wave of exhilaration and exhaustion last night after finally not only playing a home game, but winning the home game, and just *being* home after a three-game stretch away. Some of the guys on the team had gone out to celebrate, and their wives, girlfriends, and partners had joined, so it was a big party. We'd also been celebrating my buddy's birthday, so I guess I'd indulged a bit more than normal. At the end of the evening, the walk to my place had been a lot faster and warmer than enduring a car ride to wherever this woman's place was, so that had made my decision, despite breaking my rule.

Fuck. This was why I had that rule in place. *Never bring a hookup to my place.*

She'd resisted leaving last night, and my body had given in to sleep before I could be a hardass and kick her out. Now, three hours later, with my twin sister sobbing in my ear, all niceties were gone.

"Ski, hold on just a minute," I said, setting my phone down.

I glared at the girl and snatched her phone. She came alive, lunging for me with a screech. I ignored her, stepping away and putting my back to her so I could quickly go through it. I spoke as I went through her videos, her pictures—shit, she'd taken pictures of me sleeping. "You will get the fuck out. I told you to leave last night, and you refused. If I fucking have to tell you one more time, you're not going to like the consequences." I froze at a picture of my own dick on her phone.

I didn't do dick pics. Ever.

I knew it was a thing, but not for me. I was too paranoid about them being released to the press. This girl had violated my privacy. A new wave of anger crashed over me. *I don't have time for this.* Something was going on with my sister—something real fucking bad.

Every part of my body coiled tight. This girl *did not* want to keep pressing me. I deleted everything. Every goddamn picture and video from our time together. I went through her recordings and shit, deleting anything that'd been created during the time she'd been with me. This girl wasn't a problem. She was a nightmare.

Finally—fucking finally—she caught on and got moving. I watched her from the corner of my eye as she visibly swallowed, her nose wrinkling in a sneer. She threw back the sheets and stalked past me to the bathroom.

I cursed under my breath, crossing the room in two steps so I could catch the door before she slammed it. I caught it, and she gasped, twisting toward me. She began to snarl, but I had no fucks left to give. "Nope. You're not going to hide in my bathroom for the next hour or two."

Grabbing her elbow, I pulled her out of the bedroom and dragged her to the front door.

She yelled, trying to twist her arm free.

I didn't care. Not one bit.

"I need—I need my clothes, you asshole!"

I ignored her and yanked open the door.

"Hey!" she barked.

I shoved her into the hallway.

She rounded, her face red, her eyes angry. "Listen—"

The door slammed shut in her face, but I wasn't done. My two neighbors weren't currently here, and there were no cameras in this hallway, so she'd be fine for a few seconds. Marching back to the room, I swept up her clothes. Her shoes. Her purse. I did a cursory look around my place as I snapped a picture of her driver's license. She was now pounding on my door and yelling from the hallway. I still had her phone.

Crossing the kitchen, I found a glass of water on the counter. I tossed her phone into it, then opened my door and dropped the rest of her items at her feet.

"My phone—"

I slammed the door once again.

I didn't know how long it would take to ruin the phone, but I didn't want to risk it. After I figured it'd been in the water long enough, I took it out, ran a towel over it, and when it was dry, I opened the door again.

She quieted immediately, huffing, her face red. "I need my goddamn phone, you prick."

I dropped her phone into her hands, and when she got a look at my face, she edged back a step.

"If any of those pictures, audio, or videos of me get leaked online or to the press, I will slap you with a lawsuit so fucking fast, your head will spin. A buddy of mine is a lawyer, and his brother's privacy was violated by a puck bunny like you, so he has a personal vendetta against your type." I looked at her for a long moment. "I had no clue what you were about last night, but I am now wondering why my thinking was so clouded after only two drinks. Wondering if that was at your hand too?"

I didn't really believe she'd drugged me. If I did, I'd be going ballistic, but the threat was an added bonus against her.

She opened her mouth, ready to protest.

"I'm not done."

The blood drained from her face.

"Find a new drinking place. You will *not* hang out at Hook Up anymore. You are done chasing any hockey players on my team. Once I find out what's going on with my sister, I will be telling every player I know how many pictures you took of me when I was sleeping. No one will want to touch you again. Are you hearing me?"

Her bottom lip began to tremble, she jerked her head in a quick nod.

"Now get the fuck out of my building before I call security."

"I—"

I let the door slam shut one more time, then took a breath and went back to my phone. "Ski?"

My sister drew in a ragged breath. "It's about Zoey."

I was right. My twin broke my heart with what she said next.

3

RAIN

Minneapolis

It was a nice restaurant. I recognized it as my Uber dropped me off, thankfully right out front. It was mid-October and getting chillier at night. The wind didn't help, but then again, this *was* Minnesota. It could be fifty degrees one day and a blizzard the next.

Inside, there was very little light. The place seemed to be running mostly on candles, giving it a cozy and romantic atmosphere. I supposed the low lighting also allowed for more privacy, an added draw for high-end clientele.

"Ms. Connors?" A man in a business suit stepped forward from a corner as I unwrapped my scarf. He held a hand out for me. "Mal Benoit. I'm the one you're meeting."

Benoit. The name was familiar, but I couldn't place him right away. That annoyed me. I was used to knowing all the players in my professional niche.

I gave him a polite smile, a small nod. "Pleasure to meet you, Mr. Benoit."

He was a handsome man. He wore no wedding ring, but sometimes that didn't mean anything. White. Mid to older thirties. Six feet. Maybe six two? Broad shoulders. Lean waist. He had the build of an athlete. And dark brown hair he kept a little long.

As the restaurant's host led us to a table, Benoit walked in front of me, and I glanced down. I wasn't usually one to check out my potential male clients, though it wasn't that I couldn't appreciate when they looked nice, as Mal did with a youngish face and a decent jawline. He was handsome, and his eyes were shrewd and intelligent. But it was his round ass that triggered something in me.

That was a hockey ass.

I'd spent too much time with men who had similar asses. Dread took root in me, and I tried to hold it off. Mr. Benoit's rear might not indicate what I worried was coming.

Our table was in the corner, with the closest patrons five tables away, guaranteeing privacy. I wondered if he had requested this level of seclusion. Either way, I readied myself as I slid into the booth. He followed, sitting across from me.

The host left, and our server was at our side almost immediately. She brought water and asked for our drink orders. Her smile heated as she eyed Mr. Benoit. He was catnip for her. To his credit, he didn't react. He asked what I'd like to drink, and I requested coffee.

She was either interested in him because he was good looking and well-off, which was obvious, or because she knew him already. I gauged her as she went to another table where a similarly good-looking man was dining. The extra warmth was missing from her demeanor.

Okay, then. That told me she knew Mr. Benoit and *what* she knew about him made him appealing to her.

He'd been quiet, letting me look around the place before my gaze returned to him. As it did, he smiled and relaxed into his seat. "I was told you were like this." He reached for his water and paused, considering me a moment before he took a sip. "You don't miss much, do you? You scope out every detail. Is that what makes you so good at what you do?"

I measured his words, wondering if there was derision in them. I worked with mostly men. Some actively did not want women to be their equals, but I couldn't find any hint of that in Mr. Benoit. Still, I couldn't relax. I picked up my own glass of water.

His eyes sparked, noting my gesture.

Yes. He knew what I was doing, meeting him where he was. Some people did it unconsciously, matching the other person to make them feel comfortable. I did it consciously, and he was aware of this.

I'd been watching for some weakness in him but hadn't found any. I needed something that would help me categorize Mr. Benoit and prepare me for what this meeting was about.

"Is that something Justin told you about me?" I asked.

An emotion flickered in his gaze before he took another sip, then set his water back down. "No. I—"

He paused as the server returned with our drinks—along with her hopeful catnip smile. "Mr. Benoit, your bourbon. And, Ms. Connors, your coffee." She glanced my way before leaving.

She wasn't cold to me. She was merely indifferent. I was not her endgame.

I sighed and sat back. "Did you play professionally or in college? Hockey, I mean."

He sputtered into his bourbon and his eyes went wide before he schooled his features back to faint amusement. "Professional for five years." He leaned closer, the corner of his mouth lifting up. "Was it my ass that gave it away? I knew I shouldn't have walked in front of you. Though I am proud I still have it."

I didn't comment on that, instead saying, "You wouldn't give me your name before today. And I'm not a fan of small talk. Why don't we cut to the chase, and you tell me why I'm here. Please tell me it does not have to do with hockey. I don't work with hockey."

One of his eyebrows shot up. "Teams as a whole or players individually?"

"Anything with hockey. I don't do it."

He nodded but still gave nothing away. "But you know hockey. You know it very well. Don't you?"

I tensed. I wasn't a secret, but no one in my family went around telling people who I was. In the hockey world, I was considered a nobody.

When I didn't respond, he added, "You work mostly with football. American football."

I gave a short nod. Everything about Mr. Benoit told me he'd done his research thoroughly. If he knew my history with hockey, he knew about the professional football teams I'd worked with, as well as the individual players. "If you please, Mr. Benoit—"

"Call me Mal." He groaned, shaking his head. "My dad is still very much alive, and I expect him to be behind me every time you say that name."

Fine. "Why am I here, Mal?"

"You have two brothers who play in the NHL, a captain for Montreal and a center for Boston. Are they the reason you don't work in the hockey world?"

My lips parted, because *damn*. That was hella personal. That was also some serious research skills for whoever found the connection. I was estranged from my brothers and our father for a reason.

Our server approached again. Mal held up his hand, holding her off.

Irritation spiked in me. He had controlled everything about this meet.

I wasn't prepared to have him bring up my family.

"Yes, Mr. Benoi—"

"I told you—" he began. He said it nicely, but I caught a hard edge in his smile.

"To call you by your first name," I interrupted. "But I'd rather not, because I don't know you, Mr. Benoit. You have kept me in the dark this entire time, and yet you feel you have the right to bring up my family. You want to mention my brothers? Let me know that you're aware of my connection to them?" I shook my head. "I'll meet your ante using the only card I know I have. I've asked the reason for this meeting, and if you don't provide it right now, I will leave." I leaned forward. "I am good enough at my job to know that I *do not need* to be here if you're going to waste my time."

His chest rose as he drew in a breath, but then he nodded, as if coming to some decision. "You're aware that Minneapolis has two NHL teams?"

I leaned back. "I'm aware."

"Even though the Grays began a decade ago, they're still considered new to the NHL—as well as to the city itself. I represent the Grays. And you're correct, Ms. Connors. I'm aware that you worked with Philadelphia for two years before they went to the Super Bowl, and they've made the playoffs ever since. I'm also aware that you worked with Baltimore before they, as well, got to their divisional championship game. I know how many individual players you've worked with, including a certain football prodigy who struggled his first two years in the NFL before moving to a new team where he's their starting quarterback, and they've won their last five games."

He dropped all pretense, leaning forward. "I have a team with the talent, the right coaching staff, and good upper-managerial support. We have a motivated owner and possibly unlimited resources at our fingertips, within the league's rules, of course." He sighed. "I have everything on the list for a great hockey team playing at an elite level, but they're *not*. And the new owners want this team to start winning. I'm here to make that happen. I believe, Ms. Connors, I have a problem right up your alley of expertise."

From the moment he'd mentioned the team he represented, I'd been running through what I knew about them. It was very little, which pained me, but I stayed away from the hockey world. All of it.

The Grays would play against my brothers' teams. Did I want to expose myself to that? Then again, with my job, I could stay hidden in the background. It was feasible that they would never know I'd been connected to a hockey team and therefore connected to them in some small way. The nights they played the Grays, I wouldn't need to be present. There were times I didn't attend my clients' games. Not many, but there had been times.

My stomach twisted with intrigue and fear. "What exactly are you asking of me?"

He smiled. "I want you to work your magic. This morning, I received a phone call that's—well, I can't say yet what it's about. But I almost fell off my chair when I heard who might be interested in coming to us. If he pans out, we have a real shot at the Cup this year. I want everything to start moving forward for us. I think you can help ensure that happens, in whatever way you do that."

"And what's your role here? You have the authority for this?"

A hint of a smirk showed before he hid it, but he nodded. "I have the authority."

I waited, but he didn't say anything more.

"Restrictions?" I asked.

He shook his head. "There are none. We'll work with you. We're ready to give you the tools and assist you in any way so you can be effective with the team. The faster the better, as far as we're concerned."

Jesus. This was an ideal job. No restrictions? None? There were always some.

What was the catch? Because there was always a catch. Well, already this was a hockey team. An NHL team, which was a catch for me, but I knew another catch was coming. I could feel it in my gut. "If you really want me to help—"

"I do. We do."

"My methods are... I'm a woman. Certain barriers will be there. I'll have to find a way to disarm them, bring down their walls. I won't be micromanaged. If I'm doing something you don't understand, I don't care. I will not explain it to you—"

He shook his head. "I already said there are no stipulations."

I paused. *Well, good.* Moving on. "Pay?"

He reached into his pocket to pull out an envelope and slid it across the table to me. "We have it separated. A signing bonus now, plus base pay and a list of additional bonus options if we win a certain number of games, et cetera. A rather hefty payment if we go to the playoffs this year, and of course, if we get the Cup." He grinned at me. "But you'll see that the base pay should be more than enough."

I took the envelope, but I didn't open it. Honestly, when was the other shoe going to drop? "I need to do my own research, look into the team before I can make a decision."

"Of course." His grin faded. "Why don't you take the weekend? Come to the games on Friday and Sunday? Let me know your decision Monday morning."

"Who are you playing?"

He named two teams I'd once enjoyed watching. It had been so long since I'd let myself *watch* and *enjoy* hockey.

"If I agree to take this job, I will be excused from attending any games that involve my brothers' teams. That would be a stipulation. No one can know my connection to them except you and those who are already aware. Who else knows in your organization?"

He straightened, a keen look on his face. "Only myself and the investigator I hire to do all my research."

"The coaching staff?"

His lips pressed together, and he shook his head. "They're not currently aware."

"*No one.* I mean it, no one. The players. Your assistant. The press team. No one. Social media team."

"The owners?"

"No one besides those who already know." I waited, holding my breath, because so many would want to know why. This was a hint at juicy gossip. But after giving me a long and considered study, Mr. Benoit dipped his head in a nod. "That's fine."

I liked that so I said, "Box seat for Friday. Not with the WAGs. Other than that, I don't care where or how nice of a box it is. I just need to see the team from a decent distance away."

"That's easy enough."

"And right next to the rink for Sunday's game—where your team starts in the goal if there's a single seat available." I wanted to watch the way they moved together tonight, and then on Sunday I wanted to be able to see their eyes when they played.

"Done. I can do that." He nodded and must've given some sort of signal because the server began weaving through the tables toward us again. "You never touched your coffee, but do you know what you'd like to order?"

I considered leaving, starting my research now, except Mr. Benoit seemed eager to assist me in any way, so I nodded instead.

When the server approached, I asked for one of their

salads, along with a side of roasted vegetables and a glass of wine.

He ordered a steak, and his eyes held a hint of approval after she left. "You drink red wine?"

I smiled. I didn't normally, but today, I would.

4

TYLER

Minneapolis

"Are you sure you want to do this?" My agent stood next to me, his shoulders taut.

Brian had been with me from the start, and while anyone else would look at him and find him the epitome of relaxed, I knew that was not the case. He was known for his poker face, and that's what everyone else would see right now. His features were impassive, his stance casual. Yet his eyes were constantly moving, taking everything in around the empty locker room. I knew my agent.

He was anxious.

I leaned down to check my skates, one of the last things I did for my routine. I cast him a quick frown. "Kinda late for that question. The ink is dried. I signed the contract."

It had been a whirlwind since I'd called Brian a couple days ago and told him what I needed to do. After I'd talked to Ski, I had no other choice. An offer materialized for me very soon thereafter. It was generous too, and a surprising one considering this was one of the newer teams in the league.

I'd been shocked. So shocked I'd had to sit down when he'd called to let me know.

He had told them the reason for the sudden transfer was family. My former team hadn't wanted to give me up, and I didn't want to leave. I'd been with them since I was drafted. I respected them, but they also respected me and letting me out of my contract was the biggest show of that respect. Once I told them the reason, they didn't balk.

Leaving my teammates and friends, however, had been another matter. Since everything happened so fast, most of the guys and their partners came over to help me pack. We'd loaded up what I needed for a few weeks, and I'd figure out what to do with my house later.

Along the way there'd been beers, food, and lots of idle chatting, as all of us were in some level of denial about me leaving the team. Nolan, my best friend, broke first, demanding to know the reason. We were all close, so I told them the truth. Some of them got weepy.

Nolan's eyes had gone glossy. *"Fuck, man. Zoey?"*

I'd nodded, my vision blurred. *"Yeah, man. So, I gotta be there."*

Nodding, he'd crossed the room, wrapping me in a tight hug. *"I got it. Zoe's your girl."*

Yeah, she was. My niece. My goddaughter.

Even so, Christ. That goodbye was one of the hardest things I'd had to do.

Although going to see Ski and Zoey early this morning had topped it. When I saw Zoey in the hospital, her arms so thin and tangled up in all sorts of cords, I almost lost it.

But the Grays had wanted to move fast. So here I was. I hadn't even practiced with my new team. We'd had an early warmup skate this morning, so I went straight from the hospital. I'd met the guys, met my new coach and the rest of the coaching staff, then was swept off to sign my contract. After that, things had been a blur.

I'd had lunch with the team, followed by a meeting with the coaches. They'd explained I'd be on third line tonight but would be moved to first almost right away. I understood. A morning warmup and lunch didn't make up for the fact I hadn't practiced with this team yet.

There had been no announcement of my trade yet, either. It hadn't slipped to the press. I knew my old team wouldn't let it out, and I guessed my new team was solid too. I wasn't worried. All the people I cared about knew what was happening. Everyone else would find out when they made the announcement as I stepped onto the ice for warm-up before the game.

Brian spoke again, moving closer. "I can do something. Claim something. You want out, I got you. I'm just saying. This is a new team. They aren't... They aren't what you're used to, and there are always loopholes."

Just then one of the Grays' managers popped his head around the corner and smiled at me, though it was tense. "They're, uh, they're ready for you, Mr.—"

I shook my head, stepping past him. "Griff is fine."

One of the team's PR people was ahead as I rounded the corner, smiling widely. She took a deep breath. "Ready when you are, Mr.—"

I just growled and cleared the chute. I looked back once, saw her tap something on her phone, and stepped onto the ice as the loudspeaker blared.

I was officially a Gray Wolf now.

5

RAIN

Standing at the arena's platform, I watched the ice below, feeling rather overwhelmed.

I'd forgotten how much life there was in hockey. It was everywhere. Fans pressed close to the rink, separated only by a partition and some nets. Even now, during warm-ups, kids were down there—holding signs, trying to get the players' attention to have a puck tossed through the netting to them.

I'd forgotten.

I ached to go on that ice, to feel the smooth slide of it underneath my own skates.

Some of the players were dancing to the music, joking with each other, stretching on the ice. They were playful. Some kids thought it was funny when they wiggled their hips. This game was so fierce. So fast. Possessive. Loyal. Violent. But there were moments of hilarity. It was endearing and addictive.

A deep ache bloomed inside of me as I let myself reminisce about the parts of this world I loved, the parts I missed. I hadn't let myself feel it in so long. I wiped a tear before it fell.

Enough. I took a deep breath and began compartmentalizing. Everything that had been surfacing went back in its own drawer.

"HOLY SHIT!"

I jumped at the sudden explosion that boomed from the guy next to me. I'd ventured down the steps without realizing it, migrating closer to the ice. A murmur rose through the crowd as he stared down at his phone, his mouth hanging open.

Something had happened. Something big.

The air grew thick with excitement. Some people were cursing.

"What?" A woman gasped near me, breathless. "What's happening? What's going on?"

"I—holy fuck. I can't even—how did this happen?" The guy was stunned. "I—we're screwed. We're so totally fucked if this is true."

"There he is!" someone screamed.

The volume in the stadium cranked up, and the air was throbbing. Heady. I noted that the guy who already sounded defeated was wearing the rival team's jersey.

This was probably about the new player Benoit had mentioned.

Suddenly there was an opening in the crowd of players, and I saw him.

My head whirled.

Tyler Griffin. Wearing a Minnesota Grays jersey. Their metallic wolf was smack in the middle of his chest.

The fans were right. This was huge. *Huge.*

How did this happen?

Tyler Griffin was one of the top five players in the entire league, possibly top three. He'd been picked up by New York in the draft a few years back, and he'd never left. They'd built an entire team around him, and they'd won the Stanley Cup for the last five years. People had begun to hate them, because that's what happens when a team is on top for too long. But that doesn't mean they weren't good.

Dazed, I stood in stunned disbelief, alongside thousands who were flabbergasted right along with me. Looking up at the Jumbotron, I watched as the camera followed him around. *Tyler Griffin.*

A totally different anxiety slammed into my chest. I needed to sit down. Stat. Because if I took this job, I'd have to work with him.

I'd have to talk to Tyler.

The other shoe had officially dropped.

6

TYLER

The Grays weren't bad, though we'd lost tonight, and I *hated* losing.

I wanted playoffs. We wouldn't get there with this team.

It'd been hard to interpret the crowd's reaction when I was announced. There was a mix of boos and cheers. I also heard a lot of fucking confusion. I understood that. The sudden trade would be discussed incessantly on the hockey media and blogs for the foreseeable future, because this had been such an unprecedented move. I wasn't looking forward to the fallout. They'd question my team, whether there was a rift between me and the coaching staff, or the administration, or another teammate. All of which was false, but they had to talk about something. I didn't want them to find the real reason, though eventually someone would likely put it together. I'd grown up in the Twin Cities. My family, though small, was here. Someone might look hard enough to find that.

"Nice playing with you tonight, Griff." Jesse Ray held up a fist as he skated by. He was the Grays' current captain and also first-line left winger. I'd be first-line center soon, though there'd already been some crossover tonight since I'd chosen to stay on the ice during the penalty kills, which, shit, we'd gotten a lot of. My old team had spent a lot of time in the sin bin. That was just part of hockey, but we hadn't done it as much as this team seemed to. Giving the other team all those power plays was stupid. Sometimes shit happened, but as many as tonight? Fucking Christ. Keep your head.

But, different day, different problem.

I tapped Ray's fist and gave him a nod. "You too. I'm excited to play with you and Sunny."

Joel Sun—or Sunny, as he was called on the ice—was the Grays' first-line right winger. He heard my comment and gave me a quick grin. He seemed tired. We were all tired, because damn, this team was inefficient. There were better ways to play. Smarter moves.

But I was the new guy. Sure, my career pedigree gave me some power here—I wasn't going to get hazed—but I was still just coming in. I needed to shut my trap on all my thoughts about this team. I'd only played one game with them. I'd loved their inefficiency when I'd been playing against them. They were usually an easy win, especially once playoffs came around, because by then this team had worn themselves out.

I wasn't sure why. They had good bones—a good mix of veteran players with new talent coming up, and I'd help. I knew I would be an asset for them. Plus, their goalie was one of the best—his nickname was Brick for a reason. He was a goddamn wall in front of the goal. Nothing against Zoomie, my last team's goalie, but he was just normal for the NHL. Brick wasn't. He was a superstar.

I glanced over at Nick Bruge, a Grays enforcer. He got some heat around the league because he liked to skate with his helmet off as much as possible, letting those long locks of his fly. It was a running joke. Girls got off on putting videos of him up on social media. Some called him a show pony, saying he liked to be the enforcer because it got him attention. I didn't know him, and I'd never gotten that read on the ice, but I'd been on the other end of his fists a couple times. He could hit when he wanted to. Once the fight was called, though, he was cool. He didn't do a lot of extra chirping.

Right now he was sitting by Sun's locker, elbows on his knees, going through his phone.

I grimaced. That made me think about my own phone. I'd silenced it, but it kept lighting up with notification after notification. I hated social media. A girl I'd banged a couple times was good at it, though, and it turned out we were better as friends, so she handled most of my social media now. She was back in New York, so that meant I'd either need to do my social media myself or find someone new.

"Griffin." One of the coaches stepped into our locker area. He motioned behind him. "You're on press. Bruge. Ray. You too, after Griff."

As he left, Brick came in. "Who's the chick Coach is talking to?"

More than a few heads lifted.

"What do you mean?" Sunny asked.

Brick pointed out the door. "Benoit's introducing her to the whole coaching staff. Looks like she's someone, you know? Joining the team or something." He turned to me. "Unless she's with you? Your agent or manager?"

I shook my head. "Nope. My agent's a dude."

"Is she hot?" one of the younger guys asked.

A few others laughed.

Brick went to his station and began stripping down. "I am a happily married man, but if I weren't..." He paused for effect.

Some of the guys leaned forward.

Brick smirked. "I'd shoot my shot with her."

"Damn," someone hollered. "Brick never turns horndog."

Another wolf-whistled.

A few laughed.

"Knock it off." Bruge's tone was sharp.

The room quieted.

"That's unprofessional and inappropriate," he added. "You guys know better." And with that, he hunched back over his phone.

"Griff."

The same assistant coach was back in the doorway. He frowned at me, his tie tossed over his shoulder and some of his hair messed up.

I jerked forward. "Sorry."

Still in my jersey, I followed as he led me toward the press room. As we went past the coaching staff offices, I glanced in and almost stopped short.

Coach Hines was talking to a woman, alongside Mal Benoit, a representative for the team's owners.

Brick was right. She didn't seem like press. Coach was locked in and studying her.

She held herself apart from them, dressed in black pants and a buttoned-up black blazer. She was maybe five eight, a little taller than most women. She wasn't skinny—a lot of women were so thin, they were like twigs waiting to be snapped—but she wasn't big either. She was just strong. Firm. I knew, even from this distance, that I could wrap my arm around one of her legs and find straight muscle. Power.

I liked that look, or at least I did as of right now.

She was talking, but she glanced my way, and her eyes found mine. She faltered.

I felt punched in the gut. *Jesus.* Who was this woman?

Pale smooth skin. Dark eyes. Dark hair pulled back in a French braid, though I could still tell it was curly. She had a stunning face—long and angular, with a cute little chin. And fuck me, but I knew her from somewhere...

There was a flicker of recognition, and I could've sworn I

saw the same in her, but then it was gone. A neutral wall slammed in place.

I frowned at that.

"Griff. Seriously." Someone nudged me from behind. It was Jesse Ray. "Press, dude."

I shook out of whatever that had been to do my job. Press was part of that. There were going to be a lot of questions about the reason for the trade. But I wasn't willing to give them even a morsel of truth. I've been protecting my sister all of my life, and that went double for my niece. The company line was that I'd asked for a change in teams, and my team had agreed to accommodate my wishes. There was no bad blood on either side of this trade. But it was a bullshit answer. The press knew it. The fans would know it too, and maybe it was the wrong move because they'd all keep talking about it until they learned the real reason I'd had to switch teams and switch cities within a span of two days.

I just didn't care.

It was no one's business that a few nights ago, my sister had found my sixteen-year-old niece unconscious and unresponsive. Zoey had overdosed.

7

RAIN

I showed up Monday morning at Mal Benoit's office with two coffees. I handed him one. He seemed surprised but took it with a grin before sitting down. "You're taking the job?" he asked.

I took a sip of my drink, placed it on his desk, and sat in a chair. "Tyler Griffin," I said.

His eyebrows shot up. He rose to close his office door. "It was too big of an announcement," he said as he returned. "I couldn't risk it getting out."

I realized he'd misunderstood me. "I'm not upset that you didn't tell me. But I can't take this job without disclosing a potential problem."

His eyebrows furrowed. "With Tyler Griffin?"

"You did your research. You should know about the rivalry between him and my brothers."

"Yes." He drew out the word, seeming confused. "They're rivals. It's well known in the league, but how does that pertain to you? Your connection to them is not public knowledge, and you won't be here when your brothers play us. Unless the issue is more personal than the league is aware of?"

Right. He knew about the public rivalry between them. It was well documented on social media. And people loved it because the hatred was real between my brothers and Griffin, but that wasn't the whole story. "It began in high school."

"Your teams were rivals?"

I nodded. "We met each other at the state championship every year for a while there."

"I've seen a few of the older videos," he confirmed.

I'm sure he was familiar with the chant my school was famous for: "*Fuck you, Oakes. Fuck you, Griff.*" Social media had still been new back then, but there were videos floating around with hundreds of my schoolmates chanting those words over and over in the arena for the championship game and also later in the hotel where we'd gathered. Twenty floors, with classmates on every floor chanting, "*Fuck you, Oakes. Fuck you, Griff.*" It was... It was something.

Their school had tried to counter, but it was futile. There was a hostility in Greenville that overpowered the students from Oakes. Sometimes I wished I'd transferred to another school. I could've done it. I was already working and supporting myself by sixteen. But I hadn't wanted to waste my money paying rent somewhere else, not while our dad was still letting me stay at the house. Once I turned eighteen, he'd made it clear he expected me out of there. So I'd begun saving up as soon as I could start a job.

"I'm sure you've seen all sorts of interesting things on the internet," I told him. "But I don't believe Griff knows my connection to my brothers." I winced, realizing I'd slipped and used his nickname.

"And you're worried about that?" Mal's lip curved down. "He doesn't, right? I want to make sure about that."

I shifted in my seat. "I don't believe he does. But if he ever were to find out, we should have a plan in motion for my dismissal."

"Dismissal?" His eyebrows arched high. "You're talking about yours?"

"Yes."

"You're certain his reaction will be so negative? You won't be able to do your job?"

I shifted again, looking away. "If he were to learn of my connection, he might connect other dots. The high school rivalry got personal at times." I met Mal's gaze but made sure not to actually see him. I looked through him. It's the way I coped whenever thoughts about my family came to me. "I have no reason to believe he'll find out. Barely anyone knew back then, and I have no contact with my family. But it'd be unprofessional of me not to let you know about the situation."

He nodded. "What kind of plan are you thinking?"

"Some of my work will depend on the team, but with every job, I set different goals in motion. I'll keep those goals updated, including techniques being used and their progress. If you still want to proceed with the plan I've created, I'd feel more comfortable if there was a replacement ready—someone who could step in and finish the work toward the goals I'd have in place, especially considering the sensitivity of any ongoing work."

His eyes widened, and he took his time in responding. "Right. Well... I do want to move forward with you. Your results speak for themselves, so I'm not worried about that. Regarding Griffin, let me worry about him. Hmmm?"

"And a potential replacement?"

"Do you have a few names put together?"

"Yes." *Yes.* We were moving away from anything personal and focusing on my work. My shoulders relaxed as I held out a list for him. "Here you go. For what it's worth, I have this set up with any job I do. It's just that because of Griffin's involvement; it's a bit more relevant than with my other clients."

He took the list, sparing it a glance before setting it aside.

"Of course. That's just smart planning. I'm sure your past clients have appreciated the foresight."

I smiled. That was nice to hear.

"I can have all of this added to your contract," he continued. "But in the meantime, what do you need from me? What are your first steps?"

I ignored the sudden kick of nerves. "It's time to meet your players."

8

TYLER

"You ready for this?" Jesse Ray asked. I glanced up from my seat in front of my locker as more of the guys showed up in the locker room. When I nodded, he sat beside me and started to change for practice.

I was quickly learning that Jesse Ray was the team's go-to man. He was the greeter. He was the one people went to for questions or favors. He checked on the younger ones. It made sense why he was wearing the C. He'd tried reaching out to me a few times over the last couple days, but I'd been with Ski and Zoey. Correction, I was in Zoey's hospital room. They'd put her in a coma to help her recover, and Ski refused to leave, so yeah, my sleep had sucked over the weekend.

At least my niece's overdose hadn't leaked to the news. I was grateful for that. I'd been hesitant about being there so much, but Ski insisted she didn't care. She needed her twin, and she needed her daughter, and that was that. My sister was beyond reason. Though, who wouldn't be in her place? I just really fucking hoped my presence wouldn't make things worse for them.

I looked over again at Jesse. "You just mean am I ready for practice?" I asked.

He lifted his chin, watching the doorway. "Something's up. That chick is back. I saw her earlier, talking to the new owner."

I felt my eyes widen. "The owner?"

"Mal Benoit."

"I thought his dad bought the team."

He shook his head. "Nah, man. Mal's got the money. He got the approval from the league, but I think they've tried to keep it quiet. You didn't know when you came here?" He studied me.

I blinked, trying to clear away whatever he might see on my face. "No."

His eyes narrowed. "I kinda assumed that's why you were here. Like, he made you some big, huge offer and you couldn't resist, you know? He just took over, and he's motivated."

"Ha. No. That's not why I'm here. But they did well for me, considering the cap and all." I'd taken a small hit compared to what I'd previously been earning. But I had to be here. Simple as that. Ski never wanted to relocate to New York, and I was done being away from her and Zoey.

"Huh. I thought for sure it was because of... You know, never mind." He flashed me a grin and patted my arm before going back to dressing. "Lots of changes going on around these parts. I'll catch up one of these days."

Bruge came in and gave me a look as he went to his locker in the corner. Sunny was there, half suited up. Brick and Meester, the other goalie, were already dressed and waiting for the rest of us schmucks to finish. From what I'd seen, Meester was young and eager, but he got in his head too much. His eyes were bright and shining this morning.

The others filtered in around us, and chatter filled the locker room, along with music. Just when it was time to head for the ice, the locker room door opened. Coach Hines came in, followed by Benoit and the chick from Friday night's game.

I sat up straight. She'd been at the Sunday game too, sitting ice-rink level. I'd caught glimpses of her a few times. There was never much time to ruminate or stare at her, but I had been hoping she'd make another appearance at a game. If I got the opening, I was going to shoot my shot.

She was hot. End all, in my opinion.

But her coming here this morning changed things. Brick was right. She was here because she was affiliated with the team. Social media, maybe? But no. I remembered meeting the social media team. And no offense to her, but she didn't have the social media vibe. Her eyes were haunted, her hair pulled back in another tight braid.

"Fellas. Listen up." Coach got our attention, shifting to the side and indicating Benoit. "I know the goal is playoffs this year and I believe we have the bones to get there. We've got a good amount of talent and tenacity in this room. It's going to take work and a solid team unit, but we'll be helping you build all of that. And with that said, Mal here's got something to say." He inclined his head, giving the woman a small nod. "Someone to introduce us to."

Mal Benoit cleared his throat and stepped forward. "Yes. Hello, everyone. Most of you are aware that I represent the team's new owner, and I want to tell you that we believe in you guys. We believe in this team. And we are dedicated to doing everything we can to make you the best you can be." He glanced to the woman beside him.

She was captivating. I could finally give her the attention she deserved. All up close and personal. Yes, thank you. Her physical strength had gotten me last time, but now I could see she had strength inside her too.

She settled her shoulders back, raised her chin, and just like that, all emotion was gone. In its place was something that commanded attention. She was a good-looking woman, but it was that, whatever was inside of her, that kept my attention. I did a quick scan around the room, and half the guys were trying to listen to Benoit, but a good chunk of them were losing the battle, because all eyes were on this woman—whoever the fuck she was.

Benoit extended his arm toward her. "I'm here to introduce you to someone who will be assisting us for the foreseeable future." He smiled at her. "We didn't discuss this. Would you like to introduce yourself or for me to say a few words?"

She smiled, the epitome of professional. "I can give my name, but why don't you explain my function and your reason for hiring me?"

It was deftly put. I could understand her move. Hockey was a male-dominated field. Sure, there were women who worked behind the scenes, but she was *here*. She was in our locker room. The coach had brought them in, and the owner was saying she was some sort of resource for us? That meant she'd be working *with* us. Not around us or for us. With us. There was a difference, and I had to give her props for handling a first critical move, whether Benoit had any idea at all. My guess was no because he didn't blink an eye, just smiled and addressed us again.

"Right. I first heard about Ms. Connors—"

Connors? The name sent an alarm through me, and I wasn't the only one. A bunch of other guys shifted. This world was small, and Connors was a big name. We were all looking at her a little differently now. I knew I was.

She seemed to notice the shift in the room, and I caught a quick grimace on her face as she reached out toward Benoit and stepped forward. "Thanks, Mal. Change of plans. I'll take it from here." She looked around the room, going from guy to guy, and when she got to me, she held my gaze for one beat before moving on.

I felt singed.

"My name is Rain Connors," she began. "Call me Rain. If

you call me Ms. Connors, I will not answer. Not just because of the *Terminator* reference, though my name has an S, but also because I've learned not to use that last name. People start assuming things, like that I'm related to two other Connors in this world." She waved that away. "Trust me, I know hockey, and I am not a fan of those guys either. Any concern or worry you might have, it's not necessary. I actually come from a football background. Mr. Benoit was about to explain I am a sports psychologist."

She paused and looked around again. "Long answer, I'm hired by teams and individuals to help them achieve their optimal potential. My degree is in psychology because I have to understand you in order to locate whatever is holding you back, and then I will help eliminate that obstacle.

"What does this mean moving forward and how will this impact you? I'll be here. I'll be hanging out. Sometimes I might watch your practices. Sometimes I might ask a few questions. I'll have a few conversations. That's it. If you want to have a conversation, I'm here."

With that, she inclined her head a little and stepped back, but not before looking around the room at every single guy once more.

She saved me for last.

9

RAIN

I wanted to curl up in a ball.

The team thought I was their shrink. They thought I wanted to crawl in their heads and mess them up. I could see it. They were already closing off. I hadn't had to deal with this since the beginning of my career. Word had gotten around in American football circles, and those guys were more open to strategic meetings. But these guys? Fuck. I knew what I'd need to do to earn their respect, and my legs were shaking.

I hadn't been on the ice in almost two decades, but there was one area, one lane, where I could still go head-to-head with them. Even NHL players. I just didn't want to do it. But I needed to prove myself to these guys. They weren't going to listen to a word I said otherwise. I knew the fastest way to get them to shut up would be to actually shut them up.

And the other reason I wanted to escape? Tyler Griffin.

He was gorgeous. Seriously gorgeous.

I'd told myself I was ready for it, that I could forget the crush I'd had on him in high school when his team played against my brothers. But it hadn't gone away. And the reaction he caused in me now was very physical and very adult.

He made my core throb. I hadn't felt the need to slide down on someone like this, ever.

I didn't like it. It wasn't professional, but it was also unfamiliar to me. The sensations and emotions were too much. Combined with the repressed memories and feelings, all of it was overwhelming.

Once I was done with my spiel and Benoit had taken over, I'd slanted a sideways glance at Griffin.

He'd been watching me with unfiltered hunger.

Electricity jolted through me, because he'd been looking at me exactly the way I was feeling toward him. I had all of those unwelcome, lusty sensations locked up behind a wall, but he let me see that he had no problem with me pulling him into the nearest janitors' closet and have my way with him.

Heat spread through me. I muffled a curse, shifting because this was uncomfortable. And again—unprofessional. I had never, *ever* had a reaction like this to a player.

This was the opposite of what I strove for. Men came on to me. Sometimes women. If I ran across them in workplace environments, I never reciprocated. I shut that down. It was hard enough to be taken seriously, and if I had sex with one of the players, all that credibility would be gone.

"...I believe I've covered everything." Mal turned to me. "Anything I missed?"

I blinked, remembering where I was. "If you did, I'll cover it as I go." I cocked my head to the side, meeting the coach's gaze. "Mind if I shadow for the day?"

I almost smiled because it was clear he very much minded, but he wasn't going to go against Benoit. He held out a hand toward the team. "Not at all." Now his mouth lifted into a curve, and I readied myself, knowing something not great was probably coming. "We can just pretend you're another one of the equipment managers," he said, attempting a joke.

"Sorry, Coach. I'm a psychologist. My deep appreciation to

those who handle the equipment, because generally it's a thankless job, but that's not what I'm getting paid to do."

He jerked back a bit.

I'd put him in his place, but it was his fault. He didn't understand my job. Another strike against me however I would not be considered below the players, not if I wanted them to listen to me.

I was a woman. I was a stranger. I was not here to handle their equipment—even if one player made me want to do just that in a very unprofessional manner.

Coach dipped his head, a flash of apology in his eyes before they all headed out to start their usual Monday morning practice.

I couldn't shake this sense of dread as I followed. There were a lot of strikes against me after just the first meeting. I'd have to hit the ice with them sooner than I wanted.

I wasn't ready now, but I'd get there.

10

RAIN

I considered my options. I hadn't skated in over a decade... Where? It wasn't cold enough for me to find an outdoor rink that was empty, and I wasn't sure about driving an hour to the rink I'd used growing up. Daniel and Dane didn't live here, but they had friends who did. Some of those friends knew me. I tried calling a few local gyms to see if anyone had a rink I could rent for an hour or two, but it wasn't that season yet. Hockey had just started, but that didn't mean the rest of the city was ready to convert everything.

I really only had one viable option, and I knew I should be going there anyway. Some rinks weren't as well maintained as I knew the Grays' would be. After I hemmed and hawed and meditated and decided maybe I should give yoga a try (I hated yoga), I called Mal Benoit.

He answered right away. "Rain. This is a surprise. It's late. Is everything okay?"

I winced, remembering the time. I'd been so caught up that I forgot how late it was. "Yeah. I'm sorry. I got caught up with something and didn't realize the time. I'm calling about some ice time. Could I use the team's rink? Is there a time I could do that privately? I figure I should dust off some of my rust, you know?"

"Are you planning on skating with the team?"

I hesitated, but then again, he would hear about it. "Yeah, eventually."

"Oh. Is this something you did with your football clients?"

I almost laughed. "No. I—hockey isn't the same. It's a different culture. There are plays and strategies of course, but hockey is a bit more... This is just something I need to do. Something I *can* do, but I'd like to practice first. It's been a while since I've skated."

"Right. Of course. You met the building manager, yes? I'll send word to him, and you can confer with him about private time on the ice. They might need to clean the ice after you."

"Of course." I hesitated to ask, but since I'd started down this road, I couldn't let it go. "Any chance you could send that note this evening?"

"Oh..." I could tell I'd surprised him. Again. "Sure. I'll do it as soon as we hang up." He went quiet, and I was about to end the call when he spoke up. "Hockey's not new to me, Rain. I know that certain struggles are still shoved under a rug, but I did do my homework. If there's anything you need, I'm a phone call away. I love this sport, and one of the reasons I love it is because of the team camaraderie. I needed that when I played, leaned on it during some hard times. Anything you need—and I mean that, anything—don't hesitate."

My breath caught. "Thank you," I managed after a moment. "You're aware that I don't usually work in hockey. There are some memories coming up."

"You know, the building manager tends to do a walk-through right before he heads home, and sometimes he does it after his daughter's volleyball game. The rink is a few blocks from her school. There's a chance he could still be there tonight."

I closed my eyes, swallowing tightly. He knew. He understood what I was yearning to do. "Thanks for that, Mr.—"

"Mal, Rain. Mal."

"Yes. Mal."

"Goodnight. I'll send that note right away."

He ended the call before I could say thank you again, but that was probably for the best.

I *needed* to do this. Now that I'd decided, it was like I couldn't restrain myself anymore.

My phone beeped ten minutes later with a text from Mortimer, the building's manager.

Hello, Miss Rain. Mr. Benoit said you might be wanting to use the rink, maybe even tonight. The keys you got earlier today should get you in through the staff door. Just turn the lights off when you're done. Benji always cleans the ice first thing in the morning. He's got what you call insomnia, and we're used to the rink being used at all hours of the night. Ice is yours whenever you'd like. - Morty

Rain: Thank you, Mr. Mortimer. I may come around this evening. I really do appreciate this.

Mortimer (Building Manager): It's Morty, ma'am.

I made a mental note to get to know Morty and find out what he enjoyed, or what his wife enjoyed. Leaving the rink open for me was a big ask. Whether Benji really did have insomnia was one thing, but knowing the Zamboni would have to clean up after me was another. My throat felt thick all over again, because this was only part of the life I used to know. I had to stand in the corners and the shadows back then, but that never took away how much this sport made me feel alive.

I grabbed my skates and I was out the door.

11

TYLER

Going to the rink at midnight was an old habit of mine. It was also a bad habit. I'd slowed way down years ago, but it was still my go-to when things were a mess in my head. And things were definitely a mess nowadays.

My phone buzzed as I was parking.

Nolan calling.

I frowned, answering. "Dude. It's late here. You're an hour earlier than us. Is everything okay?"

He was quiet for a beat before he sighed. "You've not been on social media or checked your messages?"

My heart went cold.

"I'm sorry, man. Word got out about Zoey. Someone took a picture of you holding her hand in the hospital. She's sixteen, so some outlets will blur out her face and won't print her name, but you know how people are. They'll find her."

The air around me shifted. "What?"

"I just got a call from Suze," he continued. "She needs to know what our team should say. She couldn't get a hold of you." He sighed again. "Guess people will know why you switched to the Grays. They'll stop making up conspiracy theories."

I'd barely paid attention to what was being said, needing all my focus for either my family or the new team. Gossip hadn't made the list of things for me to worry about.

"Ty?"

"Yeah." I tried again, my voice coming out raw. "Shit."

"I know."

"Shit!" I pounded the steering wheel and closed my eyes, leaning back in my seat to breathe. I just had to breathe. One fucking breath at a time. "She's a kid. They're—"

"The story's going to break in the morning. They're making the rounds tonight for comment. I'm sure your new team's PR will be blowing up your phone soon."

I cursed.

"I know I just delivered a nightmare to you, but how's it going outside of that? Are you vibing with your new team?"

He was helping me get a lid on myself by switching to an easier topic. Hockey. "It's going. They're pretty tight, but they seem open to working with me. They're nice. There's one that's standoffish."

"Bruge?"

"How'd you guess?"

"He's their enforcer. Once he lets you in, it'll be all good. And Griff, he will. You're the player they need to get them into playoffs. They've been struggling. You know that."

"That's the goal."

Headlights passed over my face, and I opened my eyes. Who could that be? No car should be in this back lot, unless it was the team's PR person Nolan just mentioned.

"Ty? You still there?"

"Yeah." But I was distracted now, because the SUV parked and a figure got out, her hand reaching up to tuck some of her hair behind her ear. Rain Connors. I frowned. What was she doing here?

She hurried past where I was parked, not looking up. If she had, she would've seen me since I'd backed into my spot. I wasn't hiding. But she just went straight for the back door I'd been intending to use. She had some skates thrown over her shoulder, and if I was reading her correctly, she was frazzled.

Did her arrival here have anything to do with Zoey's overdose being leaked? Was that why she was flustered?

But even as the thought entered my mind, I shoved it aside. She didn't know me or my family. She came from the NFL world. She wouldn't care enough about NHL gossip to leak something. Or would she? *Fuck*. No. Nolan said it was someone at the hospital. If she'd been there, I would've known. I think I would've...

My phone began buzzing. "Nolan, I've got to go. My new team's owner is calling me."

"Wait. What? Are you serious?"

"Yeah. He seems pretty hands-on, but not a bad guy. I'll call you later."

"Okay." His tone grew hoarse. "We're thinking of you over here. Pulling for Zoey too. Some of the guys were talking about doing an auction, a jersey we've all signed or something, to help fundraise some money for Skylar and Zoey. Let us know."

I wasn't surprised, just moved. Touched. That sounded exactly like something my old team would do. "I don't need to ask. Do it, but could you do two jerseys? One to auction and one for Zoey? Otherwise, knowing Zoey, she'll try to bid on it herself. I'll pay for it."

He barked out a laugh. "Will do, and no, you won't."

"Hey."

"You know not to fight me on this. We got it."

I gave in. I had other battles to tend to. "I'll double the winning bid. Just let me know."

"Will do. Take care. Love ya, man."

"You too." We hung up, and man, I missed my best friend and my old team something fierce right now.

But I didn't have time to dwell because I'd missed the call from Mal Benoit, but now it came through again. I answered before the first ring stopped. "I heard."

Mal Benoit sighed, the sound eerily similar to Nolan moments earlier. "That's what I was worried about. I just got notified myself. The team will issue a statement, and I have ties to a reputable media outlet. One of the editors is a friend of mine. We can't control what the other outlets will say, but I promise that one will make it respectable. She won't print anything we don't approve. My personal opinion is that you loop her in, and then we hit hard, shaming the other outlets for violating your niece's privacy. Blurred faces and not printing her name doesn't mean anything nowadays. They all know that. You can also use this as a way to humanize what your family is going through."

I listened to everything he said, and he was right. That was the way to go, but I was still reeling. "Uh, yeah. That sounds good. When would she need to hear from me? How would that work?"

"She won't beat the other outlets. Everyone's printing in the morning, so as soon as possible, I'd imagine."

I needed to skate. I needed to clear my head. Then I'd go into damage control and figure out how to break the news to Skylar. Shit. Her world was going to fall apart for the second time in a week. "I need an hour or two. I—I just need that time."

"I'll make the call. She'll be on standby. She's local. She can meet you somewhere too."

That all sounded good. A private room where I could dictate which words were going to be used to set my family's life on fire. Wonderful. "I'll get back to you."

Next, I called the night nurse on duty and asked if she could keep an eye on my sister.

"Will do. She was sleeping the last time I checked in there."

"Good. If you can, don't let her check her phone until I get there."

After that, I turned my phone off. I needed to or I wouldn't be able to think. This wasn't my first rodeo. I needed to process my own shit, and then I'd figure out how to destroy everyone trying to hurt my family.

Heading inside, I expected the rink lights to be on, considering I'd seen the psych doctor with skates over her shoulder. But I hadn't expected to find her in the middle of the ice, hands on her hips, her head tipped forward.

I slowed to a stop and watched.

Music started, and my ears perked. She used to be a figure skater? No... Those were hockey skates on her feet. She stood on them like they were another pair of shoes to her. She wasn't some novice skater.

The music kicked up, and she pushed off, gliding forward.

She went straight to the end of the rink and flew around, completing a lap.

She wasn't a figure skater.

I kept watching, and she kept going, and going, and going. She picked up speed in the first lap, and by the time she was doing her fourth, she was whipping around the rink as fast as any pro NHL player. Fuck. She was good. She was really good.

I stepped closer to the ice.

That pull was there, like a hook inside of me. I knew her. I didn't know how or when our paths crossed, but they had at some point. Or was this something else? Like that shit some psychics talk about? Did I know her from a past life or something? Even as I considered that, I didn't believe it. No. No way. I knew her in this life, somehow.

On her next pass, she lifted her head and saw me. Her eyes

widened, and I realized that's what was messing with me. She was in serious pain. She hadn't had time to mask it when she looked up.

That's what had connected me to her. I didn't actually know her, but somehow, I'd realized she was experiencing the same agony as my twin sister.

Rain careened to a stop, turning shortly so she didn't fall—her chest heaving, her hair wild and free, and tears rolling down her face.

I pressed a hand to the partition separating us.

I let her see the storm inside of me, and after hesitating a second, she skated to stand on the other side. There was no reason to hide my pain. I couldn't. She'd know what was going on in my life the next time she checked her phone, so what was the point?

Besides, I wanted her. This was more than just a crazy connection. A need to claim her pulsed in me, and I wasn't second guessing it. I'd felt this way with a few other women, and I'd learned that the sooner I fucked them, the sooner we could all continue with our lives.

Those other women had also been in male-dominated professions, so maybe it was about that type. Strong. Independent. I didn't know. I just knew that when I got these feelings, the sex was fucking amazing, and with the shitstorm hitting my world right now, I could use an escape. Even if it was momentary and fleeting.

I showed her all of that.

I could see her warring with herself. It was too late to hide her sadness, and she knew it, but she considered it. Her shoulders rose and she pondered, her eyes darting to my hand. But then she looked back to my eyes, and it was like she decided to give in too. Her eyes flashed, lust-filled and yearning.

I leaned in, resting my forehead on the partition beside my

hand, and she bit her lip before she fitted her hand against mine. It was a perfect match. Or it would be.

I started for the rink door, and she skated to beat me there.

She was just stepping off the ice when I got to her side. "You okay with this?" I asked.

She'd been looking down to make sure she didn't fall, and when her head lifted, her eyes were wide. Startled. "With what?"

I stepped into her, my hand cupping the back of her head. She made a squeaking sound.

"This," I said as I pulled her against me, molding our bodies together. "I want you." I tilted her head back so she could look all the way up at me, meeting my gaze.

Her hands lifted to my chest. "You want me?" She seemed a little dazed. "I..." She licked her lips, and the slight resistance was gone. She sagged into me. "I shouldn't."

Yeah. Fuck that.

I bent down, and my lips touched hers.

12

RAIN

I—what? *What?*
I shoved Tyler back. *What the fuck?*

He froze, his hands still on me, but his head and chest bent away. He seemed startled. Then his eyes widened and he jerked back a step. "Wait. You're not—I thought you were—that this—" He gestured between us. "—was a thing. I got that wrong?"

He hadn't. My body told me that.

He'd looked at me, and I hadn't been totally aware of what was going on because I was so locked in on my memories. I'd been skating and flying and feeling everything from the past, and for a moment, seeing Tyler at the glass watching me, I almost thought I was back in high school. That's when I'd had such a huge crush on him. For a moment, some part of my fantasy had come to life.

He kissed me—an actual real touch. His lips were on mine. My mind had stopped thinking and my body began demanding, but then my brain caught up and reminded me that this *could not* happen.

"I got it wrong," he said. "I thought... Shit. Fuck. I thought you were giving me come-hither eyes, and I was all about the coming and hithering, but now you're looking at me like I..." He swore under his breath, raking his hands through his hair. He turned away, dug out his phone, and pressed a button. He shoved it back in his pocket, his eyes a little crazed. He turned away from me.

I still didn't fully understand what was happening, but my body protested. "I..." I went back over the events and what he'd said. "Come-hither eyes?"

"Yes," he snapped, his body rigid. "You were. But look, I'm not that type of guy. A person can change her mind, and that's obviously what happened."

His phone began blaring. Alert after alert poured in. He closed his eyes and cursed savagely. For a moment, it seemed as if the whole world had dropped onto his shoulders. Eventually, he let out a soft exhale and reached for his phone.

I caught his hand but didn't take it in mine. I kept my fingers wrapped around his wrist. He stilled. I knew he was watching me, but I couldn't look at him. Whatever this was between us, it was important. Because he wasn't wrong. I had given him come-hither eyes, because I couldn't help myself. I was already frayed at the edges, and he'd certainly returned that look.

I shook my head. There was a storm inside of me, but I shut it down. I did what I always did and put the lid on it, making everything go away. "I can't do this. My job. And even if my job wasn't a factor, I still couldn't do this. I'm not good at it."

"At what?"

"*This.*" I gestured between us.

"What? Fucking?"

"I—" I clamped my mouth shut, heat coming to my face because of course he would just be blunt about it. Why wouldn't he? He probably never struggled in this area. He was a hockey god. His problem was turning options away.

His phone continued to ping and buzz incessantly, which

wasn't helping my flustered state. Finally I reached into his pocket and pulled it out. I hit accept on whoever was calling. "He's in the middle of somethin—" I stopped because whoever was on the other side began sobbing.

Tyler had an odd expression on his face as I handed the phone to him. "It's for you."

He took it, his eyes not moving from mine for a beat before he looked at who had called. He pulled in a breath and turned his back to me as he raised the phone to his ear, "Ski?"

Oh no. Shock punched me so hard I fell back against the doorway of the rink, my elbow jamming. His sister. His twin, and I was the reason she... No, no. I couldn't go there. I *wouldn't* go there. Not now anyway. I'd been trying to work on that guilt. My therapist a long time ago had said it was misplaced, and maybe she was right, but I still felt it burning through me.

But it was yet another reason this thing between Tyler Griffin and me couldn't happen.

He spoke to her in hushed tones, moving farther away. I felt hollow inside. That feeling was always there but watching him care for someone he loved made me ache. Jealousy, real and bitter and toxic, speared me, and I once again returned to high school.

But there was no point in going backwards. There was nothing for me there. I'd been a burden since I was born. My oldest brother loathed me, and I was invisible to the other one. I could never decide which one had been worse—being ignored or receiving the hatred Daniel, my oldest brother, spewed at me. I'd gone numb to survive it all, and the only long-term relationship I had, the guy had treated me the same way my brothers did, so there must've been something wrong with me.

I thought I had accepted that no one would love me, but hearing Tyler speak to his sister that way, jealousy hit me hard.

I turned away, needing space, and slipped back onto the ice.

Getting out here tonight had been hard, but now I welcomed the challenge. I'd always been fast on the ice. Sometimes my brothers had utilized my speed. That'd been one of the rare times Daniel gave me *any* sort of attention, though I was just basically his on-ice assistant. They'd used me for drills because I was faster than them.

I'd loved those times with them, though I hated to admit that. I knew now I'd been deluding myself, scrambling for the scraps they gave because I'd had no idea what I was actually missing.

Regret hit me hard, making my knees weak as I circled the rink, because I'd let them take skating away from me.

Not anymore. Not ever again.

I pushed myself faster, needing to escape.

When I looked up again, much later, Tyler was gone.

13

TYLER

The Gray's PR manager was Kashvi Kumar. I thought I'd met their head of promotions and marketing already, but I was wrong. I'd met Kashvi's assistant and a few others on the social media team. But Kashvi, as I was now seeing in action, ran the show.

I was going to meet Benoit's reporter friend, but Kashvi had decided it wasn't going to happen at the rink. She thought a nice hotel suite had a better feeling, and I agreed. She had asked if five in the morning was too early or too late, and while it was probably a little of both, everyone had agreed.

So, after whatever that had been with Rain at the rink, I drove to the hospital, told my sister what was going on, held her until she fell asleep, and then fell asleep as well. The nurses had long ago brought in a cot, and there was also a large chair in the room, so that gave us both enough space to sleep if I stayed.

It didn't matter where we were, if I was with my sister, I could sleep. I'd learned that years ago, and it was somewhat comforting to know it was still true, even at the ripe age of thirty-one. We had a game tonight, so I still got a few hours of sleep.

When I got up to go, Skylar decided to stay at the hospital, trusting me to handle this for her. The team had a morning skate later, but there'd be time after the interview to go back to Skylar's place or the hospital for another decent nap. If I could talk Ski into going home for a few hours, that'd be the ultimate power nap for me. She needed new clothes and a shower, along with some decent rest, and I wasn't above telling her she reeked and that Zoey wouldn't want that tidbit leaked to any media outlets. How embarrassing. It'd make her laugh, but I hoped it would work too.

"TYLER." Kashvi met me in the hotel lobby, a tray of coffees in one hand, her phone in the other. She tucked the phone under her elbow long enough for us to shake, and then she had it back out and was typing as she indicated the elevator. "I got the room ready. I'm so sorry we're meeting for the first time under these circumstances. I've been out on maternity leave. Welcome to the Grays, by the way." She pushed the elevator button and the doors opened.

As we entered, I gave her a quick once-over. *Maternity leave?* She was tiny. "Uh, congrats on your baby as well."

She pushed for the eleventh floor, then chuckled. "Thank you. My wife is the one who had the baby. The Grays are progressive. They gave me maternity leave as her partner. We were both grateful, but my wife was the most. She needed to sleep. A lot."

"Wait, are you still supposed to be on maternity leave? You're not coming back for me?" I hoped I wasn't the reason her time with her family had been cut short.

She shrugged. "It's more like you're the excuse." She flashed me a grin just as the doors opened. She started down the hallway first. "I started getting antsy last week. I was ready to come back, but Cora's been in heaven having all of us together. When I got the call about your niece, I knew it was time to return."

I winced.

She shook her head. "No. None of that. Trust me. My assistant is more than capable of handling this type of thing. I came back because I was ready to get back to work. I've kinda missed the team."

"I still feel bad."

"Don't." Her voice was firm. "If anything, blame the asshole who violated you and your niece's privacy. Blame the first news outlet that agreed to run with the story. Blame them. Not yourself."

I nodded. When she put it like that, some of my guilt eased, but in its place was a stone of anger.

Kashvi touched my arm, stalling me in the hallway. "When we get in there, let me do the talking until the actual interview. When it comes to this sort of stuff, I let the veteran players say what they'd like. You've done this song and dance. When you've said all you want to, you can shoot me a look if you need me to step in. Also, I know you know this, but I'm going to say it anyway. You signed up to play hockey. Along with that came some responsibilities for being a role model to younger hockey fans, but your niece did not. Your sister did not. You do not have to say anything you don't want to in there. You control the interview, okay? Martine is a decent reporter. More than likely she won't push, but she's still a reporter. You decide what's in the story, not anyone else. Now." She looked me over and gave a nod of approval. "You look good. You ready?"

I had on a black Grays blazer over dark slacks. I didn't think the pants would be a big deal, but I wanted to represent the team by looking professional, not too casual, so jeans or athletic joggers were out. My hair was combed to the side, but I hadn't had time to shave, so my face was a little scruffy. Seemed appropriate considering my lack of sleep.

"Ready."

She knocked, and the door opened.

Here we go.

14

RAIN

I was horrified early the next morning when Benoit sent me a preview of the article about Tyler's niece. I calculated the timing and realized this story was why his phone had been going off incessantly at the rink. What a nightmare. Tyler Griffin had always adored his twin, and it'd been just the two of them for a while. I didn't know the details, just that their parents had died while they were younger. Someone must've stepped in to take care of them, but then again, Tyler was already a hockey star by then. Of course everyone did what was needed to ensure he was okay.

As I read about his niece, how her mother had found her in the bathroom, that she'd overdosed and was now in a coma, it all made sense. Tyler had come back home—no questions, no hesitation. His previous team had let him go. Family was family, and Tyler Griffin was a part of their family.

A few other outlets picked up the story as the morning progressed. Eventually it was everywhere in the hockey world. By midday, the mainstream media had picked it up as well.

I asked Benoit for Tyler's number. He didn't send it right away. Some might've assumed he was in a business meeting or something, but Mal Benoit responded to all of my texts within minutes. Two hours later, he sent it. Just the number. Nothing else.

I texted Tyler.

This is Rain. Is there anything I can do for you?

There was no point in saying anything else. Once I saw him in person, I'd relay my apologies and well-wishes, but I needed to reach out now.

I wasn't sure he'd respond, but he texted back a few minutes later.

Tyler: I wanted to escape last night. You weren't into it. I'm good. Thanks.

Rain: Liar. You're not good.

Rain: Also, can we keep this professional? I'd rather not lose my career.

Tyler: Professional, check. Is this you doing your job? If so, fuck off.

Tyler: No offense. I don't need a shrink.

I frowned.

Rain: You were dealing with this last night?

Tyler: Yes...?

Rain: That's why you were there to skate? I took the rink away from you.

Tyler: I wasn't there because the story leaked, but yeah, I was there to clear my head. Not your problem, doc.

Rain: Don't call me that.

Tyler: Why? You ARE a doc, aren't you? I know enough to know a Ph.D. still gets that title.

Rain: Call me Rain.

Tyler: Can I call you Slick?

Some nerves kicked my stomach.

Rain: Slick? Because...?

Tyler: A few reasons, but let's go the professional route. Because you're fast as fuck on the ice.

I huffed, shaking my head.

Rain: That makes no sense.

Tyler: To me it does. You can ask about the other reason later.

Rain: Do I dare take this new bait?

Rain: Later when?

Tyler: Thought we were keeping this professional.

Rain: You're being anything but professional. Just tell me.

Tyler: When I'm sliding inside of you and feeling how slick and tight you are.

Heat unfurled inside of me, smoothing away the nerves. Damn him. Seriously. Damn him, because he was right. I did want him, and this was so bad.

Rain: You can't type that to me.

Tyler: Honestly? Fuck that bullshit. You're texting me what can you do to help, and the only thing I want from you is to escape some of this shit. But I can't do that. I'm retracting everything. I don't know why you changed your mind, but you did want me. I saw it on your face. And I want you, so fuck everything else. The team hired you. Not me. I almost lost my niece. Life's short, Rain. I want to fuck you, so I'm going to tell you I want to fuck you. I guess the real question is what are you going to do about it?

My body was an inferno.

My hands shook, and despite all evidence to the contrary, thoughts blared in my head that he *didn't* actually want me. I started to shove it all aside before I drowned in my own confusion. That would've been my normal response. I liked to just ignore everything that didn't make sense to me, but I couldn't in this situation. I'd reached out because of what he was going through with his niece. That was important. She was important.

My fingers trembled, which made the next text take three times as long to type.

Rain: I don't know. I'm just going to be honest because I don't know what else to say or do. I don't understand when you say things like that to me, but I feel horrible about what you're going through with your family. If you need something, let me know.

And fuck. That was even more confusing. I sent another text right away.

Rain: I'm good at my job. Personal life, I'm a mess.

And *send*.

Tyler: What the fuck does any of that mean?

I sighed.

I should text back something polite but professional. Something a colleague would say, but I couldn't do it. If I did, I'd close the door on whatever he'd opened it to. When I said I was a mess, I wasn't lying.

If he actually was attracted to me, it was just because he needed an outlet right now. I was there. I seemed available. That was all.

I nodded, and some of the clouds began to lift.

That made sense to me—more sense than if he actually did want me.

Maybe he still thought he wanted me, but it'd pass. He'd learn how fucked up I was when it came to that stuff, and he'd walk away. I wasn't worth the effort.

Jesus. *My career* wasn't worth the effort. What was I thinking?

I was doing him a favor.

It was better this way.

I never texted him back.

15

TYLER

People were assholes. Why did the fucking media need to upend my sister's life and my niece's health crisis because they were nosy about why I'd asked to be traded? The news had broken almost a week ago. We played a Tuesday game, and now we were at it again on Thursday, and I was currently using Colorado's goalie as my personal anger outlet.

He blocked a particularly nasty shot from me and after the whistle blew, he skated out just beyond the crease and tore his helmet off. "What the fuck, Griffin? That's your twenty-third shot. We're in the second period. You got a problem with me that I don't know about?"

Was that a lot of shots? Yes, from one individual. Did a goalie usually get pissed off and confront that particular player? No, but Shetland was a friend, and yeah, he was mad, but there was also a twinge of concern in his eyes. Plus, Shetland had a short temper. Of all the goalies I knew, he'd been in the most fights.

Immediately, Sunny was between us, and Brick started to migrate our way in case he needed to handle the fight. *Yeah right.* Refs hardly ever let two goalies go at it anymore. I waved him off and patted Sunny's chest to let him know I was okay. I moved around him, going over to Shetland. One of the refs went with me, but neither of us was dropping gloves.

I didn't even know what to say to him. "No. Just—it's been a fucking week."

His face twisted behind his cage. He was already skating backward. "Let's do drinks after this, eh?"

"Yeah. Sounds good."

"You two ready to play hockey or do you need time to work out when you're going to braid each other's hair?" The ref was deadpan, lifting his whistle back to his mouth. "We got a game to play, gentlemen."

I didn't reply, just skated to the bench where Bruge was waiting to replace me. He was stone-faced. He dropped down as I stepped off the ice. Coach came over right away, swatting my shoulder. "What was that about?"

I shrugged and took the water offered to me. "Shelly snapped for a second. He's a hothead."

Sunny laughed beside me. "He thought Griff had a personal vendetta. Guess he's not used to dealing with that many shots."

Coach grunted, hitting my shoulder again with his clipboard. "You got us ahead four to one. Keep the lead and I don't care if you have a personal vendetta. We need those points. You hear me?"

"Yeah, Griff." Jesse laughed, reaching for the water. "You already got a hat trick, and we're not even to the end of the second period. Maybe let the rest of us try to catch up and get us those points for playoffs?"

I grinned. "Get ready for some fast passes."

He held up his glove, and I met it with mine as he said, "Bet."

When we got back on the ice, I gave him a fast pass between my skates, and Ray was ready, like he'd said he would be.

Right after his goal, he pounded my shoulder pads. "That's

our thing from now on, man." He held up his gloved hands, and as I hit them with mine, he added, "*Bet*."

Fucking hell. Okay then. "Bet," I agreed.

Guess it was our thing.

I had more aggression to work out, so for the next period, I worked on passing. Ray got one more goal. So did Sunny, who realized what I was doing and began to try to out-pass me. I had to admit, by the end of the game, most of my aggression was gone.

We won seven to two.

The locker room was elated, except for Bruge.

"How's it going with your new team?" Shetland asked later that evening. "Obviously something's working judging by that score tonight."

I told him the same as I'd mentioned to Nolan.

Shelly tilted his head, giving me a considering look. "I know Bruge. He just takes time to warm up to people. The team's already rallying around you. I could tell. If you guys don't get to playoffs, I'll be shocked."

"Maybe." It felt good to hear that, especially from a friend who was on a different team. I wanted to make sure I was doing my job, that the reason they agreed to take me on was being fulfilled. I was here for my family, but my career couldn't falter either.

"Was that what got into you tonight? About the team?"

I was still learning the ins and outs of being back in town, so Ray had suggested this place for a private drink. It was just down the block from where their team was staying.

I started to shrug off his question but stopped myself. He and I had done Juniors together. I couldn't do that to a friend. My phone had been blowing up all night. Nolan had called once and left a text for me to call him. I was sure he was going to ask the same question.

"It's my family." I leaned back in the booth and raked a hand over my face. "That shit that came out this last weekend. Saturday, my head was a mess. Skylar broke down again Monday when there was a new wave of media that decided the weekend news shouldn't die down. Tonight, you got the brunt of it."

Shelly frowned, leaning forward. "I'm sorry, man. I heard the news. Everyone did, but I didn't realize it was still going on. How's your niece doing?"

"They have her in a coma."

"What?" His eyes widened.

"They're going to try to bring her out tomorrow."

He shook his head and swore under his breath.

My phone buzzed, and I glanced down.

Rain: Can we talk?

Jesus Christ. This woman. She ignored me all week, staying professional and polite and distant. She was good at her job. I could see it. But there was something odd on her face every time she looked at me and didn't think anyone was watching—like an uncertainty. I didn't know what that was about, and I didn't have time for games either. But in a flash, I remembered her skating that night, how she felt in my arms, the sugar scent of her, and my cock was upright.

Tyler: You wanna fuck?

Rain: You can't say that to me.

Tyler: Why not?

Rain: It's unprofessional.

Tyler: I already had my tongue down your throat. We're past that. Why do you want to talk?

Rain: It's obvious something's up with you from that game. I wanted to see if you needed anything.

Tyler: You know what I want from you. As far as I'm concerned, you're not my psychologist.

Tyler: Look. Do you really want me to stop? I will.

I waited, but she didn't respond to that. That told me enough.

Tyler: Noting your silence. Unless it's got something to do with you and me getting in all sorts of magical positions, we can keep the business chitchat to business hours in the future. Eh?

Rain: Eh? You're suddenly Canadian.

Tyler: You Googled me? Is that how you know I'm not from up north?

Rain: No, dumbass. You were a bulldog.

I paused because yeah...if someone googled me, they could see where I went to high school and yeah, they could look up our mascot. That was possible, except fanatics did that sort of thing.

Slick wasn't a fanatic.

She sure as shit wasn't a fan of mine either.

So that meant...

Tyler: You from around here, Slick?

She didn't reply, and after a full minute of silence, I had a feeling she wasn't going to. I put my phone away, feeling somewhat odd.

"You good? Who the fuck were you texting?"

Crap.

I forgot Shetland.

16

RAIN

My methods were simple. I watched the players, got to know them, and I tried to let them get to know me. That was mostly it. So much of the focus was on winning, and that was the first obstacle for my job. If the pressure was off, if the guys were having fun, if they were focused on doing the best they could against themselves, then the body relaxed. Muscle memory took over. The focus got clearer. It always depended on the player, the team, and the coaching.

Some of the newer guys sought me out to ask questions, but the veterans were more resistant. I'd learned that was part of the job as well. Management had hired me. Not the team. Not the coach.

Except I stopped caring about that, because in a meeting, I made the observation that Sunny was holding back.

The meeting came to a halt, and all the coaches looked my way.

"What do you mean?" Coach Hines asked.

"He was trained to be the left winger, and somewhere in his mind, I'm guessing that means he thinks his job is just to assist the center. It's not. You all know that, but when Bruge was the center, Sunny matched him, every step of the way. When Bruge moved, Sunny was beside him. He's doing the same thing with Griffin, but Griff's faster. He's better than Bruge, and yet Sunny is still beside him the entire way. I think there's potential in Sunny that's not being tapped, and I also think it's an easy fix."

They were silent.

Coach Hines cleared his throat and leaned forward in his seat. It squeaked under his weight. "A simple fix?"

I tried to gauge Coach Hines to see if he was going to be offended if I continued on this pathway. I decided to proceed. This was my job. "He needs to be told that he can find openings, make openings," I explained. "He needs to be told he can also be the star, and then it's classic conditioning. Tell him, then give him a chance to do it. Reinforce when he does it and repeat. Eventually the lightbulb turns on. You'll know when he's broken through the old way of thinking because he'll walk into the locker room differently. *Then* watch how the team reacts to him. He's your first building block to changing their mindset."

I was half lying because the coaches' mindsets were also an early building block. They needed to change alongside the team.

"Griffin—" Coach began.

I shook my head. I knew where this was going, and this was part of their problem. "There can be more than one stand out talent on the team. Griffin is very aware of this. He'll be the first to get excited about this change. He's used to winning. He wants to win. Griffin is another tool to use to start changing the team's mindset. He wins. Do what he does, and when you find yourselves wanting to hold back and put up some resistance, come to me. You have two winners on your team right now, Griffin and Brick. Both *expect* to win."

As I looked around the table again, I could see they were listening.

"I'd like to spend one-on-one time with the players, and some of that might be on the ice. Benoit assured me I'd be allowed freedom for my methods, but you're the coaches. I'd like to make sure you're okay with that."

The assistant coaches looked puzzled, but one by one they turned to Coach Hines, who just continued to watch me as if I mystified him. Eventually he realized they were waiting for him to say something, and he cleared his throat. "Yeah. Uh, that's fine. Just not for extended periods of time. I don't want them over conditioning."

I smiled, giving a nod in thanks. I was aware they were going on blind faith here. They'd been told about my success with American football, but they hadn't a clue about my knowledge of *this* particular game.

IT WAS the end of the day's practice when I saw that Brick and Meester had stayed to talk to the goalie coach.

I waited until they skated off. "Brick."

He turned to look at me.

The goalie coach glanced over, so I held his gaze, trying to remind him of the meeting this morning. After a moment he gave me a nod and continued, leaving us.

"Can I shoot on you?" I asked.

Brick had taken off his helmet, so I could see that my question caught him off guard. "Uh." He looked beyond me, probably seeking out the coach before agreeing. "Yeah. Uh... You just want me in the crease?"

"Yep. Let me grab a stick and some pucks. I'll be a second."

It didn't take me long to find one of the equipment managers. "Hey, Benny."

He was a middle-aged man, and he was always on the run. He was a little breathless as he whirled toward me.

"Yeah? How can I help?" There were beads of sweat on his forehead.

"I'm going to shoot on goal for a bit. You have a taped leftie stick I could use? I promise not to break it."

He chuckled. "Griffin has some pre-taped sticks. He's a leftie, but I could try and find some other ones..."

"No. That'd be perfect."

"Okay. I'll be right back."

I went over and found a bucket of pucks and laced up my skates. Brick was doing laps when I returned, but he moved over to the goal when he saw me step on the ice.

Benny hurried down the hallway, carrying two sticks. He was out of breath as he handed one to me. "That's one Griffin prefers, but here's another in case that one doesn't work." He placed it on the bench, and only then did he see Brick waiting for me in the crease. His face went slack. "Uh..."

I took the stick and bucket with me as I pushed off. "Thanks, Benny."

"Yeah. Uh, yeah..." He remained watching until someone shouted his name, and I could hear him hurry away.

I shifted my focus to Brick, dumping the bucket of pucks on the ice.

He watched, probably wondering what the hell I was doing, but this wasn't for him. This wasn't even for me. I was doing this for anyone who had doubts.

I skated up to him and spoke plainly. "You don't need help with this. That's not why I'm here. Just...bear with me. Okay?"

He hesitated a second before giving me a nod.

"I'm going to shoot two times at you. The first will hit your chest. I want your eyes closed. Once it hits your chest, open your eyes for the second shot. Block the second. It won't be going to your chest. And we're going to go fast. Got it?"

He frowned a little but gave another nod.

I did a quick circle. "Ready?"

He closed his eyes, and I shot.

It hit his chest, as promised. He caught that first puck, tucked it down, and immediately looked for my second shot that came from the side. The drill was designed to help with rebounding goals, which was a skill any goalie could hone. Brick caught on to the speed after a round or two, and his eyes flared.

He liked the drill.

So did I, because my shots came from all angles. I went top shelf. Far side. Glove side. Corners. Sixth and seventh holes. Sometimes they got through, sometimes they didn't. But over and over, as soon as I hammered out the second shot, I circled fast around his net and grabbed the first puck again. That was my signal for us to repeat.

We did this for ten minutes until he grabbed some water.

"You want to keep going?" I asked. "Or head home? Up to you."

He licked his lips, eyes blazing. "Keep going."

I grinned. I couldn't help myself. God, I had missed this sport.

In this moment, we were two hockey players appreciating the sport and appreciating each other's abilities. I turned my brain off and let myself get lost in the skating, in the feel of handling the puck, in sweeping around the net, all of it, though I was aware we'd attracted an audience. I saw them by the bench, watching. But then I let that go too, because it meant I'd already accomplished my goal for this session. The rest of our time was for me and Brick.

We went another ten minutes, fast and furious, and when I signaled we were done, Brick was panting. His eyes gleamed. He pulled off his helmet and skated my way. "You're good."

My heart raced, and I could only manage a smile.

"Why are you not playing in the PWHL? Your snap shot is insane."

My smile grew. It was nice to hear him say that, but I did my job for a reason, and judging by the new way he looked at me, I'd accomplished it with him. I turned to see who had been watching us. Meester was there, alongside Marken, the goalie coach, and a few other players. Benny as well.

No Griffin. I ignored the dip in my stomach. He tended to head out immediately, probably returning to his sister's side. I shouldn't have been surprised because we'd been ignoring each other whenever I was around the team. Today wouldn't have been any different.

I refocused on Brick. "Thanks, but that's not the job I want to do."

I could see his confusion, which made me laugh. He was a hockey player. If someone had the skills to play professional hockey, why wouldn't they?

"You're one of the best goalies in the NHL," I told him.

His head raised.

"You will be in the Hall of Fame, but this fanbase and this team doesn't seem to realize that. I want them to be made aware of it sooner than later."

His eyebrows pulled together. "That's why we did this drill together?"

"No. We did this drill because I wanted to shake some people up." I flashed him a look. "This is my job. Everyone here thinks a certain way. They have pre-set assumptions in place, and I need to clear those out. You just helped me start doing that. Thank you."

He grunted, switching his helmet to one side so he could pull a glove off. He wiped his hand over his face. "I don't understand a thing you just said, but I had fun. I'll do that with you any day of the week." He looked over my shoulder. "I got a feeling Meester is going to be asking to do it too."

Meester was the only one still watching. He gave us a wide smile before heading to the locker room.

Brick gestured to the ice. "You want help cleaning up?"

"Nah. I got it. I'm going to do some laps anyway."

"Okay. It's been fun, Connors." He tapped my shoulder as he passed.

I quickly picked up all the pucks and skated the bucket and stick over to the bench. After that, I bent my head down and began to skate.

This time was for me, and I didn't hold back.

I skated until my heart wanted to explode out of my chest.

And I grinned the entire time.

17

TYLER

I could watch Rain skate for hours. I came from the locker room while she was working with Brick, so I settled in one of the chairs to watch. She hadn't known I was there.

She was good.

I could tell Brick loved this drill with her, and the others were surprised at her skill. They all took note. Many on the team had been resistant and closed off to the work she wanted to do with us, but whatever mojo she was working *was working*.

I needed to go. Get out of here.

I'd thought I just wanted to escape in her, use her for a short time, but more and more, I felt an awareness inside of me. It went deeper than I wanted. I needed to steer clear.

My phone buzzed, and I tensed. Looking down reluctantly, I saw my sister's name.

"Ski?" I answered. My voice was rough. *Fuck.* She didn't need to deal with my shit on top of her shit. "What's up? Are you okay?"

She'd been crying again. I could tell when she spoke. "She's awake."

"Zoey is?" Suddenly nothing else mattered.

Ski began crying again, but I swear I could hear her smile. "Yes. She's awake. Get here as soon as you can." Her voice dropped to a whisper. "Love you. My baby's going to be okay."

"Yeah," I breathed. A weight that I hadn't known was on my shoulders lifted. "I'm coming."

"Hurry," she rasped, and before I could tease her, she ended the call.

I felt dazed. This was huge. And yet I couldn't move. I didn't know how long I'd been standing there, but I was still looking down at my phone when I heard a side door open.

I lifted my head. Rain was just coming off the ice, and she looked wrecked—maybe worse than me, except under her sweat and messed hair, there was a glow to her, a spark in her eyes I'd never seen before.

For some reason, before she could say anything, I blurted out, "Zoey's awake."

Her eyes went wide. "She's—that's great!" She closed the door and traipsed over on her skates. "That happened today?"

"Come with me." I said the words before I knew I was going to say them.

We both froze, but I meant it. I wanted her there, and...I couldn't bring myself to take it back.

"What?" she asked.

"Come with me," I said again. I didn't know how to explain it or what to say about why it suddenly felt so right to have her with me, so I said nothing. I waited and watched her.

Uncertainty appeared before it slid away to reveal something else. Warmth? Longing? Then fear. She swallowed, edging back a step.

She was going to say no, so I took a step toward her and repeated my request, softening. "Come with me."

Her gaze held mine, and whatever she saw there closed her mouth. "O-okay."

Relief washed over me. "Do you need to shower? I mean,

don't on account of me, but if you want to... Do you need clothes? I keep some extra on hand."

"I..." She looked down at herself, flushing. Her hands splayed over her thighs and she laughed a little. "Yeah. Maybe. I usually keep a bag in my car, but..." She shivered. Her forehead wrinkled, determined now. "Give me a little time. Or my hotel isn't far—"

"You're still at a hotel?"

"Yeah. I mean, I'm not moving here. I'm just here for the job."

"Yeah, but won't that be the entire season? You could do a nine-month lease somewhere. Your job is to help us get to the playoffs, right? That'll take the whole season."

"Well, yeah, but I mean, it's fine. I think the team has some deal with the hotel." She looked away, pondering something. "Uh, if you tell me what hospital, I can meet you there."

I shook my head. "I'll give you a ride to your hotel. I can wait in the lobby while you change, shower. Whatever you need. I'd—I'd rather..." I didn't know what to say now because the truth was, I wanted to be in her presence. I didn't want to go to the hospital by myself.

I'd never had this feeling, this desire to be around another human being except with Skylar.

I was a mess. That's the only thing that made sense.

The trade. My niece's overdose. The coma. Her waking up. I was just wrecked. But whatever was going to help me right now, I was going with it.

"I'll give you a ride there and back. It's no problem. We have time."

"Okay then. Let me grab my bag." She gave me a small grin, smoothing her hands over thighs again before disappearing down the hallway.

What the hell am I doing?

18

RAIN

What am I doing?
None of this made any sense. Tyler Griffin was downstairs in the lobby waiting for me.

I tried not to rush as I got ready, because when I did, I got worked up and forgot something, and I couldn't let that happen. Cool, calm, and collected. That's what I needed to be.

I was having a heart attack.

He wanted me to go to the hospital with him. Why? I should get out of it, make something up.

I didn't.

I finished showering, dressed in black leggings, my little sneakers, and one of my favorite hoodies. I didn't want my usual purse, so I put a few things in a crossbody bag. I'd never been one to spend an hour on my hair. Put in some product and it would dry just fine. I was lucky in that aspect. A little makeup, and I was ready to go.

My palms were sweaty as I rode down the elevator, questioning everything all over again.

His sister would be there. His niece. And he wanted me with him? I couldn't make sense of it. God. I knew his sister had suffered a brain injury, and I knew how she'd gotten it. I didn't think that was common knowledge. I should not be going with him. Anyone but me. And yet—I laughed, feeling a little unhinged as the elevator doors opened—here I was.

I stepped off and turned toward the lobby.

Tyler was there, surrounded by a bit of a crowd. He was signing autographs and chatting, but as soon as he saw me, he excused himself and pushed through the group to head my way. As soon as he was beyond them, he dropped the public smile and his face hardened. He nodded as he passed me. "Ready?" His knuckle grazed my arm, sending a tingle through me.

I croaked out, "Ready."

If I was going with him, it should be in business mode, but I glanced at him sideways as we walked to the parking lot. I considered that, tried summoning the professional inside of me, and it wasn't there. A part of me wilted, or melted, because that was gone. I wouldn't be able to go back to being his sport psychologist. Then again, maybe I never had been, from the beginning? Our past had already condemned that, even though he hadn't a clue about how intertwined our lives had been at one point. I could consult with him, be his equal, but even before accepting this job, I knew Tyler Griffin didn't need any help from me. He already knew how to win. No. I was here in a totally different capacity, one a lot more private and personal, and my mind was yelling that I should stop and go back to my hotel room. But my body had no intention of turning around. We were going with him.

"Is this a rental?" I asked as we settled into his truck, my voice cracking a little.

"Mmmm? Oh, no. It's mine. A buddy drove it out for me."

"That was nice of him."

He pulled out of the parking lot. "Yeah," he said.

After that he was quiet, focused on merging onto the interstate.

He drove fast, but he was controlled. My brothers used to drive like bats out of hell. Daniel had been the worst, and if I cringed, he'd ridiculed me. It'd been hell anytime I needed a ride from him. I learned how to use the public bus system as soon as I could.

I stiffened, being in a vehicle with Tyler now. I couldn't help it. Some memories would probably never leave me.

Tyler didn't seem to be paying attention to me, though, so the closer we got to the hospital, the more I relaxed.

He finally looked over at me before getting out of the truck. "What are you wearing?"

I looked down. It was my favorite football team. "I'm pretty sure this is a sweatshirt."

He rolled his eyes and reached into the backseat, producing two different sweatshirts. He pushed one against my chest. "You can't wear an NFL sweatshirt." He shrugged out of his jacket and put on the other one.

"Why not?"

"Because hockey is better." He said this as if explaining basic math to a two year old.

I flushed. "I worked with this team. There's nothing wrong with this sweatshirt."

"And the optics? You're with me. There are Grays fans here. They will notice. You know the sport. You know the fanbase. They'll blow a gasket."

I groaned. He was right. I wasn't going to say hockey fans were entitled, but they weren't *not* entitled. The nicer way to say it was that they were passionate.

Very passionate.

I rolled my eyes, but changed, trying to ignore how the sweatshirt smelled like him. I eyed the hoodie he was now wearing. "You can't wear that either."

"What?" He looked down and cursed.

The one I wore was a Grays sweatshirt, but his was from his New York team. The fans would've been more upset about him wearing that than me wearing a football hoodie. I had to laugh.

He scowled. "Shut up."

But his mouth twitched as he looked through the other sweatshirts in the back. When he was still looking a minute later, I sighed and tugged off the one I was wearing. I shoved it at him and reached for my original one.

"No." He caught my hand, stopping me.

"It's better if I wear a football hoodie than you wear your past team's, and you know it."

He growled as he let me go. "Swear to God, first thing I'm doing is filling this fucking truck with Grays apparel." He yanked on his sweatshirt and glared as I finished, pulling my hair out and smoothing it down.

I paused. "What?"

He continued scowling, his eyes flicking to my sweatshirt. I started laughing again as understanding dawned. "I didn't take you for a hockey snob."

"I'm not." He shrugged, his jaw still tight. "I like football, but I'm hockey." He came around the front to where I'd gotten out. "You're hockey too."

"For now."

He scoffed, turning toward the hospital. "Someone can't skate like you do and shoot the way you do and not be hockey. You're hockey."

"Football's been good to me," I said simply. "Hockey hasn't."

"It will be."

He sounded so confident, as if he just knew. But he didn't. Hockey had been good to *him*. He couldn't know the future.

He glanced back and stopped to let me catch up.

I found myself holding my breath, a part of me waiting for

him to get mad that I'd made him wait, but he didn't. He turned and kept going. He went at my pace the rest of the way.

Once we got to the lobby, the doors slid open for him. Tyler walked briskly past the front desk and pushed the button for the elevators. He glanced over at me, giving me space. He didn't crowd me. He wasn't trying to guide me. The elevator arrived, and we stepped on.

A few other people got on with us, a mom and two teenaged boys. Tyler lifted a hand to the small of my back, but he didn't actually touch me, just directed me over slightly.

One of the teens sucked in his breath, recognizing Tyler. He elbowed his friend.

"Ouch. Wha—" The kid shot his friend an irritated look, but quieted when he looked over at Tyler.

"Guys." The mom shot them a look before her gaze followed theirs.

I didn't know if she recognized Tyler or if her breath just shortened because of how hot he was. I couldn't blame her. They were supposed to get off on the second floor, but when we got there, they didn't move.

Tyler moved me closer to the side of the elevator, his hand now touching my back.

The doors began to close again before the woman reached out to stop it. "Guys."

"Mom." One of them swung his wide eyes pointedly toward Tyler.

She gentled her voice, giving us an apologetic glance. "Let's go, boys."

"Mom..." He tried again.

"Tate, get off this elevator now."

He let out a dramatic sigh, his shoulders bunched as he followed his friend off the elevator. The mom turned back. "I'm so sorry about them. They're fans. Good luck tomorrow night."

The doors closed, and we were both quiet until we got to the fifth floor.

"Does that happen often?" I asked quietly as we emerged into the hallway.

There was a nurse's desk ahead, but only a few people sat behind it. The hallway was mostly empty.

Tyler shrugged. "People know I'm here."

That told me nothing.

He took the lead, going to the desk first.

"Tyler." One of the nurses greeted him with a warm smile. She was slender. Warm brown skin. Almond eyes. Her smile tightened when she saw me step to his side. "Your sister is beside herself. She'll be happy to see you."

"Is Zoey—is she...?"

The nurse's smile widened. "Why don't you go see for yourself?"

He continued down the hall and paused just before he could be seen through a window. I realized he was nervous. I laid a hand on his arm, and I could feel his pulse racing. He exhaled sharply and turned back to face me. "What if..." He couldn't finish that statement.

"Want me to scope it out first? I could walk past, peek in, and tell you what I see?"

His gaze clung to mine for a moment before he nodded. "Yeah. Thanks. That'd be nice. Help me know what I should prepare myself for."

This was a big moment. His niece was awake.

I squeezed his arm once before I did a casual walk by. The door was open, but my shoulders deflated because the curtain was pulled so no one could see in from the hallway. Then I heard laughter.

Two feminine voices—one older and one younger, more raspy.

I backed up to Tyler. "She's awake. They're laughing."

"Did they see you?" he asked.

I shook my head. "The curtain is pulled, but I heard them." I nudged him forward. "Go. I'll..." I looked around. "I'll get some coffee and come back. You want some?"

He was already looking toward the room and gave me a distracted nod. "Uh, yeah. That'd be great. Thank you." He stepped forward, but suddenly whirled and caught me, pulling me into a hug. He wound his arms tight around me and dipped his head to my neck. His lips grazed my skin. "Thank you. Thanks for coming. It means a lot." He took the back of my neck in his hand and gave my forehead a quick kiss.

Then he was gone, and I was left dazed, my skin tingling.

19

RAIN

I didn't know what to get, so I came back with a carrier full—two lattes, a matcha, and a regular black coffee with a bunch of sugars and creamer in the middle. I figured Tyler and his sister could pick. I didn't know if Zoey could have coffee. I wouldn't think so, but I also didn't want to assume and offend her.

The door was cracked open as I approached, and I lifted my hand to knock, but then I heard someone crying.

"...I don't know what to do, Ty. What do I do?"

That sounded personal, way personal. I began to back away but then stopped because I had all the coffee. I didn't want it to get cold. And Tyler had asked me to come, but again, I didn't know why.

The curtain moved aside, and Tyler saw me at the door. *Crap.* I didn't want him to think I was eavesdropping. I lifted an awkward hand. "Hi." I raised the coffee carrier. "I got drinks."

The curtain yanked farther back and Skylar Griffin, Tyler's sister, poked her head around to see who was talking. She didn't seem angry, just confused. I steeled myself, ready in case she recognized me. She blinked a few times and stepped around the curtain. I got a glimpse of the hospital bed behind them and was relieved to see it empty. Meeting the sister was stressful enough. Meeting the niece on top of that would've been a whole other level of pressure.

"Who are you?" Skylar asked.

Panic surged. I didn't want to tell her my whole name or let Tyler tell her, because she would put the pieces together. She'd dated Daniel. She knew he had a sister.

Tyler ran a weary hand over his face, seeming beyond exhausted. "This is, uh…"

I stepped forward. "Rain. Hi. I work with the team."

"You do? As what? Oh!" Her eyes got big. "Are you here for social media? Ty mentioned that you guys had asked about doing a post for Zoey, but it seems a bit early."

I shook my head, horrified. "No. I'm the team…" I didn't want to say *psychologist* because that'd scare her away.

"She's our team shrink."

Really, Tyler? That was worse.

"Oh!" Skylar blinked, clearly not expecting that answer.

Tyler began silently laughing behind her as she approached me, all formal now. She held out a hand, the other smoothing her shirt and hair. "Well, it's nice to meet you." Her hand closed around mine. "Rain." Her eyebrows pulled together and she stepped to the side, shooting her brother a look. "I'm kinda surprised Tyler brought you here. No offense, bro, but he's not exactly one to feel his emotions, much less talk about them." She fixed him with another piercing look. "Can you even feel more than the basic three?"

Tyler's grin turned wicked. His eyes sparked. "Which three are you talking about?"

She laughed, swatting his shoulder. "Oh, you know—anger, hunger, and being horny."

His grin turned sly. "There's laughter too, but yes, I have the basic three. Fighting, food, and fucking. Not always in that order."

His sister shook her head. "Look at you, evolving." She indicated the empty bed behind her. "You can come in. We have a few extra seats. They took Zoey for some tests, but she's going to go nuts when she smells the coffee and can't have any."

I held up the carrier, coming farther into the room, but I made no movement toward any of the chairs. They were both still standing, and this was such a family moment. I shouldn't be here. I tried to catch Tyler's gaze, to relay that message, but he was still smiling at his sister.

She took the coffee carrier from me. "Thanks for this." Skylar placed the coffees on the long, narrow lap table. Then she motioned toward one of the empty chairs as she took a seat herself. Wrapping her arms around her knee, she hugged it to her chest. "Have a seat. Get comfortable. These tests can take forever, and when she comes back, she'll be too exhausted to have visitors."

Tyler yawned but caught my look and frowned at me. He didn't say anything though. I looked away in case Skylar was studying us. But she was yawning as well, and she closed her eyes and rested her head against the chair. Both looked wrecked.

I thought one of them would say something, make small talk, but neither seemed bothered by the silence. And this did not seem like the time to get to know Tyler's sister in any capacity.

"She's doing good then?" Tyler finally asked.

Skylar gave him a sad smile. "She's... The hospital's psychologist was in to talk with me before they took her out. They..." Her gaze flitted my way, but there was no hesitation. Or caution. She shared that same sad smile with me. "They don't know if she overdosed on purpose. It's all been so quick, to be honest. Do you know anything about that stuff?"

I opened my mouth but thought for a moment first. I could go one route here, be all prim and proper, but Tyler hadn't asked me here for that. No matter what he said to his sister, I knew he had no interest in my professional skills. I pinned him with a look. "I'm more a sports psychologist. I have a basic knowledge about drug and alcohol addiction, but it's not my focus."

"Oh." She tilted her head to the side. "Then why did you...?" She trailed off when I glared at her brother, who was chuckling to himself. "You're such an ass, Tyler! You brought your team's psychologist with you because what? You're trying to get into her pants?"

"You're not wrong." He started laughing again.

"So on brand for you." She rolled her eyes but started laughing too.

Pain stabbed in my gut. I was just another girl he'd brought around, and I had no doubt I wouldn't be the last. But I shoved that down and instead focused on them. They had the same laugh, and they only needed to look at each other to start cracking up all over again. It was nice to see this sort of sibling love. There was no hatred. No annoyance. No one was being mean. No one was being pushed out or used as a scapegoat. Just love. And Tyler looked the most relaxed I'd ever seen him. He was determined, alert, and fierce at the arena, so it was nice to see this side of him as well.

But no matter how I tried, I couldn't get her words out of my head. *"So on brand for you."* He did this a lot. There wasn't anything special about me, which I knew. God, I knew that. But it still hurt.

I shouldn't have forgotten. Why had I?

Because Tyler looked at me and asked me to come with him, and I'd melted at his feet. I was able to do my job because I could put everything in its nice, neat drawer. Everything was compartmentalized. Except Tyler wasn't. He wouldn't let me put him in any one drawer. He was in one already because of our past, even if he didn't know it, and now he was trying to be in two other drawers. He kept jumping out of them, making everything blurred in my mind. I'd wanted to believe he wanted me here for him. But I remembered what he'd said earlier in his texts. He wanted to escape. That's why I was here. To help him forget the shitty situation going on with his family by what? Taking him to a janitor's closet? An empty patient room?

"You really are a dumb fuck, aren't you?" I flinched, hearing one of my brother's taunts. He'd laughed when he said that, and it became one of his favorite insults for the next few years.

Yes, Daniel. I'm still just a big dumb fuck.

Tyler gave me a curious look, so I pushed the old hurt aside, along with the new stuff, and put it all in the back of my head. Fixing a smile on my face, I tried to let him know I hadn't taken offense to anything his sister said. I wasn't sure it worked, but now Skylar was laughing about something else, and he was quickly distracted.

I needed to leave, but I didn't know how to excuse myself without making it uncomfortable.

Skylar had just begun talking about a neighborhood cat Zoey tried to adopt when a nurse came into the room. Seeing my chance, I stepped out into the hallway and waited to see if Tyler would come out with me.

He didn't. He stayed.

When the nurse left a few minutes later, I still waited.

It felt wrong to be here.

I waited another twenty minutes, but he didn't come out.

The nurse had closed the door when she left. I knew I should knock and go in there, say my goodbyes, make sure everything was fine. But I was hurt, though I knew that was stupid. I shouldn't be the one hurting in this situation. I already knew what Tyler wanted from me, so I shouldn't have been surprised.

But I *still* couldn't bring myself to knock on the door.

I shouldn't have come. I didn't belong.

I'd pulled my phone out to send him a text when the door opened. His eyes flashed, and he stepped into the hallway, closing the door behind him. "She's not saying it, but Ski needs to sleep. I wanted to stick around until they bring Zoey back, give her a quick hug, but I'm sure she'll need her rest too. Did you want to stick around until then?"

"I—no."

His face fell.

I looked away. "I think this is more a family thing. I'm going to go. Unless you need me for something?" *What am I saying? What am I doing?*

The spark came back to his gaze, but he only said softly, "If you've got more pressing matters, by all means."

"I don't." I did, actually, like trying to remind myself about my place, which was *not* here, for one.

He stepped closer, and his voice dropped again. "Could you stay then? I don't think it'll be long." He searched my face.

I needed to go. Not stay. I shouldn't do whatever this was that was happening between him and me. "I'll wait in the lobby. Take your time with your sister and your niece."

He stepped back, his eyes still searching mine. "Okay."

"Okay."

We watched each other. I wanted to step toward him, hug him. That felt like the natural thing to do, but I didn't. I *couldn't*.

"Tyler?" Skylar called from inside the room, and he turned to answer her.

I slipped away, turning off my feelings. It was an old trick I'd used when I was little. It was the way I coped. I ignored all the schooling I'd done and resorted back to my most raw self. I needed to remember what I was to him, to my family, to the world, and most importantly to myself.

Just another dumb fuck.

20

TYLER

Rain wasn't in the lobby when I came downstairs, not that I'd thought she would be. I'd been here for hours now. It took longer for Zoey to come back to the room than I'd thought, and once I'd stepped back in, Skylar had started crying all over again. She'd been okay while Rain was there, and to be honest, I liked having the break because Ski had either been sleeping or crying the other times I'd come. Maybe that was part of the reason I'd asked Rain to come with me—I knew if there was someone else here, Skylar would have to feel something else, even for a moment. Or hell, maybe it was the reason Skylar pointed out.

I didn't know, but something had happened between when Rain first stepped into the room and when that nurse came in. I thought maybe she wanted to use the bathroom or needed some air, but when I finally went looking for her, she was right there in the hallway, and something was different.

I couldn't place it, because on the outside, she looked like the usual Rain. Nice. Infuriatingly sexy. She could make my dick hard with just a glance, but whoever was in the hallway was not the woman I'd been obsessively watching ever since she started working with the team.

I wanted her. Maybe I even wanted something more than just her body, but she was confusing.

She sent me a text after a while saying she needed to get back, and she'd see me at the arena for our morning skate, but I wasn't going along with that plan.

I knew her hotel, and I knew what floor her room was on because I'd paid attention. So I went there, and as soon as I got to her floor, I called her phone. I heard it ringing from behind the last room in the hallway, and just as she answered, I knocked on the door.

"Hello?"

I knocked again. "I'm at the door."

I heard her coming. A moment later, the door opened. She wore a confused look, but also something more. Panic? Guilt? I couldn't tell, but then I noticed what she was wearing. A Grays' shirt—and possibly nothing else. Heat exploded inside of me, sending all the blood straight to my dick. She was wearing my shirt. That was my number. If she turned around, I knew my last name would be on the back.

Was this her regular sleeping attire?

She gaped at me a moment before she composed herself. Then she reached for the door, and I realized she was going to shut it in my face. I stepped inside before that could happen.

"What—" She stopped and her face went blank. "Are you okay?"

"What happened at the hospital?" Because sure as shit something *had* happened. She'd tucked herself behind whatever fucking fortress of walls she had in her mind, and I couldn't reach her anymore.

A lot of emotions were running through me tonight—frustration, need, anger. I'd had her, and then she was gone. Knowing that tipped me over the edge. Her eyes went wide as I reached for her, no longer giving a shit about the right thing to do. I didn't give one fuck about anything except that I needed to fuck her.

I needed to feel her mouth. Her taste. I was desperate to have her underneath me.

"Rain..." I groaned, my hand at the back of her neck.

She gasped, quietly, but didn't pull away.

She tracked my movement, like prey watching a hunter. I didn't want to hurt her. I wanted to taste her. My fingers curled tighter, and I stepped close, crowding her against the wall by the door. She didn't say a word, but she didn't stop me, so I kept moving until I could feel her breaths. Until her chest rose, grazing my own chest. I could smell that fucking sugar scent of hers. Vanilla cupcakes. It didn't seem like body spray or shampoo. I tugged her head down and pressed my face to it, making sure it wasn't her hair. It wasn't. That smelled like lilacs. The cupcake smell was just her.

Her pulse was pounding, and I angled my head to look in her eyes. "Do you want this?"

Her pupils dilated. The tip of her tongue darted out, wetting her bottom lip, and I was ready to burst. I slid my hand around to the side of her throat, still feeling her pulse, and slowly, so slowly, applied pressure just under her jaw, tipping her head back. Her mouth raised for me, but she still hadn't said a word.

I needed her voice.

My thumb moved to her bottom lip, and I felt it trembling. "You were there, Rain. Right there. With me." I closed my eyes, the desperation to claim her pounding through me. I stamped it down but moved another step closer. She pulled in some air, and she melted. Her body relaxed. Her breath released, and she began moving against me, brushing over the bulge in my pants. Her eyes closed, and the sweetest moan slipped past her lips.

I dipped down, my mouth almost touching hers, but I asked again. "Rain? Yes or no?" I ground against her.

"We shouldn't," she said quietly.

I bent down to catch her words and held still. I made myself hold still.

The yearning for her clawed at me. It was a primal demand, a need to claim her. To have her. I tried to think of things from her perspective. Her career...

My arm shook. Jesus. I'd never felt this before.

Suddenly, she moaned again and her eyes opened, wanton need shimmering there. Her lips parted and finally I heard her hiss, "I'm going to regret this."

That was all I needed.

I crushed my mouth over hers.

21

RAIN

He tasted like the rainbow after an F5 tornado had run through my home. A much-needed respite, reminding me that the destruction was over, that there were new things on the horizon. Better things.

Was that what I needed? I didn't know, but I knew I needed him.

I twined my arms around his shoulders as my body molded against his. We were kissing, but this was more, so much more. I felt drunk just at the feel of him. "You..." I began, but I stopped because *what was I about to say?*

I never lost myself. Even if I drank, I was always controlled. I had to be, because what if something slipped out? This was my secret—how lonely I was, except I was now realizing I'd kept it a secret from even myself.

I was *so* lonely.

I had deprived myself of touch, from connection, but now Tyler was here, giving me everything I'd told myself I didn't need. I'd lied to myself because I just knew no one would want to give this to me, so I'd learned to live life without it. Now he was here, but I had to remind myself that it wouldn't last.

Tonight. Maybe a few more times. Until he got tired of me—and he would. Everyone did. Everyone discovered what was wrong with me, and they walked away.

I ached, but my body shook.

He frowned. "What is it?"

I shook my head, and my throat spasmed. I couldn't talk. I wanted him. I wanted this.

Could I have it? One night? One week?

Was it worth losing my credibility over? Him? Just for however long this lasted?

When he left, would it devastate me?

"Hey." He dropped his mouth to my cheek, tasting a tear. "What's wrong? Did I do this? I'm sorry if I did."

I shook my head. It wasn't him. It had been everyone else, yet I couldn't tear myself away from him. I couldn't.

It'd been so long since someone touched me like this. I needed to push him away, tell him to leave, and close up so I wouldn't get hurt again. But I *couldn't*. He'd asked me to go to the hospital with him. He'd showed up here, and now he was holding me and wiping away my tears, even as he still eyed me hungrily. This was a gift.

He'd already torn me open. There was no mending anymore. But I would stitch myself back together. I would. I looked at him. He was so confused by me. I was fucked in the head, but I couldn't stop this.

One night. One time. Then I'd begin putting my pieces together again. But for now, I pulled him to me. I didn't just want to quiet the voices telling me I was a dumb fuck. I wanted to obliterate them.

"I have..." It hurt to speak right now. I burned for him, but he needed to have an idea what he was dealing with. "Stuff happened to me, with the way I grew up, and it's done some damage."

He shook his head. "Rain—"

I stopped him, putting a hand on his chest. "I don't want to stop this, but you need to know that when it comes to personal stuff, I'm messed up in the head. I never got that out of me."

He stared at me. Long. Hard. His eyes moved over my face, searching me, and he came to a decision. He rested his forehead against mine and breathed out, "Rain, right now, I just want to fuck you. That okay?"

Pleasure burst inside of me. I caught his shoulders as I lifted my legs to wrap around his hips. *"Yes."*

He kissed me again.

His hands hooked under my legs, adjusting me higher, and he walked to the bed. We both went down together, but he caught himself so he didn't crush me. We continued kissing.

He tasted so good. I writhed underneath him, growing more heated. Lifting my hips, I moved against him, and that felt fantastic.

He ran his hand down my side and slipped it underneath my shirt, pushing it up so I could feel more of him against my skin. "Can this come off?" he asked.

I pushed up and whipped it off, winding my arms tight around his shoulders again.

Tyler's body was so lean and built. Strong. I could feel every muscle shifting as he touched me. He slipped a hand down to my underwear and cupped my ass as he toyed with the small piece of fabric covering my pussy. Moaning, he buried his head in my neck. "Fuck, you feel so good." His finger moved inside the strap, and he circled me.

I shuddered. "I want you to fuck me, Tyler. Not toy with me."

He laughed, lifting his head to meet my gaze. He smirked, though his eyes were smoldering. "Sex can be good and fun, Connors."

I growled. "We're on a last-name basis when we fuck? Good to know, Griffin."

He laughed again, but his eyes darkened as he slid a finger inside of me. "You like that?"

I stretched for him, feeling him slip deeper, and I nodded, biting my bottom lip. That felt insanely good. He shifted up so he could see as he slid a second finger inside.

Carnal pleasure moved through my body, wrapping around my spine, and I panted, wanting to touch him back.

I knocked his hand away, sliding his fingers out of me. He paused, surprised as I pushed him back on the bed and climbed on top to straddle him.

"Rain?"

I tugged off his joggers and whisked them away, along with his boxer briefs. His dick was long and hard, and it had a lot of girth. I wrapped my hand around it and dipped my head, taking the tip of it in my mouth.

He surged up, his hands sliding into my hair. "Fuck. Shit. Are you—" I swirled my tongue around him, tasting him, and opened my throat, sucking him all the way in. I held there for a beat. I liked this, touching him this way.

He reared up, his hands fisting my hair now. "Shit, Rain. Shit. Fuck. That feels so good."

I moaned, enjoying making him tremble, and began sucking, bobbing my head over him. He laid still, shaking and twitching, and I kept going. When I nibbled along his tip, flicking my tongue over him, I used my hands to keep pumping. Then I dipped below, tasting his balls, and he cursed again, spasming. "Shit, shit, I'm going to come. Rain. *Baby.* Don't—"

I moved over him again, taking him all the way down my throat and cupping his balls with my hand, and it was enough. He exploded, cursing in guttural gasps. I kept my mouth in place, drinking up all of his cum, and then I swallowed before lifting off of him with an audible pop.

He cursed again and tugged my head up to look in his eyes.

He looked drunk as he tried scolding me. "I was planning on doing that to you, not the other way around."

I grinned, feeling a little drunk myself, just knowing I could make him come like that. "That was fun. I liked that."

He growled as he hoisted me up.

I squeaked in surprise and then I was straddling him again, and he tugged me forward to rest on his chest. He tucked some hair behind my ear, the touch tender. "I wanted to fuck you tonight."

I slid a hand down his chest, palming his dick. "We can still do that."

He waited a beat, uncertainty in his gaze. "About what you said before, about the personal shit—"

I shook my head. "I don't want to talk about it. You just needed to know there's shit in my head."

"But—"

I shook my head again. "I don't want to think. That'll come after."

He stared at me for a moment before sighing. "Okay, but I'm going to google everything I can find on 'personal shit' the second this is done, just so you know."

I grinned, ducking my head to his chest. "That's totally okay with me." I caught his hand in mine and rolled, pulling him on top of me. Holding his gaze, I slowly pushed his hand between my legs. "Now your turn."

He flashed me a grin so wicked, so carnal, that I caught my breath. "I'm going to make you *scream*, Rain."

I was already throbbing. That sounded just fine to me.

22

TYLER

My phone buzzed, lighting up the room, and it took a moment for me to remember where I was. That ceiling was not mine... And it all came back. I looked over and Rain was still in bed with me. She was curled away, as close to the edge as she could get, with the sheet pulled over her.

Buzz! Buzz!

I leaned down and snatched my phone to quiet it before I studied Rain again. She'd said some shit last night, something about what had been done to her and the way she grew up. I hadn't thought much about it at the time, as long as she was okay with fooling around, and last night had been good. It'd been fun. I wanted to do it again and again, and I still really wanted to rail her. We'd done everything but that last night, and it had been incredible. The sighs. The moans. The way she'd stroked me. The feel of her mouth, with those beautiful, fuckable lips wrapped around my cock.

I was not prone to falling in love. I barely liked people, but if a girl could make me fall at the sight of her sucking my cock, that girl was Rain. I wondered if she'd been conscious when she'd pulled away from me last night and tangled herself up in the sheet. Because I hadn't been. I wouldn't have let her do that.

My phone buzzed again.

Irritation stirred in me because I didn't want to be distracted from Rain. She was a kaleidoscope of puzzles. Every interaction yielded a different flash of pretty and confusing colors. I wanted to piece them together and figure out the painting underneath. Something had gone massively wrong with her, and I didn't like it.

I rolled out of bed as gently as possible. Her bedroom was separate from a living area and kitchenette, so I eased the bedroom door shut and moved to the living room before accepting the call.

It was Skylar.

"Hey."

"Why are you whisper—oh my God. Did you go and fuck that girl from the hospital? Also, since when do you bring girls with you to see your twin sister and your niece? You don't bring women around us, but it is so like you to sleep with your team's shrink. You won't use her for her job, but you'll get between her legs. Though, it's usually them coming on to you."

I cringed. "You have way too much energy for this conversation at whatever fucking time it is right now. Why are you calling? I was asleep."

"Oh." She laughed. "The nurse just came to check on Zoey, and I couldn't get back to sleep. I keep thinking about what the social worker said earlier. They want Zoey to go to a mental health clinic."

My sister was fully awake. Now that Zoey seemed out of the woods, she was returning to her usual self, and that was happy. She was happy almost all the time, which was annoying because I was generally *not*. I guess we balanced each other out.

"She needs to go to a mental health clinic, Ski."

"What? Why?"

I closed my eyes. "Because she overdosed. She almost died."

"But it might've been an accidental overdose."

"Does it really matter? She overdosed. She did drugs. Maybe it's not so uncommon for a teenager to do drugs, and maybe it was just one time, but I think it's better to proceed with caution. Did she say anything about it yet?"

"No." She sighed, sounding glum. "And I know Zoey. We can't force her to talk."

"This is why you called me?"

"They want to start paperwork tomorrow. I'm worried. If she goes in, she'll be away from me for even longer."

"Ski." I gentled my tone. "Zoey's not impulsive. If she'd only done drugs once and she overdosed by accident, she would've told you. It would've been one of the first things she said because she wouldn't want you to consider the alternative."

My sister started crying. I hated that.

"Talk to the social worker," I told her. "See if she can go into a clinic where you can see her or if there's a compromise. Money isn't a problem. I'll pay for it. You know that. I think it'll be good for Zoey. You two have always been close. You're a great mother, but Zoey's always been sad. If anything, it might be good for someone to look into that. It could be connected."

"You fuck a shrink and suddenly you're Dr. Phil?"

"Ski—"

"Forget it. We'll figure it out by ourselves." She ended the call.

I pulled the phone away to stare at it for a second. That wasn't my sister's normal behavior, but with the stress and the disruption to her sleep, any person would've lashed out. My sister also had a brain injury, so that could be a factor as well.

I knew what she was thinking. I was pushing for Zoey to spend time away from her, and my sister couldn't see how it was for Zoey's good. She was only focusing on them being apart. Again. The overdose and the coma had shattered my sister's heart. It shattered mine too, but eventually Skylar would calm down. She'd rethink how she spoke to me.

She'd regret it... Eventually.

Tyler: I love you, and I love Zoey. I'm not saying this to hurt you or her. I hope you know that. I really just want the best for you both.

Skylar: She needs to be with me! Not some stranger. You don't understand. You don't have kids.

No, but I raised you, didn't I? I wanted to tell her that, but I couldn't.

Tyler: What if it happens again? What if you don't find her in time? You need to focus on preventative measures. No matter what, the overdose happened. She's underage. She needs to get some help.

I didn't want to send that because it was so direct. Too harsh. Even if Zoey wasn't my kid, she was the most vulnerable in this situation and needed help the most. Losing our parents had been a blow. Skylar got pregnant. That was another blow. Then she was in a car accident and emerged with a brain injury. A third blow. I'd always done what I could for both of them, but it'd been hard for us. We'd gotten some breaks with a neighbor and when my billet parents decided to take us in, but I'd always tried to minimize how much we leaned on them. They were supposed to just host me during the hockey season. They hadn't needed to say yes to all three of us. It wasn't fair. They were good people, but a year later I turned eighteen, and I'd been taking care of Skylar and Zoey ever since.

Thank goodness for hockey and thank goodness for my sponsors that helped with the costs to get me through my training. Finally I started earning enough to afford a tiny apartment for us. The other guys roomed together and took in the newer teammates. Because of my situation, I never got that help, but fortunately Skylar's brain injury didn't prevent her from getting a job. She was high functioning, though her emotions were sometimes too intense for her to regulate. She didn't think rationally and couldn't calm down at times either. There were other things, but at a time like this, I couldn't pull my punches. I had to think of Zoey first.

I sent the text.

As I waited for her response, I used the bathroom and tried to brush my teeth with my finger. She hadn't replied by the time I was done. Leaving the bathroom, I eased open the bedroom door.

Rain hadn't moved an inch, but man, the room was cold, and that sheet looked thin.

It was almost five in the morning. If I got back into bed, I wouldn't be able to sleep, and I didn't want to wake her up. Between the midnight skating and the bags under her eyes, I wondered how much sleep she got. But I also couldn't leave her the way she was. I pulled up the blanket I'd been sleeping with and draped it over her.

When she didn't move, I snuck out, grabbing my things as I went. We had a game tonight. Morning skate was in a few hours. I needed caffeine. Lots of it.

It was going to be a long day.

23

RAIN

Tyler left a note for me.
I found it as soon as he left because I'd heard him moving around before the far door clicked shut a moment later. I'd laid there only briefly before I got up, padding to the bathroom. Starting the coffee machine, I read the note as it began to brew.

I had a great time. Can we do this again? Call me. Text me. Wink at me. Whatever you want to do, I'm down for it. -Tyler

The note made me grin, but then I remembered hearing his sister's voice through the bedroom door. I hadn't been intending to eavesdrop, but I'd gotten up and stood at the door because I thought he was gone. But he wasn't. She'd been upset while he spoke calmly back to her.

Before I could hear too much, I'd gone back to bed and rolled over the way I always slept—curled up in a ball on the farthest side of the bed.

I poured some coffee and looked at the clock. It was half past five now.

I didn't think I could sleep anymore, and it was a game day.

Morning skate was at nine, and I wanted to go in and lay some more groundwork with Sunny. I was eager to see if there'd be any change in his playing tonight, and there were some other dynamics I'd noted within the team, but my thoughts were a little muddied. I needed to take some time, write them out, and then go from there.

I looked back at the note. Tyler was right. Last night was fun. And I'd told him I struggled with personal relationships. I'd hinted at something that made me vulnerable, and I didn't like that. Letting someone in never ended well for me. Ever. I tried over and over again in my twenties until I'd finally accepted that I'd never have a close group of friends or a partner. Being a loner was the safest route for me.

This was going to end in destruction. Mine. My career.

For a moment, self-loathing hit me. It hit me hard, and I let it.

We shouldn't have done what we did last night. I shouldn't let it happen again, but I remembered how I'd felt in his arms. My body was going to give in, no matter what my mind might say. And I wasn't going to delude myself and pretend it wouldn't happen again. It would.

I'd been starved of touch for so long, and here came Tyler Griffin, barreling down all my roadblocks. Yeah. This was going to end in devastation, and I wasn't going to do one thing to stop it. I was helpless against him.

Maybe it was just time I had the final blow?

No. I could minimize the damage. I'd need some walls around me if I was going to do this with him again. How could I turn him down? I couldn't. No one would.

I shook my head, clearing it all away because the more I pondered, the more my messed-up mind would cause problems for me.

I went down to the hotel gym.

A good, hard run would help.

24

RAIN

Something was wrong. The Grays were playing *horribly*. Sunny kept shooting on goal and missing. Ray was passing to the other team, and after the third time, the crowd began booing. The only one who seemed solid was Brick, but Brick was always solid. Hence his nickname. Even Tyler was off. He wasn't connecting with his line. He was too fast, and when he tried to adjust, he was too slow. The second line was getting double the usual playing time in the second period.

I couldn't wait anymore. Making my way down to the bench, I watched as Coach Hines held Sunny back and sent Davie out with Tyler and Jesse. He turned and saw me as I stopped next to Meester. There was frustration and a bit of accusation in his eyes.

Great. He blamed me for this.

I tapped Sunny on the arm and motioned toward the tunnel. He followed, and once we were out of sight, I asked, "What's going on?"

He pulled his helmet off, his face flushed and sweaty. His frustration was evident. "I suck. That's what's going on. What else do you want me to say?" He glanced back when a boo rose from the crowd. Bruge was on the ice, and Tyler had stayed. They were both centers. That'd be interesting.

I focused on him. "Look. Stop it. This is my job. Let me in your head. I know you may not trust me but give me a chance. What's going on?"

"I don't know! Coaches got me all fucked up. They told me to shoot more on goal, but that I didn't have to. They said I could if I wanted, but I didn't need to. They just keep repeating the same shit, and I don't know what's going on. Am I getting traded? My contract is coming up for renegotiation, so I'm just spinning. It ain't something you can do anything about, doc."

Doc. I cringed at the nickname.

"No, Sunny. They—this is partly my fault."

He eyed me dubiously, toying with his mouthguard. "How's it your fault?"

"It was my idea, but I'm not to blame for the execution."

He winced.

"Listen, with my job, sometimes there are ways around people—techniques and such—but sometimes just straight-up truth yields the best result. We had a meeting earlier in the week, and I told them I think you have hidden potential."

"The fuck?"

Thud!

The crowd went wild. I glanced back to find Bruge had slammed one of the opponents into the glass. They were circling now, chirping at each other. The opponent's gloves dropped. Bruge was tugging off his gloves. The cheers were deafening.

I moved closer to Sunny, speaking so he could hear me. "You match whoever your center is. You hold back on goals, making an opening for your center."

"That's my job."

"No. Your job is to bring up the left side and work with your line. That's it. I want you to stop holding back so your center can shine. My guess is that someone told you your job was to make openings for them. But you're first line with Tyler fucking Griffin. Trust me. If you start shooting goals and making them, Griff will match you. He'll be ecstatic about the change."

His eyebrows furrowed, still flipping his mouthpiece in his mouth. He caught it between his teeth and shifted it to the side. "You're saying I hold back, but that's insane. No hockey player holds back. We all want to win."

I shrugged. "And yet you are. And yet it happens. In football, there are different roles. A running back can't be the quarterback. But basketball and hockey aren't like that. All of you can make goals, and if you're able to match Bruge and now match Griffin, that tells me you haven't been pushing yourself." I slapped his chest. "Push yourself. Surprise me. Get the fuck out of your head and start playing hockey the way you did when you were five."

"What?" He grinned. "Asking for snack break?"

"You know what I mean. You *played*. You had fun. No one could tell you what to do because you were going to play and you were going to score. Right?"

He got quiet, then finally he gave me a nod. "Yeah. I got it."

"Make it a game. Try to outshoot Griffin. See if he catches on."

He smirked. "He's going to love that."

"Yeah. He will."

He nodded again, and one of the coaches yelled his name. He returned to the bench where Coach Hines bent down to have a word with him. Sunny listened, and then it was time for their line again. He went with them this time.

Coach Hines straightened, meeting my gaze, his jaw firming before he turned back to the ice.

I moved closer to the bench but stayed out of the way. On the ice, there was suddenly an opening. One of the defensemen shot the puck forward, and Tyler took off to meet it, but his stick was still on the ice behind him. He rushed by the bench, grabbing the stick Benny held out for him, and he was off, taking the puck to the goal.

And Sunny was there. He was with him.

The opposing team's two defensemen closed in, going to block Tyler, except he circled the net. He didn't have a shot, so he passed to Sunny. One held back, considering Sunny, but I could tell they didn't think he'd shoot. They expected him to pass back to Tyler, who was trying to cut close again to the goal.

Jesse Ray was there by now, along with another defender. When Sunny pretended to pass to Ray, they fell for it. The goalie too. Sunny shot on goal instead, and he hit net. *Goal!* The red lights went off, and the crowd was on their feet again.

That was goal one.

Through the rest of the period, Sunny shot six more times. He got one more goal. Third period was a repeat, except there was a new energy coming from the team. Sunny shot. Tyler shot. They went head to head, and Tyler was grinning wide. The energy was addicting, and soon Ray was matching them, as if it was only the three of them on the ice. The other team folded under the constant barrage.

The Grays won six to three.

I heaved a breath when the siren blared at the end of the game, and Coach Hines made sure to meet my gaze. He dipped his chin in acknowledgement.

I'd passed my first test. Now I had to keep building on it.

25

TYLER

After the game, the locker room was lit. Some of the younger guys were dancing. Sunny was just grinning at everyone. Bruge scowled, but when Meester clapped him on the shoulder, some of that faded. He looked a little sheepish before bending his head and focusing on getting changed.

Coach came in and said a few words, and I noticed Rain lingering in the hallway. As soon as he was done, he motioned for her to follow him and the rest of the coaches into his office. They liked to have their own meeting after each game. She looked up as she turned to go, meeting my gaze for a second before ducking inside.

I couldn't read her.

I didn't like that.

We didn't talk much at the rink except for that one midnight skate. And I knew she was focused more on other players, but I didn't like that I couldn't talk to her. She'd had some hand in our win tonight. I wanted to tell her that.

Everyone had seen how she pulled Sunny aside, and after that he'd played with a new mission in life. He loved it. I loved it. Ray had joined in, and the whole team was infected. Meester had complained that there was only so much he could do as the second goalie.

And speaking of, Meester moseyed over now, his hips doing some sort of bounce to the music blasting through the locker room. "Hey, man."

I continued undressing. "Not going to take anything you say seriously while you're doing a bad impersonation of Shakira."

His hips stopped. "Who?"

Jesse had just come back from the shower, holding a towel around his waist. He promptly bent over in laughter. "Shakira! Meester, your hips don't lie."

Meester's eyebrows shot up. "My hips don't what?" He seemed offended on behalf of his hips. "I am no liar."

Brick snorted in laughter.

Bruge walked past, shaking his head. "It's a song, dumbass."

Meester put his hands on his hips, continuing to frown as a faint flush came to his cheeks. "I knew that."

Bruge called over his shoulder. "No, you didn't."

"No, he didn't," Jesse agreed, starting to get dressed. "But he's going to come in for practice tomorrow singing that damn song."

One of the younger guys came over. "I like Shakira. She seems feisty."

"She's from Argentina, right?" Brick called.

Bruge shook his head. "She's from Spain."

I had ceased undressing since this conversation was occurring in front of my locker.

"Anyway." Meester focused on me. "We're going to Halbrechts. You should come. Tonight's game was epic. We need to celebrate."

I glanced around, noting that most of the side conversations had ceased. Even Bruge had stopped to look at me.

They'd invited me before, but I hadn't gone. I'd always gone to the hospital.

I stood up. "Uh, yeah. My niece isn't in a coma anymore."

I heard a sharp inhale around the room.

Meester blinked, and his mouth stretched to a grin. He held up his fist. "Well, all right then. Another reason to celebrate."

I met his fist with mine, suddenly really looking forward to meeting them out for a drink. I hadn't been able to enjoy that sort of thing since the trade.

After I was dressed, Rain was still in Coach's office, and I considered inviting her along. But I knew she wouldn't go. I doubted any of the coaches would go, and she was considered an extension of them.

I still wanted to see her.

Tyler: Going out with the team for a drink. Can I swing by after?

"Ready?" Brick came over.

Most of the others had left. I'd been stalling to see if I could get a word with Rain, but that wasn't happening.

I stood. "Yeah, man. All ready."

26

RAIN

Around the conference table in Coach's office, we'd run through the logistics of the game like usual—what worked, what didn't, brief ideas to expand on at a later time, thoughts to ruminate over as we headed home—but now we were getting down to my business.

"Good call on Sunny," Coach Hines said, nodding my way.

"Thanks. Glad it helped."

I could feel the other coaches' eyes on me, but glancing around, I didn't see any hostility. Thank goodness. I struggled a bit with the beginning part of a new job, where I had to prove myself. Then after that, I'd navigate anyone who didn't like a girl knowing the sport as well as they did—if not better. I didn't sense that here, and hope began to rise inside me. That meant good things for the team. They were open to change. That was everything.

"Mind sharing what you told him?" Javier, one of the assistant coaches, asked. He'd played hockey until a knee injury ended his career in the AHL. After that, he began working his way up the coaching ladder, and this was his first year working with an NHL team. Young. Lean build. Brown skin. Dark eyes.

He was the kind of guy who was attractive but wasn't focused on his looks. He was only focused on his job. That made him somewhat intense at times, but it seemed he wanted to learn anything and everything to do the best job he could. I liked that about him.

I relayed a brief summary, and they all stared.

Coach Hines finally cleared his throat. "We should've been more clear in our instructions."

I shrugged. "Sometimes the best thing is just to lay it out for them. That worked today for Sunny, but I don't think it was mishandled initially. You guys planted the seed. That means some things were unearthed. I just came along and began weeding, in essence." I added, "The end goal is always to win. Obviously. However, I've never subscribed to the method of just telling them to win. I've found that when you switch their mindset to competing with themselves, trying to beat their personal records, or making a game of it, that eases some of the pressure. It's also a bit more fun, and we all know that when hockey players are having fun, generally they're going to play their best."

Marken nodded along as I spoke. "Brick loved the exercise you did with him. Meester's already asked if I'd do the same with him." None of the other coaches seemed surprised, so he must've already shared this with them. "I'm going to be honest; your slap shot is a helluva lot more lethal than mine. You interested in working with Meester on that?"

I gave him a small smile. "Yeah. I'd like to spend some one-on-one time with him anyway. He's in his head a lot, I can tell."

Marken nodded. "He is."

Coach Hines cleared his throat again. "Our first line is working well together. Let's focus on the second line. Bruge and Markie are struggling. Keeting seems adaptable to both." He glanced at me before turning to Javier. "If you have thoughts on smoothing them out, I'm open to suggestions. But let's cover that tomorrow morning. Any more general thoughts about the game tonight?"

It seemed we'd covered things for now, and when the meeting came to an end, I slipped out to use the bathroom. As I returned, Coach Hines was locking his office. The locker room lights had dimmed, so everyone was gone already, except the equipment managers. Games usually ended late, so people liked to get home. I wasn't surprised to find we were the last ones around.

At hearing my footsteps, Coach Hines looked my way. He waited by his door as I approached. "Did you know that before I took this job, I used to coach at Minnesota? The U of M."

I shook my head, lying. I did know that about him.

He studied me a moment, and I thought I caught a flash of amusement there. "I did. So I was local for a good long while. I was here when Griffin was a rising star, but there was a set of brothers as well. The Connors brothers. They're also from around here."

I tensed.

"Back then, their pop was pretty active, making sure they got the best coaches looking at them," he continued. "He liked to drop hints about their practice schedules. One day, I was in the area and thought, *what the hell*? So I stopped by to watch. They didn't know I was there. I never said anything. Just came in, took a seat in the back, and watched their practice." He looked at me carefully. "The funny thing is, their dad wasn't with them. There was a girl with them on the ice, though. She skated just as fast as they did, acted as their goalie at times. I watched them for a full hour. I didn't intend to watch that long, but I liked what I was seeing. I never knew who the little girl was, because she wore a helmet, but I always figured it was a sister. Maybe a cousin. Didn't seem like a girlfriend. Neither of the boys was particularly kind to her, or to each other really. They were straight business."

His eyes grew distant, and he nodded to himself. "After that day, I always thought I'd be hearing about a Connors sister. My daughter played back then. She went to college, got a scholarship, so I had an ear tuned, you know? But nothing. I never heard about a female Connors playing the sport. Always wondered though." He waited a beat before his eyes found my face again.

My throat had tightened in slight panic at the memory of being a hockey bitch for my brothers.

"Mal made sure I was aware that you wouldn't be at the games when we play Montreal and Boston," he added. "Both teams have a Connors playing for them."

I had to turn away from the knowing look on his face.

"I have three girls. All three played hockey, and none of them played because I wanted them to. They took to the sport like blood-thirsty Amazonians, and they got that competitive streak from their mother. She was all-state in track two years in a row. I love my girls, all of them, and if any of them had wanted to play golf or be a mathlete, I would've been just as proud of them. So, if you ever want to talk, about anything, my door is open. And if not, that's just fine too." He patted my shoulder, starting down the hallway. "You have a good night, Rain. Do something fun to celebrate. We've got a long road ahead of us."

I stood there in the hallway, my feet rooted and my legs going numb. He was almost to the door when I heard myself asking, my voice a little hoarse, "Was it my last name?"

He reached for the door but looked back.

I started after him, my feet stumbling. Cold sweat trickled down my spine. "Hockey's a small world, but I didn't think a last name would be that obvious. The Wolverines have two Henrik Gustavson players. They aren't related, but maybe I'm fooling myself."

He shook his head. "I know a few other Connors in hockey,

and none of them are related, so no, it wasn't the last name. You've got the same slapshot as both your brothers."

Humiliation burned through me. I should've known, should've thought of that.

He opened the door for us and stepped out first, giving my arm another pat as I moved past him. "Don't beat yourself up. I've seen you skate twice now—against Brick the other day and back then with your brothers. I wouldn't worry about anything."

We fell in step as we moved toward the parking lot.

"Should I be expecting a call from Keith Connors if word gets out about you working with us?" Coach asked.

"No." I shook my head. "He won't call, but Daniel might. He won't be happy about me being here."

That was an understatement. Daniel would be livid. He'd probably try to get me fired—throw his weight around, make some threats. I'd heard him do it enough times in the past.

Coach grunted. "Got it." We continued walking in silence until it was time to separate. "Never liked the eldest Connors boy. Always thought he had an attitude problem. Still do." He gave me a last wave before heading to his vehicle.

That conversation had just about ended me, but I couldn't stop smiling all the way to the hotel.

27

TYLER

I tried sending Rain another text, but she wasn't responding. She wasn't even reading them.
I tried again.
Tyler: You're missing out. Brick does karaoke. He sang and Meester was his back-up dancer. What are you doing?
I was frustrated. I wanted to see her, but I also just wanted her here. With the team. She deserved to be a part of our celebration. She was part of the reason we won, and everyone knew it.
A twinge of alarm ran through me. We weren't exclusive. We'd just hooked up. That was it, and I'd left before we had a conversation about anything. I hadn't even considered having a discussion because this was hella early—and hella unheard of for me. But...what was she doing? Did she meet someone else for drinks? Was she with that person right now?
Kissing that person?
Maybe someone else was in her hotel room?
Jealousy, hot and bitter, burned inside of me.
I had never wanted to lock someone down so they could only see me, except for right now. I wanted to stake my claim all

over Rain. I wanted to mark her so everyone would know she was taken, except I couldn't because I was the idiot who'd decided to leave this morning without waking her up.

Stupid.

Bruge slid into the seat next to me, placing his beer on the table. Half the guys had gone home by now, and most of the remainder were starting to say their goodbyes. A few looked ready to stay as late as possible, but Bruge was married, so I was surprised he was still here.

"Hey, man." I tipped my beer toward him.

We clinked bottles before we both took a pull. He set his back on the table, playing with the label.

I waited. It seemed he had something to say.

"It's good you joined the team."

I arched my eyebrow.

He shrugged. "I wasn't sure at first, but I was wrong. You don't have an ego. You're helping the guys, making them believe they can win. You're good for the team." With that, he picked his beer up, saluted me, and walked away.

And. Well. Okay then. Good talk.

Sunny slid into his empty seat, his coat over his arm. "What was that about?"

"Said I was good for the team."

Sunny's eyebrows went up, and he shook his head. "I'm heading out. You want a ride somewhere?"

"Nah." I slid my beer away and stood. "I've been nursing the same drink the whole time. I'm good to drive. I'll walk out with you."

"You need to settle your tab?"

I shook my head. "Nope. I cashed out after I ordered."

We said our goodbyes to the guys still there, and once we were outside, Sunny eyed my truck. "You still staying at a hotel?"

"For now." I took my keys out and began fidgeting with them. "Just been too busy with my sister and niece."

"How's that going?"

I lifted my shoulder, trying to seem nonchalant. I didn't want to talk about my family. And not because I didn't trust Sunny. He was still new to me, but there was already a level of trust. He was in the NHL. He was hockey. He understood this life and how hard it could be. He wouldn't say anything about my niece to someone else. I guess because of that I found myself saying, "The hospital wants to send her to some sort of clinic."

"That's good, right? She overdosed, didn't she?"

I hadn't told the team those specifics, but he knew what had been leaked to the press. "Yeah."

As if sensing my reluctance, he squeezed my shoulder. "I'm sure whatever they recommend is what's best for your niece. My little brother's an addict. He's been sober for three years, but we were there, smack in the middle of his struggles. None of it got leaked to the press, though. I'm not as big a deal as you, so people aren't as nosy about me. I wanted you to know I understand. I'm here if you want to talk."

"Thanks, Sunny. I appreciate that." We headed for our vehicles. Right before we parted ways, I asked, "With your brother, how old was he?"

"Oh. Uh..." He paused. "He was twenty-two when he got help and it stuck, but he did drugs all through high school. I'm surprised he graduated, to be honest." A shadow crossed his face. "I've always felt guilty, like part of it was my fault. I was the hockey star and got a lot of attention he didn't—golden child/forgotten child, that sort of thing." He flashed a sheepish grin. "My sister's in graduate school for therapy, so she spouts a lot of that shit. Sometimes it sticks. Makes sense." He rolled his eyes. "Don't tell her that."

I smiled. The situations weren't totally the same, but it felt good to know someone on the team had an inkling of what I was going through.

"But you know, we do have a psychologist for the team now," he continued. "I bet Rain would be open to talking."

My gaze had fallen to the sidewalk, but my eyes flicked up to him now. Did he know about us? I couldn't see any sort of hint there, so I let it go. "Yeah, maybe."

"She seems to know what she's doing. Has she approached you for anything yet?"

I gave him another searching look before I shook my head. "No, not really."

He clapped me on the shoulder and stepped away. "Consider yourself warned, because I'm sure it's coming." He held up a hand. "I'm off. When you're ready to get out of that hotel, let me know. I've got a realtor who can help with whatever you need. Apartment. Condo. House. Rental. She knows her shit. Okay, see you, buddy."

I raised a hand and got into my truck, but as he drove away, I didn't move.

He'd opened the door, asking about Zoey. I checked my phone, but there were still no calls or texts from my sister. I'd pissed her off, but she'd be okay. I said what needed to be said, and when she processed it all, she'd reach out. Or I'd just show up and annoy her until she broke and forgave me—not that I needed forgiveness here. It hadn't felt right to talk to Sunny too much, but I did want to talk to someone.

I pulled up my thread with Rain and saw a text from her. She'd sent it thirty minutes ago.

Rain: Congratulations on the win tonight.

That was it? Nothing else? No what am I doing now? How's it going with the team? Call me when you're done? Swing by and fuck me until we both black out?

I expelled a ragged breath. What had I been expecting? I couldn't expect anything. That was the point. I couldn't just expect Rain to want me every time I wanted her. And she'd said there were things she struggled with, so that made this even more complex.

Plus, her job. Jesus.

Her job.

A battle raged within me. My gut said to go to her hotel, that I needed to be the one to push her, pull her out of her head. My brain said to restrain myself, not to be an asshole.

But I *was* an asshole.

I swung my truck around and headed for her hotel.

28

RAIN

Just as I started to fall asleep, there was a knock on my door.

I'd been wired after talking with Coach Hines, so wired that I'd given up trying to go to sleep. I'd gone back to the rink for an hour of skating. I'd read Tyler's texts, but what was he thinking? I couldn't go to the bar with them. How would we act around each other? The first words he'd said to me were asking if I was okay with him kissing me. We hadn't spoken to each other in front of the team. So again, *what was he thinking?*

I'd just texted back something general. We could talk more in person tomorrow.

But now there was pounding at my door.

"Rain! Are you asleep? Let me in."

That was Tyler, and when he continued knocking, I hurried out of bed. Rushing to the door, I lectured myself in my head. *Who else were you expecting? Why are you in such a hurry to let him in when this is a* terrible *idea?*

I unlocked the door, swung it open, and pulled him inside. "Stop."

As soon as the door was closed and locked, I turned to him, and his hands went to my face. He stepped close, and the air left my lungs as he backed me against the door. He didn't give me a moment to acclimate myself. He was there, right there, and he was breathing my space. My heart lurched as my body got hot.

He plastered himself against me and bent down, but he didn't kiss me. He just held there.

"My mind's been buzzing all night, thinking about why you weren't responding to my texts," he said. "I got worked up. Were you with someone? I shouldn't ask, but were you? I don't want that, for the record. If we keep doing this, it's just you and me. Can I ask that? I'm asking. I'm saying it. Just you and me. Fuck. I never do exclusive, but the thought of someone else touching you?" His hand went to my hip and slid under my shirt, resting against my skin. His forehead fell to mine and he breathed me in again. "I was going fucking nuts."

His pulse raced and his eyes were dilated. I got a whiff of beer from his breath, but he didn't seem intoxicated. I reached up, wrapping my hands around his wrists as I pulled his hand from my face. I stepped back so I could better see him. "Are you drunk?"

"No. One beer that I didn't even finish." He took my hands in his, pinning them to the door above my head.

Whoosh. And just like that, I was throbbing for him. I could feel my heartbeat in my pussy. "Tyler, what are you doing?"

"I want you." His eyes were molten, so dark. His gaze fell to my lips, and hunger flared. "I haven't been able to get you out of my head all night. What were you doing? Tell me you weren't with someone else." He moved against me, and I could feel how hard he was. That was for me. Because of me.

I struggled against the surge of feeling that bloomed within me. Power.

Tyler wants me.
But for how long?
"Rain," he whispered as he bent over, his lips finding my throat.

And just like that, I ceased thinking. "Yes."

"Thank God." And he picked me up, moving us to the couch. He sat, his hands sliding under my shirt. "I want you to ride me, just like this. Do you want that? Feel me sliding inside of you? You're in control."

I wanted it. I was panting for it as his hand slid into my shorts, finding my clit and rubbing there. I closed my eyes, struggling to breathe. Every touch felt so good. Had it been like this the last time? I was struggling to remember. I could only concentrate on how he was making me feel this time. Tonight.

"I want to be in you," he murmured against my throat, switching to the other side. His hand slid up under my shirt, raising it before I reached down to whisk it off. I didn't have a bra on tonight and he gazed at me, looking intoxicated even though he said he wasn't. "Goddamn," he whispered, one hand palming my breast. "You are beautiful."

He didn't notice how I froze at his words, groaning as he leaned forward to take my breast in his mouth. His tongue flicked over my nipple.

Stop thinking, Rain. Stop waiting for the other shoe to drop.

I did just that, giving myself over to how he was making me feel.

And he was making me feel so good. So wanted. Every touch sent tingles through me. I began moving over him, grinding down on him, and his hands cupped my hips, squeezing me. "Holy shit, that feels so good." He tilted his head back, his eyes dazed with lust. "Condom?"

The sensations were distracting and it took a moment to think about a response. I remembered and cursed under my breath. My forehead went to his, resting there gently. "In the stand by my bed." Which meant we would have to move and I really, *really* liked where we were right now.

"Got it." Tyler held onto me, and I had a moment's notice, feeling his body shift under mine and then he was standing and taking me with him.

"What?" I clamped onto him.

But he had me. His arm moved around me, keeping me in place and he walked into my bedroom and bent down enough to open the bedside drawer. He pulled out a handful of condoms.

"Really?"

He smirked at me and I swear I felt that smirk all the way to my core.

He returned to the couch, sitting and adjusted me so I was straddling him. He leaned in once to give me a long, drawn out kiss before letting his head fall back so we could see each other. "You sure you want to do this?"

This. Like this was so different from what we did last time?

And he didn't know who I was—*stop, Rain. Just. Stop it.*

This one time. It'd be the last.

Then we'd stop.

"We can't keep doing this."

"We won't." His hands went to his pants and I shifted so he could pull them down, along with my shorts. "I'm usually one and done anyways."

I muttered a curse, my forehead falling to the side of his neck. "Not what a girl wants to hear before you're about to put your dick inside her."

He was sliding on the condom, and he paused at my words. A husky laugh slipped from him. "Sorry. I meant that to be reassuring. Last time, right?" His hands went back to my hips, helping me lift up and move over him.

This was wrong. All the reasons this could be wrong, it was.

Still, I reached down, positioned him, and then I slid down. Both of us were groaning, panting.

"Christ, you feel good. Tight."

I put a hand over his mouth. "Stop talking."

"Okay," he said, muffled behind my hand.

I began to ride him.

29

RAIN

He came over the next night.
I opened the door and glared at him. "Last night was supposed to be the end."

He flashed me a wicked grin before shouldering his way past me and into my room. He was carrying a bag of take-out. "Who said I'm just here for sex? Maybe I'm here for you to shrink me?"

He winced at the same time I growled. "Not the right words to say, buddy."

He relaxed, giving me that grin again. "See. Buddy. We can do this." He held up the bags. "I have food and I know there's a rerun of Harry Potter happening on TV."

"You're a fan of Harry Potter?"

He gave me a look. "Duh. I'm a Griffin."

"I don't know what that means."

He'd begun taking out the food, but stopped and raised his head, alarmed. "Do not tell me that you've never watched Harry Potter?"

I narrowed my eyes at him. "You know it's not just the movies, right? That they're based on books?"

He waved that off, continuing to pull out the containers of food. "Books shmooks. I know the movies are great to watch on the plane when we're going to our away games. Gets me out of the mindset of only hockey, you know?"

I moved closer. "What do you mean?"

He paused after popping one of the containers open. It was filled with noodles and another bag looked like there were egg rolls inside. He gave me a look before shrugging. "Nothing."

"Hey." I moved even closer, my hand going to his arm. "What do you mean?"

He tensed under my touch. "It's nothing, but..." He was back to watching me, a bit warily. "I'm still fitting in. Or I'm still waiting for the team to fully accept me. Or, I don't know. Maybe they have? Bruge sat down with me, said it was good I joined the team. That felt important."

"It is." I was going over every interaction I'd witnessed from the team and was coming up empty with anyone still unsure about Tyler's place on the team. "Tyler, where is this coming from? The team is doing better because you're on it. Trust me. This is my job. I'm paid to watch and assess. The team from last year is not the team this year. You've upped the ante. Your whole expectation that you're going to win is infectious. You *expect* to win, not in an unrealistic way, but in a way that's just is. Like tomorrow is another day. It's fact. You're that good and you're going to win. Fact. But it's more than that. You believe in the team and they see that."

He was so still, his chest barely moving. His eyes were glued to me, and he was listening to every word I said. I encircled his wrist, feeling for his pulse. It was pounding incredibly fast under my touch.

I hoped he could hear the sincerity in my tone. "They're taking their cues from you. And your cue is that you're all in with them. That's breathing new energy into them. It's as if somewhere down the line, someone told them they were only going to go so far and they believed them. They let themselves get locked into that box, except there was no door for them to get out. You didn't just break into the box to release them. You obliterated the box for them. They're starting with new belief in themselves and that's because of you. You believe in them. They see that. They're starting to believe in themselves too and they're having fun. Athletes always play the best when their bodies are loose, when their minds are clear, and having fun is the best way to make that happen. You brought that back to them. That's no small feat. Give yourself that, at least."

He didn't reply right away. His throat was tightening before he said, gruffly, "Thanks for that."

I shrugged, releasing him and stepping over to grab some plates. "Just the truth." I turned away, giving him a modicum of privacy because I could see what I said had an effect on him. His head bent before I turned away and I heard him draw in a ragged breath.

"It weighs on me."

I slowed in pulling the plates out from the cupboard. "What does?"

"Coming here. Trying to juggle a family crisis but wanting to do my best as a player too. As a teammate. I like them. I like this team a lot. I want to do the best for them, be the best that I can be."

I glanced over my shoulder. He was watching me back, a raw vulnerability to him that was making my heart pound in my chest. I murmured, "You already are."

He closed his eyes and nodded, his chest rising. "Thanks."

I shrugged again. "Like I said, it's the truth. I'm not blowing smoke up your ass."

His lips tipped up, curving. "I've never had that experience."

"And we're back to our regular programmed Tyler show."

He chuckled. "Not quite. Let's eat and watch the Sorcerer's Stone so you get the full effect of the Harry Potter world."

"Learn what a griffin is?"

The look he gave me was all suggestion, all heat, and it had me clenching for the table because it was making me all too unsteady. "You can learn what a Griffin is any day of the week, but yes. You'll learn the difference between a griffin and a hippogriff."

"A hippo-what?"

HE CAME over the next night after the game.

He also came over the next three nights after that.

Sometimes we had sex, though I was aware every time I heard his knock and every time I opened that door it needed to be the last night. I still opened the door.

I was fast losing the ability to stop this.

Some nights he brought take-out and crawled in bed with me to watch the rest of the Harry Potter movies. He was right. Griffins were awesome. We moved onto *The Lord of the Rings* and he was still coming over almost every night.

There would be a time when I needed to end this. I knew it.

Except every night I kept thinking to myself, the next time. I would tell him the next time. Then he'd reach for me, roll me underneath him, and that thought would melt away because no matter what, I loved how he made me feel.

He made me feel wanted.

30
TYLER

I dropped down to the bench, exhausted. That loss *sucked*.

"Hey, man." Sunny sank down next to me. "That was shit."

I grunted. It'd been a shut out for them. Four to zero. Meester had been in goal and he was currently sitting in front of his locker, his head hanging down. He was still learning, but I said, "Not getting an argument from me."

"Yeah." He was just as glum as I was. We begin silently undressing.

If I wasn't thinking about hockey, worrying about Skylar, who still wouldn't respond to me, then my mind trailed to Rain. She was fast becoming an addiction.

I liked her. I did.

I shouldn't, but I did.

It wasn't just the sex, which was hot. It was more. It was her. Talking to her about my worries, she'd been there for me on numerous occasions by now. Going to the hospital with me, not injecting her own judgments into what my sister should do, and then saying all that to me about how I was helping the team. I felt safe with her.

Who was I kidding? I just wanted her. Any way I could get her, I would take it. She felt good in my arms, felt right. The last two nights I hadn't even left after sex or after the movie. The first night it happened, we'd both just fallen asleep. The second time it happened, she'd fallen asleep and I was the one who made the decision. I stayed.

I *liked* staying and I liked waking up next to her.

Who was I becoming?

Bruge thudded over to us and stood there, folding his arms across his chest. He glared down at us. "Boston is playing against L.A. Our game was early today. We have time to watch. You come over to do that. I'll make food." His gaze indicated both of us. When neither of us argued, he clipped his head down once. "Good. Be there in one hour. I'll text you my address."

He moved on, saying something similar to the others.

I glanced at Sunny. "That happen often?"

"Bruge's orders?" He grinned. "Sometimes. If we've had a particularly brutal loss." He slapped my shoulder. "Come on. Let's shower and stop on the way for drinks. Bruge only ever has water or tea, maybe beer leftover from another gathering. We can pick some up."

Quite a few of the team was there when Sunny and I showed up. We rode together. I liked it when Sunny made the suggestion. It reminded me of when my old team would get together. Nolan and I rode together a lot of times. Sunny reminded me of Nolan, except Sunny was nicer. Nolan had more of an edge to him, which was probably why he and I were best friends. I understood him.

"We brought beer." Sunny held up the case.

A bunch of guys cheered from the living room.

Bruge met us in the kitchen. He took the beer, putting it in the fridge and gave the protein drink in my hand a sneer. "I said I'd cook for you. I cook for you. You don't need that." He gestured to his stove, which had a plethora of meat. "See. Lots of protein."

Sunny was grinning. He nabbed a beer and slipped away before I could figure out how to shift the attention to him.

"Uh." My mind was blank. "Sorry?"

Bruge grunted. "Shoo. I like cooking. My wife is gone. Girls' trip, so I do all the cooking for the week. Italian and Greek today. The team needs the nutrition and time together. Go watch your nemesis. Give us a cheat sheet on how better to play against him. He's a slippery eel. Mean. Fast. And slimy. I don't like him." He waved for me to leave so I followed suit, grabbing a beer as well. Going to the living room, I saw space in front of one of the couches next to Meester. I sank down and the camera gave a close-up of Dane Connors's face. Immediately my attitude soured.

"I hate that guy."

I thought I'd been the one to say it, but it was one of our defensemen. He added, "He's dirty."

"He's not as dirty as his brother. Daniel Connors is a nightmare to play against. He'll high-stick you every time the ref's back is turned. Guaranteed. Just start expecting it. Messes with your mind." That was Ray.

"They hate you." Sunny was studying me.

"Yeah, man. I've never seen a rivalry like what they make it out to be between you and them. What's the backstory? Anything we should know for when we play them next week?" Jesse asked.

I knew the NHL liked to build up the rivalry between us, as did social media. I'd stopped listening to anything or going online the week leading up to a game against either of the

Connors brothers so because of that I somewhat forgot how big of a deal it still was to others.

I shrugged. "I don't know. All of us grew up here, but at different schools. We were high school rivals. As far as I can tell, Daniel just hated me off the bat."

"Cause you're better than him." Meester raised his beer, taking a pull.

"Maybe. No. I'm sure that's part of it, but it got personal when he dated my sister."

"What? No way."

I don't know who said it, but a bunch of the guys leaned forward at that information.

I went back to glaring at the television. They really did love talking up Dane Connors. "Daniel did. They got in a car accident, his fault from what I was told. She was in the hospital and he ghosted her. The fucker gave her a brain injury and then said he didn't have time for her anymore."

"Holy fuck," Meester commented.

"Dane's not much better."

"Well, they hate you. That's for sure." Jesse was on his phone and noticing everyone looking his way, he handed his phone over. "Daniel made a post. 'Stick it to Griffin, little brother. Remind him he's in our hometown next week. Not his.' The post has over a thousand likes."

"Shit." Sunny shook his head. "That's next level hate."

I refocused on the game. "It's just Daniel being Daniel. Best revenge is beating Boston." I gestured to the television. "Dane is fast, but he's got a tell."

"He's hard to read."

"Nah. He's got a tell. Watch his eyes. When he's going to shoot, his elbow will jerk, just a tiny bit, in the direction he's going to shoot or pass."

"Hard to watch his elbows. If we take our eyes off the puck, he's already past us."

"You'll get a read on him. Promise. He doesn't like to go to the goal without Engler in the vicinity. Those two are almost conjoined twins. Watch their tapes and focus on them. New York has its own rivalry with Boston so I got good at reading both of them. Engler will always look for Connors before he'll cross the blue line, but Connors won't shoot on goal unless Engler is on the other side ready for the rebound."

For the rest of the night, we watched and everyone made a sound when they started noticing the pattern. Bruge's spaghetti was delicious, but I needed this time with the team.

I was one of them.

It clicked for me tonight.

I *was* a Gray Wolf.

31

RAIN

I knew that knock was coming before it came.
It was another night. The first before the week that everything inside of me was going to get overhauled. I was already unsteady when I opened the door and Tyler shoved in. It was late. They had an afternoon game today, but he sent a text saying he was heading to Bruge's to watch Boston's game.

The mention of my brother made me want to upheave the little I'd eaten today.

"Damn. You look good." There was no food in his hands and he crowded against me, kicking the door shut behind him. He was here for sex and that was first and foremost on his mind. My stomach dipped as his hands went to my hips, sliding under my shirt.

But, no.

I couldn't do this. Not tonight.

I needed all my reserves to handle the next week, knowing Dane would be in town.

I held up a hand to his chest and moved back, giving me some space. My heart leapt, then it sank because I couldn't do this.

God...

I was about to break my own heart, but no.

Enough was enough.

"Tyler."

He stopped. "What? What is it?"

We'd gone too far.

I couldn't go further. He needed to know who exactly I was.

Maybe it wouldn't be so bad to tell him?

Maybe he wouldn't react the way I always assumed he would, with hatred and loathing? Maybe he'd be like Coach Hines, just a quiet understanding. But I knew I was deluding myself. I wanted to believe I could still have him, but he'd look at me with such disdain.

And my job... I'd already gone too far. My career was over if this got out. And then what would I have? Nothing.

My chest grew tight as my throat closed off, but I had to tell him. It was the right thing. I moved his hands back to his sides. He watched as I pushed him back, creating more space between us.

"We can't do this."

His gaze clouded over. "What? Why not?"

"I..." It hurt to talk.

Was I really going to do this? Tell him? Give my enemy who didn't know he was my enemy the ammunition against me? But he hadn't felt like my enemy this whole time.

No. He had to know.

"You don't want me?"

Pain already began trickling through me. "No," I said gently. "It's not that. I—I need to talk to you."

He moved back in, appeased by my answer. He reached for me, but I ducked out of his hold and stepped aside.

"Tyler—"

"What is this?"

My throat hurt. A knot had settled there. "I have to..." I

shook my head, trying to clear the pain away so I could speak. I needed to pull away, dissociate. I needed to numb myself enough to think clearly. "We *shouldn't* keep doing this. We both know that, even though we *keep* doing it. It's like we can't stop. I can't stop."

My throat swelled up.

He was so still. "It's reciprocated, you know. We've not had a conversation, but I'm coming over here for a reason. It's not just for sex."

"I know, but..." My voice was failing me. I pushed through it. "But if you want to *keep* doing this, I have to tell you something. It's not right if I don't."

"I don't care."

"Tyler," I tried again, my voice hitching.

"I don't. I just—" He stepped toward me again but stopped when I jumped.

I bit my lip. I had reacted that way because of how fast he'd moved, not because it was him. Everything in me wanted to just shut up, to let him touch me, kiss me, and deal with the consequences tomorrow. But I couldn't. It felt like violating his trust.

He cursed, scrubbing a hand over his face. "I didn't come here with the intention of making you scared of me. *Fuck*. I'm making a mess of all of this."

He closed his eyes and sank into one of the chairs.

Tentatively, I went to the couch and sat across from him.

"Okay. I'm good. I'll restrain myself." He grinned crookedly. "I'll be a good boy, just this one time." He motioned to me. "Go ahead. I'm all ears, but I came here for another reason. Besides sex and movies. And cuddling."

He was?

He caught my look and amended, "Or not totally for sex. Sunny asked about Zoey a while ago. I didn't get into it with him, but I realized I do want to talk about her. That's big for me. I usually don't want to say shit to anyone. I'm learning that maybe I *can* open up. I mean, I did with you before and that was great. Then I felt connected to the team tonight and that was really great. That all just made me want to open up more, share more. Ski's mad at me because I told her Zoey should go to a mental health clinic. That's up your alley, right? All the psychology and shit."

Psychology and shit.

He looked so proud, beaming about this new thing for him, which was normal for most people. It was normal to talk about what was going on in your life. My heart pinched because it was something I deprived myself of.

He was handing me all the excuses not to come clean.

A lesser person would jump on that because it was a good thing that he wanted to talk to someone. But I was about to shove all that progress away.

I cleared my throat, my voice growing hoarse, but I started. I had to, otherwise I didn't think I'd ever be able to tell him. "You need to know things about me. Especially if you want to keep opening up to me. I can't let you do that until you know everything." My knees were trembling. So was my voice. "My first name is not Rain. It's Dylan. My dad really wanted another boy, so he was set on my name even before I was born."

Here we go.

"My name is Dylan Rain Connors."

His eyes darkened, narrowing. "What?"

"I use my middle name because it's from my mom. I like to think she loved me. Maybe I should've changed my last name, but I went to school as a Connors. I got my degree as a Connors. I was already known in my field as Rain Connors before I could make any sort of switch. I stayed with it."

"What are you talking about?"

The pain tripled, growing stronger. I tried to numb it all away. "My last name was never an issue when I worked with the NFL. I went that direction to get away from hockey, but I'd forgotten how much I used to love this sport. It's been bittersweet coming back, but my name..." I couldn't bring myself to look at him, so I focused on the floor. "I can't be involved with you unless you know who I am and are okay with it." I readied myself. He wasn't going to be okay with it. I had to tell him anyway. "I was supposed to be their third boy. Dylan Connors. Daniel, Dane, and Dylan. Daniel and Dane Connors are my brothers."

I waited a beat, expecting *something*. An exclamation. A threat. A reprimand for not coming clean before.

Nothing came until I heard a soft click.

I looked up and felt as if a knife was just shoved into my gut.

The room was empty.

He was gone.

32

RAIN

They'd made me an office in a room previously used for storage near the administration offices. I was working on a few individual plans—step-by-step ways to work toward achieving a goal. I had them for almost all the players now, as well as for the team itself and the coaches. I was working on one for Meester when there was a knock at my door.

"Come in."

The door opened, and Mal Benoit poked his head in. He flashed me a smile, in dress slacks and a button-down shirt. The collar was pulled out and it was sans a tie, but he looked the epitome of a rich business owner. "Bad time?"

"Uh, no." I saved my work and closed out of the program, shutting my laptop. "Come in." I indicated the loveseat on the other side of my desk. When and if a player came in, I liked having them comfortable. As Mal took a seat at one end, I said, "I have a mini fridge. Would you like water? I also brought in my Keurig. I can make a mean cup of coffee."

"I'm good. You do know there's a whole cafeteria where any of the staff can go for water or coffee or hell, even a latte, I'm told." He was teasing, but I saw some tension on his face.

I had an inkling of what this was about, but I asked anyway. "What brings you to my corner of the Grays' world?"

"What happened with Tyler?"

Yes. That.

Since I'd told Tyler my secret, he hadn't spoken a word to me. That'd been a week ago. I hadn't been certain what to expect from him, but it wasn't this silent treatment.

I'd tried telling myself it was fine. We never talked around the team, but this felt different. If I entered a room, he left it. If he had to be in a room with me, he kept his eyes somewhere else. It was to be expected, and maybe even for the best, except it *hurt*.

He had every right to be angry.

We couldn't have kept going the way we were.

I kept reminding myself it was for the best. It worked after a while, after I'd learned to numb myself before coming to the arena every morning and to give myself a few hours every evening to turn off all of the hurt.

But I was miserable at work when I was around the team. Around him.

I'd shut down more and more. I shouldn't have been surprised that Mal had heard about it, or that he was concerned enough to make an office visit.

My heartbeat picked up. This could be the start of them having to make a choice: Tyler Griffin or me.

"Griffin found out who I'm related to."

Whatever Mal had been expecting, it wasn't that. His face went blank in surprise. "He—what?"

My hands began to shake. I tucked them under the desk, folding them together in my lap. "That's why you're here, right? Because of the way he's been ignoring me?"

He coughed and straightened in his seat. "I mean, yes. People have noticed and brought it to me, but..." He gave me a befuddled look. "How'd he find out?"

"I told him."

He pulled in a sharp breath. "What? You what?"

"I told him." I said it again.

"Why?"

For a moment, a very brief moment, I considered coming clean about our potential personal relationship. That would've been career suicide. I'd be fired. He would have no other choice. I'd be forcing his hand. I was self-aware enough to know I wanted to punish myself—that's where that impulse came from. I wanted to push myself down even farther. But I didn't do it.

Mal was still waiting for an explanation.

I didn't have one. "It came up in conversation."

He leaned forward in his seat. "Walk me through that conversation."

I opened my mouth, ready to tell him I couldn't.

"It affects the team and your ability to do your job," he countered before I'd even spoken. "You need to walk me through how that came up." His face tightened. "You were the one who warned us about this scenario."

I swallowed the words that wanted to come up. "He asked me to go to the hospital with him one night, to see his sister and niece. His sister didn't recognize me, but I knew if he continued wanting me to be involved with his family situation, it was only a matter of time. She dated Daniel for a short period and was aware that he had a sister. I felt it was unethical. He needed to know who I was if he was going to trust me with such personal issues."

It was plausible. It was also a lie.

"Christ, Connors."

"Rain."

"Right. Rain. Sorry." He grimaced. "Do I need to know the full history of Griffin and your brothers?"

A snort left me before I could stop it. "All you need to do is visit YouTube. The videos will pop up. I'm sure your P.I. already looked into it, right?"

His gaze was measured. "I'd rather hear it from you. His sister dated your brother?"

"That won't come up on YouTube."

"You know what I mean."

I did, and I closed my mouth. I was self-destructive, but not that self-destructive. "I don't know much about her relationship with Daniel. He... I can only imagine. Daniel wasn't the most pleasant person to me. And they didn't date long."

"Is your brother pleasant to anyone?"

My mouth twitched. "Daniel? I have no idea. I didn't lie to the team when they met me. I truly don't know my brothers, either of them."

Mal gazed at me with concern, but he didn't comment on whatever he was thinking. After a moment, he asked, "Is it affecting the team? Griffin's silent treatment of you?"

I was sure some noticed, but I shook my head. "We rarely interacted around the team before he found out, so not much has changed. I'll let you know if I think it's affecting my productivity."

I was saying all the words to appease him, but Mal wasn't stupid. He looked at me long enough that I grew uncomfortable.

Then he switched it off, and a professional mask slipped over him. "I have no idea what your family dynamics are like, were like, but I can imagine—based on your requests and now with Griffin's reaction. What I do have an idea about is you. You're kind. You have no ego. And you care. You care about your job. You care about the players. You care about the sport itself. If Griffin's treatment continues, we'll have to talk to him. I don't want to lose you here. You're helping. Everyone can tell."

My eyes burned as I nodded. "Yes. Thank you."

"You're here for the team, but we're here for you. Don't

forget that. My job is to give you whatever resources you need. My door's always open."

This time my smile was a little less forced and the pain lessened, just a fraction. "Thank you, Mal. Again."

He said goodbye, and I sat at my desk, feeling my world slipping out from under my feet. I'd fought for so long to keep hockey out of my life. But now that it was back, I didn't want anything to take it away again.

I finished my reports and my plan for Meester, and as soon as I was done, I headed for the ice. The team was gone for the day, so it was quiet when I got to the rink. By now, Morty was quite aware of my routine. After the third time of asking him if I could skate since the ice was clean, he told me he always came early to clean the ice, whether it needed a cleaning at five in the morning or not. *"Either myself or Benji cleans it. It became a part of my routine when my wife was battling cancer and the kids were in school,"* he'd told me. *"I used that time to get myself ready for the day. My wife's been cancer-free for ten years, and my kids are now starting to have their own little ones, but I like that peace in the morning. I'll be there if you skate or if you don't, so you don't have to keep asking me for permission. That ice is there to be skated on, and my job is to keep it clean. Let the ice and me both do our jobs. You can always skate, Miss Rain."*

Hearing that helped. After that, I hit the ice just about any time someone else wasn't on it.

Today, I had two needs warring inside of me. One was violence, and the other was escape. Hockey could fulfill them both.

For the first, I wanted to feel a hockey stick in my hand, and I wanted to use it to hit the puck as hard into the net as possible. I wanted to do that over and over again. For the other, I needed to skate fast. I needed the world to slip away, and I wasn't going to stop until my legs gave out.

I linked my earbuds to my phone, tucked it in my pocket, and began.

33

RAIN

Tonight was the Grays' first game against one of my brothers' teams since I'd been with them. Everyone was focused on the rivalry between Tyler and Dane so hardly anyone noticed me. They didn't see how I was a mess in the days before. I had planned for my reaction, and I fully was prepared to spend the evening in my hotel room.

Except I messed up.

I followed my routine without thinking and came to the rink in the morning.

I forgot. I just totally forgot.

Boston had gotten into town the night before, and *of course* they would have morning skate. It's what both teams did. How could I have forgotten? I couldn't explain it, but I did.

I was heading down the hallway to my office when a bunch of the Boston players crossed ahead of me, going to their locker room.

I froze, panic rising. Dread lined my stomach.

Everything happened in slow motion.

Marcus Engler passed, Dane's best friend, and right behind him—because the two were inseparable—was my brother. He turned back, laughing at something their goalie was saying. He didn't see me, but he would have if he'd looked down the hallway they were crossing.

My stomach heaved.

I shoved my way into the closest bathroom and emptied anything and everything I'd eaten that morning. I left home when I was eighteen. It'd been twelve years since I'd seen Dane in person. Both of my brothers were NHL stars, so it was almost impossible not to see their faces on anything advertising hockey, but I'd sequestered my life into football. Tom Brady, Jason and Travis Kelce, Tyreek Hill, Pat Mahomes. Those were the faces I encountered over and over again. I was part of that world.

But no longer.

A soft knocking sounded on the door, and I cursed, trying to push myself back to my feet. "Ho—hold on, please." My legs were unsteady. This happened whenever I was sick like this.

"Rain?" It was Mal. "Someone told me you darted in here. Are you okay? I didn't think you'd be here today."

My stomach spasmed, and I got scared I was going to puke again, but then it settled. I let out a breath of relief. Flushing the toilet, I backed up and let myself slide along the wall. Leaning over, I rested my shoulder and the side of my head against the door. "Do you need to use the bathroom?"

"No, but can I come in?" he asked.

I hesitated. "It's gross in here."

"You're my employee. I'm okay with gross. As long as you're okay."

"I'm okay."

"I'd still feel better if you let me come in. Please? Just for a moment. I'd like to get eyes on you, reassure myself."

Reaching up, I unlocked the door and he pushed in, easing the door gently until he spotted me. He came in and locked the door behind him. He turned the water on, testing the temperature. "Do you have the flu?"

His eyes were too knowing, so I wasn't going to bullshit him. I shook my head. "No."

He grabbed a bunch of paper towels and put them under the water. When he was satisfied, he turned the water off and handed them to me. As I used them to wipe off my face, he checked the toilet. The only other place to sit was by the toilet. He leaned against the wall in front of me. We both avoided that area.

"You saw your brother?"

I nodded, wordless, crumpling the paper towels in my hand.

"Is this..." His face was a storm of concern and other emotions. "Can I be frank with you?"

I held out a hand, indicating for him to go ahead. My tongue was too heavy. My throat hurt. I wasn't going to talk unless I absolutely needed to.

He let out a soft sigh. "I wasn't completely honest with you when we first met for dinner. When we found the connection between you and your brothers, we were confused about the secrecy. We went digging. We talked to some high school coaches, teachers, and even some neighbors. The picture we began to get wasn't... It began to tell a story, and I knew we needed to stop if we were going to respect your privacy. We tried. I promise we did. I wasn't surprised when you asked for your family connection to be kept secret and said you didn't want to be here when we played their teams. But after your reaction today, I feel I need to ask..."

I waited, holding my breath.

"Would you like the opportunity to talk to someone? If seeing... If there was abuse of any sort in the house... It's obvious something happened, and I'd hate it if this job was reopening old wounds."

My eyebrows went up at *abuse*, but it made sense. I shook my head. "No," I rasped out. Clearing my throat, I spoke again. "There was no physical or sexual abuse. Nothing like that. I never worried about my safety or having enough to eat. Nothing like that."

"Oh." It was clear that wasn't what he thought I'd say.

I grimaced. "But you're right. Coming back to hockey has brought up old stuff, and after seeing my brother just now, I'm sure I'll be shaken for the rest of the day."

His eyes clouded over again.

He deserved some of the truth. "There was neglect." I looked away because this made me feel exposed. "There was extreme neglect in some aspects. Some verbal abuse. And some emotional abuse. It's not the type of abuse that gets talked about, but there are wounds. Dane..." Shit, even saying his name out loud was difficult. My hand began shaking, so I tucked it under my leg. "He wasn't as bad as Daniel, but there was no kindness either."

Mal snorted before he flashed me a rueful grin. "That was unprofessional of me. I apologize, but I just thought that was appropriate, considering how he plays hockey. He's not as much of a bully as your oldest brother, but he's still a mean son of a bitch on the ice."

I laughed, which felt good. "I'm not so fond of him, so no offense taken."

He chuckled with me before he grew serious. "I'm sorry about this stuff, that it's opening old wounds." He hesitated. "If you ever wanted to talk to someone, I could be there for you. Lend a listening ear over a glass of wine, that sort of thing." He held my gaze. "A friend if you'd like."

I drew in some air, silently, but he saw my reaction.

His face became a mask of professional warmth. "Or not. That's entirely up to you. I just wanted you to know that someone could care, does care." He coughed. "I do care. And yes, if anything, as friends. *Friends.*" He said it again, more firmly. "Is there anything you need right now? I can send someone to bring you water? Your things? Mouthwash?"

I barked out a laugh. "No. I'm good. I promise."

"Okay, but Rain, just in case you need to hear it, you're wanted here. I've said it before, but I'll say it again. People care about you. If there's anything you need, let me know. We're all one big family. This is hockey, remember?"

Yes, it was. I thanked him, and after he left, I remained in the bathroom.

A hockey family.

I'd never understood what that word meant growing up. It was tossed around a lot, but it meant something different to me than it did the rest of the world. I'd needed to watch others in school, in college. I'd needed to see how their families treated them to realize that other families weren't like mine. Other parents weren't like my father. Other siblings didn't loathe each other. They didn't ignore each other, treat each other with disdain. Some siblings even loved each other. That was a novel concept to me, but by the time I began to piece together what was missing in my life, too much time had passed. I was too broken already.

Still, Mal's words stirred a sliver of hope inside me.

Was it possible?

34

TYLER

Rain wasn't at the game. Why the fuck wasn't she at the game?

Benny rushed past me through the locker room, and I grabbed his sleeve. "Benny."

"Yo!" He had a pair of gloves in his hands, but he swung around to come to a stop in front of me. He was always rushing and always out of breath but always smiling. "Griff! What's up? What can I do for you?"

"The team shrink."

He had to think for a moment before his face brightened again. "Miss Rain. Yes. Do you need her?" His eyebrows scrunched together. "I think there was an email stating that she would not be present or available during games against Montreal and Boston. We're playing Boston tonight, so I don't think she's here. I could call her. Do you want me to do that?"

It'd been a while since Rain told me about her connection to Dane and Daniel Connors, and we hadn't spoken since. Well, I hadn't spoken to her. I couldn't handle hearing who she was, so I'd shut it all off. Now there was a white-hot hatred for her brewing underneath everything. Pure hatred. Except hearing she wasn't here because we were about to go against one of her brothers, that tugged at me.

Why?

It didn't make sense.

"Griff?"

Benny was still waiting for my response, and he wasn't the only one. Sunny and Ray had both stilled, looking over at me. Confused. I shook my head, forcing a nonchalant expression. "Nah. That's fine. I was just wondering."

I sat back and finished dressing, but Benny lingered. "Uh, okay. Are you sure?"

I nodded, fiddling with my arm pad. "I'm good. You're busy enough as it is. Thanks, Benny."

He still seemed uncertain, but then he was off.

Sunny nudged me with his glove. "What was that about? You need to see Rain? You could probably just call her. She's chill. She'll answer."

I shook it off. "It's nothing."

He continued to stare at me, so I gave him a shrug. "Just a question. I can ask it tomorrow. It's no big deal."

I bent down to double check my skates. I couldn't keep playing with my arm pad or I was going to mess it up. Benny did a good job getting our equipment ready for us and keeping it exactly the way we wanted. I didn't want to make his job more stressful by fucking something up and asking for a replacement.

The team was on edge, and I knew it was because of me. Everyone knew about the tension between me and the Connors brothers, and we'd begun our round of games against the eastern teams. Tonight I'd face Dane. He was first line, too, so we'd be spending a lot of time playing against each other. At least this was a home game, so not many Boston fans would be heckling me, but I wasn't stupid. The ones who were here would be loud and proud. They hated me. So far, the Grays fans hadn't experienced true hate for one of their players.

They were about to.

Coach Hines came into the locker room before warmups. Everyone grew quiet because this was unusual. He cleared his throat. "Okay. So tonight's a little abnormal for most of us. Having said that, we're going to do the same thing we do every night. We go out there. We warm up. We pay attention to our team, and we keep it moving. Don't let the fans get in your head. Don't let the opposing team do the same. Got it? Warm up. Have fun. Laugh. Keep your minds clear. If you find yourself getting riled, you focus on the guy to your left and your right. You lean on each other." He surveyed the team one more time before nodding. "All right, gents. Get out there."

I readied myself.

As soon as I appeared, the crowd went from cheering and happy to an undercurrent of boos and loud heckling from the Boston fans. I ducked my head and concentrated on going through our usual routine.

Brick did his thing on the side for a moment, letting Meester have some time in the net. He skated over to me. "Seats are usually still half empty during this time, with people getting their drinks or whatever. But it looks like Boston made sure to get their asses camped for maximum chirping time on you. And the signs." He whistled under his breath. "Taking the negative shit out of it, you gotta be impressed they hate you this much. They're fans, except because you're a rival, it goes the other way. If you ever joined their team?" He laughed to himself. "They'd be pissing themselves at how lucky they were to have you."

I shook my head. "I'm used to it. Both Connors are assholes, but Dane isn't as dirty as Daniel. Consider this the preshow before we get Montreal later on."

"Yeah, but these are Boston fans. They raise 'em different. That city and Philly." He grimaced. "I really hate Philly fans."

My grin came easier. "That's the way they like it."

He grunted before hitting my shoulder. "Don't sweat it. We're going to have fun tonight."

I held up a glove. "You know it."

He hit it with his before heading to the net for his turn.

Ray and Sunny both made sure to stay near me during warmups. I appreciated it. Judging by their dazed expressions under their helmets, they probably needed my protection more than the other way around. It made me smile. This was their taste of the real, *passionate* fans in the hockey world. Heckling was a normal part of the sport, but this was another level.

As we finished, Bruge came over. "Coach changed the starting line. Second line's going out first."

Ray cursed around his mouthpiece. "Are you shitting me?"

Bruge glanced his way, and Sunny came to join our circle.

"They're starting their bruisers, so he wants us to meet them," Bruge continued. "We'll get the initial fight out of the way and then play hockey."

Sunny swore. "They want a shit show, huh?" He bumped my shoulder. "All for you, Griff."

To start the game with their fighters first? I glanced toward their bench, trying to get a read on their energy. A couple of them were standing to the side, talking and looking our way, but the rest were doing their usual pregame stuff. Was this really about me or was it something else?

Was this about Rain and the rest of the team didn't know it? I found Dane, but he wasn't part of the group talking and watching us. He was in line to hit the puck into the net. When it was his turn, he rounded behind the goal and came to join the other line. I got a glimpse of his face, and he looked normal. No unusual rage.

I shrugged to Sunny. "Guess we'll find out."

"We got your back." Bruge moved in, making sure I heard him.

I gave him a nod, and we dispersed to do our thing.

When we left the ice, for the first time since Rain had told me her connection, I wondered if there was something more to it than I'd thought. I'd grown up hating Daniel Connors the most, but Dane was included. If she was one of the Connors too? Done. Simple as that. The loathing extended to her too, and it ramped up because she was in my world. She was in my space. She'd made me want to touch her. She'd made me want to open up in a way I never did. But she was dead to me now. I'd never sought her out before, but I knew the guys had noticed my newfound contempt for her.

A few had asked if there was something they should know. I didn't want to fuck up her job, which would fuck up the team, and because I hadn't decided yet whether I wanted her fired or not, I'd just told them there were things going on with my niece and I had a newfound loathing for all shrinks. They'd gone back to listening to her, attributing my issue to my family business. Only a couple of the younger guys remained wary around Rain, but as far as I'd noticed, she handled it just fine.

Now, though, knowing she wasn't here and that according to Benny, she wouldn't be at any of the games against her brothers, I began to question myself.

Was there something I'd missed?

35

RAIN

"GRIFFIN, YOU SUCK!"

The guy next to me was screaming, and the teams had just left the ice after warmups. The game hadn't even started. After my debacle in the bathroom, strangely, I couldn't bring myself to leave the rink.

I also couldn't bring myself to be here in a work capacity. I was too strung out, too much of a mess. I knew Mal would've let me watch from the owner's suite. And I could've gone down and watched from behind the bench, in the tunnel and out of sight, but either way, there'd still be people watching me. With Mal, there'd be pity and concern, maybe something else. With the staff, there'd be confusion. I couldn't handle either, so I ended up purchasing a single seat, which put me in the middle of a bunch of Boston fans.

Holy shit, they hated Tyler. I'd known they did, but this seemed extra. Maybe it was because he'd left the eastern conference for Minnesota?

"Sorry," the same fan said as he took his seat. "I just honestly hate that bastard. He's a rat for leaving his team the way he did."

The fan glanced my way and apparently mistook my confusion for ignorance. He grunted, shifting his popcorn aside as two of his buddies came back from getting drinks. And snacks. Their arms were full of food and beverages. As they sat, he explained, "He used to play for New York, and if you know your geometry at all, you'd know New York isn't that far from Boston. He was basically one of us. And the way he left? Within a day? It wasn't right. It just wasn't right. He did New York dirty."

The press had leaked the reason Tyler was traded. Was this guy that heartless? "He transferred because of his family."

The guy flicked his hand in the air. "Pffft. That sad story about his niece overdosing? Fake news. His PR team made it up. The real story's out on the blogs. He demanded more money, and his team was capped. They couldn't give it, so he walked—like a big, dramatic baby. We should call him rat baby."

His friends thought that was hilarious. "Right on, Bobby," one of them said. The other laughed along with him, his mouth full of hot dog.

They fist-bumped each other before Bobby looked my way again. "Don't be embarrassed about believing what the mainstream media is reporting. It's all bullshit anyway. Do yourself a favor. Don't believe it."

With that, the lights went down and the hype video cued up. After that, the players would be back on the ice for the anthem and then puck drop.

I suddenly needed a drink. Standing, I ignored whatever Bobby was about to say and spoke over him, "Be right back."

He leered at me.

"Little girl's room."

That leer intensified.

"I have my period. Need to change my tampon or we'll have a situation here."

The leer vanished. He looked a little green and shifted as far away from me as he could.

I tried suppressing the satisfaction that bloomed in me. Not caring if Bobby saw my grin, I headed up the aisle. Most everyone was hurrying to get to their seats now, so I hoped the concessions lines would be short.

But everyone else must've had the same thought because they weren't.

I still had my employee badge, and I eyed the stairs, knowing there were better bathrooms up there. They were out of the way. I'd been lying about needing the bathroom, but now it seemed like a good idea. I decided to go for it.

I dug out my badge and flashed it when I came to the stairs that led to the suite floors. The administration offices were clear on the other side of the rink. I didn't have enough time.

The guard let me pass, and I hurried up the stairs.

Coming to the first women's bathroom, I ducked inside and found an empty stall. As I sat, I could hear the click of heels entering, along with some little girls giggling.

"Dylan," a woman's voice scolded. "Don't do that. Here. We can wait for the next stall to open up."

I froze.

The toilet next to me flushed, and the woman left. The little girl and her mom both entered, and the mom continued to speak to her daughter. "Go to the bathroom quickly. Then we'll wash our hands and go see Daddy play. How's that sound?"

"Can I have some candy, Mom? We should take something to Grandpa."

I sat paralyzed on the toilet. I didn't recognize their voices, but what were the odds?

The woman chuckled. "Of course, you adorable little munchkin."

"Mom!" Dylan giggled. "Only Daddy can call me that."

"Oh really? Only Daddy gets to call you that? I don't think so."

A burst of shrieks and giggles pitched through the air until the mom suddenly seemed to remember where they were. "Okay, okay. Let's finish up, and then we'll grab treats to take back to Grandpa Keith."

The stall began to swim around me.

"Yay! We need to get the licorice he likes."

"We will."

I stayed quiet until they'd both used the bathroom and the sinks. I left my stall just as they were leaving. I stepped out in time to get a brief glimpse at the little girl's face, and I was speechless. Stunned.

Dylan, which was my name. Grandpa Keith. Licorice, which was my father's favorite thing to eat at hockey events. He liked popcorn for football games. Hot dogs for baseball, but hockey was his favorite, so he ate his favorite candy. Red licorice.

This was the VIP floor.

We were playing Boston.

That little girl could've been my twin at her age.

I was pretty sure I just saw my niece for the first time.

36

TYLER

The puck dropped, and three seconds later, so did the gloves.

Bruge squared up against one of Boston's enforcers. The problem was that the Grays had one enforcer. Boston had four on their team. The Grays only played against Boston twice in the season, playoffs not included. But New York played them a lot more, so I was used to their enforcers. When the first penalties were handed out and Bruge went to the box, along with one of Boston's players, my line got on the ice.

The crowd went nuclear. "YOU RAT BABY, GRIFFIN!"

I lined up for the face-off against Rain's brother and bent over, ignoring whoever that fan was. I was impressed with his volume level, but not his taunt. I'd heard that one when another of their players got traded to Florida. They needed new material.

"How's it feel to be a bigger loser than you already are, you defecting piece of shit?"

I looked up, met Dane's ice-cold eyes, and realized they were the same as Rain's. Except there was a void in Dane's while Rain's were warm. Kind. There was so much humanity in hers, along with pain. I realized that with a start too.

"Is that what they're saying about me?"

"You boys ready?" The ref held the puck between us, waiting.

Dane ignored him. "Isn't that what you did? Running back home to your family? I don't believe it for a second. What are you hiding from, you fucking coward?"

I didn't understand any of what he was saying and shook my head. "As if you can talk about family. At least mine's proud of me."

He straightened abruptly. "What *the fuck* does that mean?"

I straightened too, and the crowd went nuts again, thinking their star had decided to take on enemy number one, forget using the enforcers.

"You know exactly what that means."

He skated forward, his chest bumping mine. "No," he spat. "I don't. Enlighten me."

"That's a big word for you, Connors. You sure you used it correctly?" I taunted right back. Fuck him, I wanted to fight. I didn't usually go out of my way to start them, but if something needed to go down, I was ready and willing.

"Okay, boys." The ref got between us. "We already did that. We're not doing it again. Sully. Ray. One of you is up."

Connors continued to glare at me. I smirked as we moved to our new starting places and our replacements took the face-off.

A second later, the puck dropped. Boston won it.

I pushed off after it, because that was going to be the only thing Boston won for the rest of the game, if I had anything to do with it. Tonight, the thirst for good, old-fashioned violence was in my blood, and I looked forward to unleashing it on the ice.

God, I loved this sport.

37

RAIN

Someone was pounding on my door. Again. I had fallen asleep on my couch, and it took me a moment to decipher what was going on.

Pound! Pound!

"Let me in, Rain." It was Tyler. "Now!"

What was up with this asshole? Nothing for too long and then back to pounding on my door?

Something was on me, leaning against me, and I shoved it off because I didn't like being touched like that. Oh, shit. It was a bottle. It was filled with liquid.

Oh, *shit*. It was rum.

I'd forgotten.

I must've fallen asleep with the bottle in my hand.

"Rain!"

My phone started ringing.

I snatched it up, trying to save the rum and the bottle. My couch was going to be drunk.

I put my phone to my ear. "Hello?"

But the phone was still ringing.

It was the hotel landline. Well, that wasn't good.

I tossed my cell on the table and grabbed the cordless phone as I went over to the door. I opened it and answered the phone at the same time. "Hello?"

"Ms. Connors, this is the front desk—"

Tyler had lifted his hand to continue pounding. He dropped it now, his face furious as he shoved his way into the room.

I focused on what the front desk was saying, "—a disturbance." They stopped talking.

I stared at Tyler, my brain working hard to process it all. "Oh," I said. "I'm okay. That was an asshole at my door, but I opened it."

There was quiet for a beat on the other end. "Are you in need of security, Ms. Connors?"

I stared at Tyler, whose gaze had fallen to my rum. He took it from my hand and tipped it back, taking a good swallow. "No. He's inside now."

"I'm aware, Ms. Connors. I'm asking if you would like us to send security to your room."

"Why?"

"For your safety. Do you feel safe, Ms. Connors?"

"Not emotionally."

Tyler wiped the back of his hand over his mouth, glaring at me as he took another drink. "What the fuck are they saying?"

"They're asking if I feel safe."

He rolled his eyes upward and turned away from me, going into the bedroom with my rum.

"Ms. Connors?"

"I'm fine. I don't need security, but if you know a good couch cleaner on staff?" I looked over at the piece of furniture. Too much of that bottle had leaked out. I'd gotten home, started drinking, and probably passed out after two swigs. *Lightweight.*

"What was that?" the front desk asked sharply.

"Nothing. Everything's fine." I ended the call and tossed the phone in the direction of its base. There was a thud and a crash, but I was beyond caring at this point.

When I went to the bedroom, Tyler was sitting on the edge of my bed, still drinking and scowling at me.

"You're one of them."

I readied myself, or tried. "I'm too drunk for this."

"Pfft. What? You had two shots of this? You're not drunk."

"I feel drunk."

"You look tired."

"That too."

We fell silent. I watched him. He watched me. We were at our first standstill until the storm moved over his face. "You're a fucking Connors."

I swallowed. "Not by choice."

"You are, though. What? Were you laughing at us behind our backs? Sharing all the neat little tidbits to your brothers? To fucking Daniel?"

Nausea rode over me. "I would never."

"Wouldn't you? You're a Connors. That's what they would do!"

"But I'm not a Connors by choice! I'm only a Connors because of my mom." My voice broke. "Trust me. I've thought about changing my name, but she held me in her arms and told me she liked my name and it's the last thing I have from her."

He was quiet. "Your mom?"

"She died when I was six."

He looked away. "I'm sorry."

"Yeah. Well. We all have our things, right?" I gave him a pointed look.

He closed his eyes tight and let out a rueful exhale. His hand gripped the bottle so tight while his other raked through his hair. "Daniel fucked my sister's life up. You know that, right?"

"I know that." Guilt flooded me. He had no idea how much I knew that.

"I have had to deal with your brothers all my fucking life. I couldn't get away from them in high school because they were there. They were there in Juniors. They were there on the national teams. They were there in the NHL. They're everywhere I go and now they're in my *fucking bed*?"

"No." I stepped toward him. "Don't you—" My voice went guttural. "Don't you dare fucking go there. They are not here. I —I *cannot* stand them. I didn't lie to the team. I don't know Daniel and Dane Connors. I never want to know them."

"That doesn't make sense."

"It doesn't make sense to you because you love your sister. Mine don't love me. I do not have the type of relationship with them you have with yours. When it comes to family, you are the lucky one. *Trust* me."

Silence grew thick in the room. I felt my words echoing around us. Pounding.

"Where the fuck were you tonight?"

I shook my head, stopping in the doorway. "I grew up with a brother who was meaner than you. Nothing you say will penetrate. Did you know I have a niece? I didn't. I haven't talked to my brothers in twelve years, and tonight, I not only found out that Dane has a daughter, but he named her after me. *Me*." My voice rose. "Why the fuck would he name her after me? He hated me growing up."

"You haven't talked to your brothers in twelve years?"

"Now you want to ask questions? After giving me the silent treatment for how long?"

He frowned, ignoring what I said. "Your brother hates you?"

"I just told you they do."

"How'd you find out about the niece?"

I gave him the abbreviated version. "In the bathroom."

"Bathroom?"

"VIP section. On the suites level."

"The fuck are you talking about?"

I was done answering questions. Stalking over to him, I swiped my rum back and returned to the living room. What was I going to do with that couch? I'd need to call someone because I didn't want the hotel to charge me for cleaning. They'd overcharge me.

Tyler followed. "So you were at the game tonight?"

"You grew up here. Do you know a couch cleaner I could call?"

He stared at the couch alongside me. "My sister probably does, but she's not talking to me right now."

I grunted. "Lucky her."

"What?"

I ignored that. "How do I find somewhere to clean it?"

He gave me a sideways glance. "I don't think you take couches to the cleaners. They're not really portable."

I grunted. "True." I took another shot of rum and changed my focus. "What are you doing here?"

"Why weren't you at the game tonight?"

"We've already established that I was."

"But not as part of the team. You weren't working." He said this like an accusation.

"It's none of your business, remember? You left. You haven't talked to me lately. You have no reason to be here, and even less reason to ask me those sorts of questions." I pointed at the door, the rum swishing in the bottle from the motion. "Get out."

"You don't mean that." He still glowered, but it was lessening.

"The fuck I don't." I took a step toward him. "Get. Out."

He didn't move, his eyes tracing my movements. He bent down so he could see right into my eyes. One more inch and my chest would brush against his.

I had no bra on.

I was suddenly aware of that fact.

When I got home, I'd pulled on the clothes on the top of my dresser—a Grays hoodie and my tiny shorts. I hadn't expected guests. I only wanted to get drunk, numb some of the pain, and sleep. I really wanted to sleep. I always struggled with that, but it'd been worse lately.

As if following my thoughts, Tyler noted, "Morty said you've been skating every night."

I shrugged, taking a step away from him, because this was pointless. Tyler wasn't going to leave until he took his pound of flesh, whatever that meant for him.

He grabbed my arm.

I froze, looking down at his hold. "What are you doing?"

His thumb began stroking my skin, and he took the rum from me, placing it on the table. "I hate your family." He tugged me against him, and I could feel how hard his dick was.

I looked down.

He cupped my cheek, tilting me back to look at him. Holding me in place, he slowly, purposefully, directed me backward until I hit the wall. He followed, his body against mine, but he was so still, watching me with a cold gleam in his eyes. His finger moved to rest over my pulse point, holding my chin in place. He pressed against my carotid. "I don't think you understand the magnitude of how much I loathe your family members."

"I have an idea," I said, my heart beginning to spike. "I was around back then."

"You see." He leaned over me, his gaze now jumping from my eyes to my mouth. "That's the part I can't understand. Because where were you? I never heard of a Connors sister. Your brothers are huge assholes. I would've heard if they had a weak spot."

Anger flamed hot in me. I shoved him back...or tried. "I'm no one's weak spot."

His fingers pressed harder against my chin. He growled, ducking his head, and I felt his words against my neck. "I'm starting to think you might be mine."

I stilled. What did that mean? "Tyler?"

His hand suddenly found my hair, fisted a handful of it, and tipped my head backward. I cried out in surprise, but it didn't hurt me.

My core throbbed. I wanted him. He was *such* a dick, but I *wanted* his dick.

He continued to glare at me with such hatred, pure loathing. "I don't know the situation with you and your brothers, but tonight, I don't care." He opened his mouth, tasting my neck. I gasped, surging against him. "Not right now." His hand slid down and grabbed under my leg, lifting me, giving him better access to grind against me.

I bit back a moan because it felt so good. "You stopped talking to me." I evaded his kiss when he lifted his head, his mouth searching for mine.

His gaze met mine, hot with repressed need and frustration and lust. "Because I'm pissed. I was about to open up to you, and then suddenly *you're* the enemy."

"You're my brother's enemy." Both of them. I was their enemy as well. "That's why I told you." My annoyance was dissipating, replaced by a frenzied desperation for him to shut up. I wanted his hands on me. Touching me. "I wanted you to know who my family was if we were going to continue the way we were going."

"Well, we're not," he snapped. His jaw clenched, and I could see a vein pulsing there.

"Your actions tonight say otherwise."

He broke, lifting me with a snarl, and I yelped, wrapping my arms around his neck. He dropped me on the bed and lowered himself on top of me. He tugged my hoodie off and tossed it to the side. He caught the side of my jaw in his hand

and glowered down at me. "I want to fuck you." He waited for my permission.

I flushed, my entire body a volcano for him. "Now you're asking my permission?"

"I'm an asshole."

"That's been established," I shot back.

He didn't react except to drop his groin and rub up into me. *Holy*—I had to bite back another groan. It'd been a long time. I began panting as he dropped his mouth to my neck, sucking long and hard.

Fuck. He was really good at that.

His hand smoothed over my waist, sliding into my shorts and underwear. He slid a finger to my clit but held back. He was waiting for me.

"You don't fight fair."

He scoffed. "You wouldn't have let me anywhere near you if you didn't want this tonight, and you know it."

He was right. "I'm drunk," I countered. I wasn't. I wished I was.

"Then we both are, because I drank more than you did since I've been here."

"This is wrong."

He slid one finger inside me.

I couldn't hold back the moan this time. Just as I remembered how to breathe, he slid a second finger inside. *Why does that have to feel so good?*

I fisted his sweatshirt, yanking his face to mine. "Listen here."

His eyes blazed.

"You lost your chance to get to know me. But this." I wrapped my legs around his waist, mashing us together with his hand still between us. He smirked as his fingers began sliding in and out of me. I struggled to hold on to his hoodie to make my point, but I tried valiantly. "We're just going to fuck and then you leave. Okay?"

His eyes flashed again and his lip curved up. "Sure." He dipped his head toward my neck.

"I mean it. After we're done, you go."

Dark triumph gleamed back from that beautiful fucking face of his. "Not a problem." His mouth lowered to cover mine, and as I was swept up in the kiss, I had a feeling I'd been outmaneuvered.

His tongue slid into my mouth, and all that other stupid shit left my mind.

38

RAIN

Damn if he wasn't taking his time. Oh no. No, no, no. That wasn't how this was going to go. I pushed at his shoulder, turning him over so I could climb on top. I glared. "This isn't going to be a whole tender moment. I didn't let you in here for slow sex."

"You didn't let me in. I walked in."

"I let you stay."

"Because you want my dick."

"Yes. So use it."

He scoffed, staring at me.

I stared back at him, and damn. He was something to stare at. Something to memorize—that gorgeous face, those smoldering eyes, the cheekbones. *Ugh*. I bit back a sigh because those cheekbones... All chiseled and defined, like the rest of him. His tan and toned body. His abs. His fucking abs. I ran my hands over his chest and slipped them under his hoodie, pushing it up. "I want this off."

He sat up a little and whisked the sweatshirt away. As he laid back down, his hands went to my hips. "You don't want slow sex, fine with me. Do something about it." He said this in challenge, and fuck him, because my body reacted. The inferno kept building and building, and I rocked over him, taking my time.

After a moment his hands flexed against my hips. "I thought you didn't want to go slow," he said through gritted teeth.

"Shut up." I rocked over him again, carnal pleasure spreading through me, and closed my eyes for a moment. I rocked again, both of us reacting. He groaned, sounding hoarse, "Jesus. That feels good."

It did. It really did. Opening my eyes, my hands went to his pants, and I began tugging them down.

"Up." He patted the back of my ass.

I shot him a dark look, which he chuckled at. Sitting up, he helped remove the rest of his clothing, and before I sat back down, he pulled mine off as well. He laid back down and helped settle me over him.

My eyes went wide. "You're ridiculously good at that."

He smirked, but wanton lust swirled in his eyes. "Thought you wanted a quick fuck."

I smiled. Something eased in me with the banter. That hadn't changed, and it's what I needed right now. It anchored me so I didn't float away on my feelings, mistaking this for something else. I was already wet for him, but only because it'd been a while. And this, between him and me, was just unfinished business.

That helped settle me further. I trailed my fingertips over his hips, over his obliques. As his dick bobbed, I wrapped my hand around him.

He hissed. "Goddamn. That feels good too."

Triumph flared in me, and I began stroking him, watching him through hooded eyes.

He swallowed, his muscles bunching under my caresses. Because of me. I gave him that pleasure, and it made me feel a certain way. I kept stroking, looking down to watch my hand moving over his cock. I ran my thumb over his tip, and he jerked up with another hiss. This time was louder, more pronounced. His eyes were closed. His hands were at my hips, just holding me. But I'd had enough waiting.

Reaching over to my nightstand, I pulled a condom from the packet. His eyes opened and watched me when I settled over him. He drew in a sharp breath as I rolled it down his length.

"Hey," he said quietly.

I looked up, meeting his eyes. I didn't respond, instead sliding down over him. We both grunted as he entered me, and I waited a moment, adjusting to him until he was all the way inside. A whimper left me because he was so big. He was always so big. Resting my hands on his chest, I rolled my hips forward.

"Holy shit. You're tight," he gasped, helping me move over him. "I think I forgot. How could I have forgotten?"

There was nothing emotional about this, I told myself as I picked up speed, slamming against him. No. I impaled myself again, pumping harder. Harder. Fiercer. Jesus. I was railing him, and I was breathless, because this felt amazing.

"Damn, Rain. I need to touch you."

"Yeah," I panted.

His hand moved toward my clit, but I grabbed it. "Not there." I sat up, tilting my head back as I closed my eyes. "Not yet. I want to ride you longer."

"You're killing me." I could hear how breathless he was, and I grinned, savoring the effect I had on him. I felt his hand moving over my stomach, exploring me. He caressed me. Up my side, around to my back, down my spine. Tingles of sensation trailed in his wake, and then he shifted to sit up. One of his arms wrapped around my waist. His heat burned against my front as he bent down, his mouth finding my throat, teasing and tantalizing as he explored there, moving down until I felt his mouth close over one of my nipples.

I surged up, barely suppressing a cry.

He groaned, deep in his throat. "Keep riding me, baby. Keep going."

I grabbed a fistful of his hair and yanked. "I am not your baby."

He grinned at me. His eyes were wild, lost in hunger. "Right now, you could tell me you want to be called the Easter Bunny and I'd do that. Whatever you want, ba—little Connors."

That was worse. I lifted myself up off of him, and as he protested, I slammed back down.

He groaned, closing his eyes, and his forehead hit the side of my neck. He clawed at my back, struggling to find a hold because we were both sweaty messes by now. "Shit, woman. You feel so good." He tipped his head back and grinned again. "I think I might already be addicted to you."

Something dark and determined flashed in his eyes. Suddenly I was holding my breath, unsure. He rested his forehead between my breasts. His hands returned to my hips, and he began moving with me.

An explosion was stirring. I felt it building at the bottom of my spine, in my core, and as he yanked me over him one more time, lifting my body in the air. I came, a scream ripping out of me.

He cursed, dragging me over him a few more times before I felt him release inside of me. My walls constricted around him and he whimpered. He didn't seem aware of the sound.

I collapsed on top of him, riding out the wave of my climax.

We stayed there like that until reality came back to me. Until I remembered what I'd just done and who I'd done it with. I welcomed the cold that now invaded me. It pushed out the warmth. Swiftly, I swung myself off of him. Clambering to the side of the bed, I bent down and grabbed the first hoodie I touched. I yanked it on and rose from the bed.

"Rain—"

"We fucked. Now get out."

I left the room.

Only later did I realize I'd grabbed his hoodie.

39

TYLER

A week later

I was just leaving practice when my phone rang. I didn't even need to look at the screen once I heard the Batman-theme ringtone. I swiped to answer, a big smile already coming to my face. "Nolan. My man."

"Hey!"

He sounded good. Cheerful. It felt good to hear his voice again. I missed him. I missed my old team.

"It's been a minute," he added.

"Yeah." I unlocked my truck and opened the door to toss my things inside. I rounded to the driver's seat, and as I pulled out of my parking spot, the phone synced up with the dashboard. Nolan's voice transferred to the speakers.

"—to catch up, but I was calling for a reason."

I frowned. "Yeah, man. What's up?"

It wasn't that Nolan and I didn't keep in touch. We texted and sent each other funny memes or reels, but we'd not had a discussion of all the details going on with our lives in a while.

I'd been too busy with Skylar at first, then I was distracted by Rain, and now, well, I didn't have a good reason.

"When's the last time you talked to your sister?"

My gut churned. "Uh, it's been a while. Why are you asking?"

Ski knew Nolan. When she and Zoey visited me in New York, Nolan was over all the time. He took to Skylar as if she were his sister, and Zoey was his niece.

"She's been calling me."

"What?"

"Yeah, buddy. I'm sorry. I wasn't sure what to do at first. The first time she called, she cried almost the whole time. I just listened. At the end, I told her to let you know she'd called me. She said she would, but I never heard from you. I know you. You would've reached out. I meant to shoot you a message, let you know myself, but you know how it is. Hockey."

Games were almost every other night. Traveling. Practices. We were busy.

"Anyway, it's been a few weeks, and she's still calling."

I turned in to a parking lot and swung for the closest slot. Letting the engine idle, I sat back. "Ski's giving me the silent treatment. She got pissed when I told her Zoey should go to a mental health clinic."

He was quiet for a beat. "Interesting. She didn't put it in those words."

"How'd she put it?"

"She said you thought she and Zoey should be separated. When I asked her for the specific wording, she just started crying. Again, I know you, and I was reading between the lines, but she's not doing so well."

I pulled up the last few texts I'd sent my sister.

Tyler: Can we talk about this?

Tyler: Please.

Tyler: I miss you. I love you and Zoey. I just want what's best for her.

Tyler: I'm learning that maybe therapy isn't such a bad thing.

Tyler: Can you let me know what you decided?

Tyler: Do you need anything from me?

Tyler: I came here for you and Zoey.

Tyler: What the hell, Ski?

Tyler: We're not fourteen anymore.

That last text had been a threat. If she didn't respond, I was going to start looking for them. I hadn't sent it, but it was still there in the drafts.

I sighed. "She's upset because the hospital wanted Zoey to go somewhere for treatment because of her overdose. I agreed with them, but I told her she could try to find a compromise program where she'd still be able to see Zoey. She hung up on me."

"Huh."

"I'm almost afraid to ask for the update."

"Well, she was really worked up about a text you sent her. Something about if it happened again and Zoey couldn't be found, it'd be her fault."

"What?" That came out strangled.

"Her words, brother. Look, I know you didn't mean it that way, but that's how she took it. When's the last time you guys talked?"

"Too long."

"Shit."

"Yeah."

I suddenly felt the world on my shoulders again. "I've been busy, but they're the reason I came out here. I'll go around to her place, and if she's not there, I'll try tracking her down. I shouldn't have left it this long. If anything, I need to check in with Zoey and see how she's faring. I don't think Skylar gave

Zoey her phone back. She mentioned she was going to keep it, see if that would help her."

Suddenly antsy, I pulled out of the parking lot and returned to the road.

"Sky said she was staying with a friend," Nolan noted after a moment.

"And Zoey?"

"She won't answer my questions when I ask about Zoey. I haven't pushed because I'm scared she'll stop talking to me."

"I know. You don't have to be the bad guy."

"Listen, we play you guys next week, so I'm in town for a night, at least. I can help. If you want to be bad cop and I'm good cop, I'll do it. An intervention? Whatever you need. If Zoey is getting help, I think something needs to be done for Skylar too. The stress, her TBI—I don't think she's handling any of this very well. After some of her messages, I'm concerned. I'm sorry to call you about this."

"No. You're family, Nolan. I'm glad she called you, and I appreciate all you've done. I've been slacking on my end. I'm sorry you were put in this position. I should've been more on top of this."

He sighed. "It's not on you. I've been beside you when Sky's cut you off. I know how it goes. I've got two sisters of my own."

I grinned. "Yeah, but both your sisters mother you. You'd be the one to cut them off."

He barked out a laugh. "As if they'd let me. They'd drive down and threaten to take my balls if I pulled that on them." He quieted. "It's different with your situation. You know that."

"Did she say what friend she was staying with?"

"No. She knew I'd tell you."

I cursed. "Ski's got a lot of friends."

"She does, which is normally a good thing."

"Okay. Thank you for letting me know, and I'll start doing

the rounds. Ski forgets that I used to live here too. I know her old haunts."

"Try the hospital first. Maybe they can help you somehow?"

"Skylar doesn't have me on any of Zoey's paperwork. I'm on some of hers, but not for this. I'll call and see, but I'm not holding my breath that they can help."

"Keep me updated and loop me in when I get to town to beat your ass on the ice."

We ended the call on a chuckle, and it was then that I realized I'd driven to Rain's hotel. I hadn't even thought about where I was going. Autopilot had brought me here, but considering the situation, I couldn't bring myself to leave. Rain and I hadn't talked since the last time I was here, which had been a week ago for our hate fuck. I didn't know what else to call it. I would never stop hating her brothers. And I wasn't sure about my feelings for Rain anymore. The time when I could've asked questions about her relationship with them seemed to have passed, but I knew Rain grew up here as well.

I didn't think she'd still been at the rink when I left.

Pocketing my keys, phone, and wallet, I hopped out of my truck.

This should be fun.

40

RAIN

I was headed down the hall from my hotel room, planning on using the hotel gym for once, when the elevator doors opened and Tyler stepped out.

I stopped in my tracks as he headed my way.

Backtracking, I tried to return to my room, but the door had already swished shut behind me. Panic flared as I grabbed the door handle, leaning into the door, but it had locked, and my key card was in my bag. The end result: my forehead hit the door.

"Ouch." I rubbed my head.

Tyler chuckled behind me, dark and ominous.

I gave him a side eye.

He folded his arms over that leanly muscled chest of his. "Did you forget something? It looked as if you were leaving your room. Could there be a reason you'd suddenly try to go back in?"

I scowled. "What are you doing here?"

He dropped his grin. "My sister's avoiding me, and I just got a concerning call from a buddy of mine. I need to find her." He nodded toward me. "You're local. Thought you might help me look for her."

"My apartment is in Kansas City. I'm here for work."

He frowned. "Wait. What?"

I didn't want to have a conversation about me. "What's going on with your sister?"

He walled up right away. My tactic worked. "I just gotta find her, check on her." He turned and motioned for me to follow. "Come on. She knows my truck, so you're driving. You got a rental car, right?"

I didn't move, just watched as he went to the elevator. When he noticed I wasn't following, he gestured impatiently. "Let's go. What are you waiting for?"

Such a dickbag.

I didn't need to do this. But if something was wrong with his sister...

How much help could I be anyway?

"Rain." Tyler stopped at the elevator.

Fuck.

Fine.

I was going to regret this.

"Hold on." I pulled out my keycard and went back into my room. Stuffing my phone in my purse, I tossed my headphones on the table and grabbed a hoodie from the chair. Minnesota was having an abnormally warm November, but it was still chilly at night. I exchanged my shorts for leggings and found my car keys.

When I returned, Tyler was waiting in the same spot, except with his back against the wall. I faltered for a moment. Jesus, he was hot. He wore a black Grays hoodie and black joggers. No one who played hockey should look like he did. It wasn't fair. Then he turned those cold eyes on me, and I remembered that even if we fucked again, he hated me. He'd *always* hate me, just on principle, which I was loathe to admit I understood, but I did.

The hatred was deserved.

I shut the door and headed down the hall as he pushed the button for the elevator.

"Where do you want to start?" I asked.

He grimaced. "She won't be at her place, but we'll start there."

Awesome.

41

RAIN

I drove while Tyler was on his phone. Most of the people he called answered, and they sounded like old friends of his sister's. They were excited to hear from him. Most wanted to catch up, but he tried to keep it short. We checked an apartment building first, and he ran in by himself. He came back out five minutes later, and off we went again.

At the end of the seventh call, he said, "Yeah. No. It's great to hear your girls are doing well. Yeah. Yeah. Okay. Thanks. Yeah, if you hear from her, give me a call. Thanks again." After hanging up, he cursed, rubbing his forehead. "Fuck's sake. The problem with my sister is that she has a whole network of people I don't know. Some of them don't even have phones. I've called all the people I can think of, but I've not been back here to socialize in a fucking decade."

I needed to concentrate with the traffic. I couldn't sort through this with him at the same time, so I turned into a cafe's parking lot.

"What are you doing?"

I pulled into a slot and put the car in park. "Let's go through the basics. Her best friends."

He held up his phone. "I called them."

"Okay. Family members?"

"It's just her and me. And Zoey."

"No cousins?"

He shook his head. "No one. The woman who helped us didn't have family or kids. And that was only for a few years. She's down in Florida. It was really just Skylar and me growing up. She didn't get close to any of my billet families."

Their parents died in a car crash.

My chest squeezed, and I cleared my throat. "Okay, work friends. Who are they?"

He thought for a moment. "She has two jobs. She works at a bar part time. She doesn't need the money, but my sister is stubborn. I bought their condo. I pay for their medical insurance. She works so she has something to do while Zoey's in school, and now she's getting older. Her social life is more active. She also works full time at a nursing home."

"Your sister or Zoey?"

"My sister."

"You don't know who your sister's work friends are?"

"Do you know your siblings' work friends?" he shot back.

"Yes, because it's blasted on Instagram and TikTok. I'd rather not know, but when I took this job, that meant I had to tune into the lovely world of the NHL again."

He stopped short, frowning at me before he burst out laughing. "Jesus." He chuckled. "The joys of having celebrity brothers, huh? You and my sister could probably vent over a whole box of wine."

"I'd rather not." I gave him a pointed look.

He cursed softly. "Shit. I forgot that Ski and Daniel dated. I mean, I didn't forget. I hate that fucking asshole. He's part of the reason she got hurt, but I keep forgetting the details. Does that make sense?"

Ski. I'd heard him use the nickname before, but my mind

had been caught up with other worries. Now, more memories flooded in.

I must've made some sort of face because he asked, "What?"

I shrugged. "It's nothing. Just...Daniel used to tease her about being called Ski. I heard him sometimes in the house, bitching about it. He didn't understand it, and she wouldn't let him use it. Said it was just for you." I laughed, but it was bitter. "He hated that, being told he couldn't do something. Sad part is that he didn't even really care. Not about your sister. Not about the nickname. He just didn't like being told no."

"Oh."

"Can we go to one of your sister's jobs?"

He nodded. "Let's try the bar first. She works in the kitchen at the nursing home, and she's adamant about not letting people know she's related to me, said her co-workers wouldn't handle it well. She's more likely to make friends with co-workers at the bar."

I nodded as he looked up the address, and once he typed in the name, I knew where it was. I pulled out and swung my car around in the right direction.

"You know the place?" he asked.

"I'm assuming there's only one Hank's Tulip in Oakes, Minnesota, so yeah. I know where it is."

I pulled out onto the street. I didn't tell him it was the bar a couple friends and I had tried to sneak into in high school. That was when I was still trying to make friends, have friends, keep friends. That was before I learned friends were not worth it.

My phone rang. The dashboard announced that Mal Benoit was calling.

I reached for the ignore button, but Tyler got there first and hit accept.

I cursed under my breath and hit him anywhere I could reach.

He tried to dodge my hands, but he was too busy laughing.

"Hello?" Mal said when no one said anything.

"*You little fuck,*" I mouthed at Tyler.

He laughed silently and pointed to the dashboard.

"Rain? Are you there?"

I cleared my throat. "Yes. Hey. Hi, Mal. How's it going? I'm in the car."

"Hi. I wanted to check in. You know, see how you're doing. And if you wanted to grab that glass of wine sometime?"

My hands tightened on the steering wheel, and for a moment, I was transported back to that bathroom, back to that moment I'd seen Dane. I pulled in a ragged breath. "I'm, uh..."

Tyler's eyes narrowed.

I ignored him. "I'm okay, Mr. Benoit."

"Mal. Please. After—please call me Mal, Rain."

"Of course." I smiled. "Mal."

Tyler rolled his eyes. "*Mal?*"

I gave him a look as I straightened in my seat. "Anyway, I'm doing fine. After what we talked about."

"Of course. That's good. Listen, uh, there's another reason I was calling. First, I meant the offer as a friend. I can't imagine—"

I coughed to shut him up and raised my voice. "Yeah. It's okay. I don't want to rehash it."

"Of course. Of course, but..." He cleared his throat. "We've got more of the eastern teams coming. We're playing Griffin's previous team early next week and then Montreal after Thanksgiving. With the holiday, and knowing about your situation, I wondered if you wanted to watch the game with me? In the owner's suite." When I didn't reply right away, he added, "No one has to know you're there. Just you, watching the game."

A tornado took root inside of me, churning and twisting and causing all sorts of damage.

Daniel.

He'd be here, the day after Thanksgiving. They were playing that Friday night against the Grays.

Dane was one sort of monster. Cold. Ignoring me. But Daniel. He was a different beast.

"I..." I forgot who else was in the car for a moment. My voice dropped, and I held onto that steering wheel so tightly, trying to focus on my driving. "Maybe. Maybe? Can I make a decision later?"

"Of course. And I meant it about a glass of wine as well."

"Thank you, Mal."

"Of course. And if there's anything the team or I can do for you, just let me know. Have a good night." He signed off first, leaving the car in silence.

Daniel.

If I went to the game, I'd have to see him again. In person. The day after Thanksgiving. Our dad had been there for Dane's game. Would he be at Daniel's too? Did our dad even still live in Minneapolis?

"Mal, huh?"

I sighed and closed my eyes. "I almost forgot you were in the car. Can we rewind a few minutes?"

"Har har. So..." He turned to face me.

I glanced over. He wasn't going to let this go. I was still going to try. "Can you not?"

"Not a chance. You and the owner of an NHL team? Why'd you fuck me when you can fuck him instead?"

My mouth dropped open. "Tyler!"

He raised an eyebrow. "I said what I said. What are you doing with me?"

"Well, right now, we're looking for *your* sister. Or did you forget Skylar?"

"I raised my sister. I'd never forget her." He thought a moment and cringed. "Except I did for a bit, but I was distracted. By you. You distracted me."

I was about done with members of the opposite sex blaming me for their mistakes. "You might want to rephrase that statement. Right now."

He continued to study me. "I said what I said. What are you doing with me? He's a billionaire, you know." He leaned closer, dropping his voice. "And if he says he wants to be friends, he's lying. He wants to fuck you. He just might keep you around a bit longer afterward. That's all that means."

"You are such a jackass."

"Yeah. I am, but I'm not lying. That man doesn't want to be friends. Are you fucking him already?"

"Stop talking. Please." The bar came into view, and I hit the turn signal. I'd never been more grateful to see a bar in my life. "We're here."

Tyler kept quiet until after I parked and shut the engine off. Then he leaned over. "If you're fucking us both, keep it clean. Safe sex and all." He was out of the car before I could even process what he'd said. His door slammed shut.

As soon as I did, I exploded after him. "Hey!" I yelled.

He ignored me, already halfway to the entrance. He'd shoved his hands into the front of his hoodie, pulling the sweatshirt tight around his shoulders. He'd put a ballcap on low and his hood up over the back of his hat.

All signs indicated that he wanted to go in under the radar, but just as I caught up with him, the front door opened and a bouncer stepped out. "If you're going to call me a slut, then use the actual word," I hissed. "Don't be a passive-aggressive little bitch about it."

Tyler whirled around.

I swallowed, meeting his gaze head on.

"Pretty sure I was clear," he said. "You fucking him or not?"

"No, I'm not." I stepped closer, digging my finger into his chest. "For the record, I have done *nothing* since I met you. I told you who I was. I was honest with you."

"Not fucking fast enough."

I winced as if I'd been slapped.

He cursed under his breath. "I didn't mean that."

I shook my head, woodenly. "No. Say it. You meant it, and I am sorry it took me that long. I did tell you, though. I came clean. Right now, you're the one with the problem. You're the one who can't choose, so I'm saying it. Either get your head together and choose to move on—with me or without me. I am *so done* with being shit on by hockey players." I stepped away from him, ignored the bouncer, whose jaw was on the floor, and went inside Harry's Tulip.

I took a moment to absorb the giant flowers on the wall and all around the bar. Techno music blared, neon lights pulsed. Many of the guys were walking around shirtless. My heart rested easy, because no matter the jackass behind me, I felt safe here.

Tyler stepped up next to me, also looking around. "This is a gay bar."

42

TYLER

We went to the bar, and the bartender took one look at us and began shaking his head. He was slim, maybe six feet tall with a pretty-boy face. The guy fought back a grin. "What can I get for you?" Giving me a once-over, he turned to Rain, indicating me. "No offense, but first time?"

Rain smiled. "We're looking for someone. Skylar Griffin."

The change was immediate. He stiffened. His eyes hardened. "Who's asking?"

A table of women were now eyeing Rain. I stepped closer and placed my hand at the small of her back. She tensed in surprise and glanced at me. This was a gay bar. Those women could be straight, and usually I'd be the one getting the attention. I wasn't, and a possessive streak rose within me. Rain was mine.

"I am. I'm her brother."

His mouth formed a small o. He reached for a rag on the counter.

I took some comfort when he didn't outright lie and say he didn't know her, but he looked torn.

"A buddy told me she's been calling him, and he was

concerned enough to reach out," I continued. "If you know my sister, you know that generally she and I get along."

His shoulders softened. "Yeah. I—" His eyes clamped shut. He hissed under his breath, "Fuck."

"Look, a compromise? Call her and see if she'll talk to me. Or see if she'll come here. She feels comfortable in this place. It's her territory."

A guy whose skin was covered in glitter, joined us, draping himself over the counter. "This looks fun. What's happening here?" He had dark eyes and black hair with rainbow highlights at the ends.

The bartender motioned to me. "This is Sky's brother. He's looking for her."

The guy's eyes lit up and a wide smile came to his face. "Well, no shit." He leaned an elbow on the counter, facing me. "Sky never told us what a hottie you are. Look at you." He sounded flirty, but his eyes were cold. "She's been holding out on us. You're coming off all straight and manly. Just my type." He winked, but I wasn't fooled.

The guy was also a watchdog. The bar wasn't too full, and we were attracting attention from the people around us. As soon as Sky's name came up, he'd gone into full protection mode.

The bartender gestured to us, now with his phone in hand. "Maybe we should call her, Eric. He seems concerned."

Eric snatched the phone from the bartender. "We will do no such thing. *You* will do no such thing, Paul. If this guy is looking for Sky, there's a reason she doesn't want to be found." The two shared a look. Eric's was heated. Paul's was still torn.

One of the women smiled at Rain.

I pulled Rain in front of me, fitting my chest to her back, and my hands found her hips. She drew in a sharp breath, but her hands rested over mine. "Okay," I said. "You guys don't want to violate Ski's trust, and we get that, so we'll let it go. We'll try to make sure she's okay another way. Since we're here, how about a drink?" Rain pressed back against me, her nails digging into my hands.

I muffled a grunt as she moved her ass over my groin. And just like that, my pants got a whole lot tighter. Rain could draw blood if she wanted. I wasn't moving. She felt damn good in my arms.

"I'll take a beer," I added.

"I'll take whatever you like mixing," Rain said.

That earned a smile from Paul, and Eric slid onto the barstool next to us. He continued to watch us with narrowed eyes. "How long have you known Sky?"

Paul frowned, but Eric didn't notice. He was fixated on me.

"Well, we're twins. So my whole life."

Paul laughed.

Rain tensed all over again.

Eric didn't react. "Uh-huh. Twins, you say. Who was the oldest?"

I stared at him, trying to figure out his game. "I was, by twelve minutes."

The guy jerked away from the bar, smirking. "So not your *whole* life."

Paul placed Rain's drink in front of her. "Dude. What is your problem?"

Eric gazed at him, wide-eyed. "What? We're conversing. I'm trying to get to know Sky's big brother. What's wrong with that?"

Paul narrowed his eyes. "You're interrogating him, and you don't know the circumstances. He and Sky might be good in a few days."

Eric snorted, folding his arms over chest. "We're talking about Sky here. She's the queen of grudges."

That made me laugh, and both turned to look at me,

seeming startled. My hands dug into Rain's hips. "Sorry, but yeah. You know my sister."

Paul looked torn again. "I know her better than Sherlock Holmes here." His eyes flickered to Eric. "And I know how much she adores her brother."

Eric jumped in, "Which brother? Maybe it's a different one."

Paul groaned. "She's only got *one* brother. Her twin brother. And she gushes about him all the time." He raised his eyebrows at me. "What kind of beer would you like?"

"Whatever's local. Right now a beer is a beer for me."

"Ha!" Eric practically yelled. "If you knew Sky, you'd know how opinionated she is about different beers."

"Fuck's sakes." Paul pinched between his eyebrows. "I'm going to call her. She can decide if she wants to talk to you *herself*."

I relaxed. "Thanks, man. Appreciate it."

"Yeah, yeah." Moving away from us, he pulled out his phone and lifted it to his ear.

After Paul began talking, Eric hummed. "I just wanted to protect her." He huffed to himself. The fight seemed to have left him. "You two are adorable, but you don't have to be scared of us gays. We don't bite." He winked again and this one felt genuine. "Unless you ask nicely."

I realized my hands had slipped under Rain's shirt, my thumbs smoothing over her hips.

"Oh. No. I'm not holding onto her because of that." I gestured toward the table of women. "I'm a jealous fucker, and one of those girls was giving her a lusty look."

Eric grinned, glancing over.

Rain jerked forward. "What? Where?" Her head tilted to the side. "Oh."

"Oh?" I tipped her head back to look at me. "*Oh?*"

She laughed, and I went still at the smile on her face. She

was radiant. "I mean, she's hot, if it's the one I think you're talking about."

I growled.

Eric laughed.

"What?" She gave me a look before turning to Eric. "He's a really good brother, but this whole thing is confusing to me. We had hate sex a week ago."

"Rain," I snapped.

Eric's eyes went wide. "Hate sex? Tell me more."

Rain laughed. "Part of it's my fault—"

She stopped abruptly because Paul had returned, sliding his phone into his pocket. He grabbed me a beer from beneath the counter.

"Bated breath here, dude," I said through gritted teeth.

He was silent until he'd delivered the beer with a flourish. "She'll be here in fifteen minutes." He beamed at me. "Cash or credit?"

Eric slumped. "And they call me dramatic."

I tossed my card on the bar. "We'll start a tab."

I knew my sister. Fifteen minutes was an hour and a half in Skylar-speak.

We might as well get comfortable.

43

RAIN

Thirty minutes later, I was buzzed.
I was supposed to be the driver, but I was too buzzed for that. We'd just been drinking and chatting, even though Tyler didn't want me to share all the weirdness happening between us. And Paul kept refilling our drinks.

Actually, no. Wait. He'd been filling *my* drink, and Tyler got water. *Grrr*. I didn't like that move. But I drank them. They were delicious fruity drinks.

The bar had gotten busier, and now the dance floor was hopping. Eric thought we should definitely join the dancing. I wasn't convinced, but Tyler just kept watching the door.

With a shrug, I slid off my stool.

Eric caught my hand and pulled me into the middle of the group. Soon we were a sweaty mess. It was fun. A few guys came over to dance with Eric, but he wrapped an arm around my waist, pulled me close, and shook his head until they moved away.

I wasn't sure how long we danced. It was long enough that I felt a lot less intoxicated when Eric patted my hip and swung me around.

"Look."

It took a minute for me to see what he was pointing at, but I found Paul. He nodded discreetly toward the door where Tyler stood. His sister ducked out as he continued to hold it open. He was looking for me. His gaze swept over the dancers until he found me.

Our eyes caught, and something fluttered in my chest.

Oh. No, no, no.

This wasn't supposed to happen.

I wasn't supposed to get feelings. Not these types of feelings. Sexual feelings—arousal, lust—yes, those were fine. But not the kind that made my heart feel like it was floating and all sunshiny.

Tyler indicated that he was going outside, and I nodded. He disappeared out the door.

"Ow. Sweetie." Eric held up our hands and tried to disentangle the tight grip I had on him. "I need this hand for things, you know, like washing and basic daily living."

I released immediately. "Sorry. I..." I glanced back to where Tyler had disappeared with his sister. "I..."

He wrapped his hand gently around my arm. Moving in, he rested his head against my shoulder. "It's like that, huh?"

I sighed, placing my head against his. "Apparently."

He laced our fingers. "For what it's worth, he's dreamy."

"I know." I sighed. "That's the problem." Eric knew about the hate sex. Now he knew about my feelings. "Did we just become best friends?"

His smile was blinding. "I'd love that. I'm a testy bitch, but I'm a loyal testy bitch."

"I believe you."

We laughed, having a moment.

"I could use a friend, to be honest."

"Girl." He squeezed me from the side. "Consider me caped up."

I didn't know what that meant, but I liked the sound of it.

"Come on." He started through the crowd, still holding my hand. "Let's go eavesdrop."

"Ah. You're that type of friend."

He flashed me a grin over his shoulder. "I never said I wasn't nosy."

He took me past the bar, where Paul did a doubletake at our joined hands, to a side door. Easing it open, he stepped past a couple workers having a smoke outside. One snorted, shaking his head. "I don't even want to know, Eric."

"Yeah? And keep it that way, Bertle," he shot back.

Bertle tipped his head back, taking a long drag and letting the smoke drift out as he drawled, "I'd like to keep it another way."

They held a long and intense stare before Eric blinked and shook his head, as if to clear his thoughts. "I'm down for that," he said, his voice a little husky.

Bertle let out another puff of smoke, his eyes smoldering. "Good."

Eric continued staring, as if in a trance, and I had to nudge him.

"Right," he said. "Sounds like a plan." He tugged me down the alley to the parking lot, and we both leaned forward

"—didn't need to do all this and track down my coworkers. We're fine, Zoey and me." That was Sky. She sounded angry, but tearful at the same time.

"I was worried. I am worried. I didn't say that stuff to—I'm not coming at you, Ski. I'm not saying it's going to happen again..."

Oh. I fisted Eric's shirt sleeve. They were talking about Zoey's overdose.

Tyler's tone was ragged. "How is Zoey doing? What's the plan?"

There was silence.

"Skylar."

She made an exasperated sound. "Fine. She's home with me, but she is talking to a therapist. Or, they're talking. She's not talking to me."

"She hasn't said what happened?"

"She's a teenager. And she came from my loins. It's like herding cats to get her to talk to me. She won't do it." She choked back a sob. "I'm at my wit's end, Ty. I don't know what to do."

"Come here."

Eric and I both craned our necks. Tyler wrapped his lean, muscled hockey arms around her. She almost disappeared in his hold. They stood like that for a minute before Skylar stepped back, sniffling. She wiped her face and hugged herself, looking at the ground. "But what if you're right?"

Tyler went still.

"What if it happens again?" She lifted her head. "What if I'm too late the next time?"

Tyler shook his head. "That's—that's not what I meant when I texted you. I meant that as a worst-case scenario." He sighed. "I meant that *we* need to be proactive and preventative so there won't be a next time."

"But she's not talking to me."

His voice came out gentle. "I think if you ignored what she did, that worst-case scenario could happen. But you're not ignoring it. She's talking to a therapist. You might not be privy to what they're talking about, but she's talking to someone who knows what they're doing. That's something. And you're not going to stop. I know you. You're going to keep harassing Zoey until she has no other choice but to finally open up and let you know what happened that night. I mean, shit. Your methods work."

She snorted. "Maybe it's a twin thing. You're at a gay bar

looking for me. If that doesn't say dedication, I don't know what does."

"It's not that big of a stretch. It's not a common hangout for me, but I've been to gay bars before."

"You have?" she said.

"Yeah. North Allistair's gay. Remember? He's a buddy."

Eric gave me a questioning look.

I shook my head, trying to relay that I'd explain later. North Allistair had been the first NHL player to come out as gay last year. I'd been sequestered in my NFL bubble, but even I'd gotten wind of the story. It was an announcement made bigger by the fact that his father was a governor in a state where the politics ran red.

"Oh. That's right. I forgot you were buddies with North." Sky laughed. "Eric and Paul would piss themselves if you walked in with him and they found out he was gay."

"Yeah," Tyler said. "Real buckets of fun, those two."

She laughed again, sounding more sold. "They're both sweethearts. Eric especially. He's all vinegar at first, but then he gets sweet and melty. Wait. Paul said you were here with someone. They're with Eric now?" She suddenly seemed alarmed.

"Yeah. Why?"

"Who is it?"

My hand tightened on Eric's sleeve. We rose carefully and started to step backwards.

"Eric was on the dance floor with my friend."

"Your friend?" Skylar rasped. "What friend?"

"The, uh..."

"The same *friend* you brought to the hospital with you? *That* friend?"

"Yeah. Why?"

"Are you *fucking* serious? What are you doing? Still haven't screwed her or just haven't had your fill of her? Tyler, you don't know who she is. Come on!"

She grabbed his arm and dragged him back inside Harry's Tulip.

Eric turned to look at me, a question on his face. "Do you know what that's about?"

I sighed. "Yeah. Unfortunately."

He waited.

I didn't want to explain the worst parts of my life, because who would?

"And?" he prompted, just as there was a short, shrill whistle from behind us in the alley. His gaze moved past me.

"My brother used to date Skylar," I began to explain, feeling a little faint.

"Bert, I swear to *God*, I'm not just going to steal your phone, I'm going to snap your SIM card if you don't tell me where Eric is. And you know I'll do it."

Skylar's voice rang out behind us.

We both turned to look as Skylar's gaze moved past Bertle, who was no longer smoking, but had remained in the alley. He was alone. Tyler stepped out to stand next to Skylar.

When Skylar saw me, I had a flashback to the first time Tyler saw me after finding out who I was. Such hatred. It wasn't a fun déjà vu.

I braced myself as Skylar came our way.

"She didn't recognize me the first time we met," I told Eric under my breath.

He nodded. "I think it's safe to say she's remembered now." He stepped in front of me and raised his voice. "Skylar! Hello. You decided to scurry off of Bertle's couch and join us. I'm so happy. I held them off as much as I could, but I need to warn you that since then..." He shot me a questioning look.

Ah. My name. "Rain."

He swung back to beam at Skylar. "Since then, Rain and I have become friends. If you're going to lay into her, just know that I'll be at her side, and you know more than most how I am with my friends. Also," he chided softly. "We can't choose our families, honey. Please remember that. And with all that said..." He stepped aside and waved in my direction. "We were *just* looking for you both."

44

TYLER

"Yeah. Right. You *just* came looking for us." My sister snorted.

Eric didn't bat an eyelash. I had a feeling this wasn't the first time they'd gone head-to-head. But Skylar was in a mood, and she wanted to fillet someone. Probably Rain.

Rain stood behind Eric, wariness in her gaze, along with other emotions. Pain? Anguish? Torment?

Why were those there?

Why hadn't she talked to her family?

Why didn't she know she had a niece?

Suddenly, I was *done* with all of this. I wanted to take Rain to her hotel and demand answers. But I couldn't, because at the end of the day, it was *her* brother who'd given my sister a brain injury. It was unforgiveable, too much to get over that.

But...

Fuck it all.

"We're leaving." I said it so abruptly that Eric and Skylar jumped.

But not Rain.

She didn't move a muscle. She wasn't surprised one bit at

how harshly my words came out. I shouldn't have been grateful about that connection, because at the end of the day, she was not mine. She could never be mine.

"Tyler," my sister murmured, drifting closer. She touched my arm.

I knew she was asking if I was all right, but I shook my head and brushed past her, past Eric, whose eyes were wide. Rain nodded at me, and that was enough.

I turned back to Skylar. "I'd like to see Zoey."

My sister's face flooded with uncertainty and fear, but she jerked her head up and down. "Of course."

"No more hiding?"

She swallowed. "Not from you."

"Skylar."

"What? No. Fine. No more hiding." She swallowed again. "I'll stop avoiding your calls." Hesitating a moment, she asked, "Could we come to one of your games? Maybe next week. You have some at home."

"My old team will be here next week. That one? You could see Nolan."

Eric went rigid all of a sudden. "Wait a minute. You're a hockey player?"

I frowned. Had Skylar not mentioned that? Judging by her pinking cheeks, nope. She hadn't.

Eric's eyes were like saucers. "Oh my God. You're Tyler Griffin. Like, the NHL hockey savant, Tyler Griffin."

I frowned.

Skylar rolled her eyes. "I mean, let's not get ahead of ourselves here."

I grinned. "I'm good. You can keep going."

Ski laughed, and something eased in my chest. We were on the same page again. Our twin page.

"Can we get tickets?" Eric breathed out in wonder. "Wait.

Fuck that. I don't need free tickets." He turned to Skylar and touched her arm. "We're coming."

Skylar now looked wary. "Uh..."

Eric waved that off. "Too bad. You're the one who decided to avoid your brother, and because he loves you so much, he came looking and that brought him to Hank's lovely Tulip, and now you're stuck with all of us knowing, because dear Lord." He was breathless. "Some of us are huge hockey fans. Paul's going to flip out."

"Again. Let's not get carried away here."

He stared at Skylar. "Bertle."

She winced. "Him too?"

"We're all going. Deal with it." He turned to me. "Don't worry about their tickets. On me. But be prepared. There's going to be signage."

"No." Skylar stomped her foot.

"Oh yes. Lots of signage. I'm so fucking excited. And you." He pointed to Rain, making her jump a little. He held out his hand. "Phone."

"What?" She looked over at me.

"Phone. Now. I'm getting your number. When I said we were friends, I meant it." He snapped his fingers. "Let's go. Give it to me."

She did, unlocking it for him. He was on her phone for a second before an alert sounded from his pocket. He handed it back. "There. Now I've got your number, and you've got mine, so we can decide what we're doing together on our friend date."

"Okay." She seemed dazed as she slid her phone into her pocket.

And I'd officially had enough. I wanted to tell myself it was because I had morning skate tomorrow. That I needed eight hours of sleep. But in truth, I was done sharing Rain with others. Even my sister. I wanted to take Rain away from here and get lost between her thighs. And because I couldn't, I had no more patience.

"Let's go. I mean it." I reached into Rain's pocket and found her keys. She inhaled at my touch, but if anything, she leaned into it. As I withdrew, I grazed my finger up the back side of her arm. I wanted that extra touch. I felt her shiver.

Images of us together pushed to the forefront of my mind. The feeling of sliding inside her, of her walls as she squeezed me when she came. Her little gasp when I pulled out and she reached for me, needing me back inside of her.

I'd been standing here too long, but I couldn't make myself move.

I bit back a moan.

Or I tried.

Rain heard it, and she looked up at me.

I couldn't hold back the lust I was feeling, and her eyes widened, flaring before she hid it. How she did that, I didn't know, but I didn't like it.

Screw this.

Wrapping an arm around her waist, I brought her flush against me. "We're leaving."

"Yep. That's what you keep saying. Thought you would've been gone by now." Skylar tried to sound bored, but when I met her gaze, she was anything but. She did give me a smile.

"Say goodbye, Rain."

"Bye." She waved to them, and we started walking. I kept her in my arms, making her walk in front of me.

The other two parroted together, "Goodbye, Rain." Then they laughed.

Rain chuckled, her breath hitching when I readjusted, clamping my hand over her thigh. "Ooooh."

I groaned. "Do not make those sounds right now."

She leaned even more of her weight on me. "Why not?"

"Because I'll bend you over the back of your car and fuck

you for anyone to see. I won't be quiet. I'll make you scream, and I'll make you beg, and I'll make you want to beat me bloody because I'll keep you from coming over and over and over again. Are you getting me?"

She saw me. Read me. And gulped before whispering, "I got you."

"Fucking good." I gave up the pretense and just bent down to hoist her up in my arms.

I carried her the rest of the way to her car.

45

RAIN

Tyler had positioned himself in the driver's seat of my car, and his knuckles were white as he gripped the steering wheel. He was livid.

Uneasiness flip flopped in my sternum. "Are you mad at me?"

"No," he said.

Okay... "Who are you mad at?"

He cursed, making a concerted effort to loosen his grip on the steering wheel. "I'm not mad at anyone."

"But you *are* mad."

"No."

I scoffed. "I grew up with Daniel Connors. Anger is his profession. I can *tell* you're mad. Why?"

"I'm not mad at any person. That's what you were asking. I'm mad at the situation."

"What situation?" I asked. I had a feeling I knew.

"What situation?" He shook his head. "What situation do you think I'm talking about? I want to fuck you again, and I can't. I. Can't," he seethed through gritted teeth. "Why haven't you talked to your brothers in twelve years?"

He seemed genuinely confused, and my heart sank. From his point of view, his sister was everything. His niece too. But it wasn't the same for me—or for lots of other people. He had no idea that I'd been left out for as long as I could remember. I looked away, because if I kept looking at him, I'd spill all the sad and lonely details, and that wouldn't help anyone. "Why do you care? I thought I was your enemy."

He was quiet for a few blocks, and then we merged onto the interstate. It wasn't until we neared my exit that he sighed. "I'm starting to wonder if that's actually the case."

The same flutters that had buzzed in my stomach at the Tulip, when he'd made sure I was okay before going outside with his sister, stirred again. I took a deep breath. I couldn't afford to let those feelings grow. "Well, don't waste your time," I said harshly.

He didn't reply, and my heart constricted at his silence, but that's what I wanted. There were things between us we could never get past. This was for the best.

His phone buzzed. He dug it out, giving it to me. "Can you tell me who that's from?" He used his finger to unlock it.

I had to suppress the fangirl in me when I saw it was from Nolan Everwood. "Nolan."

"Can you read it?"

I cleared my throat. "Based on the full minute of yelling your sister left in my voice messages, I'm guessing you found her? Let me know what you need from me."

He laughed before motioning to the phone. "Do me a favor? Call him and put it on speaker."

A second after the ringing filled the car, Nolan Everwood answered, sounding amused. "I hope you're still in one piece. Do I need to rouse some people I know in Minneapolis and send them to patch your ass up?"

Tyler took the phone from me, raising it to his mouth, but he kept it on speaker. "We found her."

"*Good.* Is everything okay?" Nolan asked.

Tyler slid a look my way. "We can get into the specifics later. I'm not alone right now, brother, but I think things will be okay. I'll see Zoey tomorrow."

Nolan fell quiet for a moment. "It sounds like we need to catch up."

"Yes, we do. I'll call you this weekend. It'd be good to talk before we beat your ass next Wednesday."

Nolan laughed. "We'll see about that. I don't know what else you have planned tonight but try to stay out of trouble."

"Can't promise that." Tyler smirked.

My hotel was just ahead, and Nolan ended the call as Tyler turned into the parking lot, pulling into a spot at the far corner. I thought he'd want to talk, but he just got out with me, and as I took a step toward the hotel, he shoved his hands in his sweatshirt and turned away, heading down the block.

I watched. He obviously didn't want to be around me any longer, despite what he'd said in the truck, and I knew I should let him go. Right now. Right here. This was a defining moment. If I let him go, whatever fucked-up situationship had developed between us would officially be done. Over. I felt that in my gut. That's what needed to happen. *Let him go.*

I didn't move.

Turn around, go into the hotel. Remind yourself why he hates you...

Except I headed after him. My feet moved of their own volition. I heard myself call to him. "Where are you going?"

He turned back, stiffening when he saw me, and shook his head. "No." His nostrils flared. "Leave. Go to your hotel. Go to your room. Forget me, Rain."

I took another step toward him.

His eyes closed before opening again, tormented. "Stop," he said, still harsh. He gestured down the block. "There's a bar there. I'm going to get obliterated, and I'm going to forget you.

I'm going to forget everything about you, and then I'll take an Uber home. I'll wake up to go see Zoey. If I feel like it, I'll fuck someone else tonight."

Pain sliced me. "You don't mean that." I took another step in his direction.

This was stupid. I was being foolish. Rash.

He didn't move away, breathing hard.

"You should," I said, feeling myself peel away from my body. I was dissociating. "You should go and do all of that."

We continued to stare at each other, chests heaving. He cursed under his breath. "Why do you think your brother hates you?"

I winced, but I was exhausted. He'd already asked once. I didn't have the strength to deflect it again. I shrugged. "I don't think it. I know it. He's always hated me." My hands went up in a helpless gesture. "There's no great mystery to it. As far as I know, I never did anything. I was just born, and I wasn't supposed to be there. That's all I can say."

"That's messed up. He named his daughter after you. How can you explain that?"

"I can't. But I guarantee if Dane ever saw me again, he'd look right through me like he always did. Maybe you're right. Maybe Dane doesn't hate me. It was always a more cold indifference. I never existed to him growing up. That will never change. I know my place, and it's not in that family."

Tyler slid his hand around my neck to the back of my head, drawing me close.

I put my hands on his chest, feeling his heart beat through his sweatshirt. He pulled me even closer, smashing the space between us until only my hands kept us apart—my hands and our clothes.

He let out a soft breath, lowering his forehead to rest on mine. His fingers slid into my hair. "This is a bad idea."

I focused on his mouth, how close it was to mine. If I lifted up on my toes, just a little, I could taste him again, and suddenly that's all I wanted. "Agreed," I whispered.

Yet we stood like that, in an embrace that wasn't an embrace, and we breathed each other's air. He muttered, "My sister's going to have to get over it."

My eyes jerked to his. Determination flashed there, like steel. "Wait." I pressed back, my pulse going wild. "She can't. What Daniel did—"

"Not the car accident, not her injury. You. She's going to have to get over the fact that I want you, because Jesus Christ, Rain." He shifted directions and backed me against the building behind us. His hips pressed against me. "I want you, and I'm fast losing the strength to stay away."

I licked my lips, salivating to taste him again.

His eyes darkened. "Don't do that unless you want me to do something about it."

"We're on the street," I said weakly.

"It's late. Anyone from our organization is in bed asleep." He let go of me to pull his hood up. "Thank God hockey players aren't so recognizable." He cupped the side of my face and tilted me toward him as he lowered his mouth. "Are you ready to deal with this? I can't stay away anymore."

I clutched his shoulders. This time we were choosing. There was no going back.

"I'm sober."

He paused. "I didn't even think of that. You can consent?"

He began to pull away, but I yanked him back. "Yes. Now shut up." I fused his mouth to mine and stopped thinking.

46

RAIN

I didn't want to want it, but I did.
As soon as we were in the hotel, we were at each other. My body was against his. He was pressing me against the hotel door. Our hands were fumbling for each other's clothes, shoving down our pants.

It was going to be quick. Fast.

He got my pants down first. My underwear was ripped away. I had no idea where it went, then his finger was rubbing around me. I slowed, moaning, and began rocking into his hand. That felt good.

"You like that?" His tongue demanded entry before kissing down my throat, then to my ear.

His finger slid inside of me.

I was forgetting what I'd been trying to do.

A second thrust up into me. I began moving with them, trying to ride his hand.

"Jesus." He breathed against my throat. "I love when you ride my hand. Ride my dick. Ride me. I'll never be tired of watching you do that, because you do it for me. Right? Just me. No one else." He nipped at my ear.

I squeaked, and he took advantage of my distraction to slide a third finger into me.

I exhaled, melting against him. "Tyler."

"Yeah. Say my name. I want you to scream it." He nipped at my throat this time, shoving those fingers so deep inside of me.

"Fuck. They're so—Tyler. I can't—"

"You can," he said, breathing hard. "I promise you that you *will*."

He kept pistoning his fingers into me, but my brain started working again and I remembered what I'd originally been doing. I lifted up a foot, shoved down his pants and hooked my foot inside of them enough to step them down all the way. His boxer briefs went with them. My hand wrapped around his cock. It was long and hard and fully upright.

He slowed in his ministrations as I gave him one long smooth stroke. "Shit," he said under his breath.

I liked that sound. I liked it a lot. "You like this?" I was almost goading him.

He'd closed his eyes as I gave him another stroke but opened them again to gaze at me. They narrowed. A sudden spark showed and I paused, not sure if I liked whatever that meant, but a mean glint pulled at his mouth.

He taunted back, "I think tonight's about what I want. What do you think about that?"

I opened my mouth, a retort on the tip of my tongue, but he pulled his fingers out and flipped me around. I was facing the door before I could comprehend what was happening. In that space of time, he stuck his fingers back inside of me, positioning my ass out toward him.

My hands went to the door.

My heart was pumping.

"Tyler—"

I heard the sounds of a condom wrapper, then felt him move between my legs. His fingers slid out, and his cock slid in.

He went all the way to the hilt, until I felt him bottom out. "Oh. God. *Tyler.*"

He held still, panting against my shoulder. "Jesus Christ, you feel good. Why do you feel like this? Every fucking time?" He began moving inside of me.

I groaned, loud and low and felt it all the way to my stomach. "Oh. Tyler. Oh. Fuck," I hissed as he began going faster.

I could only brace myself, except my palms were sweaty so I couldn't get a good hold on the door.

Tyler repositioned me, picking me up a little and he kicked my feet apart, settling more comfortably between my legs. He pounded into me. His hips were hitting me. Over and over again. He was fucking me so *fucking* good.

I gasped, trying to catch my breath. Resting my forehead on the door, I looked down, but the view was of our joined pants on the floor. His feet were there. His hands gripped the sides of me, and he just kept thrusting.

God.

I couldn't—I gasped for air.

Pleasure was blasting me. It was a continuous onslaught.

I didn't want it to end.

I wanted him to keep fucking me. All night long. Every night.

I heard myself begging, "Tyler." I didn't know what I was asking for, but it was a whispered plea in my throat. He paused, stopping, and I flailed at him behind me. "What are you doing?"

"Holding off," he grated behind me. His hand shifted, going to my clit and rubbing me.

I was almost crying. "No. No. I—"

He shifted me again, holding me even more upright off the floor and away from the door. He was almost completely holding my weight, standing firmly on his two planted feet. "What do you want?" He kept one arm wrapped tight around my waist, holding me in place for him, but the other slid up my front to wrap around my throat. He didn't squeeze me. He just cupped me there, his thumb brushing over my neck. Soothing. He pressed a hot kiss to the back of my neck. "Tell me what you want?"

"I want you," I mewled, my head falling forward.

"Babe." He began rolling my hips over his dick. He was using me as his own personal sex toy. I didn't know how he was doing this, but my mind was exploding.

I needed to come.

I didn't want to come.

I wanted this to go on forever.

I needed him to let me release.

All the demands were hitting at me at once and I couldn't talk anymore. I could only make choking sounds, though his hand hadn't moved. I could breathe freely.

"Tyler. Please."

"What do you need?" He kissed my neck again. His hand fell from my throat, sliding to my breast and his thumb rubbed over my nipple.

I arched my back. They were so sensitive, too sensitive.

"What do you need, Rain? You need to tell me."

"I—"

He began lifting me again, a few more pumps, before he plastered me against the door once more. If anyone was out there, they would know what we were doing. The thumps. The sounds. They would have no question what was happening just on the other side of the door.

I couldn't talk anymore. I felt like his dick was all the way up into my stomach.

My body began quivering. Sweat rolled down my spine.

Pleasure accosted me in waves, but still, I wasn't coming.

"You need to tell me." He was having fun, saying that, and slowing his thrusts, as he kissed the back of my neck. He moved his mouth, tasting around to the front of my throat, his hand tilting me further back for his angle.

"I need—let me come. Please." My legs were shaking.

"You'd like that, hmm?" His hand rubbed between my legs again in strong slow circles. "Like you like that too?"

I hissed, trying to get away from his touch. It was too much, but he was firmly inside of me and I didn't want to go anywhere. I wanted his touch. I wanted it forever. But I also needed to release. He was playing with me. It was maddening.

He chuckled in my ear and the sound was so dark, cruel. "You have no idea." He nipped at my ear again, then circled my clit so much until I was exploding. I screamed; my body went taut. He held me in place, waiting as my climax rode through me and I sagged, my knees unsteady. He held me in place, but he was still fully erect and inside of me.

"Now you're going to find out what we're going to be doing all fucking night." He gripped me hard and began thrusting up into me, as if I had never come, as if we were just starting. He gutted out, "We're going to be going all night like this. I'm going to pound into you like this until you start recovering from your release, and then I'm going to stop and make you come. Then I'll wait. I'm a professional fucking athlete. I have the endurance to last a *long* time. But I'm going to hold off every time until you come. You got that? It's my version of edging."

I moaned, so low. "You're going to fuck me to death."

"Exactly. So get ready because here's your second release coming soon."

And he delivered.

My second.

My third, still against the hotel door.

He moved us to the bed, laying on top of me while I was on my stomach. He slid inside from behind, and he just kept moving inside of me until he felt another climax coming my way. It was torture and I was crying by the sixth for him to just come.

"You want that?" He was moving, his whole body stretched over mine.

I balled my hands into fists, pinned to the bed next to my head. "*Yes.*"

"You sure?"

"Yes. *Please.*" My mind was scrambled. My body was a mess. I was shaking all over. It was the best night of sex I'd ever had, but it was also the most tormented as well. I couldn't handle much more.

He held still, then bit out his own groan. "Okay. I don't think I can hold off anyway." He reared back and began slamming into me. It was rough, and hot, and it felt dirty. I felt like he'd fucked my soul out of my body. I couldn't move as he was riding me this time. He was merciless. Then, thank God, my walls clamped down on him one last time and I felt him exploding inside of me.

He cursed right before he collapsed on top of me.

I felt relief, except when he pulled out, I felt empty. I was awake just long enough to feel him tenderly rolling me over. There were soft, soothing touches after that. A washcloth was between my legs.

My hair was being brushed off my forehead.

Gentle kisses.

Then I fell asleep.

47

TYLER

A phone began ringing at five in the morning. Cursing, I tightened my hold around Rain before recognizing the ring as my phone. I reached over to silence it, and my heart sank as I saw *Kashvi PR* on the screen.

I sat up, swinging my feet off the edge of the bed to the floor. "Hello?"

"The publicity surrounding your niece wasn't enough? You needed to go and screw the team shrink too?" Kashvi's voice was alarmingly alert for this time of the morning. "I've got a blogger calling me with a picture of you sucking tongue on the side of the street, taken a few hours ago."

Rain shifted, and I looked over, finding her awake. She watched me, eyes wide with concern. Sitting up, she yawned and ran a hand through her hair.

"This is from last night?"

"This morning, you mean?" she snapped. "As of right now, you were identified thanks to your *so*-conspicuous Grays sweatshirt, which helpfully has your name and number on it. The hotel is blocks from the arena. The girl has not been identified, but she will be. It's only a matter of time. What were you thinking?"

Kashvi was speaking loud enough that Rain could hear everything, and she clambered out of bed and toward the bathroom. I put the phone on speaker as the door shut. "Do you actually want to know what I was thinking, or was that more a rhetorical question?"

"Rhetorical unless you have something that'll assist in me convincing the team's owner you're still worth it. Right now, only the hockey sites are running with this. Once Ms. Connors is identified, this shit's going to explode."

The bathroom door opened, and Rain stood there brushing her teeth.

"It'll explode because of her connection to the team?"

"Yes! A team shrink sucking face with our newest acquisition? That'll be a scandal for the mainstream media to pick up."

Rain paled.

I cursed. "I need to call you back."

"Wha—"

I ended the call and pinned Rain with a stare. "Who knows about your family connection?"

She wavered on her feet, grabbing the doorframe for balance.

I jumped up, steadying her, and maneuvered her to the bed. Grabbing a washcloth and a cup of water from the bathroom, I brought them to her. She finished brushing her teeth, and I took the toothbrush as I placed the water on the nightstand, along with the washcloth. In the bathroom, I rinsed her toothbrush and returned with an empty glass. She used the water to rinse her mouth and ran the washcloth over her face before lifting sad eyes my way.

A need to protect and reassure her surged through me. I knelt at her feet and took her face in my hands. "I do not give one shit what happens. You hear me? I won't regret last night.

We made a decision to stop fighting, and we both knew there could be consequences. I heard Mal Benoit on the phone with you. He cares. He won't have you fired."

"My career is over." She wrapped her hands around my wrists. "You're not going anywhere. You don't have to worry about your place with the team."

"Neither do you." I shook my head.

"No, Tyler. I'm done." She sounded way too resigned. Way too fucking calm about it. A dejected look came over her face. "No team will reach out after this kind of scandal. I have money saved. I can go underground for a while. Then maybe individual players might reach out in a few years. I can see if I can build back up."

"Some teams won't care."

Tears shone in her eyes. "You know that's not true. They'll all care. I'm done. No one's going to want me."

"I want you."

Her eyes flashed, and the tears spilled over. "Good to know, but you can't fix my career now that you've fucked me. Now that everyone knows you fucked me." She whispered, "This is going to get bad."

Dread settled in my stomach. She was right. This was only the beginning, but we needed to move into damage control. "We need to tell Kashvi who you are. Your brothers. Everything. She needs to be prepared. The team will have a plan moving forward." I moved to sit next to her, and she rested her head against my shoulder.

I wrapped an arm around her, hugging her close. She trembled in my arms.

I sucked in a breath and held it, because damn. *Damn.* I needed to do something to protect her. For fuck's sake. Hours ago I'd hated her. I truly had but needing her had tipped me over. I needed her more than I'd hated her. And now we were here.

"I'm not letting you burn for this."

She lifted her head from my shoulder and let out a soft sigh. "You should call her back."

"Yeah." *Fuck.*

I called Kashvi, and she answered immediately. "Should I take it that Ms. Connors is with you?"

Rain leaned closer to the phone. "This is Rain."

Kashvi was quiet for a beat. "Ms. Connors, I would highly recommend that you consult your own media team as well as a lawyer."

I tensed. "Now wait a minute—"

"It's for her protection, Tyler. I'm not saying anything other than that."

Rain cleared her throat. "There's more you need to know. The team will need to be prepared if other information comes out."

"More than if and when you're identified as the team's sports psychologist?"

"Yes," Rain said.

So fucking calm, so fucking resigned. Her eyes seemed tired. Her shoulders slumped, but her chin was up. She was enduring.

Kashvi went quiet again. "Okay. I think you both should come in. I'll loop in Mr. Benoit, so he's aware of the situation."

"Mal knows."

"What'd you say?" Kashvi asked.

"Mr. Benoit knows what I need to tell you. It was one of the conditions for me taking this job."

"Conditions on the team's part?"

"Conditions on mine. You'll understand once I tell you."

Kashvi sighed. "Why does this seem like just the beginning of a big storm coming our way?"

Rain didn't respond, just gave me a tight-lipped smile, so I took over, brushing a hand over her hair and down her back.

"We'll come to the arena," I told Kashvi. "Be there soon."
Kashvi ended the call.

I turned to look at Rain. "I made my decision last night."

Her bottom lip trembled, but she held my gaze.

I said it again, resting my forehead against hers—that seemed to be our thing. "I know who your brothers are. I don't know the specifics, but you told me who you were. And Skylar knows who you are. Even though she was pissy last night, she knows what it meant that I brought you with me to look for her. That means my family knows. The only thing they can get mad about is our sexual relationship, and I will say whatever the fuck I need to say so everyone stays off your back. If that means you and I are in a loving and committed relationship, so be it. If we need to make a trip to Vegas, I'm game. I mean it. I'm not going to let them fuck you over."

"Stop." Her hand pressed against my mouth, but it was shaking. She looked so sad and beaten, and I hated it. "It won't come to that but thank you. It means a lot that you'd be willing to lie for me."

I didn't say anything to that, but as we got ready to leave, a question bounced in my head, and I couldn't get rid of it.

Were those lies? I wasn't sure anymore.

48

RAIN

It was going to come out. All of it.
I felt numb as we drove toward the arena. Tyler stopped to get us coffee. He was dressed in the same clothes as last night, so then he drove over to his hotel and quickly changed.

When he came back, he was wearing joggers and a white thermal long-sleeved shirt. He must've showered as well because his black hair was wet. He finished the drive and ran a brisk hand through it as we walked into the arena.

He led the way, calling the elevator to take us to the administrative floor.

When we stepped off, a few people from the social media team were walking around. They paused to watch us as we passed. Tyler opened the door for me and his hand grazed my arm as he led the way to Kashvi's office. I could hear her on the phone as he knocked on the door.

A moment later, it swung open. Kashvi stepped back, her face tight with irritation, and motioned for us to come inside. As we did, I saw Mal was already there, sitting on a couch in the back corner. He gave me a sad smile but didn't say or do anything else as we came inside.

Kashvi closed the door, still on the phone, and walked behind her desk. She didn't sit but turned her back to us as she continued talking. Her office overlooked the ice with floor-to-ceiling windows. I assumed it was the kind that could only be seen through one way, so she could watch the games or practices from here, if she wanted, without disturbing anyone. It was a good office.

"I'll have Stephanie at the front entrance waiting for you," she said. "Thank you for this. Yes. I'm going to inform them right now." The call ended, and she put her phone down and turned back to regard us both. Her eyes lingered on me before she took a deep breath. "Your contract will be considered terminated as of this morning."

Tyler shot forward in his chair. "Wait a minute—"

She spoke over him and kept her eyes trained on me. "There is a moral clause in your contract. You were caught having a sexual relationship with one of the team's players. No matter how this plays out, your position is terminated. Once you're identified, this could get ugly. The women take the blame. Always. If we're lucky, mainstream media will not pick up the story, but hockey fans won't forget. Your days of working with the NHL are done."

"Except..." Mal spoke from behind us, sounding almost casual. "She accepted the job before she was aware Tyler would be on the team."

I spun in my seat, mouth parting in surprise. What was he doing? That wasn't true.

He refused to meet my gaze, raising an eyebrow at Kashvi. "That's a loophole Ms. Connors could use to counter her termination. She could claim it was wrongful because she disclosed potential personal issues concerning Tyler Griffin after she accepted the job."

Tyler studied Mal, his jaw clenched tight.

"What personal issues?" Kashvi demanded. "Were they fucking before he joined the team?"

Tyler twisted forward in his seat again. "Yes."

"No, they were not," Mal said at the same time. "But she raised other concerns."

Kashvi's eyebrows furrowed, and she turned to me. "What is going on here?"

"Rain isn't losing her job, so make a different plan," Tyler said heatedly.

I was in shock.

Kashvi looked from Tyler to Mal before returning to me. "Are you fucking them both?"

Tyler shoved up out of his seat. "Take that back—"

"Ms. Kumar," Mal exclaimed sharply, but he remained sitting.

Kashvi waved them off, still focusing on me. "If we're moving forward with you remaining with the team, I need to be brought in, and I mean all the way. I need to know everything. The dirty. The gritty. Everything. You hear me?"

No. I didn't, because I didn't want to do this. I didn't want to expose the years of hatred I'd endured, but I met Tyler's gaze and turned to look at Mal. Both had offered me their support. I needed to reciprocate, so I nodded. "I'll tell you everything."

"Good." She pulled out her chair, sitting.

"You want me to stay for this?" Tyler asked.

I nodded, wishing I could hold his hand. It wouldn't have been appropriate in these circumstances, but I'd process later everything he'd said.

"There's potential fallout coming that doesn't just include the Grays, but also Montreal and Boston, because Daniel and Dane Connors are my brothers," I began. "We're estranged, and only a handful of people are aware of my connection to them. Cyber sleuthing is a real thing nowadays, and if they're looking into me, it could come out at any time."

Kashvi sat quietly, blinking at me. I could understand her shock and also her new alarm because while Dane tended to avoid publicity, Daniel did not. His marriages, affairs, and divorces, plus all his fights and issues with the league, were popular clickbait for hockey blogs. He wasn't known to be a drinker, but he was often filmed going into bars and leaving with a new woman on his arm, whether he was currently married or not.

"Okay." Kashvi cleared her throat. She leaned forward and pressed a button. A moment later the door opened and one of the women from the social media team popped her head in.

"Yes?"

"Stephanie," Kashvi ordered, "I need you to do a deep dive on Daniel and Dane Connors. I want to know everything there is to know about them, including family members and their family life. In a separate file, update everything that comes up regarding their rivalry with Tyler Griffin. I believe it started in high school."

Tyler's eyes closed, and a hint of regret pulled at his mouth. His sister. This could push all of that into the public eye again. My hand began to shake. I needed to touch him, hold his hand, reassure him. But I couldn't, so I tucked it under my leg.

"What would happen if I resigned?" I ignored Tyler's exclamation next to me or the way Mal seemed to go rigid behind me. I only looked at Kashvi. "What could happen then?"

A flicker of something showed in Kashvi's gaze. "If you were lucky, nothing. Maybe someone would still identify you, but it would likely stop there if you didn't remain working with the team. That's the best-case scenario. The more realistic possibility is that someone will still dig for your name. Tyler's hot news, especially considering his recent bout in the public eye. People like him. Fans want more of him, and if there's anything to find, they'll find it. Based on my time and experience in this business, you need to plan for everything to come out. I mean everything, and yes, you will still have to take me through it all so I can figure out the team's best course of action moving forward."

My heart sank.

"Jesus Christ, Rain. You're not going anywhere. I won't let you." Tyler glared at me.

"I also won't allow it, Rain." Mal's statement was quieter, but just as effective. "On this matter, Tyler and I are on the same page. Don't let your brothers take this away from you too." He leaned forward, his eyes flicking to Kashvi before returning to me. "You're not the bad guy in this scenario. Kashvi doesn't have all the information, but once she does, I have no doubt she'll agree. Let's direct blame elsewhere. None of it belongs with you or any member of the Grays organization."

He lifted his gaze to meet Kashvi's once again before I heard her say, quietly, "I see."

My brothers weren't the reason I slept with Tyler. That's not what Mal was insinuating. He was giving her a new narrative. Blame my brothers. Distract from this story and give the media sites a different one, with different bad guys.

I stared at Mal with wide eyes, because what *did* he know? He'd said his investigator did a thorough job, but how thorough? Did they even understand what they'd unearthed?

He stood and nodded to me. "Call me after this, please. Kashvi, keep me updated."

"Oh." She laughed. "You don't have to worry about that. I've got a feeling I'll be blowing up your phone after this meeting."

"I'll look forward to the call."

As he left, her phone rang. "Kashvi here," she answered, putting it on speaker.

"Ms. Kumar, there's a Martine deBlanc here. Says she has a meeting with you." I recognized Morty, sounding hesitant. He was here this early to clean the ice.

"Yes, Morty. Could you escort her to my offices? The girls will get her comfortable in one of the conference rooms."

"Will do, ma'am."

"Thank you." She ended the call, and Tyler reached over to take my hand. He looked defiantly back at Kashvi. "I'm holding her hand."

Amusement moved over her face. "Get it out of your system, because we need to get ahead of this story before we decide what to give Martine. Now." She focused on me. "Start talking. And remember, I want everything."

49

RAIN

"I'm estranged from my family. I want to be able to tell you there's some big scandal, but there's not. It's just... I think it started when my mom died. I was six when she had a brain aneurysm that burst."

I looked at the floor as I slowly began to go numb. "I remember laughing before that, so she must've loved me. I don't remember my dad when I was little. But I remember moments with my brothers. We watched movies together, and it wasn't bad. We'd make popcorn. It didn't get bad until after Mom died."

Suddenly I was back there, sitting in that hot funeral home. The bench was uncomfortable, and Daniel had snapped at me so many times. I never knew what I had done wrong.

"At the time, they didn't tell me how she died. She was just gone one day, and then we were at her funeral. My dress was itchy, and this strange woman kept pinching me, making sure I was quiet. I had to sit so still. I remember that part."

My throat hurt. "I saw her in the casket, and that's how I knew she wasn't coming back. I tried waking her up. Daniel hit me, told me not to be stupid."

Kashvi inhaled sharply. "And your dad?"

I shook my head. "You know, I can't remember him ever giving me any attention. He certainly didn't after my mom died. Whoever that woman was, she went through the house and took down all the pictures of my mom. Those were the only pictures of me too. And he never interacted with me after that. He referred to me as 'the girl'. If there was anything that needed to be conveyed to me, Daniel was given that task." My numbness wasn't quite enough. I paused to breathe for a moment. "He was so mean to me."

"Daniel? Or your dad?" Kashvi asked.

I looked up, meeting her eyes. "Daniel. I didn't exist to my father. There was just nothing. The best way I can explain is that I had a room. I was given food. A woman was assigned to look after me until I was older and could start doing everything myself. Laundry. My own meals. All of that."

"And what age was that?"

I shook my head, shrugging. "I think I was eight or nine?"

There was a long silence before Kashvi asked, "You were doing laundry at eight years old?"

I nodded. "I was doing everything by that age, except driving of course." I grimaced. "Though if I could go somewhere on my bike, I did."

"Did your father pay for your things?"

I shook my head. "No." Shame trickled in. "Daniel had money. I don't know how he had it. To my knowledge, he and Dane never worked, but they always seemed to have money. I stole from him."

There was another silence. "You stole from both of them?"

"No, just Daniel. He left his money out all the time. He never counted anything. I was smart. I took small bills to get by, ate the food that was in the cupboards. Cereal is a great thing when you don't know how to use the stove, but once I figured that out, I was able to make other stuff. Mac and cheese.

Spaghetti. I just had to make small amounts of spaghetti because the pan got too heavy for me sometimes."

"And then?"

I shrugged, stripping away the layers and looking at myself from the outside. "And then nothing. I grew up, and I raised myself." My throat tightened. "The woman, whoever she was, eventually stopped coming around. I don't know if she was hired to take care of the house or if she was a girlfriend, but she went away and another woman came who I know was hired to clean the place. She came every morning in the summers. Cleaned the house. Cooked meals."

"Now, you little sweetheart, Mr. Connors told me not to worry about you, that you can make your own meals, but that's not right," she'd told me once. *"You're the sweetest little thing, and you never say a word, but you deserve better. Here."*

She'd shoved food into my hands and wrapped her arms around me. The memory brought tears to my eyes, and I blinked them away. "Mrs. Calinther. She made me food sometimes. I think she made it at her house and brought it for me, so my father never suspected she was using his groceries to feed me."

"What?" Kashvi's eyes were wide.

"It's confusing." I shook my head, trying to decipher everything. "He was fine with me rummaging through the cupboards when I was little, but when I was ten or eleven and could make my own meals, suddenly she couldn't make enough food for me? I didn't understand it. I still don't. He never yelled at me, but there were times he caught me leaving the kitchen with food, and he stormed off in a huff. Then Daniel would come in and yell at me. God, Daniel hated me. He loathed me."

"Was there other abuse?"

I shook my head, aching. "No, nothing like that."

"Verbal abuse?" Tyler asked.

I looked over at him, shocked to see tears in his eyes. He asked again, "Verbal abuse?"

"*You stupid little bitch. Such a waste of space. You're lucky to have a room in this house. I swear to God, Dad needs to just toss you out with the trash.*"

"Yeah," I managed. "Daniel was verbally and emotionally abusive."

"And Dane?" Kashvi asked, gently.

The silence. I remember it as clear as day, as if I was back in that household. I shook my head, another piece of me splintering off. I didn't want to feel any of this. "Dane was like my dad. He ignored me. Daniel was the only one who talked to me, and when he did, he clearly hated that he had to be the one dealing with me. He told me so every time."

I swallowed a knot in my throat. *Get this done.* "I went to the same school as they did, but by the time junior high came around, I could bike everywhere. I got a job that paid me under the counter. I used that money to get by, and then as I got older, I got better jobs. Made more money. I kept all my checks until I was old enough to open a bank account. Thank goodness they didn't do direct deposit back then, or I don't think I'd have kept any of my money. Got my own car as soon as I could—paid cash for it. It wasn't anything great, but good enough to get me from one place to another. A neighbor down the road must've had an inkling what was happening, because she took me to get my driver's license. My dad relayed through Daniel that if the school ever needed him to sign anything, I could just forge his name."

I shook my head. "The message was loud and clear. My dad wanted nothing to do with me. I didn't exist to him, and that's how I grew up. As a burden to them. When I turned eighteen, they expected me to leave. And that's what I did." It still hurt. All of it. "I put myself through community college, and then I used scholarships to finish my four-year degree. It took me longer, but I worked my way into this field. I've not seen my brothers since I turned eighteen, and even the morning I left, they were eating breakfast when I came downstairs with my bags. My dad was there too. All three of them looked up, but only Daniel reacted. He said, '*Good riddance.*' That was the last time I saw Daniel and my father in person. I saw Dane at the game last week. I haven't paid attention to their careers or followed them on social media, but they're franchise darlings, so I can't miss some things."

"What about hockey?" Tyler asked.

"What about it?"

"You have a nasty slap shot. Did you play?"

"Oh." I shook my head. "No. But if Daniel and Dane had to go to the rink for something hockey-related, I was expected to go with them. Carry their bags. Clean up the ice after them. If they needed a goalie, I suited up and played the position."

Numb, numb, numb. I didn't want to remember anymore. I didn't want to feel anymore, but I couldn't help admitting, "After my mom died, those were the only good memories I have of my brothers, and it was because of hockey. I loved the sport. I *love* the sport. It's the only time Dane looked at me—when he had to, because I was their goalie."

Finally.

Complete numbness achieved.

I'd ceased to feel anything. It was bliss.

"As an adult, when I look back, I realize my emotional development was neglected. But that was it, so can I really complain?" I laughed, the sound hollow. What was worse? Being seen and abused or not being seen? I couldn't think of anyone who would choose the first option. Being unseen was an invisible prison of its own, but considering the alternative...

Kashvi's voice shook a little. "Is there anything else I need to know?"

Yes. That I'm the reason Tyler's sister has her brain injury.

But I couldn't bring myself to admit that. I just couldn't. I shook my head, lying. "That's it from my end."

"That's not it," Tyler said. He raked a hand over his face. "You can pull up all the history between our schools and our rivalry. Daniel dated my sister the summer after he graduated, which was before our senior year."

Kashvi now stared hard at Tyler. "Are you shitting me?"

He shook his head. "They didn't date long, and they broke up after they were in a car accident. She got a brain injury from that wreck."

"He dumped your sister after that happened?"

He laughed bitterly. "I believe the excuse he gave was that he was leaving to join Juniors, so why stay together? But yeah, he dumped her while she was still in the hospital."

Kashvi's eyes slid my way before returning to her notepad. "What a swell guy." She took a moment before she shoved back in her seat. "Jesus Christ, you guys. This could blow up in a big fucking way." She looked between us. "I need to know how you want to play this and what you're willing to do."

I frowned. What did she mean?

Tyler looked over at me, a low heat simmering in his gaze.

My lips parted. I got an uneasy feeling.

Tyler turned to Kashvi. "I think it's time the world knew what pieces of shit the Connors brothers are, don't you?"

Kashvi laughed darkly, but there was a warning on her face. "I'll be very honest here. There are a lot of ways this story could go sideways, and the blame could land on either your sister or Rain. Women get blamed. That's how society is. If you want the narrative to go the way you want, I suggest you be the one to say everything. Or have this ready to go if we decide to use it."

Tyler's response was immediate. "Sign me the fuck up."

My lungs ceased to work as fear gripped me. They couldn't... Were they talking about...? I couldn't process that. Both turned to me, waiting for my decision. I needed to say something, but didn't they see how hard it had been to even tell them?

I had grown up as nothing. I wasn't worth this fight, and people would see that. The public would see exactly what my father knew, what Daniel knew, what Dane knew. Didn't Tyler see this? It wouldn't go the way he was thinking. The public would hate me, and then they'd hate him too.

I shook my head, getting up from my seat.

I couldn't do that to him.

He'd link himself to me if we did this, and eventually he'd see whatever was wrong with me. He'd identify what my family had seen right away, and then he'd be bitter. I couldn't stick around and wait for the day he looked at me with the same hatred Daniel had—or worse, the day he looked *through* me the way Dane did.

Suddenly I was back in my apartment in Kansas City. I was at my kitchen table, the gun I'd bought in my hand.

Christ, I wished now that I'd used it. None of this would be happening.

"Rain?" Tyler stood with me.

I shook my head, backing away. "I can't..." I whispered. I couldn't get my voice to be any louder. It was physically impossible. Something was strangling me, choking my ability to breathe. "I can't do this. I'm sorry." I looked at Kashvi. "I resign."

50

RAIN

I got as far as the parking lot before Tyler burst through the door that had just closed behind me. "You're going to run? That's your answer?"

I stopped abruptly.

I had to face him. I knew this. Some deep sense told me that if I ran now, I'd be running forever. Tyler wouldn't stop. He was a fighter. That's what he did in every situation. And right now, he was fighting for me.

I turned, my chest heaving, and I tried not to think about what that meant. "You don't understand."

"No?" His face twisted in fury. He didn't give one fuck who could overhear us. He stepped closer, looming over me. "I don't understand? What don't I understand? Hardship? You think I have no clue about that sort of thing?"

He laughed in my face, and I recoiled, because it was so hard, so bitter, so real.

"You think I have no idea what it's like to lose your parents in one day? To worry about the foster system, whether they're going to separate me from my sister? To just automatically write off hockey, because what fucking kid in the foster system can afford hockey? Or no, that's not enough. What about when my sister comes to me when she's fifteen and tells me she's pregnant? *Fifteen.* Or to have people look at me with disdain, as if I were the one who fathered her kid? That's incest. And *disgusting.* And they thought that shit about me. But you're right. I have no idea what it's like to struggle through life. Not at all. Not when my twin sister has a baby when she's a sophomore in high school. Or when she decides to keep the most precious gem of our lives. Not to mention that the piece of shit who got her pregnant dumped her the first second she told him about their child."

"We got lucky with someone who agreed to take both of us in," he continued. "I got sponsored. My sister was dealing. Then comes along a new boyfriend, except he's a dick of a boyfriend. He's angry and he's volatile and he hates me, but Skylar thinks he's the king shit. Then, because the asshole doesn't want to learn how to drive, he gets them in a car accident and my sister walks away with a brain injury. Guess what happens with that boyfriend? Just like the last one, he leaves her in the dust. Now it's me, my sister, and my niece, plus a brain injury. She's high functioning, but she still has a fucking brain injury and a host of abandonment issues. I swear to God, but you're right. I have no idea about hardship. Or pushing through it. None at all." His anger came at me in waves. "Fuck you for bolting. Fuck you for leaving the first second you got a chance. Fuck you, Rain."

He turned to walk away.

I should let him go.

I should...

But I couldn't.

God help me, I can't.

"You don't understand. *Everyone* leaves," I yelled, my voice cracking.

He stopped before slowly pivoting around. "Everyone leaves? How fucking cliché can you get?"

I winced. His jab hit its bullseye. "Never mind." I started walking.

"You're so fucking oblivious. It's driving me insane."

I grimaced at the second jab. I stopped, but I didn't turn around.

He drew closer. "The whole time in there, I listened to you talk about a life devoid of love. You never got that, and then you apologized to Kashvi that your life wasn't worse than it was. What the fuck are you smoking?"

I jumped at the force of his anger.

He spat, "I don't know what kind of psychological torment you're in, but don't discredit it. My sister loved me. Our parents loved us before they died. We got them for a full fourteen years. I remember them. I know how my mom used to laugh. I know how my dad used to roll his eyes at my mom, before he gave in to whatever she was asking him to do. I have those memories. Life sucked afterward, yeah. But I had my sister. I was loved. I know what that's like. I don't question my place in life, but I have to imagine that's what you do. Is that it? Do you question whether you matter to people? When I laughed, someone responded. They either laughed with me or they told me to stop laughing. But there was something there. I meant something. It doesn't sound like you ever got that."

He paused a moment, gathering himself. "Who let you know you existed? No one. Who validated you, praised you, told you that you were worth something? Who loved you?"

Every word he said was painful, but he was right.

"What are you doing, Tyler?" I whispered, hanging my head. "I'm not worth this."

"Bullshit."

"I'm not. You don't get it..." I trailed off. He kinda did. And how did he? "I'm *not* worth this."

He took a step closer, tilting his head to the side. "Maybe you are to me."

"No." I shook my head, falling back a few steps, and when he followed, I held up my hand to stop him. "Everyone leaves. I'm not being dramatic when I say this. Everyone *has* left. My brothers. My father. We had no relatives that I knew about. I've tried. I really have. I've dated, but after a year or two, they learn. There's something inherently wrong with me. They figure it out, whatever it is, and they realize I'm not worth it. No one stays. The only ones who do are the ones I keep at a distance, the ones I don't let in. I don't allow them to get close enough to find out what's wrong with me. Because I know the second I let them in, they'll see it and they'll go. You'll see it too. I am doing you a favor right now."

He scoffed. "This is the biggest pity party I've ever seen in my life. That's what you're doing."

I felt slapped in the face.

He thought he knew better, but he'd learn. *Why can't he see that?*

I shook my head. "I'm going to ruin your life. I'm telling you, and you don't believe me." This was emotional torture in ways I couldn't explain. I said it again. "I'm not worth this. Throw me under the bus for your career. At least I'm of some use that way."

Had this been worth it for me?

To touch him. Feel him?

I looked at him, really looked at him, and it hurt. He was everything I wanted, and he was standing in front of me, trying to fight for me, but I knew I would lose him. I believed that with every fiber of my being. So. Was he worth it?

The answer hit me hard. It was the same reason I had let myself fall in the first place.

Yes. Being loved by Tyler, just for one night, two, or however long it would've lasted, that would've been everything. But *I* wasn't. He couldn't see it now, but he would eventually.

I had to make that decision for him instead.

He softened and stepped toward me, his hands out.

I shook my head. "Don't do this. Trust me. You will regret it later on, and it'll be too late by then. I'll have ruined you. Toss me aside now. Please."

His hands cupped my face. "Oh, baby girl," he said tenderly.

I winced. "Don't."

He leaned his forehead against mine. "I'm asking for an interview right now. That's it. I will give you the universe, if that's what you want, but I know that's too much for you to believe. It'll spook you, so let me do this. Do the interview with me. You are worth burning down the world. Give me that pleasure. Do it for Skylar. Do it for me."

Tears streamed down my face. "Don't, Tyler."

"I'm going to do the interview with Martine. I'm going to tell her everything. It'll come out no matter what. This way, we're telling it your way. My way. Let's do it together." He found my hand and laced our fingers. "Let's burn your brothers' worlds down."

51

RAIN

I worried I was going to vomit, but I did it. Somehow, I made it through that interview.

I didn't put all of my family's business out there. I just couldn't, so I was vague about parts of it. I didn't give examples of the things Daniel used to say. I just said Dane and I didn't have a relationship growing up. As for my dad, I was honest. Everything I told Kashvi and Tyler, I told Martine.

She asked at the end if I could summarize what it was like growing up with my dad, and my answer was, "It was lonely. Because he refused to speak to me directly, I did not grow up with a father. I grew up in someone else's home, and while they were kind enough to allow me to eat their food and know that I was physically safe under their roof, I do not know what it is like to have a father or a mother. When I lost her, I lost him. Though, to be honest, I don't have memories of my dad before my mother passed either, so it might've just been that I lost my only loving parent when my mom died."

Martine seemed a bit stunned, blinking a few times before she moved on to more questions. The majority of the interview was about the high school rivalry, which had Martine salivating. There was a hungry look in her eyes.

After the interview, I felt dazed. Had I really said all of that?

"Some people are going to be sympathetic," she told me. "Some people aren't. These are hockey fans. They're mean. Of course most people, if they really put themselves in your shoes, would cringe at the thought of growing up the way you did. Being fed and sheltered is great, but kids need a lot more than that."

I shrugged. "There was no physical or sexual abuse."

"It's sad that you've made that your baseline, and that's why you don't feel you have a right to be upset." She included Tyler. "I'll write it so there's minimal blowback on the women, but I'd also like to talk to your sister. Is that an option?"

Tyler raked a hand over his face, standing. The bags under his eyes were more pronounced after the interview than when it had started, as if going through everything had aged him. "I'll reach out to her and ask. I'll be honest. I don't know if she'll want to talk to you, but I'll explain the situation, and we can go from there."

"That's all I can ask. Thank you." She gave us both a nod before leaving. As she did, Kashvi came in, her arms raised. "I have good news. We killed the story."

"What?" I gaped.

"We bought the rights to the original image. The person who took it can't sell it elsewhere or say anything further. They signed an NDA as well."

Tyler stood next to me. He didn't seem entirely relieved. "What does that mean?"

"Well, we have some time even if the story does eventually drop. Martine messaged me while you were talking to her and said there'd be a lot to research. So, there were two potential scandals we wanted to get ahead of. First, you kissing your team's shrink, and from the Grays perspective,

Mal will state that Rain took the job before knowing you were part of the team. The other scandal is Rain's estrangement from her family. The Connors brothers are franchise stars and good click bait. Hockey fans love the fact that they're brothers. Mix in a secret sister caught kissing their longtime rival, that's a good old fashioned *mess*." She shook her head and brightened. "But now we can control the narrative, as long as you two can keep your hands off each other in public."

I glanced at Tyler, startled to see him staring right at me.

"What?" I asked.

He didn't respond, turning to Kashvi. "We can still see each other?"

She snorted. "Are you asking for permission? You? Tyler Griffin?"

He didn't blink. "Not really."

"Didn't think so."

"Wait. What's the bad news?" I asked.

Both focused on me again.

"You said the good news. That means there's bad news too."

Kashvi shrugged. "I guess the bad news is that this story still has the potential to drop, and we may not get a heads-up next time. But we've done our part to cover us if that happens. I'll talk with Martine about the timing of her story, but right now, I wouldn't worry. Don't worry until you have something to worry about, you know?" She gave us a wry grin before gesturing to the door. "It's still early. I'd take off if I were you."

"I resigned."

She huffed. "Considering that Mal is backing you up, I also wouldn't worry about that. But you can stop by his office, if you'd like. They'll probably have guidelines for both of you." She waved us off. "Now go. Get out of my hair so I can do my job. You have to fly out today for the game tomorrow."

Tyler's hand came to the small of my back and guided me

out the door. Once in the hallway, he asked, "Did you want to stop in and talk to the owner?"

"Not particularly. I'm a bit raw right now," I told him. "I'd rather wait to have that meeting."

"Coach will probably have something to say."

"Yeah." My stomach churned. I wasn't looking forward to the fallout there. I'd crossed the line. I had a sexual relationship with a player, and any credibility I might've had was gone. There was no point in even being here anymore, but I still owed Mal and Coach Hines a meeting. "I need to regroup a little, build up my walls, and then I'll reach out."

Tyler's hand pressed against my back in support, and he pushed open the door for me as we spilled out onto the parking lot. "Until then, I need a nap, coffee, and breakfast," he said. "Maybe not in that order. You get to choose."

I doubted I could sleep. "Coffee first."

Then I'd figure out my next steps.

52

RAIN

My next steps came in the form of a text message I received while Tyler was napping. We were at his hotel room for once.

Mal Benoit: I do not accept your resignation.

Rain: I don't understand.

Mal Benoit: It's simple. You are still working for the Grays organization as a consultant. If you insist on resigning, it won't take effect until after you and I have a meeting to discuss everything. Right now, I'm on a plane to Dubai, so that meeting will have to wait. Continue with your duties as normal. I'll see you when I get back.

I stared at my phone. It seemed I somehow still had a job. For now.

LATER THAT AFTERNOON, I was writing a report when Coach Hines slipped into the seat beside me at the front of the plane. The team took up the entire back with the other coaches a few seats behind us. We had some privacy.

"I had a visit from Benoit earlier today," he said. "He told me you and Griffin will be disclosing a personal relationship."

Well. *Shit.*

I closed my laptop, putting us both in shadow. "Uh. I resigned for a few minutes there."

His eyebrows shot up. "You what?"

"But Mal informed me that he doesn't accept my resignation."

"You don't say."

I forced myself to meet his eyes, my emotions all twisted. "I'm a bit of a mess right now. Coming back to the hockey world has dredged up a lot of not-great memories. I apologize if I'm not being as professional as I should."

"You have Sunny getting an average of two points per game. That's *per game.*" Coach shook his head. "He's up fifty percent from the previous year. Because of that change and the way Griffin is matching him, you got Ray skating faster and with an edge I've never seen in him. I didn't know it was there, because I'd never seen it before. And you've got Meester challenging shooters instead of holding back between the posts. A great goalie knows how to read shooters and adapt accordingly. His productivity is up thirty-three percent. I don't give a fuck about your professionalism right now, because you're getting results."

A warmth washed over me. "Thank you, Coach."

"It's not ideal, you and a player, but Mal and I had a long conversation. He insisted you took the job before you knew about Griffin joining the team, and that you disclosed that there could be issues. He also made sure to emphasize that the team hired you, not the individual players, so that's a loophole in your contract. With all that said, just keep it professional, both of you. Griffin's never come to you in a patient role, has he?"

I scoffed. "Tyler? You've met him, right?"

"That's what I thought. You can continue consulting with

other players, but in that respect, you and Griffin should continue to steer clear of each other. If that's how things go, then for now I'm fine with it. I'll let the two of you decide if you want to disclose to the team."

I managed a nod, and he dipped his head in goodbye before getting up to return to his seat.

I released a shaky breath, and my hands trembled a bit.

What is happening?

Could it actually be like this? This easy? I wasn't sure, but Kashvi's words came back to me. *"Worry about that when there's something to worry about."*

I opened my laptop and went back to my reports, though my stomach was still unsettled. I was skating on thin ice, and eventually the ice would break.

My phone buzzed a moment later.

Tyler: Was that Coach I saw talking to you?

Rain: I told him I resigned. He told me not to worry, except you're no longer considered my patient.

Tyler: Ha. I knew I liked him.

Tyler: He's a good coach. Fair. Not biased.

Rain: Seems so.

Tyler: I want to see you tonight.

Rain: I don't think we should. We haven't even had our own talk.

Tyler: I thought we did? Fuck everyone else.

I stifled a laugh.

Rain: Is this our talk then? Are we dating? Just having sex? If the article comes out, we'll have to act as if we're dating, but is that what you actually want? I meant everything I said. I am not worth this.

Tyler: Shut. Up.

Rain: Tyler...

Tyler: You and I can get into it later. Right now, we're on a plane. Maybe you should let me make my own decisions?

Tyler: I'm a simple guy.

Tyler: If I want something, I just want it.

Tyler: I want you.

Tyler: I don't see that going away. So we can use whatever word you want.

Tyler: I want to be the guy in your bed. I want to be the guy who gives you a ride somewhere.

Tyler: I want to hold your hand and get cuddles from you and I want your smile turned my way.

Tyler: And I don't want to do that with anyone else.

"Damn, Griff. Are you writing a novel? Who are you texting?" I heard someone ask him from a few rows behind.

"Fuck off," Tyler growled

A few guys laughed.

"Who's the girl?"

"Or guy! He could be texting a guy."

"Whoever it is, it's your honey. Right? There's no one in my life I'm texting a complete novel to unless it's *my someone*. You got a someone, Griff?"

It got quiet. My phone buzzed just as Tyler said, "Yeah. I got a someone."

"Good for you, man."

I read his last text.

Tyler: I liked you, and then I thought I couldn't like you, so I hated you. Except I didn't actually hate you. I just wanted to hate you, and now I know for sure I don't hate you at all. I like you. I don't want to fight it anymore.

Tyler: So there.

Tyler: Also

Tyler: Will you be my someone?

My heart squeezed as fear, panic, and something else flooded me.

Falling. *Fuck.* I was still falling for him. I don't think I had ever stopped.

Rain: You know my head is messed up when it comes to personal relationships. I believe I mentioned that.

Tyler: Baby, that's the most shrink thing you could've said to me right now. FYI, I don't care how messed up your head is. Talk to me when you're questioning something, and I think we'll be okay.

Fear still pulsed through me.

Tyler: Rain?

Rain: I have never been someone's baby.

Tyler: You're mine now.

A tear slid down my face.

Rain: Okay.

Tyler: Yeah? Is that what I think it is? We're doing this?

Rain: We probably should've had this conversation before getting called into Kashvi's office.

Tyler: Pft. This is what Griffins are like. We do everything backwards and upside down. This is totally normal to me.

Tyler: Now.

Tyler: What are you wearing?

I almost barked out a laugh but caught myself at the last second. Tyler was going to be the death of me.

53

RAIN

The knock came two hours after the game against Seattle had ended. The Grays won, and I knew the guys wanted to celebrate a little in the hotel bar. Tyler slipped into my room last night for a bit, but he hadn't said anything about tonight. As for me, I just operated as I would under normal circumstances. I worked.

Meester had played well tonight. Occasionally he still hesitated to challenge, but it was getting better. He still wasn't as good as Brick. There weren't a lot of goalies who were, but Meester had the potential.

The team as a whole was operating a lot more seamlessly than before. There was still something holding them back, but I couldn't place it.

I went to answer the door and quickly moved back as Tyler slipped inside.

"Wha—"

His mouth was on mine, swallowing my question.

"I need you. I know we were going to wait, but I need to fuck you so bad right now." His hands were a little frenzied as they ran down my back. He picked me up, pushing me against the wall as his mouth trailed down my throat and a hand slid under my shirt, lifting it so his mouth could find my breasts.

Holy shit. He sucked on one of my nipples, and I arched my back. My hands went to his hair, holding him close. "Tyler," I gasped. I wrapped my legs around him, feeling how hard he was for me. That felt so good. I moaned.

His fingers dug into my thigh, and he raised his head, his eyes heated. "Can I fuck you here? Right now?"

I opened my mouth to respond as his other hand slid inside my shorts. I had already dressed for bed. His finger circled my clit and my vision blurred for a moment.

His finger slid inside.

God. That felt delicious.

"Please, baby? I've been wanting to fuck you since you put your reading glasses on and chewed the end of your pen. I've been dying."

Wait. *What?*

I tried to think, to remember where I'd worn my reading glasses. I rarely used them. And then all thought ceased again as he slid two fingers inside me.

"That was at breakfast."

He sucked at the skin just above my breast. That was criminal. I writhed against him.

"I know," he breathed. "I had to keep thinking of my best friend's grandma to keep my dick down. I need my fill of you so hockey doesn't break my dick." He tugged down my shorts. My thong. "Right here. This exact angle. I want to go as deep as possible. Can I?"

I tightened my legs around him before relaxing and letting him pull my clothes off. As we parted a moment, I pulled him out of his pants.

He did me one better, shoving his pants and boxer briefs off and then stepping completely out of them. His eyes darkened as he took in that I was wearing his jersey.

I felt a little shy. "I can't wear it at the game so..." I began to pull it off.

He stopped me. "I want to fuck you in it."

"Oh." That sent a surge of heat through me. I felt a little dizzy.

His hand fisted in his jersey. "Can I?"

I nodded, losing the ability to talk for a second.

"Condom or—"

"Are you negative?"

He nodded, his eyes full of need.

I licked my lips, suddenly parched. "I'm on the patch too."

His eyes flared. "Baby," he said quietly, and that was a caress all by itself. He closed the distance and for a moment, we just stood there.

Some sort of tenderness swirled in me, making me feel wonderful.

But then I shut it down and reached for him. "I want you to come inside of me."

His eyes went black, and a second later, he thrust up into me. I'd never felt as full as I did then. I wrapped myself around him and whispered, "Fuck me *good*."

54

TYLER

After I felt Rain shatter in my arms and released inside of her for the second time that night, I pulled out gingerly and rolled to my back, my chest heaving.

Damn. I was never going to get better sex than this. I already knew that, because it was Rain. It was because of the way I felt about her. That terrified me. Something was happening to me, but I couldn't face it. I wasn't ready yet. Once I did, nothing would be the same.

Because of that, I forced myself to get up.

Rain looked over at me. "You're leaving?"

I smiled at her, brushing a thumb over her forehead and smoothing her hair back. "I don't want to rock the boat. Better if I don't stay. This way, we can get a little sleep."

Her face fell, but she nodded. "Oh. Okay. Yeah. Good call."

I went to the bathroom to clean up. When I came back, she hadn't moved except to pull the blanket over herself.

I tried to tell myself that was okay. It was normal for her to cover herself. Maybe she was cold. But my gut flared. I didn't like that she'd hidden herself from me. Not *me*. I pulled my clothes on, and she didn't say a word as I dressed. When I turned to her, she wasn't looking at me.

Concerned, I approached the bed. There was a vacant look in her eyes. "You okay?"

She blinked, and it was gone. "Yeah, yeah. All good. I'll see you on the plane tomorrow."

I cocked my head to the side.

She was too...something. I didn't know. Closed off? No. That didn't feel right. I couldn't tell.

I took her hand in mine and sat on the edge of the bed. "I can stay? Fuck what Coach says. No one will know. Maybe I should stay." The more I said it, the more right it felt.

I regretted that I'd even said I was leaving in the first place.

"Let me stay."

She blinked again and shook her head, her hand cupping the side of my face. It was such a gentle touch. "You were right the first time," she said. "We shouldn't sleep together. Further complicates things."

I frowned. My gut screamed that I shouldn't walk out that door. "Rain? What just happened?"

She smiled. "Nothing happened." After a moment, it bloomed over her face, filling her up.

My chest eased.

She shoved me, grinning. "Leave before I change my mind."

I stood. "Are you sure, though?" I was still tense. Something still didn't feel right.

She harrumphed a laugh. "Go. I'll see you on the plane."

Right. I started for the door but paused before opening it.

Looking back, she yawned and her whole body stretched. When she finished, her grin turned sleepy.

I made sure I had everything before reaching for the door handle. "Tomorrow."

She waved at me. "Ugh. Just go. We don't need to do a whole

Minnesota goodbye. I'll see you tomorrow. Text me in the morning."

That helped push away the last of my uneasiness, and I sent her one last grin before slipping out into the hallway.

Checking my phone on the way to my room, I found a text from Zoey.

Zoey: Isn't this your friend? The shrink mom mentioned?
Oh no.
I clicked on the TikTok link.
My heart sunk.

55

RAIN

I'd been getting weird looks all morning when I got on the plane. I just kept ignoring them.

The team was... I didn't know. I couldn't explain their weirdness. But there had been odd looks from some of the hotel staff too. And now the assistant coaches seemed uncomfortable as I took my usual seat.

I shifted around. "What?"

They shared a look before Marken, the goalies' coach, leaned forward. "Have you been on your phone this morning?"

"No. It died last night. I forgot to charge it. Why? What is it?"

They glanced at each other again.

"What?" I was getting impatient. *Fine.* I pulled out my laptop. I'd look myself.

But then a hand shut my laptop and Tyler swung into the seat beside me. His face was grim. "Not that way."

"Wha—?"

He handed me his phone. It was open to TikTok. I suddenly didn't want to take it. "What is this?"

"There's no good way to tell you, so you should see it for yourself."

I took his phone, but my fingers were numb. I couldn't feel them. My heart sped up. "What is this, Tyler?"

"Word's out about you and your brothers."

I felt the floor drop out from beneath me. My hand shook as I pressed play.

A girl popped up on the screen with a screen behind her. On it was a picture of when I'd talked to Sunny just inside their bench, by the tunnel. A fan in the stands must've taken the photo. The girl in the video pointed to it. "Listen up, people! I know everyone loves the Connors brothers. How could you not?" The picture switched to a slideshow of Daniel and Dane in their hockey uniforms, playing against each other, playing individually, posing together before a game. Then it switched back to the picture of me and Sunny. "But hold up because did you know that they have a sister? There's a Connors sister! And what's this?" The image zoomed in on where my hand rested on Sunny's shoulder. "Okay. I have questions. One, what is this? This is not just a fan here. This is Sister Connors, and she's *just* come from the tunnel. Is she working with the Grays? Also, *where did she come from?* There are *no* pictures of her *anywhere* from when Daniel and Dane were kids. Did she even grow up with them? Did she grow up somewhere else? Is there a secret Connors family we don't know about? Are there *more* Connors brothers?"

Pictures flashed on the screen. High school pictures of Daniel and Dane playing hockey, playing golf, with their friends, with their father, on their Juniors teams. There were more recent images that were taken at a family event. "None. I repeat, none of these images include Sister Connors. Where are you, Sister Connors?"

The screen changed again to an interview with Daniel. "Daniel was recently asked about his sister, and this is what he had to say." The reporter asked, "Is it true that both you and Dane are estranged from your sister? What do you have to say about the rumors that she's working with the Grays, the team your long-time nemesis, Tyler Griffin, recently joined?"

Daniel scowled. "I don't give two f-*BEEP*-s what that girl does. She wanted nothing to do with us growing up and still doesn't, apparently. Good riddance to her."

"So you're saying the estrangement is her choice? She *chose* to be estranged from you?"

He glowered back in annoyance. "She's had a chip on her shoulder all her life. We could never make her happy, and it's not my fault she chooses not to have anything to do with her family or her nieces." His eyes gleamed as he leaned into the camera, dropping his voice. "Do better, Dylan."

The image flashed back to the girl on the TikTok, and her eyes were dramatically wide. "There you have it, people. Who is Dylan Connors, and what is she doing with the Grays? People want to know. Also, how is this going to affect the upcoming game between Minneapolis and Montreal? I've got a feeling things are going to get bloodier than normal. Don't forget to subscribe, like, or follow for more about this story."

I couldn't think, speak, or function. I only sat there as Tyler pulled his phone away and typed on it.

"Come on, you little piece of shit. Such a waste of space. Let's go. You're going to make us late."

I winced as Daniel's voice came back to me. He'd been angry at me for making him late to school, but I'd been on the steps waiting for him. He'd come out, stopped, and glared at me. "What the fuck? Next time fucking speak up. Tell me you're there. Did you start my truck? Could've been useful to get it warm. Christ."

My mouth had dropped open, because just the day before he'd growled at me, *"Listen, you little shit. I want you on the steps here every morning, ready when we need to leave for school. I'm not going to be late because of your ass."*

And two mornings later, when I'd taken his keys and started his truck, warming it for him, he'd snapped at me, throwing his bag into the backseat and almost hitting me on the way. *"What the fuck? You stole my keys? You don't ever fucking touch my keys and start my truck. Waste of gas and waste of space. Now shut up and let's go."*

I could never make him happy. Had never made him happy.

I felt myself spiraling into panic.

Daniel was going to put everything on me.

After takeoff, Tyler put his phone away. "Dane hasn't said anything."

"Shocker," I mumbled. "He never did."

The weird looks now made sense. Fuck. The team had asked me if I was related to Daniel and Dane, and I'd evaded them with a vague lie. A bubble of laughter worked its way up my throat. I'd been worried about losing my credibility because I was in a sexual relationship with Tyler—even last night, I'd seen the hesitation on his face. I watched him pause and shut down. I knew he was going to leave, and I'd dissociated in that heartbeat. I had to be ready, because no matter what he said, he *was* going to reject me. He was going to leave.

But now this happened?

My relationship with Tyler hadn't even been disclosed yet.

Once we reached altitude and the seatbelt sign turned off, Coach Hines came over to stand by our seats. "The team's confused. Whatever you're thinking, don't. Put your own work into action here. Give the guys a chance, and if you want to say something to them when we arrive, they'll listen."

I nodded. That was the least I could do. "If they could go into the locker room, I'll say my piece there."

He nodded. "Done. Good." He gripped the back of my seat. "Speak from the heart. That's the only kind of advice I can give at a moment like this. This shouldn't be a story. An estranged sister? It's getting attention because it's a brother duo and you're with us. That's the only reason. Fans love to hate Daniel, but they like Dane. My own girls have crushed on him, so I understand the appeal on that app thing. All the TikToks these days and reels and apps." He rolled his eyes. "What's next? I can't even imagine. Chin up, Connors."

That was easier said than done, but I tried. "Thanks, Coach."

"You need anything?" Tyler asked.

I shook my head and looked away, waiting until his attention returned to his phone. Then I wiped away a tear.

Did I need anything? I needed to disappear.

56

TYLER

Skylar was blowing up my phone, but I was worried about Rain.

She was pulling away. I could feel it. I'd felt it last night, too, and it was getting worse. If she could've disappeared inside herself, she would have. The flight attendant asked her three times if she wanted something to drink, and finally I answered for her. I don't think Rain even noticed that interaction. Her eyes were flat, walled off. And when we landed and began to deplane, she moved like a robot. The guys noticed as well, shooting me confused and concerned looks.

Coach glanced at her a few times, but didn't seem shocked. I wondered about that. Had he known about her relationship with her brothers? I felt like I was still learning, and the more details that came out, the more I was concerned. She had paled, but she'd been listening to the TikToker until the interviewer asked Daniel about her. She jumped in her seat at his words, and her eyes had started glazing over.

Dissociation. I didn't know much about it, but Skylar had used the term a few times.

I think Rain had mentioned it as well. Was that what was happening here? I'd googled it on the plane and didn't like the definition, a mental process of disconnecting from reality, or their feelings, thoughts. It was a coping mechanism for trauma.

I needed to learn as much about dissociation as possible.

My phone buzzed again.

I assumed it was Skylar. Her last texts had been about Rain. She had been anti-Rain until Zoey sent me that TikTok thing. Now her tune had changed.

The text was from Kashvi, though.

Kashvi: Martine reached out. She's got the article ready. I'm sending you and Rain a copy so you can read over it.

Kashvi: document attached

Kashvi: I'm keeping abreast of what they're saying about Rain on the hockey sites, and the news is traveling faster than I anticipated. It's only a matter of time until speculation starts about you and her. Normally I'm not into outing a personal relationship, but you're always a hot ticket for clickbait. All the old tapes are going to come out from high school. My advice is to bite the bullet and get ahead of it before Daniel gets more people to hate Rain. So far that's what's happening. The TikToker who made the first video has been approached by his people. They are pushing his narrative, and it'll keep going the way they want.

Kashvi: Rain isn't responding to anything. Are you with her? Can you talk to her about this?

My phone vibrated again. This time it was a text from Nolan.

Nolan: Dude. WTF is happening on your team? Is this true? Is Sister Connors working with you guys?

"Everyone," Coach Hines called for our attention as we headed toward the locker room. "I know everyone is excited to get home, but Rain has asked for a chance to say something. If you all will sit and give her the floor? Thank you." He inclined his head to her.

We went inside, and instead of grabbing our things and leaving, everyone stowed their bags or dropped them on the floor and got comfortable.

Rain stood to the side and looked down at the floor until it was dead silent.

My chest tightened. She looked like a little girl right now, and I ached at the thought of how Daniel had treated her growing up. She was gone. I could tell. Her mind was somewhere far away. I found myself praying she wasn't going to resign then and there. And not just for her, but the team too. The guys cared about her. They could rally around her. I knew it. But she needed to stay. She'd made too many inroads with too many of the guys.

And I... Fuck.

I was in love with her.

I had to admit that. I was in love with her. It'd been growing for a while. That was the sensation last night that had made me uncomfortable, but *damn*. It was true. I loved her. Heaven help anyone who tried to hurt her. They'd have to go through me now.

She cleared her throat and lifted her head.

I tried not to wince at the sight of her face. *Dissociation*. That word again. I was staring at it in present tense. Her body was here. Her mind was working. She looked at us, but she wasn't seeing us and even though she was about to speak, I knew she wasn't with us anymore. I loathed my new understanding.

"I guess I'll start with an apology," she began. She looked around, making eye contact with each guy—or appearing to. "Some of you asked in the beginning if I was related to Daniel and Dane Connors. I lied by omission. I am related, but I was honest when I said I do not know them. I have no relationship with Keith, Daniel, or Dane Connors. I left that house when I turned eighteen, and until Dane's game against you guys last week, I hadn't seen any of them in person since. What Daniel said on the video is untrue. We are estranged, but it's because of them. I kept my last name because of our mother, but that's it. Keith Connors has never once wanted anything to do with me, and considering he decided that when I was six and my mother died, I have a hard time imagining that I did something to make him decide to turn his back on his only daughter. You all know my brothers. Daniel has always been an asshole. I've never done anything to him. I know what that video is saying and how it's being spun, but I think the only thing I can say to you is that I'm sorry for not coming clean about my relationship with Daniel and Dane Connors from the beginning. I wanted it not to be a factor, not to be part of my life, but it seems that's not going to be possible. And I'm sorry. If you can't get over that, please let me know. You need to be able to trust what I say in order for me to continue to do my job."

"What?" Meester squawked before someone hushed him.

Rain's eyes found mine and stayed.

There. She was back in her body. I could see her again.

"I would like to remain working with the Grays, but you all need to know about one more thing. Tyler and I are in a relationship."

My mouth fell open.

She—wow, yeah. She just laid it out there.

A buzz swirled among the guys, but I didn't dare look at them. If one of them looked at her wrong, said one wrong word about her, I would lose my shit.

Coach Hines straightened abruptly and took a step in my direction.

But Rain wasn't fucking done. "Now that you know that, I realize there might be an irreparable rift between me and you. I feel it's only right to ask whether you guys want to continue working with me. The organization should convene and let me know if I should stay or take my leave." Her eyes flashed with apology, and I felt that all the way through my soul. She was saying goodbye in more than one capacity.

Damn it.

She knew what she was doing.

She was burning all the bridges. Every single one of them.

I was going to lose her.

She was leaving. I could see it in her eyes, in the way she stood. She was saying goodbye to me without the actual words.

But I couldn't lose her.

I *would not* lose her.

She looked to Coach Hines. "I'll do whatever you decide is best."

His eyebrows pulled together, but he didn't respond. I screamed silently at him to reassure her, to tell her that of course she needed to stay, but he didn't. They'd have a meeting no matter what, weigh the pros and cons of working with her. But she was one of us. Didn't they see that?

Dammit. Damn them all.

She was one of us.

She was a part of me.

She was mine.

They couldn't let her go.

And yet, as she walked out of the locker room, everyone was quiet.

The door closed behind her, and I *snapped*. "Are you fucking kidding?" I snarled.

And the world went black for me.

CRASH!

Thud.

Blood.

My voice felt hoarse from yelling.

I was still the one yelling.

Something broke, and I was the only one yelling.

After a moment, I came back to myself.

God.

The locker room benches were upended, paper strewn everywhere. A mirror tilted off the wall. There was glass on the floor. All over.

What had I done?

Then I felt another surge. "Rain..."

I inhaled, and the world slipped away once more.

WHEN I CAME BACK the next time, Bruge and Brick held me against the wall

I couldn't get enough air, though my chest was heaving.

There was blood.

Where was Rain?

I searched for her, ignoring the team who stared at me in stunned silence.

Had she come back? Was she in the room? She wasn't. I couldn't find her anywhere.

"You need to get a hold of yourself, man." Bruge shoved me.

The guys stood in a semicircle, staring at me in shock.

I held up my hands, and blood streamed down my arms. I should've felt pain, but I felt nothing.

Except loss.

I needed to get to Rain.

I struggled against Bruge and Brick. "Let me go."

"No, man. You went complete psycho just now," Bruge said. "You gotta chill, and you need to let a trainer look at your hands."

I growled.

Brick barked over his shoulder. "Get Hunter in here now to look at his hands."

After a moment, the trainer rushed in, carrying his medical kit. He seemed winded, running over to us. "I'm here. Okay. Let me see."

Bruge and Brick didn't move.

Brick asked, "You going to go psycho again?"

"Rain." I hung my head.

Bruge leaned closer. "We're not letting her go, so calm the fuck down. Maybe trust us to have your backs, hmm? Now, are you going to be all calm-like and let Hunter patch you up?"

I held his gaze. He seemed to be telling the truth. I nodded, and both relaxed at the same time, taking a step back. Hunter cringed when he got a look at my hands. He touched one, turning it over, and used an alcohol swab to begin cleaning the blood.

Both Bruge and Brick hissed, but I wasn't feeling a goddamn thing.

Hunter turned toward Coach Hines. "Our X-ray machine is down for repairs. The guy is scheduled to come later today, but Griffin will need X-rays. I don't think we should wait. I should take him to the hospital."

Coach Hines glared at me. "Do whatever you need to."

Sunny stepped to the center of the room, his chest lifting. But Bruge spoke first. "One of us should go with him. I'll go."

Sunny's chest deflated. He shot Bruge a confused look, but he didn't say anything else.

Coach Hines nodded. "Go. Hunter, keep us updated."

"I will, Coach." He and Bruge made sure to walk beside me, a hand out if I needed them.

I didn't need any of them.

The only person I needed, I had let walk out of this room by herself.

My mind whirled a mile a minute.

She was gone. Or she was leaving. She said she'd stay if the team wanted her to stay, but I'd come to know Rain. A part of her was gone. Daniel had done that to her. I didn't understand it. But I knew it had happened, and it happened on my watch. It happened when she was right next to me.

There was only one way I could think of to keep her.

"I need my phone."

Bruge held up my bag. "I'm assuming it's in here?" He looked at my pants. "Or is it in there? Not sure I want to be that buddy-buddy with you..."

I glowered at him as Hunter began laughing.

I touched the front of my sweatshirt with the back of my arm and felt the familiar bulge of the phone. "It's here." I held up my arm. "Can you grab it for me?"

He growled low in his throat.

Hunter held up some keys. "You guys stay here. I'll run and get the car. Just stay. Don't leave." He darted off across the parking lot. We'd just stepped outside the rink.

"I'm doing this under protest, but hold still, you complete psychopath." Bruge stepped close as Hunter took off. He pulled the front pocket of my sweatshirt away from my body and angled his head to see inside. Spotting my phone, he slid a hand inside to grab it and held it out for me. It kept buzzing, but he just looked at my hands. "I don't think you can do much on it right now."

I shook my head. "I need you to open it for me and pull up my texts from Kashvi."

His eyebrows went up, but he didn't say anything.

I held up my finger. He touched it to the screen and unlocked the phone.

"Fuck, Griffin. I get like ten texts a day, and three of those are from my agent. You have forty new texts just this morning."

"Ignore them. Pull up Kashvi's and show me the screen."

He did. The last text was the one I'd already read.

Kashvi: Rain isn't responding to anything. Are you with her? Can you talk to her about this?

"Text her back for me. Tell her to release it."

His head jerked up. "Release what?"

"Just type it."

"No." He began to put the phone away.

"Goddammit, Bruge! Just fucking type it. We're losing her. It's the only way to keep her."

He didn't respond for a moment, but his eyes narrowed. "You're talking about Rain?"

"Yes," I clipped out. "What she said in there is just a hint of the fucked-up shit her family did to her growing up. I don't understand it, but I know it was psychological torment. She's gone unless we do something drastic. I have something I *can* do, but you need to type that for me. Please."

His eyebrows smoothed out. "You love her."

"Of course I fucking love her. I went all Hulk just now in the locker room because you assholes are going to let her walk. As long as she's here, we're not going to lose her. I can't tell you anything else because I don't understand it. But this is what my gut says we need to do. What *I* need to do. Send the fucking text, Bruge."

His lips pressed into a flat line, but he typed it out before showing me the screen.

Tyler: Release it.

I gave him a nod.

He hit send.

We waited. I could feel my tension ramping up with every second it took for her to respond.

Just as Hunter pulled up in his car, my phone buzzed with Kashvi's response.

Kashvi: Done. Get ready. I'm assuming you and Rain both agreed?

Hunter got out and came around to open the passenger

doors for us. He stepped aside. Bruge ignored him, staring at me in silent condemnation.

I breezed past Hunter to get into the front seat. "Don't give me that look," I told Bruge. "It was the only way."

Bruge got into the back. "Did you have to take the front seat? Such a fucking diva."

57

RAIN

I didn't stick around after my goodbye to the team. It wasn't technically a goodbye, but for me it was.

They'd release me from my contract.

This was strike two, and there'd be more coming. I had no doubt Daniel's team wanted me to disappear completely. That's how I'd felt growing up. If I'd simply left when I was a kid, no one would've looked for me. Others in my position might've run away, but I'd had a house and food. I was physically safe. Why risk facing the dangers out there until I absolutely needed to?

I think a part of me stayed because that'd been the house where my mother lived. She'd hugged me. Cuddled me. She'd loved me.

And I didn't want to leave until I was forced out.

I tried telling myself Daniel couldn't hurt me anymore, but it wasn't true. If it was, I would've had the courage to turn my phone on.

We'd returned on Monday. It was now Wednesday. The Grays were playing Tyler's old New York team, and I had no idea what the fallout was going to look like.

I'd changed rooms at the hotel, but that was it. My phone had stayed off. I'd asked the front desk to hold any other calls.

I was hiding.

I didn't even watch television.

In all honesty, I had no recollection of what I had done since I got into my new room Monday afternoon.

I'd finally woken up today. That's the best way I could describe it. I'd come back to myself, my reality, and I was all too aware of the time. The Grays were playing in thirty minutes.

I couldn't watch.

I couldn't not watch.

Drinking. That was a solution. I could do it drunk, so I showered, pulled on leggings, a Grays sweatshirt, and a ball cap. I'd get more attention if I wasn't wearing some form of Grays apparel, but the cap should help hide my face. I went down to the hotel bar, and it wasn't too busy. A few louder fans sat at the bar, so I chose a booth in the corner. I slid in with my back to the room, facing one of the TVs mounted on the wall. An old Vikings game played on one of the other televisions, along with an MMA fight, so to keep the confusion down, everything was muted.

"Can I get you something to drink?" A server appeared at my side.

Recognizing the voice, but not placing it right away, I tilted my head up. It was the server from my first dinner with Mal. Different establishment though. Of all the ironies...

She gazed back at me with the utmost indifference, and I knew she had no interest in who I was. I gave thanks for the small gift of disinterest.

"I'll take a water and a..." I caught sight of a purple martini being handed to someone in the booth across from us.

That looked delicious.

I pointed at it. "I'll take that."

She looked over. "Got it. A lavender lush martini coming up."

"And water."

"Mmmm-hmmm. You want some food?"

My stomach rumbled, but I shook my head. My body might be hungry, but I wasn't. I wasn't sure what I'd eaten since Monday. The martini would flatten me, but there were calories in there. I'd be just fine. "No. Just the drink and water."

"Awesome," she deadpanned before pivoting away. A moment later I heard her exclaim, "Well, hey there, Mark! How are you doing?" She was a lot friendlier to Mark. Good for Mark.

The subtitles said they weren't talking about Daniel anymore, though the rivalry was always big news, and his game was on Friday. The thought of him being here again, in the same city as myself, where we'd grown up, made it hard to breathe.

I needed to turn my phone on, but I couldn't make myself do it.

After the game. This game.

Or tomorrow.

Yes. Tomorrow. On Thanksgiving.

I'd deal with whatever the fallout had accumulated then.

My drink was delivered by a different server.

"I had asked for water as well," I noted.

He smiled brightly, "Oh! I can grab that for you."

He placed it on the table just as the face-off began. "Anything else for you?"

"Could you be my server?" I asked.

He laughed nervously, glancing toward the bar. "You know... I'll see what I can do."

"Thanks."

"I'll check on you later."

He left, and the puck dropped.

The game began.

58

RAIN

I was two drinks in by the end of the second period, and the Grays weren't looking the best. First line was all over the place. There was no unity. Sunny passed where no one was waiting. Jesse went the wrong way half the time. Tyler looked as if he needed to win the game by himself. Fortunately, their defensemen were playing well. If they hadn't, the Grays would've been trailing by more than two goals.

Meester was in the net, and after the second one got through, he looked ready to break his stick in half. Bruge skated over and seemed to talk him down.

I was thankful again that the television was muted. Based on the subtitles, the announcers were talking over each other, complaining about how the Grays were a different team tonight.

I frowned. Was this because of me? No... I wasn't that important. I rolled my eyes at myself, slipping away to use the bathroom. I asked the server for a third martini on the way and let him know I was coming back.

He gave me a bright smile, as he had the whole night.

I didn't want to look in the mirror as I washed my hands. But I did, forcing myself.

God. My lips parted.

She was so sad.

She frowned back at me, and there was such pain in her eyes.

Me.

That was me.

I looked miserable.

I closed my eyes, willing the tears away, and when I looked again, I seemed more my usual. But even so, I winced at the permanent wall I lived behind.

I was so tired of being alone.

But that's how it's always going to be, because that's always how it's been, a voice whispered in the back of my mind. I bent my head, tearing my gaze away from the mirror. I didn't want to look at her. I didn't want to see the destruction I had allowed to reign over me throughout my life.

I'd left the house when I was eighteen, and my brothers were still affecting me. *Still.*

Enough.

It was enough.

Maybe there was something wrong with me, but what if there wasn't? What if I just sought out people who were going to leave me in the end because that's what I believed would happen?

The door opened, and a girl teetered inside on her heels. "Whoopsie daisies!" She laughed as she almost fell backwards. "That door moved a lot easier than I thought it was going to. Either that or I gotta work on my tolerance for those pink martinis." She laughed again, coming to stand next to me and fluffing her hair. "You okay, darling?" She touched my arm.

It was the softness in her voice, and I crumbled. "No."

"Oh, darling." Her voice dropped. "You want a hug?"

I shook my head, forcing a smile. "No. I'm good. But thank you."

"Okay. Well, I'm here if you need me." She indicated the bathroom stall before laughing to herself. "I mean, not *here* here. But here in the bar. I'll be at the bar. Look for my big poof hair. You just walk over and give me a nod, and I'll be hugging you before you know it. Got it?"

"Got it." The knot lessened in my throat. "And thanks."

She gave me another smile as I left and returned to my booth. Almost as soon as I sat down, Peter brought over my martini. "I didn't want you to worry about an unattended drink, so I waited until you came back," he explained. "Here you go."

"Thank you."

"Anytime. I'll grab you another water."

He moved away, and that's when Mal Benoit slipped into the seat across from me.

59

RAIN

"Mal." My lungs were on the verge of collapse. "What are you doing here?"

"I have a cousin, but she's like a sister. We raised her in our family. There were reasons she couldn't live with her own parents." He gazed back at me, stoic, resigned. His hands folded on the table, and he glanced down before he continued. "Not many know about her." His gaze grew distant.

The original female server I'd had, chose this moment to remember I was her customer, but Mal waved her off as she approached. He only had eyes for me, very business-like and somber eyes. There was a reason he was here, telling me this.

"There are five years between us. Miriam's quiet. She's always been quiet. I think she grew up that way because she had to. We have money. That's obvious, but we didn't grow up with nannies or housekeepers. No staff. Just family. And maybe it's because of that, I don't know. Our parents were busy. They weren't—it's not that they didn't love Miriam or they loved her less for any reason. She was family. They just...took her for granted. How sweet she was. How kind. She was empathetic and sensitive, and she enjoyed reading books in her room. Of course there were times she didn't want to do the dishes or didn't want to take the trash out, because we had chores. Both of us, though later she got the brunt of them because I was in college and our parents were both working. Miriam was in high school by then. They said she could take care of herself." His voice grew thick, and he had to stop, getting himself under control for a moment.

My insides began to boil.

"She called me from time to time. She wanted to know how I was. She wanted to know what was going on in my life. When I asked how she was, she generally didn't say anything. I thought that was weird, but I just chalked it up to her being private. She didn't want to share. I wasn't going to take it personally. Then one day she called, and we went through the usual conversation. I was going into a meeting, so I rushed her along. I remember thinking, *Why is she calling me now? It's the middle of the day*. I told her how my day was, and when I asked about her, this time she got quiet. I thought for a split second I heard her crying, but then she said, 'Oh, you know. Sometimes I miss everyone.' Then she laughed it off, said everything was fine, and we ended the call."

His eyes shone with tears as he continued, hoarsely, "I was glad when she ended the call because the meeting was important. We had to turn our phones off. It was that important. When it ended, my assistant was in the hallway. She was crying. She saw me, and she broke down all over again. When I turned my phone on, it beeped with a text from my sister, and I was confused. That was it. I was just confused. I wasn't concerned. I didn't think to question why Miriam, who always tried to call when it was convenient for me, had called in the middle of the day this time. I never thought about any of that, and I didn't click to read her text. I was wrapped up in how well the meeting had gone, and I was worried about what was going on with my assistant. And I was irritated that Miriam was interrupting me."

I pulled in a ragged breath.

"I couldn't tell you what that meeting was about today, but I can tell you every word Miriam said on that call. And we were wrong. She couldn't take care of herself. She shouldn't have had to, because that was *our* job. My parents. Mine. We took her in when she was five years old. We raised her. She was our family. It was my job to call her, check on her. It was my job to ask her how she was doing, and if she didn't want to talk to me, it was my job to help her open up. But I failed her as a brother. I was the golden child growing up. I got the attention. Miriam came along, and she was timid, so timid, and she was pushed to the background. My mom was stressed, so Miriam didn't want to upset her by asking for things. My dad was gone, and Miriam didn't want to be selfish and ask him to stay. She put us first. She put our family first, and we never reciprocated." He raised his head and blinked rapidly, trying to keep the tears at bay. "I have agonized ever since, because that's all I have right now. *The aftermath.* What did I miss? Was she asking for help and I wasn't listening?" He shook his head, face haunted. "She was a good kid, but she didn't have a lot of friends. I thought she'd grow into her own. I never considered—" He broke off. "Her last call was to me. And her last text said, *I'm sorry. Don't blame yourself. There was nothing you could've done.* We lived in a high rise. We were on the top floor."

Pressure squeezed my chest.

"She jumped."

I closed my eyes.

After a moment, he continued, quietly, "I *have* a sister, and I visit her grave every goddamn week because I will never forget her again."

"Mal," I whispered. "I'm so sorry."

"I first heard about you from Justin Gathaway. He's not why

I hired you. Obviously, when we looked into you, the results spoke for themselves. You were good. You are good. Justin sang your praises, so I wanted to meet you. I didn't go to that dinner intending to hire you. I wanted to meet you first, but I believe in my gut instincts. My gut said I couldn't let you slip through cracks. I never once regretted making you that offer. You told me ahead of time about your personal connection with Tyler Griffin. I've been around the business before. You are a beautiful woman. I'm aware that Tyler has a lot of female fans, and they are die-hard fans. So I wasn't altogether shocked to find out about your relationship with him."

"What?" My mouth opened.

"As if Tyler Griffin isn't going to take one look at you and not snap you up. Please. Griffin did what I expected him to do, and he did it because he's new to the team and he didn't yet have the respect for us that might've held him back. He has it now, but I can see you're both too far gone."

"You knew about us before it came out?"

"No."

The female server tried again. This time, Mal gave her a scathing look.

She wilted away.

He returned his focus to me. "Miriam kept video diaries, and I had a psychologist analyze them. She didn't leave a note, other than her text, so we didn't know why she jumped. I wanted to know." He paused, gathering himself, and reached for my water. After taking a sip, he set it back down but held on to it. "The psychologist explained that in dysfunctional families, everyone takes different roles—the scapegoat, the golden child, the hero. Then she told me about the lost child or the invisible child." He needed to take another moment. "She believes, based on Miriam's diary, that's the role she took on, or it was placed on her. She told me Miriam might've isolated herself. Which she did. That she suppressed her own emotions, kept them hidden. That she probably wanted to avoid conflict, so she tried to stay under the radar. She shut down. That she probably internalized feelings of being invisible. That she was neglected." His voice broke. "She didn't believe she was worthy of being loved. She wanted to minimize her presence. That was her way of not adding to the family problems or the stress the rest of us felt." He drank the rest of my water and rattled the ice. "She felt flawed. That's what the psychologist said. She felt fatally flawed. I've read more on the lost child. And according to what I've read, my cousin's needs weren't met. Her needs and her voice were discounted. I don't—I swear to God, I don't remember doing that, but does it matter anymore? The research said she probably questioned her right to even exist. That it wouldn't be obvious, but she didn't share what was going on with her life because she didn't think she mattered. To me. That she didn't matter to me.

"The research says she probably felt she didn't matter to the world, that she was 'inconsequential'. That she was 'insignificant'." He shook his head. "My cousin wasn't insignificant, but she felt she was, and that was my failure." He laughed, hollow, his jaw clenched. "Want to know what else we failed at? Seeing her. I don't know how we did that, but we did. I was too busy with my own life to praise Miriam for five goddamn minutes. She told me she missed everyone, but she never gave any indication that she struggled. I missed it. *We* missed it. My parents were always on the brink of a divorce, and Miriam got swept to the side because she was so fucking sweet." His head hung low. "We did that to her because we weren't looking at her."

I couldn't move.

He lifted his head, no longer hiding his tears. "My P.I. looked into you. You know that, but after you were hired, I had him look into you more. I wanted to know what might be coming down the road with your family. He couldn't find a thing. I had him do a deep dive. He talked to your teachers. He talked to staff at your school. He talked to your neighbors. Your bus drivers. You want to know what they all said about you?"

I felt numb.

"They said you were sweet. They said you were quiet. A lot of them worried about you because you were always alone. Some said they tried to get you to talk, but you always said you were fine. And if they pushed, you'd smile, shake your head, and say it didn't matter." He looked into my eyes. "You were being conditioned to be invisible, weren't you?"

I wanted to disappear. I wanted to be forgotten, because he was right. That was my comfort zone. "Mal," I could barely get a whisper out.

"Did you know that you were what my cousin was? Did you know from your schooling?"

I shook my head. Everything hurt. "I—that's counseling and family therapy. It's not my specialty. I—I didn't know."

He glanced down to the table and was quiet for a moment. He was so still, his shoulders drew in on themselves. I found myself waiting, my muscles primed, because what else was coming my way?

His shoulders lowered and his head raised and I saw a sheen of emotions staring back at me. He tried blinking away the wetness, but they wouldn't leave. When he spoke, his voice was so rough. "My P.I. also found something else." He closed his eyes, drew in some air, and delivered, "For a short period of time my father knew your mother."

"I—" I closed my mouth. Mystified. "I didn't know." I shook my head. "I know very little about my mom. She died when I was six and no one talked about her to me. How did they know each other?"

"He took piano lessons. He taught me growing up, said it was something he learned to teach my grandmother before she passed. She had dementia, but she loved the piano. It was a time when she was a bit more coherent. He said he always felt it soothed her soul. So he took piano lessons from a local teacher. Your mother."

The wetness dried away and he was staring at me clearly. So focused. "My parents' marriage was always on the brink of divorce. Apparently, that never changed. There were moments of infidelity on both sides. There was even a stretch where they were separated." His head inclined a little, but he kept his eyes on me. "During that time was when he met your mother. They had an affair."

My insides were wheeling.

"I didn't know until my P.I. was looking into your family. He looked into your mom. My dad is the one who told me about the affair. He said my mom was aware of it, that they were separated, but your mom ended things between them. She apparently had gotten pregnant and wanted to try again with her husband. He asked if there was a chance the child was his, and she adamantly denied that possibility." His voice softened. "I'm sorry. I had my P.I. do a DNA test. You look like my dad."

I'd been staring down to process all of this but then looked up.

He tried giving me a smile. It somewhat fell flat. "I'm your half-brother, Rain."

60

RAIN

I sat there for a full five minutes, trying to comprehend all of this. Mal came in, took hold of the floor underneath me, and whipped it away. I was no longer grounded. I was floating in the air and feeling like a fish trying to get oxygen that wasn't there.

"You're my brother?"

"Half."

"So." I was thinking about what else this meant. "Dane and Daniel are my half brothers?" Was this why he hated me so much? My father—no. Not my father. Keith Connors loathed me growing up. Was this why? Was this the "bad" thing about me? What was so inherently wrong with me? Because I wasn't actually his child.

As if he were following my train of thought, Mal leaned closer and spoke, "As far as my P.I. could find, Keith never knew. He stepped out regularly on your mom, but from what my investigator could find, the only affair she ever had was with my father. Keith would've had no reason to suspect your mom of cheating on him. My investigator couldn't find anything indicating Keith knew you weren't his real daughter."

"Other than how he treated me."

"Other than that, yeah. But knowing how Keith Connors is, he would've said something to you. He never did?"

I shook my head. He was right. Keith would've shoved that information in my face the second the funeral was done. "He would've kicked me out if I wasn't his kid."

"I know this is a lot."

I started laughing. It was high-pitched and tight, and my goodness, I was having a nervous meltdown in this bar. In front of my boss who wasn't just my boss, but also my brother? And oh my God, I had a dad. A real dad.

"Your dad—" What did this mean? All of it.

Mal's smile was so gentle. "He'd like to meet you, but only when you're ready. He's a good dad. He wasn't a great husband, but after we lost Miriam, he made a lot of changes in his life. His family was his first priority. He and my mom decided to end things, but both are happy. They're in good relationships with new partners. It's why I took over the team. It was a family venture, but I'm the CEO of the family businesses." He paused another second. "When we found out about you, we had you added to the business. Technically, you own a small fraction of the team as well."

My mouth dropped all the way to the table. "*What?*"

His grin was small, but authentic. "It's a small percentage. Not enough where you really have a say so you're not in violation of any ethical concerns. The team's board met and decided to terminate your contract with us, effective immediately. They're using the morality clause, saying you violated it not only once with your relationship with Griffin but twice because of 'whatever Daniel Connors is referring to.' Those are their exact words."

I couldn't stay numb any longer. I was trying, but something had changed. Now I felt all the pain, all at once.

"Want to know what the team had to say about that?" Mal asked.

My eyes lifted.

"They told the board to fuck off. Griffin led the charge, while he was also going nuts because he couldn't get ahold of you. Everyone else added their agreement. Bruge. Meester. Brick. All of them. Including the coaches. Every single one of them. I wasn't aware of the board meeting. It was done in my absence. I just got back from Dubai. Want to know what I told the board?"

My heart was frozen, not daring to beat.

"I told them to fuck off too." He leaned forward. "I informed them of our connection and that you had a small percentage of ownership as well. It was pointed out to me how this is also a conflict of interest, but frankly, I don't care. If you want to remain working for the Grays as a consultant, I can have my lawyers draw up a contract that in the event where you might actually have a small say in some vote, that you'd defer because of your employment as a consultant. We can do it that way, if you'd like. Would you like to continue working with the Grays?"

At this point, I didn't even know where I was sitting anymore. If I was still sitting. But I heard myself saying, "When I take on clients, I stay for a season. I'd like to see the season through."

"Then that's what we'll do. I only got Griffin to calm down enough to focus on the game tonight because I told him I knew where you were. I promised I'd bring you back." He glanced up at the game on the screen. "I've already paid your tab. My car is outside waiting for us. Will you come back with me?"

I felt entirely flabbergasted by everything he'd just said. All of it.

"Rain?"

Tomorrow, I promised myself. Tomorrow, I'd start my research on the lost child.

I looked at him. "Is this real?"

"It's real."

"You really want me to continue working with the Grays?"

"*Yes*. Family connection aside, Rain, we're hockey. I saw your face when I first mentioned I was representing a hockey team. It was a look of absolute yearning, and knowing now what I know, I get it. Hockey's family. If you come back, you're accepting that you're part of our family. I'm opening the door. I need you to step inside."

I shook my head. "This doesn't feel right. My job—"

"One of the coaches went through a divorce last year. He struggled, started drinking, started gambling, started doing other bad shit. Coach Hines is the one who drove him to rehab, and he's the one who picked him up, bringing him right back because they needed to get to work. That's the definition of a hockey family. You're one of us. It's time to accept a new family."

My hands shook. Was I actually going to do this?

Gingerly, I slid from the booth. I couldn't meet his gaze. My eyes watered, and I couldn't get them to stop.

"Rain," he murmured. "I didn't hire you because of my cousin or because you're my sister, but I'm also not going to let you go. Let me help you, in any way you need it, because I didn't help her. And I am going to be damned if I lose another sister."

I struggled to breathe but managed to jerk my head in a nod. He looked wrecked, but I was sure I was a mess as well.

"We've still got third period," he said.

I barked out a laugh. My voice sounded strangled.

We left the hotel. A man opened the back door to an SUV as we approached. Mal slid inside first, and I followed. As the doors closed and the vehicle pulled away from the curb, I told him, "I would've liked to meet Miriam."

"I'm going to her grave soon. You can come along."

"I'd like that."

We fell quiet after that, because we were only a few blocks from the arena, and I needed to regroup. I was raw on the inside, but whether he knew it or not, he'd cleared the table so I could start putting myself back together. The right way this time.

When we pulled into the players' entrance, Mal hesitated. "When was the last time you checked your phone?"

"I haven't. I couldn't bring myself to turn it on. I was..." Embarrassed, I realized he knew exactly what I'd been doing. Isolating. Pulling away. It's what his cousin did.

An odd look crossed his face. "Tyler doesn't know about our connection. No one does except the board, my PI, and our father. The board won't release that information. They're all locked in with iron-clad non-disclosure agreements. And my father won't say a word. He's just hoping to meet you sometime. But regarding everything else, Tyler went public. He had Martine publish the article."

"*He did* what?"

61

TYLER

The crowd booed us. I sighed, skating up for the face-off. I couldn't blame them.

We were a mess. We'd been a mess the whole game. And I couldn't find it in me to care. Mal said he knew where Rain was, that'd he go check on her during the game. That was the only thing that kept me sane today.

Martine's article had dropped yesterday, and I hadn't heard one word from Rain. I'd gone to the hotel, but she wasn't there anymore. I kept calling and calling and nothing.

"You okay, buddy?" Nolan asked, stepping up across from me.

I hadn't even had time to consider that we were playing my old team. But it was comforting to see the guys again. Especially Nolan.

The ref skated up, but he waited for my response.

"Yeah. Life's just a fucking shitshow sometimes."

"Life lesson learned. Now, you boys ready—" His words faded as a sudden roar came up from the crowd. It also drowned out the music.

"Griff!" Sunny hissed beside me.

"Dude. Look!" That was Karasvota, one of our defensemen. He pointed up.

I looked, and then immediately skated backward because the camera had found Rain. She sat beside Mal, giant sized on the Jumbotron.

Nolan also turned.

Jesse smacked me on the shoulder. "Your girl's back."

Relief poured over me. I'd been so worried I might never see her again. But Mal had delivered what he promised. He'd brought her back. She was here in the arena.

I bent over, hands on my knees, letting that knowledge sink in.

"Are we ready to get back to hockey, boys?" the referee asked.

"Ready." I got into position.

Nolan followed suit. "Ready."

The ref dropped the puck.

62

RAIN

After we got to the owner's suite, I turned my phone on, and my notifications went crazy. There were a hundred, at least. Most were from Eric—my new friend from Hank's Tulip.

Eric: GIRL! GIRRRRLLLL!

Eric: Okay. Honey darling. Where are you? We need to do our friend date. Remember?

Eric: OH MY GAWD! YOU'RE SISTER CONNORS? WHAT?

Eric: Call me. Jesus. I never have to work this hard to get a girl to call me.

Eric: Okay. Officially mad. And hurt. And mad again. I don't mean to toot my own horn but in the friends department, I'm kind of a big deal. You are going to miss out on all this. (Pretend I'm gesturing to my well-kept body because I work out. I take care of myself. I'm my own temple.)

Eric: Um. Okay. I just got a call from Skylar, and she told me a bit more about what might be going on. I'm so sorry if you're going through it. I'm here for you whenever.

Eric: Still here. Just staying. See? I'm a loyal bitch.

Eric: Well. Okay then. I'd like to say this. Your asshole brother puts out that video saying you're not the greatest and your man is like, "Hold my beer." And bam. The article conveying ALL OF THE NASTINESS drops, and your brothers are now the most hated players in the league.

Eric: I get that you got shit going on, but honestly, for the love of my manhole, call me.

Eric: Not for the love of my manhole. That was a weird autocorrect. I meant for the love of all that's holy, and my phone is also gay apparently. CALL ME

Eric: Skylar said that according to your man, you are not responding to anyone. I'm here. We're here. We care. Where are you, honey?

Eric: Waiting you out, but until then -- WE HAVE SIGNS! (for the hockey game tonight) We're going. Will you be there? Please show up and bam, you'll suddenly be on the jumbotron and everyone is going to go nuts. I know I will. The article about you and your brothers and all of the history with Skylar and her brother, it's making a wave among the die hard fanatics.

Eric: I SEE YOU! YOU'RE HERE! YOU'RE HERE! LOOK AT ME. CAN YOU SEE ME WAVING?!

Eric: HIIIIIIIIII, BITCH! *(smiley face emoji with tears)*

Eric: We're behind the opponent's goalie. I maybe should've told you. Hehe

I looked up at the sudden roar from the crowd and holy shit, Eric had called it. We were on the Jumbotron, me and Mal.

My mouth fell open, and that sent another roar through the crowd. A chant started, "Griffin's..." I couldn't make out the second word.

Mal leaned over and said, "They're saying Griffin's woman."

I was officially dumbfounded.

This was just a temporary thing. A fad. That was it. The hockey blogs loved Tyler already, and they loved to hate my brothers, and mix in good old-fashioned scandal, and this story was a hot ticket. The hockey news must've been slow this week. By the next game, all of this would be forgotten. Except then I remembered that the next game was against Montreal.

Daniel's team.

I blinked back tears, but the game started again, and the jumbotron moved on. Thankfully. It came back one more time before the end of the game. This time, I got myself under control enough to give a small wave and smile to the camera, trying not to come off as an ungrateful asshole. I just couldn't fathom the attention.

Tyler glanced up a few times, but with his helmet on and the game in progress, there wasn't a chance to really make eye contact.

"He's playing better," Mal noted. "They all are."

I agreed. I'd missed the entire second period, but caught the first one. "That *was* because of me?"

Mal shrugged. "A lot happened this week for them. Someone they'd begun to rely on disappeared. But it's not all about you. They've been worried about Tyler, and I think some of them are already thinking about playing your brother in two days. The rivalry between your brothers and Tyler took some of our players by surprise. Plus, it's the holiday. Some of them are missing their families. All of that's combined together, I'm sure."

Guilt washed through me. "I messed up."

"None of that." Mal reached over to squeeze my arm. "Right now, you're not working. You're off the clock. You're here as part of the Grays family. Got it? Let us rally around you."

I nodded, but my stomach remained unsettled. I was embarrassed to have caused all of this.

"Can I tell Tyler about Miriam?" I asked. "To help him understand?"

Mal's face softened. "I already did. That's how I got him to trust that I'd bring you back. He knows about Miriam."

Tears sprang to my eyes again, but no, no, no. I would not let the Jumbotron catch me sobbing. I wiped them away and was grateful when they showed an image of Wolfie, the Grays' wolf mascot, dancing with a drum in one of the fan sections.

During one of the breaks in the game, I pulled my phone out again and debated clicking on Tyler's name. My finger trembled. I was scared to see what he'd sent me, but there was no avoiding it.

Tyler: You need to come back, baby.

Tyler: I have things to say, and I can't say them unless you're here. I need to say them to you, not to this phone so you need to come back.

Tyler: Come back to me.

Short, but to the point. Powerful.

There were so many other texts and calls and voice messages, and I'd get to them. I would. But I wanted Tyler's to be the last one I read for now. Tucking my phone away, I sat back and watched him until the last buzzer sounded. As soon as the game ended, with New York winning five to one, Tyler skated to the middle of the rink and took his helmet off. He stared straight up at me. Standing, suddenly so nervous, I stepped to the edge of the suite. He raised his chin when he saw me.

I gave him a little wave.

"You came back," he mouthed.

I wanted to cry again, but I only drew in a sharp breath and gave him a jerky nod.

He continued looking at me until some of the other players tugged him toward the locker room. Once he was out of sight, trailed by Bruge, who had a hand on his shoulder, Mal sidled up next to me.

"That exchange is going to be all over social media in five minutes."

I drew in more air. "I have no idea how to respond to that."

"I have a feeling your time being in the background is over."

There was a knock on the suite's door. "I should warn you that my phone's been blowing up since our first appearance on the Jumbotron," Mal said. "There are a few people here who'd like to see you."

"Who?"

"I believe one goes by the name of Eric..."

I was already smiling.

He motioned to the door, and one of the staff opened it.

Eric came through first, rushing to throw his arms around me, lifting me up in a hug. Paul was next, holding up a hand in a much more calm wave.

Skylar and Zoey followed, holding hands, and both seemed to be fighting back tears.

Bertle was the last. He only glanced our way, his hands in his pockets, as he veered over to the counter to order a drink.

"Girl!" Eric set me back on my feet. "Do not ever do that again."

"Do what?"

"Disappear." He scowled at me, his hands still on my hips. "You got it? And you need to respond to my texts. You're not the only one with abandonment issues."

"I'll respond. I promise. It's been..." I felt light-headed. "It's been a lot."

"You okay?" The scowl vanished, and his eyes filled with concern.

I began to nod, then paused and asked myself the same question. Then I continued nodding. "Yeah. I will be."

"Good." He sniffled and pulled me in for another hug. "There are others who want to hug you, but I need to show you our signs from the game. And we're going to Friday's game too.

We all already asked for the night off, because no way in hell are we going to make you see your asshole brother by yourself. Daniel Connors is going to learn he's not welcome in the Grays's arena. He's going to be shocked by what we have in store for him."

I tensed, but Eric didn't seem to notice. He moved aside and then Skylar hugged me. "I'm sorry about how I treated you the other night. Tyler tried to tell me it wasn't what I thought, but I didn't listen. Then that article came out, and after reading everything, I realized I should've stopped to think about how Daniel would've treated his sister. I know how he was with me, and why would he be any different to anyone else? I pity his two little girls, that's for sure."

My eyes widened. "He has two little girls?"

Her face fell. "Oh. You didn't know..." She nodded. "I'm so sorry. Yes. He has two girls from two different marriages."

"Wh-what are their ages? Do you know?"

"I think eight and four?"

Dane had three girls. Daniel had two. I had five nieces.

I began laughing.

Skylar chuckled too, but she didn't seem sure if she should be laughing. She moved back to Zoey's side, holding her hand again.

"It's just..." I couldn't get over the irony. "They *only* have girls."

The universe was funny sometimes.

63

TYLER

Coach didn't ream us out. He should've, but maybe he took pity.

"Okay, boys. Tonight wasn't your night," he said instead. "I won't say much more on that except, let's take Thanksgiving to forget about it. Spend time with your family, and if that's not possible, all are welcome at my house. Missy cooks for sixty people, so no worries about having enough food. You might have to put in some time with the little ones, but they'll tucker out for their afternoon naps. So, let tonight's game go and focus on what's ahead." He gave us each a meaningful look, then waved to me with his clipboard. "Griff, they want you on press. Ray. Bruge. You're after him. Everyone, get going."

"Coach, some of the players don't have your address," Bruge called.

"Right. I'll send it out in the team text and add it on the board."

Marken picked up a marker. "I got it, Coach."

Meester stood. "Yo! We're going to Halbrechts after this. Back room. Coach, you all are invited." He looked my way, and I knew he'd made a point of inviting them so Rain didn't feel out of place going. Or at least I hoped she'd go. Maybe I was getting ahead of myself. Press first. Shower next.

One of the assistant coaches came over. "They want to let press back here. That okay with you?"

Bruge and Jesse both nodded. "Fine with us."

I gave a nod. But I reached for my phone before the press could get to me.

Tyler: Where are you?

Rain: In my office. Just got here. Also, hi.

Tyler: You have an office?

Rain: Omg.

Tyler: I'll find it. Give me a few. They want me to do press and then shower.

Tyler: Meester said everyone is going to Halbrechts tonight, coaching staff too. They'll want to see you.

Rain: I know. I'll come. I'm going to talk to Coach Hines now. Mal said they tried to fire me, but he stopped it.

Tyler: Coach did? He has that power?

Rain: No. *(eye roll emoji)* Mal did. He's the owner. I'm assuming he has the majority share.

Tyler: That makes more sense. I'd be a terrible NHL team owner. I'd just fire everyone who wanted to fire you.

Rain: I don't think that's how it works but thank you.

Rain: I have things to say to you too.

Tyler: Press is coming. Be there SOON

The reporters came in. They were usually hand-picked by Kashvi so they weren't too scandalous, but I knew tonight was going to be different.

The first asked, "Tyler, what are your thoughts on your team's loss tonight? Do you have any regrets?"

I kept my face deadpan. "My thoughts are that we were a mess. Obviously. We didn't win, so there are always regrets there, but we'll move forward and keep our focus on the next game."

General question. General answer.

The next one asked, "Speaking of the next game, what strategy might you have so you don't get a repeat of tonight's game?"

I almost laughed but kept the same deadpan expression instead. "Strategy will be to stay focused and to make sure we all play as a cohesive unit."

The third had a gleam in her eye. "Given the recent media storm surrounding your team's consultant and your personal relationship with her, are you worried about facing her brother?"

I liked this question, and I grinned, knowing it likely looked chilling. "I've never been worried about facing Daniel or Dane Connors on the ice. Wasn't worried in high school and that's not changed. In fact, I'm looking forward to facing Connors on the ice."

She had a follow-up question. "Any words for Daniel Connors if he's watching right now?"

"Yeah." I looked right into her camera. "Fuck you, Daniel."

The reporter's eyes went wide, and I knew that would get bleeped out on certain streams, but I'd gotten my message across. I gave them all a smirk before standing to grab my items for the shower. "Now, if you'll excuse me."

When I came back from showering, half the guys were gone.

I checked my phone before dressing.

Nolan: We're flying back in the morning. Want to meet up tonight?

Tyler: The team is going to Halbrechts down the block. I want to talk to Rain first. If she and I are okay, we'll put in an appearance.

Nolan: Okay. Your sister's hitting up my phone. I'll mention Halbrechts to her.

Tyler: I'm going to shoot her a text too.

I switched threads and clicked on my sister's name.

Tyler: Plans tonight? Team is going to Halbrechts. I mentioned it to Nolan. I'm sure he and some of the other guys will come out with us.

Skylar: He just texted me. The guys are coming. Eric is obsessed with Rain, so be thankful he only likes dick. Have you talked to her yet?

Tyler: I will in a minute. I think she's still with Coach.

Skylar: Zoey brought a friend tonight. She's going to go back and stay at her house so I can do Halbrechts. I think a night away from her mom will be good for her. But I think she has a crush on Paul.

Tyler: Not really liking Paul right now.

Skylar: Relax, big uncle. He was very respectful. He just has a pretty-boy face and looks like a jock. He might be a jock. I don't know. We don't talk about that stuff, but I know he's gay. But also, she's underage and Paul would never. I'd gut him if he even looked at her like that. (Not that he would.)

Skylar: Are you sure you want to come out with all of us? You won't want to spend the evening with Rain?

Tyler: The guys need to see Rain. They're worried about her too. She's made a difference with a lot of them. I can't guarantee we'll stay long.

Skylar: That makes sense. I'm going to make sure Zoey and her friend get back. Her friend's parents are nearby for dinner, so they're picking the girls up. Once they're off, we'll go to Halbrechts. Do you need us to save booths? Tables?

Tyler: Meester said we're in the back room.

Skylar: See you there. Love you, brother. Sorry you were such a loser tonight.

I grinned.

Tyler: Payback's a bitch, little sister. Payback is a bitch. Just remember that.

Skylar: So not scared. Your pranks suck. CUL8R!

I let Nolan know about the back room and also shot a text to Meester to say I had other people coming. He could find out who when they showed up.

Instead of wearing my suit home, I pulled on some jeans I had in my locker and a gray Henley, then shrugged on my jacket. It was getting cold again.

Heading out, I looked for someone who could tell me where Rain's office was. Why had I never known she had an office in the first place? It hurt to think about all the desk sex we'd missed out on.

64

RAIN

When I saw Tyler heading for the shower with the press surrounding his locker, I quickly knocked on Coach's office door. Once he told me to come in, I jumped inside before the press saw me. I sagged against the door.

Coach Hines looked up from behind his desk. Unlike most nights, the other coaches weren't in his office with him.

"No debrief tonight?" I asked as I took a seat.

"Not much to debrief. It was a shitshow, but we've got a holiday tomorrow, and I've got a feeling the guys will bring their A game on Friday." He let a little gleam show in his eyes. "A certain player on that team has pissed some of the guys off. You wouldn't know anything about that, would you?"

I winced. "Coach, I—"

He waved me off. "I'm teasing you. Now, I need you to listen to me. The only thing you did wrong was engage in a personal relationship with one of my players and not disclose it. We've already talked about that. He's not your patient. This ain't that sort of thing. You are not full-time staff, and as far as I know, there are no policies saying anything about a personal relationship with consultants. That's what you were hired as, and that is what you have been doing for this team. I know Benoit pulled something out of his ass for some sort of loophole, but I asked to see your contract, and the morality clause is vague. Missy went through the Grays' policies, and she's the one who said there's no mention of temporary positions or consultants."

"Missy?"

"My wife." He leaned back in his chair. "She's a lawyer."

"She is?"

He nodded. "A damn good one. All my girls take after her. Did you know I mentioned to her that I'd seen a girl skating with the Connors boy, all those years ago?"

"You did?"

"I did. I thought the whole thing was odd. You looked like one of them. Skated like them, but they acted like you were their equipment manager. And not in a respectful way. It never sat well with me, and I made sure to mention it to Missy."

My throat went dry. "What did she say about it?"

"She got mad. Right mad. She got on the computer and did all this research on the Connors family. She had a friend who worked the front desk at your high school, gave her a call. The two went out for martinis and when she came back that night, she was in a tizzy like I'd rarely seen."

That took my breath away. "So you knew who I was this whole time?"

"I knew, but I didn't know how to handle you. I fumbled a bit in the beginning, if I'm being honest, but I let Missy know you were back. I hope that's all right with you? She got back to work, researching you and following your career." He pressed his lips together before continuing. "She didn't share whatever she found. I asked if I needed to know anything, and she said she'd share when the time was right. She's been keeping an eye on you, and, Rain, she let me know today that if I don't officially invite you to Thanksgiving tomorrow, I best not come home tonight. You may have your own plans, but half the guys usually drop by. Missy would be tickled pink if you showed. And another fair warning, she's going to try to mother you."

My heart lurched.

"She'll try to hold herself back. She won't want to scare you away, but I know my wife. If she could adopt you, even at your age, she'll try. And she's not the type to let you go once she's got you. You hear me?"

She wouldn't let me go. That'd never been the case, not for the ones who got into my heart space. *But this time is different*, I tried telling myself. People knew about me, and they hadn't cast me out.

"Thank you, Coach."

He nodded before gesturing to the door. "I believe there's a celebration tonight to attend, and a certain person lingering in the hallway out there waiting to have a word with you."

I felt a little raw, but I stood. "Thanks, Coach."

"Rain."

I looked back.

"Should I expect you on Friday, or are you taking that game off?"

As far as he was concerned, it was business as usual. I had a job to do, and I needed to do it.

I shook my head. "I took today off. That means I'll be here on Friday and for the game that night."

"Be glad to have you back."

"Coach." I squared my shoulders. "I want to be on the bench, if that's okay with you?"

I caught a glimmer of a grin before he masked it. "That's just fine with me."

My mind was spinning as I stepped outside, but Tyler was there. He straightened from the wall, a predatory look on his face as he stalked toward me.

"Tyl—" I started to say, holding my hands up.

He bent down in front of me and tossed me over his shoulder.

"Tyler!"

He turned around. "No one will tell me where your damn office is, so *you* tell me. We've got things to talk about, woman."

Well then. I pointed him in the right direction.

65

TYLER

She thought she could leave me? *I don't think so.*

She thought she could hide from me? *Hell* no.

She thought she didn't have to turn her phone on and let me know she was alive? Over my dead body.

I planned to let her know all of this, except the second we were in her office and I lowered her to her feet, she jumped back into my arms. Her legs wrapped around me, she clung to my shoulders, and I had no choice but to hold on to her.

"Rain—"

"No," she breathed, raking a hand through my hair.

And then her mouth was on mine.

Fuck.

I could kiss this woman for the rest of my life. But I needed to—I lifted my head.

"Tyler." She fisted my hair, holding me in place. "No."

"What?"

"I—I want to say my stuff first."

Oh. Right. There were things we needed to talk about. I'd forgotten. My hands tightened on her ass. I bounced her in my arms a little bit, and oooh. That felt good. That felt really good.

"Tyler!" Rain laughed, creating some space between us.

Yes. A talk. I looked around her office and saw she had a couch. *She had a couch, and this was the first time I knew about it?* I went over and sat down, keeping her on my lap. She moved her legs to straddle me and sank down.

Yup, I had to think of anything I could to keep my dick from trying to tunnel its way into her. She smoothed her hands down my chest, biting her bottom lip. I lifted a hand, stopping her from doing that. Her eyes flicked up.

"Only I get to do that," I explained.

Her eyes flashed, but then they cooled. "Okay. Listen, I messed up." She tucked her chin against her shoulder, turning away.

I touched a finger to her chin, bringing her back to me.

Such guilt pooled in her eyes. "I couldn't bring myself to turn my phone back on, and that was wrong," she said softly. "I hid, and I isolated, and I pulled away. That's always been my go-to. I did that growing up because that's where I was safe, and I did that when I got older because I kept getting hurt, and I didn't know what I was doing wrong. But I shouldn't have done that with you." She gripped my arms. "I've been cautious my whole life, and suddenly there you are, and you came in hot and fast. The first time you kissed me, I didn't know what was happening. You woke up all these emotions in me that I didn't know were there anymore. All my attempts at relationships have failed, and I'd accepted that I'd be alone all my life."

That broke me to hear.

She rested her forehead on my chest, and I ran a hand down her hair and back, soothing her.

"You came along, and for the first time, I'm thinking there's more," she continued. Her hands slid down to the front of my shirt and fisted it. She lifted her head, and her eyes were glassy. "You are giving me *more*." She broke off as a tear slid down her cheek.

I cupped the back of her neck, smoothing my thumb over her face. Yes. There was so much more here. I bent down to rest my forehead against hers. "You can tell me whenever you want. You don't have to say it all now."

She drew in a breath and closed her eyes, some tension leaving her body. "You deserve to know it all."

I framed the sides of her face with both my hands. "We have time. You're not going anywhere." I looked into her eyes. "Right?"

She shook her head, a smile breaking over her face. "No. I'm not running anymore. I'm not hiding, but Tyler, you have to know that the way I grew up, I was conditioned to believe no one would want me. I'm messed up in the head."

"Babe," I whispered. "We all are."

She laughed.

I grinned, loving that sound from her.

She wiped the rest of her tears away. "I'm sorry for hiding the last few days."

I took that in, needing it to ground me.

Her eyes shifted down. "I shouldn't have hidden from you."

"No, you shouldn't have." I tilted her head back up again. "But that's over with, because now I know your ways. I'm going to put a tracker on you somewhere." I wasn't kidding, but she laughed as if I were. "Maybe your shoes or your bag."

So not joking.

"Look," I told her. "I have things to say to you too. Serious things."

Her face changed. "What are they? You don't want to keep doing this with me?" Pain flared in her eyes. Fresh and stricken. "I get it, Tyler. I do. I'm a—"

I sealed my mouth over hers. I needed her to stop talking. *Now.* She surged against me, and I decided enough was enough. I lifted my head enough to say, "We can talk later, but do me a favor and stop thinking I'm going anywhere. You turned your phone off. It's not a big deal in the grand scheme of things. I outed us without your permission. Of the two of us, I should be the one hiding, and for everything else, you've done nothing wrong. Your dad is a piece of shit. Your brothers are pieces of shit. You are a fucking treasure. So when your brain starts going sideways, tell it to fuck off, okay? For me? Or think, *what would Tyler tell my brain to do?*" I pressed my forehead back to hers. "Please don't ghost me again, though. I don't think I could bear it."

She studied me a moment, her cute little eyebrows pulling low. "Tyler?"

Should I...? Oh. Fuck it.

I stopped holding back and let it show on my face. "I love you."

Her eyes got big, really big. "*What?*"

"I am in love with you, and, babe, I've only ever loved five people in my life. My parents, the woman who took us in, and Skylar and Zoey. That's it." Well, some of my friends too, but that was semantics. "When I love someone, I will do anything for them, and you're in there. You got in. I love you, Rain."

More tears slid from her eyes. She stared at me in wonder. "No one's ever told me that."

"What do you mean?"

"No one's ever told me they loved me."

"Your mom?"

She shook her head. "If she did, I don't remember. I have happy memories with her, so she must've. But you're the first person I can remember telling me that." She pressed against me. "Thank you. I—"

I touched the side of her face. "You don't have to say it back just because I said it. I didn't say it for that reason. It's just the truth. I actually tried *not* to say it, because I didn't want to scare you away."

"I'll never run again," she said. "I promise."

Relief filtered through me. She meant it. I kissed her, loving how soft her lips were and the way she tasted like cupcakes. "Good, because now I'm going to fuck you, and then we need to put in an appearance with the team, because they're all worried about you too." I slid a hand inside her pants, moved her thong aside and circled her, feeling how warm and wet she was. "Baby."

She moaned, moving over my fingers and grinding down on me.

"You're all wet for me? This is for me."

Her eyes went glassy again, but with lust this time. She bit down on her lip as my finger slid inside of her. She pressed her forehead into my neck. I grasped her ass. "That's it," I crooned, urging her to keep grinding. "Ride my fingers." I slid a second one inside and a third not long after.

She bore down on them, breathing harshly into my neck.

I adjusted my position to get a better view of her as she rode me, her pink cheeks, her flushed neck, the perspiration forming on her forehead. Her eyes closed, and she bit her lip to keep from moaning. I lifted my fingers to her lip and plucked it from her teeth. A full groan filled the office.

She was glorious.

Tugging her hair, I pulled her head back to taste her throat. I needed to mark her. I wanted everyone to see me when they looked at her. She was *mine*.

"That's it. Keep going," I said between nipping and laving her skin, sweeping my tongue over her. When a good mark had formed on one side of her neck, I pulled her head to the other side and started there as well.

"Tyler," she gasped, fisting my hair.

She yanked, and I moaned. "Pull harder. I love that shit."

She did.

Fuck. The pain went straight to my dick. It surged up, trying to get into her through our clothes, and she shifted, rubbing her clit over my cock with my fingers still tunneled up inside of her.

"Tyler, I want you," she breathed, her hand pushing between us to palm my cock. "Please."

It was that one word. It came out on a whimper, and it broke me.

I yanked her up, tearing her pants and underwear out of the way. She bent and tugged my pants farther down. As soon as my dick hit air, I brought her down on me and slid inside.

I groaned at the feel of her, tight and hot and mine. All fucking mine.

Fucking Christ. I needed to rein myself in or I wasn't going to last.

Rain rested her chest against mine for a moment before she began moving over me in a slow and deep rhythm.

"You feel so fucking good." I went back to my mark on her neck. More, more, more. I needed all of my marks on her.

She yanked my hair, pulling my head up to meet my lips with hers. Her tongue slid in, tasting me. She was claiming me right back.

My tongue met hers, caressing. I was going to kiss this woman for the rest of my fucking life.

"Ty," she gasped, her hips bearing down.

Satisfaction rolled through me at hearing the nickname fall from her lips. I wanted her to say it all the time.

Running my hand over her back, I lifted her shirt, my nails scraping up her spine. She shivered, raising her head. She looked so sexy—her skin flushed and soft, her eyes hazed over with lust, her lips swollen and pink, shimmering. I wanted to see all of her and pulled her shirt off. Her bra was next. I palmed one of her breasts, leaning down to taste her.

She whimpered again, and just as my teeth scraped over her nipple, her walls clamped down on my cock. I let out a guttural moan, deep in my throat, because that shit felt like heaven, and then she was coming apart in my arms. I held off on my own release, moving inside of her slowly and watching as her climax came over her in waves. She was beautiful. When she was done and her eyes opened, her lip lifted in a tiny grin.

I smirked back at her. "My turn?"

I didn't wait for her to respond, just flipped us over so she was lying on the couch, missionary style, and then I went to town on her, pounding and thrusting, deep and hard. It wasn't long before my climax hit, and that shit felt good. Jesus. This woman. Waves of pleasure wrecked me, leaving me panting as I lifted up to gaze down at her.

She slid a hand up my chest, her fingers tracing my muscles to my shoulder, then down my arm until she intertwined our fingers. She pulled me down to lie on top of her.

"I'm not too heavy?"

She shook her head, nuzzling into my neck. "I like you on me."

I moved a little to the side so I wasn't crushing her, and as I got comfortable, I looked back down.

She'd fallen asleep.

I reached for the blanket that had been tossed over the corner of the couch and switched us so she was lying on top of me. Spreading the blanket over both of us, I bent my forehead into her neck and closed my eyes. A little nap was a good idea.

66

RAIN

Everyone was drunk by the time we got to Halbrechts. I didn't think we were going to make it. But my hotel wasn't too far away, so we washed up after waking from a twenty-minute nap and headed out. The place was thirty minutes from closing by the time we got there, and walking into the back room, Skylar saw us first.

She rushed over, her scream cutting through a break in the song.

I expected her to throw herself at her brother, but instead she threw her arms around me.

"Ooomph," I grunted, falling back a step.

Tyler steadied me, a hand to my back. He poked his sister. "Hey. Don't injure my woman. I just got her back."

I stood immobile, because what was this? We'd hugged in Mal's suite when she came up with Eric, but it still took me by surprise. After a moment, my arms lifted and wrapped around her to return the hug. When she pulled away, her hands clasped my arms and she beamed.

"I kinda love that my brother is obviously in love with you, and you ghosted him. He's not used to women running away. Feel free to keep him on his toes."

Jesus. There was that word again. *Love.*

I gave both siblings an uneasy look, because was this just some word they threw around? Though, the way they grinned at each other, their love was so obvious. Maybe they could say it because they actually knew what it felt like?

"You're coming to Thanksgiving tomorrow." Sky squeezed me again before stepping back.

"Actually, about that—" I started to say, but then other people were there.

The next body that crushed me in a hug was...I wasn't even sure, but they were big and beefy and smelled like alcohol and sweat. He stepped back and—it was Meester?

His grin was sloppy and he shook his head. "You're not allowed to go anywhere else. You can't work for any other team anymore. K?" He crushed me back to him before Tyler cleared his throat pointedly. Meester stepped away, shooting him a rueful glance. "We still need you." His gaze returned to me. "And this man obviously needs you. Lost his shit when you left the locker room, and his play sucked ass. We'll get them on Friday. Don't worry. I'm more than ready to be assertive. I mean, I'm not playing, and I was terrible today, but I'll be ready for Friday from the bench. I'll open the door like no other backup goalie ever has." His eyes grew misty. "You helped me with that."

"Okay. That's enough from you, buddy." Sunny came next, and he extricated me from Meester.

Tyler gave him a look of thanks.

Sunny nodded to him and gave me a tender hug. "It's good seeing you back, and everything Meester said, except the goalie-specific things. Ditto from me." He jerked his head in Tyler's direction. "We do kinda need you to keep this one grounded. He's our ace player."

"Aces," Meester whispered next to us, a wasted smile on his face.

"Move. Move. Everyone, MOVE OUT OF THE WAY!"

Sunny was shoved aside. They tried moving Meester, but he wasn't having it. He barely batted an eyelash, so the person darted around the side, and Eric launched himself at me for the second time tonight.

"We already loved on you at your hot boss's suite, but you have left us alone too long with all these hockey players." He scowled, but he started laughing and it gave way to a blinding smile. "Thank you so much. That's been the best holiday gift ever. Also," he whispered into my ear, "Please tell me Jesse Ray swings both ways. Is he a secret bi-baby? Can I get his number?"

Paul had accompanied him, and he now shook his head at Eric, though he also gave Jesse a heated once-over. Feeling the attention, Jesse frowned, giving Tyler a questioning look before offering me a small wave.

Tyler leaned in. "Some of my old teammates are here. I'm going to go say hi. You good?"

Eric was still hugging me, and now Meester was jabbing at his shoulder. "You gotta share. No keepsies, dude. Little dude. Little pretty dude?"

Eric stiffened. "Little pretty dude?"

Meester got him with a lopsided grin. "You know." He patted him on the head. "You're, like, compact size."

"I am not compact size," Eric growled, and he let me go to step up to Meester. "Take that back."

Meester stared down at him, confused. "What'd I say?"

Someone tugged me to the side, where more players waited to hug me.

"Don't do that again. Just. Don't," Bruge said.

When he released me, Jesse was next. "Do I want to know what the looks were for?"

I shook my head. "No. Probably not unless you're open to men. If so, I think there are some willing to help you experiment."

Paul flashed me a knowing grin and winked at Jesse. "You just name the place."

I clocked the shiver that went through Jesse. "Uh..." He swallowed. "I—I've never, I mean—girls. I like girls. Women. I—what's going on?"

Paul laughed, banking some of the heat in his gaze before nudging Jesse out of the way. "Move aside, hot stuff."

Eric and Meester were still bickering on the other side of me.

Paul hugged me. "You look like you've had a night."

He stepped back, and my fingers curled into his shoulders for a moment before letting him go. Paul was much more reserved than Eric, I was finding out. I was getting to know them, and it wasn't uncomfortable. I released a ball of nerves that had been in my stomach since we entered Halbrechts. "I have, but it's been a good night." A really good night.

A few more of the players came over. Brick had already left, but I'd see him and the rest of them on Friday or for Thanksgiving. I needed to talk to Tyler about that, because we had a couple different invitations.

Or. Wait—was I just assuming I'd be going to Thanksgiving with Tyler? No, Skylar had asked me.

Old worries tugged at me, pulling me into uncertainty. Tyler was across the room, talking with Nolan Everwood and some other players from New York. As if feeling my attention, his gaze shifted, finding mine. His eyes darkened, and he tilted his head to the side, lifting his eyebrows in question.

Was I all right?

I couldn't answer.

I closed my eyes, because I wanted to pull away. Right now. All these people were too much. They were saying such nice things to me, but suddenly I wasn't comfortable. I'd grown up in the shadows, and now I was in the spotlight, and I was making assumptions about the future, and I—*he loves me.*

That was my own voice shutting everything off.

Tyler loved me. He'd told me.

He'd *want* to go have holiday dinner with me.

I thought about it... Yes. I was sure. And just like that, my uneasiness melted away. Tyler had started to come my way, but I shook my head and mouthed, "I'm fine."

"You sure?" he mouthed back.

I nodded. "I love you."

His eyes flared. He mouthed back, "I fucking love you too."

I felt a stupid grin on my face.

It was new. All of this. Tyler loving me. The team being worried about me. Skylar's acceptance. I'm sure there'd been others in the past who'd cared about me. Maybe I hadn't given them a chance. Maybe I'd pulled away to protect myself, assuming they'd be just like my family, just like the first few relationships and friendships that had left me too? I didn't know, but this day, right here, right now, this was when things would change.

I was staying.

"Not sure what all that was about, but it's nice to see my brother like this." Skylar had found her way back to my side.

"Like what?"

"Happy. Grounded." She studied him, nursing her drink. "I've only seen him like this one other time, the day Zoey was born. That first morning in the hospital when he held her, he was content. Calm. He's always had this restless energy, like the world was eating at him and he wanted to take it on." She turned to look at me. "It's a good look on him. Let's keep him that way? He's so much easier to deal with."

"I'll do what I can." My lips twitched upwards.

Hers twitched too, and she gestured to her drink. "You want something?"

The first notes of "Bohemian Rhapsody" filled the room, and Meester took the lead. Eric did the screaming parts, along with some sort of running-man dance in the background. Meester's eyes were closed, his head tipped back. He was entirely somewhere else.

"They've been like this all night." Sky shook her head. "Those two took one look at each other, and I'm pretty sure they both saw their soul animal."

"Soul animal?"

"You know, like how dogs will sniff each other to determine if they want to be friends, and then bam, they'll start chasing each other around? Those two did some sort of thing like that. Eric's not this way with anyone. Except you, but you had to dance with him first. After that, he decided he wanted to be besties."

Tyler brought over Nolan Everwood and introduced us, then he and his sister fell into an easy teasing routine. Nolan Everwood was intimidating. He was a smart and lethal player, but he was more intimidating because I knew he was Tyler's best friend. And he seemed reserved about me, not overly warm.

Tyler shifted to stand behind me, and I leaned into him. His hand went to my hip before slipping under my shirt.

That's okay, I thought to myself. I was used to reactions like Nolan's. He just wasn't sure about me. As long as he didn't try to make Tyler change his mind, we'd be okay. Not that Tyler was the type to be influenced that way.

Still, a little tendril of fear slithered down my back. I pressed against Tyler, pulling his other arm around me.

Skylar and Nolan were chatting, and the song had changed. Paul was now on the microphone as the opening bars of "Baby, One More Time" began. Eric jumped back on stage, hip checking Paul, who only laughed, content to share the song with him.

Tyler nuzzled my ear. "You okay?"

My throat was suddenly full. I was a mess. Happy, then scared, because what if all this went away? The usual numbness started to creep in, but I stopped it. I needed to stop expecting things to end a certain way. I needed to begin thinking the opposite, letting in the positive and believing good *would* happen.

Tyler happened.

Tyler was good.

I held onto his arms in front of me with a cement grip. I would never let him go.

Mal. His dad who was *my* dad...

"I'm okay," I told him.

His arms tightened around me, and I leaned against him.

67

TYLER

Rain and I still hadn't had a real talk. After the bar last night, we crashed, but she brought me up to date about how my boss was going to be my future brother-in-law. What a mindfuck that was. Rain still seemed shocked by the whole thing but was also half falling asleep from the couple of drinks she had so I gave her a kiss, tucked her into bed, and promised we'd go over everything tomorrow.

It was tomorrow and Rain was hurrying around everywhere. I called Ski to talk about Coach's Thanksgiving invitation. After some negotiation, we'd go to Coach's house first and end the evening at Ski and Zoey's.

"That way it'll give us more time to talk," Ski explained. "Be more intimate."

I frowned at the phone. "Intimate? You sound like you want to date her. You don't, right?"

"No. Though I do wish I was more into women."

I snorted. "I wish you were more into women too."

"Men are just so... Not Nolan, though. Nolan's the best guy I've ever met."

I frowned again. "You cannot date my best friend."

She sighed. "I know, but why does he have to live all the way in New York? Not fair."

"I'm not enjoying this conversation," I informed her. "Before I forget, should we bring anything with us?"

"No. I have it all covered."

I paused. "You ordered Chinese, didn't you?"

"Yep. On your credit card."

"That's for emergencies."

"It is an emergency. It's a holiday, and I forgot to go to the grocery store yesterday. So hence, I used your card today. Thank you, big brother. I'll see you when you get here."

I was grumbling as she ended the call, but then Rain came out of her bedroom, and I was blown away. I stood, going to her. "You look incredible."

She'd been brushing her fingers through her hair and stopped to look at herself. "I'm in a sweater and jeans."

I shook my head. She didn't have one clue how beautiful she was. "It's not the clothes, babe."

"It's not?" She continued frowning at herself.

I drew her to me, brushing a kiss over her forehead. There was that same aroma—cupcakes. I caught an added underlying hint of lilac. My two new favorite smells. "Your jeans show off this seriously sexy ass." My hands dropped there, cupping her as she chuckled against my chest. "But it's just you, babe. You could be wearing anything and my dick would get hard, but I like you best in nothing. Let's skip all the parties and start our own tradition: naked Thanksgiving. I'm thankful every time you're naked for me. Let's celebrate."

She laughed, but I was serious.

Lifting a hand to my chest, she looked up at me as if she wanted to say something.

"What is it?" I prompted.

"I had a boyfriend once, my longest relationship. I used to give him compliments all the time. He made fun of me, so I eventually stopped. Looking back, I was attracted to him because he was like my family, or I knew he'd treat me the same way they had. I was attracted to what I knew. But I want to be different with you. I want to change and heal. So because of that..." Her hands flattened, fingers spreading apart. "You're hot, Tyler."

My lips curved up. "I'm aware but keep going."

"You're very hot."

I tugged her against me. "You're making me hard."

"You are sexy."

"Mmmm..." I nuzzled under her ear, feeling her shiver. "Say more. Please."

She laughingly pressed a finger to my forehead and pushed me back. "If we don't get going, we're going to be late. I can't be late for Coach's dinner."

Tugging on my hands, she led us out of there and to the elevator. There was a couple already inside. The guy recognized me, but we got to the lobby before he could say anything. I didn't mind the random fan. It didn't happen that often, but it felt weird on Thanksgiving.

On the way to Coach's, Rain was quiet. I reached over for her hand. "You okay? It's Thanksgiving. Normal families do family things. Did you want to try and see Mal at all?"

She went eerily still, her eyes going vacant for a moment before she shook her head. "No. I think it's too soon. Maybe next year."

I said, "Maybe Christmas?"

She was quiet again before she jerked her head up and down. "Yeah. Christmas. I'll mention it to him."

I squeezed her hand.

She squeezed it back. "Uh, we still need to have *our* talk."

"We will. We could leave Ski's a little early. Make time for us tonight."

"I like that idea. Us time. Tonight."

So that was the plan.

68
TYLER

Thanksgiving at Coach's was fun. Interesting. Coach's wife went nuts over Rain, which I wasn't surprised about. And I met his daughters, who looked like Amazonian women. I knew they'd played ice hockey in college, but they hadn't gone pro. Instead one was a teacher, and one was a head of physical therapy at some elite program. They were impressive, as were their husbands. Their kids were excited and hyper, running everywhere. A few got big eyes when they saw me, but they didn't come over.

And lots of guys from the team showed up. We had our own table in the kids' room.

Meester seemed right at home, sitting on the floor, eating a big slab of turkey with one hand and putting together a LEGO hockey rink with Coach Hine's four-year-old grandson with the other. One of the little girls sat on his other side, putting a dress on a stuffed dog. Every now and then, Meester would reach over and give the dog a pet, making the little girl dissolve in giggles.

More than once, Coach's wife came over to pull Rain off somewhere, and I lost track of her for twenty minutes or so.

Checking my phone, I saw it'd been at least an hour this time, so I made my excuses to the guys at the table and began my search to find her.

I moved past the back room in the basement and drew up short, hearing Rain's voice.

"—need, really. Everything turned out fine."

"But it wasn't, was it?" That was Coach's wife, and her voice was sharp. "I've been trying to work up my nerve all day to apologize. When Bruce told me about seeing a girl playing with the Connors boys, I had a feeling. It didn't sit right. I couldn't let it go. I should have stepped in. Reached out. Introduced myself to your father. Met you. I..."

She got quiet. "When Bruce said you were working with their team, I took this as my second chance. I know you're older. You're an adult, and you probably don't need a mother-like figure nosing around in your life, but if you'd like one, I'm here. This family is here. Bruce too. He told me how nervous he got when you first showed up, said he stumbled something fierce, but you righted him just fine. I was proud when he told me that. Proud of you. And so was he, even though he was embarrassed." She sniffled. "I wanted you to know that."

There was a beat of silence. I wondered if I should make an appearance, maybe pull Rain out of the situation, but then she said, "There was nothing you could've done."

I stayed where I was.

"I should've tried."

"No. I'm—he never would've let me go, because it could've come back as an embarrassment on him. He didn't want to deal with me, but he also didn't want to look bad. Does that make sense?"

"That doesn't matter. I should've—"

"I wouldn't have trusted you," Rain said.

It got quiet again.

"I was conditioned to be a certain way, think a certain way,"

Rain explained. "I'm an adult, and I'm just now starting to change those thought processes. Back then? Around the time you would've stepped up for me? Even if he had let me go to live with you or something, it wouldn't have mattered. I would've slept in your house. I would've played my part, not drawn any attention to myself. I would have sat at every meal uncomfortable and sweating, worried my answers to your questions could be turned against me somehow. If my family talked to me, that's what they did. I was too far gone. I think I'm too far gone now."

"Rain. No. Don't *ever* think that. Please."

There was another moment of quiet, and when I heard Rain draw in a quiet breath, I knew she was struggling.

I stepped around the corner to find her fighting tears.

Both women looked up.

"Tyler." Mrs. Hines patted under her eyes with her fingertips, giving me a slightly uneasy smile. "I must say, you've been a welcome addition to the team. Bruce told me you brought a no-nonsense, why-the-fuck-aren't-we-winning attitude. I believe that's how he put it." She smiled more genuinely now. "He said the other guys needed that."

I checked on Rain, asking without words if she was all right. She gave me a little smile, but as I stepped closer, she moved to my side and sagged against me.

She wasn't okay.

I wrapped an arm around her and smiled at Mrs. Hines. "The guys are good. I think we'll go far this season." I held Rain tightly against me. "I came to find Rain because we actually have another meal to get to. My sister is hosting a Thanksgiving thing as well."

"Of course. I hope your niece is doing so much better." Mrs. Hines began leading the way back upstairs. When we got to the first floor, she motioned for us to follow her into the kitchen. "Can I talk you into taking some leftovers with you?"

She didn't give us a chance to respond, just began putting together four plates of food, filling each one to the brim. When they were done, she wrapped them in plastic wrap and put all four in a bag before handing it over.

We thanked her and then said our farewells, making the rounds in each room. The Minnesota goodbye was a real challenge here, but finally we got to the door. Mrs. Hines moved in to hug Rain, and I could see she was struggling not to cry all over again.

Coach gave me an apologetic look before tugging his wife away. He rested an arm around her shoulders and nodded. "We'll be seeing you for morning skate. And you asked to work tomorrow, so I'll expect you bright and early as well, Rain."

"Got it, Coach." Rain answered for both of us, stepping outside. Suddenly the weather was normal again. It was cold as fuck. Once the door closed behind her, she went pale. I didn't think the weather had anything to do with it.

"Rain?"

She tore off, hurrying to my truck.

I hustled after her, hitting the unlock button so she could get in without waiting. I hit the start button too, so the engine was rumbling before I got behind the wheel.

Rain was bent over, her fists pressed against her eyes. She rocked back and forth, a raw sound coming from her that didn't sound altogether human.

I touched her back. "Rain?"

She flew upright at my touch, exploding, "She would've adopted me! That's what she told me in there. If she'd known exactly what my situation was, she would've tried to adopt me. She knew enough, knew something wasn't right, but she didn't push. She…" The fight suddenly left her, as if she'd deflated.

"You told her it wouldn't have mattered."

"I lied," she said flatly. "I said that to make her feel better, but I lied. Yes, there would've been a time period where I didn't trust them. But eventually, if they'd stuck it out with me, it would've helped. It would've made so much difference. But even as I say that, something in me thinks, *why would they have wasted that on me?* I had shelter. I had food. I was physically safe. Others had it worse. They should've adopted someone else if they were going to help anyone."

"Rain..." I started, not totally sure what to say.

"And he wasn't even my father. Not my real one. I didn't know! I wished I had known. Why did my mom lie to everyone about that? She could've—things could've been better." She was back to whispering, her voice coming out sounding so tiny. "He didn't know I wasn't his and he *still* treated me like that. I—why? Was it just because I was a girl? Did he actually know he wasn't my real dad? Maybe he could sense it, but no. He would've kicked me out. I know he would've. And if someone questioned him, he would've told them I wasn't his kid so why did he need to put up with me?" Tears kept streaming down her face. One silent trail after another. She wasn't even fighting them. "What was so wrong with me?"

I reached over, cupped the back of her neck, and held her tight. "You did nothing wrong. There *is* nothing wrong with you. The problem lies with him. With them. Not you. You hear me? Not. You. I don't ever want to hear you say that again. There's *nothing* wrong with you. There is *only* good in you. You got me?"

"Tyler," she whimpered, closing her eyes and letting her head fall forward.

Christ. I wanted to take the world on for her. She didn't deserve to feel this. Not her. I meant what I said. She was only good.

"You went to the hospital with me."

"What?"

I said it again. "You went to the hospital with me. You went there not knowing what you were going to walk into, and you still went. You were by my side. You went to get us coffees. You are everything that's right in the world, and you don't have one clue about it. You are my sunshine. Day one, I wanted you. Day two, I never wanted to leave your side. You've become my foundation and baby, I'm generally rock solid. I don't really need a foundation, but I'm addicted to you. I can't leave you. Like, literally. Ever. There are not enough words to tell you how much I love you, how much I need you. You steady me. You are brave. You inspire me. I want to be better for you, because of you. You make me a better person and that says everything about you. You might be slow to letting people in, but that's the only flaw I can see in you and I don't think that's even a flaw. I got a feeling that when you love, you love hard and I will sign up any day and every day for some of that goodness from you." I squeezed the back of her neck, gently. "Do you believe me?"

She held my gaze, a few more tears sliding down her face, but there was a hole in her pain. Some of the sun I knew in her started to peek out. She said, "Yeah."

"Good."

"It's all fresh."

"What is?"

"This. Me." She pointed at her head. "This shit that's in there. I didn't know there was a name for it." She was quiet a moment. "I told you about Mal, how he found me at the bar yesterday. He told me about his cousin." She looked up at me as I began massaging her neck. "Ty, Miriam was like me. We didn't get into that last night, but she was like me." Her eyes filled with tears again, along with a flash of annoyance. She wiped savagely at her face. "I've not cried in years, because there was no point, and now for the last twenty-four hours, I can't stop crying."

She closed her eyes, and I knew she was going to get lost in her head.

I let go of her neck and took one her hands, pulling it into my lap. "Tell me about Mal's cousin."

She gazed back at me with such sorrow, the words coming out in a whisper, "I can't. I—I just can't, because if I do, if I tell you the name, and you look it up, it's a road map to my entire childhood. But it makes me feel less crazy. It makes me feel that a part of me was normal, and maybe if I'd grown up in a household like that, I might not have..." She trailed off, looking toward Coach's house.

"You might not have what?"

She shook her head, looking my way again. "Tonight? I'll tell you everything tonight."

I laced our fingers together. "Okay. Tonight."

As I put the truck in drive and eased away from the curb, she whispered, "Please don't leave me after you find out how messed up I am inside."

I squeezed her hand so tightly, only loosening my hold when I worried I might break her fingers. "I'll never fucking leave you because of something that was done to you."

"Promise."

"You're only sunshine, cupcakes, and lilacs to me. Only good in you. That's the easiest promise I've ever made in my life."

I was really, *really* looking forward to the game tomorrow against her brother.

69

RAIN

"How was the dinner at Coach's house?" I overheard Sky ask Tyler in the kitchen.

They were washing dishes while Zoey and I were in the living room. There was a movie playing on the television, but I wasn't paying attention.

"My mom said you were a counselor?" Zoey asked, her eyes wide as she curled up in the corner of the couch. She had a pillow and blanket pulled over her lap, and she looked almost as if she were trying to hide. Her brown hair was piled in a messy bun on top of her head, and she wore Tyler's jersey. She and her mother were matching, actually. Sky said they'd changed as soon as their first batch of company left. When we got here, they'd thrown their hands in the air yelling, "Ta da! We're thankful for you."

I'd never seen Tyler smile so wide. It took my breath away. After that, we'd sat down for a drink and snacks, though no one was hungry. All of us were stuffed from our earlier meals.

I sat up a little straighter to answer Zoey. She was asking for a reason. I shook my head. "I didn't go to school specifically for that." I smiled. "My specialty is sports psychology and team dynamics."

She tucked her blanket under her chin. "My therapist said going to therapy doesn't mean something is wrong with me. It just means I'm brave enough to try to separate the ouchies on my inside from the ouchies on the outside." She made a face. The blanket slipped down to her lap. "I think she mostly talks to little kids, but she's the one my mom feels comfortable with me talking to." She furrowed her brow. "But there are different specialties?"

The professional in me took over, and it became clear in my mind. I was here for one reason right now, and that was Zoey. "Yes," I told her. "There are lots of different specialties. Family therapists, sex therapists…"

She giggled.

My lips curved up. "There are counselors for eating disorders, addiction, alcoholism. All kinds of things. And there are psychiatrists, psychologists, mental health workers, social workers, and occupational therapists. But their main goal is always to help. Are you enjoying talking to your therapist?"

I did not miss the way she looked toward the kitchen. Tyler and Sky had quieted, but the water continued running. They were still washing dishes.

Zoey picked at her blanket. "It's okay."

Right. Okay. I felt like she really wanted to say something.

Zoey was not a player or an athlete. She was Tyler's niece. I needed to adjust my approach and bring myself more to the forefront. "Listen, it's not my place to speak on your mom's behalf, but I can tell you that she's an adult. She probably has a whole plan for how to help you, but the bottom line is that she just wants to help. That's it. If you don't like your counselor, there are other counselors. Other therapists. But the biggest thing is you. Your mom's not a mind-reader, though it would be awesome and terrifying if she were." Zoey's lip twitched, and I mirrored her grin. "I think you just gotta tell her what's going on with you."

She nodded, going back to picking at her blanket. "Yeah. I know."

God. I didn't know this girl. We had no relationship to lean on. I didn't know the right words to say, but I sensed so much pain. I had to wonder for a second if it was mine. Or if it was hers and somehow, I was feeling it? There'd been times when that sort of thing occurred with me.

"I was at the hospital," I told her.

She looked up at my words. She went so still.

"I was really nervous."

"*You* were?" She tilted her head.

I nodded. "Yeah. Because your uncle and your mom didn't know who I was at the time, who my brother was."

"Oh." She tugged the blanket up again. "He dated my mom, right?"

My throat swelled up, painfully, as I nodded. "He was mean."

She went back to picking at the blanket, not looking at me. "That's what she said. He was mean to her, and he ghosted her after the car accident."

A sudden clarity washed through me. I didn't know why or where it had come from, but I almost laughed. "You know, I used to blame myself for that car accident."

Her eyes were so big. "Why? Were you there?"

"No." I did laugh this time, because it was so silly, what I had let Daniel put in my head. "He was mad at me that day." I rolled my eyes. "I never got to watch television, and back then, we didn't have all the different things you could watch TV on now, or at least I didn't. My brothers always monopolized the television, watching tape or games. But for once, I'd gotten it. Our other brother was gone, and I knew Daniel was leaving for a date, so I was excited to watch a movie. But then he came down and demanded to check the scores for whatever game was on that day. I don't know why he couldn't check on the computer or his phone. I think he was just pissed that I looked comfortable in the living room. He liked to make me go to my room as much as possible, but since no one else was around, I refused to change the channel for him. I was adamant that it was my turn, and I was going to watch the movie I wanted to watch. He was so mad at me. He stormed out." I looked over at her. "That was the night he and your mom got into their car accident." I shivered, remembering how I'd enjoyed that evening. I'd watched the movie and gone to bed. When I woke up later that night, Daniel was standing in my doorway. He was covered in blood. "He blamed me."

"*What?*" She inhaled. "How?"

"Said it was my fault he was in such a pissed-off mood, and if he hadn't been so angry, he wouldn't have missed the stop sign." *Jesus.* "I believed him for years—until just now, actually, which is sad in a whole other way. But it didn't occur to me that he had driven that route so many other times. They were going to his favorite restaurant. He knew the stop sign was there. He rolled it because he liked to roll through stop signs. The other driver had been drinking and hit them, but if he hadn't rolled that stop sign, they wouldn't have been hit. And he was in an angry mood because he was always in an angry mood. It had nothing to do with me. But he blamed me because that's what he did. He always blamed someone."

"Wait. So..." Zoey frowned and moved to sit so she was facing me. She drew her knees up against her chest and wrapped her arms around them. "That's the car accident where my mom got her brain injury?"

"Yeah." That accident was not my fault. The weight of it lifted from my chest. It wasn't my fault. Skylar's brain injury *was not* my fault.

She shook her head. "That's messed up. That's, like—your brother was an asshole."

I laughed. "Yeah. He really was. He really is."

"I'm sorry you thought that this whole time. My mom didn't blame you, did she?"

"Oh no. I've never said anything—"

"Because she wouldn't." Zoey's gaze was so fierce. She leaned toward me. "I know my mom, and she would never say it was your fault. Ever."

I grew warm inside and my voice softened. "Yeah. I know that now, but for the longest time, I didn't. I never told anyone that Daniel blamed me. I never even thought to share that with someone."

I saw it on her face, when a light suddenly came on. She chewed her lip as she rocked back against the couch cushion. "Oh. I see where you're going with that."

"I didn't do that on purpose. That's just from many years of bringing a conversation back on topic." My grin turned sardonic before it went sad. "Like I said before, I'm not a counselor, but the stuff I went through as a kid feels very fresh to me right now, so I can tell you that I didn't talk to anyone back then, and I wish that I had. I really, *really* wish I'd said something to someone, and if they didn't want to listen, I wish I'd kept trying until I found someone that would. If your arm is broken, and you don't tell anyone it hurts, no one can help heal your arm. It'll heal, but probably in the wrong way. You know? I'm just now starting to heal from some of the stuff that happened to me, and I don't want you to go through the years of silent suffering that I went through. Your mom loves you so much. Your uncle too. I just met Eric and Paul, but I've got a feeling Eric would literally kill someone for you."

She laughed. "Don't forget Bertle. He drives everyone crazy, but he takes care of them all. They just don't know it."

"I don't really know Bertle, but I'm looking forward to getting to know him more."

The corners of her mouth lifted in a timid smile, but I saw the fear that blazed in her eyes as well. I had laid the foundation, set up parameters so we could talk about the scary things here. Now I needed to see what she'd do. I'd told her something about me. I'd showed her trust, and then I'd changed my voice so it was strong, soothing, and I'd tried to reassure her that I was an adult and was here for her. I was steady. I could handle whatever she wanted to say to me.

In the back of my mind, I knew the water had stopped running in the kitchen. There was absolute silence except for the movie playing on the television.

She looked up, her eyes shining with unshed tears.

I went for it, speaking in a low tone, "Zoey? Can I ask you something? About your overdose?"

Time seemed to stand still, until she finally nodded.

I took a breath. "Was it accidental?"

Tears fell, and she crumbled, shaking her head.

My heart pounded. "You tried to..."

I didn't need to keep going. She jerked her head up and down, her tears flowing.

I sat still. I allowed her to sit with her emotions and feel them, feel whatever she needed to feel. She needed to express it, and if I moved to hug her, that might change our course.

She opened her mouth, but she was gasping for breath.

"You can take your time," I murmured.

She hung her head, and those tears never stopped. "It hurts to talk." She patted her chest.

"Sometimes the more important the words are, the harder it is to say them."

Her knees fell, and she sat cross-legged. Finally, in a small voice, she said, "I went to a party and I—" Her chest heaved again.

I waited.

She sniffled. "I went to a party at a friend's house and went to her mom's bathroom. There were pills in there and I..." She took another deep breath. She looked up and cleared her throat. "I took them home because I wanted to—" She began crying again, giant sobs crashed through her, one after another. "I didn't mean for my mom to find me. Not her. I didn't—"

Movement came from beside me as Skylar stepped out of the hallway.

Zoey paled. "Mom. I—I—I'm so sorry. I didn't—"

"Baby." Skylar rushed to her, pulling her into a hug and smoothing a hand through her hair, rocking her back and forth. "Oh, baby. I'm so sorry."

The dam broke with Zoey, and she sobbed into her mom's arms. Her cries were loud and guttural, and they broke my heart.

Then Tyler was there, blinking back his own tears, his eyes on me.

I studied him. Was he angry with me? There was such torment on his face as he blinked and turned to his sister and niece. He moved past me, but his hand came to my knee and squeezed before he sat on the other side of Zoey. She was sandwiched between her mom and her uncle.

Skylar didn't lift her head from where it was buried in her daughter's neck, but she reached out with one arm to clasp onto Tyler. He reached back for her, and the three of them were together. That's how they sat for a long while, like a family.

70

TYLER

Later that night, Rain was quiet on the way back to her hotel. I glanced over, the sound of the wipers filling the air. We hadn't turned the radio on, and it had started to snow. Tonight had been *a lot*. The previous twenty-four hours had been a lot. *Fuck.* The whole week had been intense. Rain was quiet, withdrawn, and looking out the window I was suddenly really tired of going to a hotel in order to be with her.

"I need to get an apartment."

"What?" She frowned at me. "You didn't sign just for a year. They locked you in for five years, right? You should get a house. Move Skylar and Zoey in with you."

I shot her a look. She wasn't including herself? "Thank you for tonight," I told her.

I hadn't said it earlier, but I'd felt it. Zoey hugged Rain before going to bed, and then Skylar had hugged her so tightly I worried she might break my woman's bones. As soon as Zoey's bedroom door had shut, Skylar broke down and clung to Rain, thanking her profusely.

Rain had smiled, hugged Skylar back, and said, "I just nudged the door open. That's it. She wanted to say it. Sometimes it's easier to tell someone who's not so close, someone more impartial. I think it would've come out soon anyway."

Skylar had needed to hear that, and she'd thanked her for saying that too.

We hadn't stayed much longer, as things felt a little surreal and heavy. Now the air in my truck felt just as heavy. Was that an emotional hangover from what Zoey had confessed? I gripped the steering wheel. "She's going to get her help."

Rain turned my way.

"We didn't have time to get into it, but she's going to get Zoey all the help. Not that she wasn't before. She was just—Ski doesn't trust a lot of people, but there was one social worker that helped us. Helped her, really. I don't understand all that stuff, but I know you helped tonight. And you're acting all impartial about it and chill, but it was a big fucking deal what you did. You helped Zoey, and you helped my sister, and you helped me, and I don't get why you're sitting there all cold—"

"I wanted to kill myself too."

I stopped breathing as those words echoed in the truck.

Fucking Christ.

I hit the blinker and pulled into the nearest parking lot. As soon as I knew I wasn't going to crash the truck, I put it in park and turned her way.

"When you were a kid too? A teenager?"

Rain faced forward. Her eyes weren't on me. I didn't like that. I wanted to see her.

"No," she said after a moment. "I still had hope back then. I don't know how or where it came from, but I wasn't done yet."

Jesus. A vacant expression came over her. Her words sounded empty. "I'd bought a gun the day Mal Benoit called me. I decided I was *done*, so I went and bought a gun and brought it back to my apartment. Then I just stared at it."

She laughed, though she still wasn't looking at me. "I freaked out. The phone rang, and I came here and took this job and..." She stopped talking. She just looked like a statue. "You—when I met Mal for dinner and realized the team he wanted me to help was a hockey team, I had so many feelings rushing through me, but I wanted it."

She finally turned my way, that beautiful, haunted face finally looked at me. I saw the spark in her eyes. I saw the hunger.

"I wanted it so badly because I'd forgotten how much I loved hockey," she said. "I'd loved it too, and they took it away from me." Tears filled her eyes. "My brothers became these fucking NHL superstars, and I had to hide because I didn't want anyone to know I was their sister. Fuck them. *Fuck them*. Mal offered me a chance to come back into this world, and I took it, and I don't regret it. Not one *fucking* bit."

Her eyes pled with me, as if asking for permission.

I reached for her hand. "You can feel however you want. They've taken enough from you."

She squeezed my hand. "Daniel found out I'm here. I don't know how, but that TikTok was him trying to scare me away."

"I know."

Her knuckles were white. "They conditioned me to believe I didn't matter. I don't know if they did it on purpose. I doubt it. It was just something they did. My dad didn't want me, and my brothers followed suit." She looked at me a moment. "You're my brother's enemy, but so am I. Daniel did that. *He* made me his enemy, and I never knew why. What was so wrong with me? Daniel saw me, hated me, and emotionally abused me. Dane just never saw me."

She glanced my way. "I went into psychology to try to fix myself, but I couldn't. I just thought—I thought I wasn't worth anyone loving me." She closed her eyes, and her head hung down. "I've carried that with me all this time—that I don't matter, that something's wrong with me, that no one will love me. I gave up. I accepted that I'd be alone for the rest of my life, but I was *so lonely*." She shook her head. "I was lonely, and I was so tired of being alone, and there was no reason to keep going. There was no hope anymore. So I bought a gun."

She turned away.

I didn't have one fucking clue what to say or how to respond. Jesus Christ. *What should I do?* "Rai—"

"But there's a name for how I grew up. A name." She looked at me, her eyes shining and alive. "That means there are others like me. They've been researched and identified. There are enough of us to make an identifiable list of our qualities, our characteristics. I'd accepted that I was alone." Her voice rose, but it shook. "I thought I was the problem, and Mal gave me a name, a name I should've known, but I didn't!"

"But you know now."

She was breathing hard now and she nodded. "I was going to kill myself. I bought that gun. Sure, I freaked out, but I know what I would've done. Eventually I would've pulled the trigger. But Mal called. That call, coming here, coming back to hockey, meeting you—you saved my life. That call brought me to you. Brought me to another brother and maybe... It wouldn't have been enough just to have hockey again. I needed you."

"Baby," I said, brokenly. "I have no idea what to say or do. I've got no clue how to be here for you."

She shook her head, holding on to my hand. "You don't have to say anything. I'm not Zoey. My stuff is different. I was resigned to dying. I just didn't see why I should keep going, but Zoey's different. I think hers was an impulsive decision? I don't know. That's for Zoey and Skylar and whoever she ends up seeing as a professional to unpack. They'll dive into that and help her. She will get help. Saying it is always the first step. And it's terrifying." She gazed at me. "It's really terrifying."

"You're scared now?" I reached for her, my hand sliding along her jaw, cupping her face.

She blinked and nodded. "Yeah," she said quietly. "I feel like a fraud."

"What? Why?"

"Because maybe I shouldn't be doing what I do considering—"

"*Fuck that*," I growled. "In one sitting, my niece told you she'd tried to kill herself. In one fucking sitting, you got her to open up. You've helped me. What you said to me about the team, they meant everything. And you know as well as I do what you've done with the team—what you've done with countless teams. Stop that line of thinking. No one is perfect, Rain. Not one person. And it's harder for women sometimes. I get that. I see it, but you and Skylar are the two strongest people I have ever met. Whatever you're thinking about, whatever spiral you want to fall into, just stop it." I leaned over, resting my forehead to hers and holding her face in my hands. "I need you here. I want you whole, and I'll be with you every step of the way, to help in any way you need it. You hear me? I got you. The team has you. My sister will never let you go now. You're not going anywhere, and all you need to do from now is do your job and take care of yourself. That's it. The rest of us will have your back, okay?" I lifted my head but held her gaze.

Her eyes searched mine, and after a moment, they changed. "Thank you."

"For what?"

She shrugged sheepishly. "You were here for me." She smiled and reached for me. "For me, you being here, listening to me, letting me talk, seeing me, hearing me, that's all I need. That's all I needed. You see me."

"I will always see you. I love you."

"I love you too." She glanced away for a second. "I'm going to find a professional to talk to, someone who specializes in the lost child role."

"That's the name?"

"Yeah. The lost child syndrome. Or the invisible child. For me, it was the same thing." She nodded to herself, seeming determined. "It helped a lot to find out the name for what I was. It's helped so much, even in a short amount of time, but I'm not going to lie. I am hard-wired to believe you don't love me. I've been conditioned that you and everyone else will eventually leave, that you'll suddenly realize I'm not worth it. Please be patient with me. I'm going to be fighting myself. And it's...it's going to be hard."

"Rain." I leaned in, finding her mouth. "I'm going to do so much research and studying and talking to your professional person," I told her between kisses. "I'll be able to take one look at you and know what you're struggling with. That's my goal. And you need to know that in the Griffin family, we're one for all, like those Mouse people."

"Mouse people?"

"The Mousksters. Those people."

"The Musketeers?"

"Yeah. Those people. You're the fourth one. Don't tell Eric. Ski says he thinks he's the fourth member of the family, now that he's met me and you. I think your days of hiding are over. You've got too many people who'll put out an APB if you try isolating yourself again."

She grinned at me. She looked good.

She gave me another kiss and murmured, "We can go home, baby."

I liked hearing her call me that. I liked it a whole lot, but a new type of worry sprang to life. I never would've thought she was the type to buy a gun and consider what she was going to do. Never. I'd met her and wanted her. She'd seemed good. Beautiful. She looked capable. Strong. Assertive. Now to find out she'd been wanting to die for years? I would've had no idea if she hadn't said the words to me tonight. Not one inkling.

"You don't think Zoey's like..."

"Like what?" she asked.

"The way you were treated growing up—you think Zoey's treated like that?"

"No!" She grasped my hand and shook her head fervently. "God, no. I don't know why Zoey felt the way she did. It could be because something happened at school. Or she suffers from depression? I don't know, but Zoey is not me. Zoey is loved. She's seen. You switched NHL teams and moved across the country because your family needed you, because she needed you. Trust me. Zoey is not me." She peered at me intently. "She will get the help she needs. I have all the faith. You and Skylar, you rallied around her. I really think she's going to be okay."

Some of my fears lessened. "And you? If you're ever thinking of doing something again?"

That's what worried me now. She could hide it so well. She had hidden it, but maybe that was part of the invisible kid thing? I didn't know. I needed to learn about it.

She drew in a breath. "I think with me, it's going to take time. I need to find someone who can help me. Then I'll know more about how you can help. But I can tell you I don't want to do anything with that gun anymore. I have you. I have hockey again. I have friends. I have hope. I'd lost hope. The world went gray and stayed gray and I didn't see any more color coming. But then it did. If I ever do have those thoughts, I'll come to you."

"Promise me." If she was suddenly not here one day? "Promise me, Rain."

"I promise," her voice went quiet again and she repeated it. "I promise." She released her seatbelt and clambered over to me.

I hit my seat, pushing it as far back as possible so she could straddle me. Her forehead came to mine, and her hair fell like a curtain around us, cocooning us in our own world.

I breathed her in, cupcakes and lilac, and knew I'd want this world with her forever. "Don't ever leave me," I said raggedly.

"I won't." Her mouth found mine, and I was swept up in all things Rain.

It rattled me, thinking about a world without her, a life without her. "I want to marry you."

She stiffened before lifting her head. "What?"

"I..." I closed my mouth. "Well, fuck."

71

TYLER

"Yo." Bruge skated up to me the next afternoon and held out his gloved hand. "We got this." He glanced my way but turned his attention to the Montreal skater I'd been watching for the last couple minutes.

It was warmups. I wasn't supposed to be standing on the red line, but I couldn't bring myself to leave. I hated this fucking guy, Daniel Connors. The second he'd taken the ice, he was skating around with his helmet off, eyeing our bench. Like he was daring Rain to come out.

"You should be stretching if you're going to stand here."

I grunted at Bruge.

"Coach is starting my line."

"What?" Now he had my attention. Bruge was our enforcer. "Why's he doing that?"

"Why do you think?" He went back to watching Montreal's captain. "Same as with Boston. Both teams know what's going to happen."

"What if he doesn't fight?"

Bruge laughed. "Are you kidding me? I could make him fight me right now."

I smirked. "Do it."

Bruge shook his head. "I've got a feeling Connors has no idea what's in store for him tonight."

"What was that?" The guy we were speaking about had skated past us but now pivoted back in a tight circle. I'd been dealing with his assholery all my life but knowing how he'd treated Rain growing up just made me angrier.

Before Bruge could say anything, I was in Connors's face. "Step the fuck back, Connors. We can say whatever we want about you until that puck drops."

"Oooh. Big guy, huh? You're so tough now?" he taunted.

The crowd noticed what was going on and began cheering. Boos broke out as well. They wanted blood, and we were in our hometown. They wanted Connors's blood specifically. The sport was brutal sometimes.

"Okay. Enough of this." A ref was between us in no time, his hands up. "Save it for the game. Get back to warmups."

"How's my sister? She still a brat like she always was?"

I saw red. Reaching for him, I tried to yank his jersey since the fucker didn't have his helmet. I wanted him close so when I hit him, it would land. I didn't want him to be able to skate out of the way.

The crowd went nuts.

"Hey! Stop it. Both of you." Two more refs got between us and shoved us away from each other.

"Keep fucking talking," I told him. "Keep doing it."

"Dude." Sunny skated over, shoving me back. "You're mic'd. Are you crazy?"

Shit. I'd forgotten. What a game to be mic'd up.

Connors was laughing. He craned his neck around the ref and his teammates that had come over to help. "I have a better question. How's *your* sister doing? I'm in town for the holidays. Maybe I'll give her a call. See how she's doing myself."

I went for him again.

"Fuck. Griffin. Stop." Sunny and Jesse both helped the ref push me back.

I needed to get my shit together. If I didn't, the refs were going to give me a penalty before the game even started.

Daniel continued laughing, loud and caustic-sounding, then suddenly it dried up. His eyes got unnaturally big, and he froze in place. His gaze moved past me.

I looked, cursing when I saw that Rain had stepped out into the bench along with a couple of the other assistant coaches. Her eyes were on her brother, but they held no fear. She wasn't shaking or trembling. She'd told me she could compartmentalize, and I was seeing it in action. Her chin lifted, and her eyes were cool. Rock solid.

She took in the scene before her eyes returned to her brother. "Still the bully, I see. You have two little girls, Danny. Do 'em a favor. Grow up for them."

Rage transformed Daniel's face. His nostrils flared. He looked like a bull about ready to charge, and he lunged for her. But there were too many people between him and Rain—me, Bruge, Sunny, Jesse, three refs, two of Daniel's own teammates, and now Meester and Brick as well.

"You shut up about them. They'll never meet you—"

"Hey!" One of the Montreal's coaches got on the ice, holding his clipboard. He stepped close in front of Daniel, and Daniel did nothing more except shoot Rain a nasty look and skate away. The coach turned around and focused on Rain. He didn't approach, but his gaze cut past all of our players to find her. "Keep to your bench."

"She *is* on our bench." Marken bristled next to her.

Rain, to her credit, didn't look ruffled at all. "How about this?" she said. "You control your player, and there will be no problem."

"Hey." Daniel had returned, slinking behind his coach. He

lifted his gaze to a corner of the stadium, giving it a meaningful stare before grinning almost maniacally at Rain.

She followed his gaze, and when she saw whoever he wanted her to see, she paled. The blood drained from her face, and she swallowed.

He laughed at her. "It's a family reunion, little sister."

I cursed under my breath. There, in one of the suites, I recognized Dane Connors. He was wearing his jersey and had two little girls and a woman next to him. She held an infant. There was an older man with them as well, and I knew in a heartbeat it was their dad. He and Daniel had the same reddish hair, and there was a jawline all the Connors shared. He wore Daniel's jersey, as did two other little girls in the suite and another woman.

"I'm going to fuck you up," I growled, going at him.

People pounded on the partitions and started a cheer, but I couldn't make out the words. I just wanted to hurt him, as badly as I could. I wanted to feel his blood on my hands.

Suddenly Bruge was in between us, his back to me, and he went after Daniel instead.

The refs had to scramble again. Bruge was our enforcer for a reason. He was big and efficient. When he swung, his hits landed every time.

All of the refs were between us now, and more of the Montreal staff joined the fray.

Coach Hines came out and barked, "Clear out. Everyone. I mean it. Griffin, you need to warm up."

One by one, we skated away, reluctant. The refs lingered, having a word with Coach and the other coaches who had stayed with Rain. I shot at the net and then circled behind to get in line from the other side, but my focus was still on our bench. I could see Rain shaking her head at something the ref had said. Daniel's teammates formed a physical barrier so he couldn't go over to our side.

For the rest of our warmups, I went through the motions, but my attention was on the other team. Daniel kept trying to skate by our bench, his face twisted in a cruel smile, and no doubt he had some form of taunt ready for his sister. He looked like he was living for this moment.

"Shows you right there what a piece of shit he is." Sunny sidled up next to me, both of us looking over. "That's how he talks to his own sister?"

We got the alert we needed to head off the ice, but Bruge stopped in front of us, skating backwards as we started for the locker room. "I'll take care of him." His dead-serious eyes found mine.

I wanted to be the one to take care of him, but I nodded. "Yeah."

Sunny laughed. "You really think he's going to be good with fighting just one of you?" He whistled under his breath. "This entire game is going to be on replay for the NHL highlights. It'll live forever on YouTube. I can't fucking wait."

Rain was still on the bench, going over something on her tablet. She didn't look rattled anymore. Annoyed, maybe.

The guys went past me, heading for the locker room.

I lingered when I reached the bench. "Hey," I said softly.

She lifted her head and fixed me with a chilled stare.

I fought against wincing, because it wasn't there because of me. I knew that. Yet I couldn't prevent how my stomach twisted up at seeing it.

I didn't say anything else, but she read my question on my face.

"I'm good," she said. "Go ahead. Coach Hines has things to say to everyone."

I nodded. She was in full professional mode. She was fully locked in.

But how big would the fallout be after this game? I

supposed we'd deal with it later. Until then, I was going to fuck up her brother.

72

RAIN

Coach Hines was finishing up his pregame speech when I slipped inside the locker room. He looked over at me and extended a hand. "Is there anything you wanted to include?"

I nodded and stepped forward. I made sure my words came out clear and calm. "Today's game is no different than any other game you've played before. If you think it's different, your brain is going to start looking for the differences. It'll look for other information to fill in, and that's not what you need today. This is a game like any other." I looked around, meeting their eyes. "I don't want your focus on the other team or my brother, though he *will be* an asshole to you. He thrives on conflict and tension. That's how he operates. Know that. Expect that from him. But there's nothing special about Daniel. He's just another bruiser trying to get in your head, so you do what you always do. You shut him out. You play the game. And with respect to whatever Coach Hines has told you, I want you to have fun out there. Don't focus on the score. Don't focus on what they're doing or what they might be doing. Focus on *your* game. Yours. Do *your* best. Compete against yourself. Beat your personal best. This is hockey. You grew up playing it. They don't want you to have fun. My brother doesn't want you to have fun. So go out and do exactly what they don't want. Remind yourself why you *love* this game."

I nodded to Coach Hines, hoping I hadn't overstepped.

He gave a nod of approval. "Okay, boys. Let's go out and do this. Have fun out there."

They rallied with a cheer, and Bruge stepped up to say a few words, which had them rallying even louder. "Let's fucking go!" he shouted, hitting the wall as he stepped out of the locker room. Each player hit the wall in the same spot as they passed, and the coaches followed.

The crowd was deafening as we came through the tunnel, and the noise went up another decibel when Brick hit the ice. Assistant Coach Marken gave me a rueful grin. "That never gets old."

Coach Hines held me back as the others moved into the bench. "They're rallying around you."

I shook my head. "Like you didn't set that up when you asked if I wanted to say something."

He shrugged. "You did good." Then he clasped me on the shoulder before joining the rest of the staff on the bench.

I lingered a little for a moment, watching from the tunnel as the players zipped around the ice before lining up for both countries' national anthems. The lights dimmed. The starters went to their spots as they were announced. The Canadian anthem played, followed by the United States' anthem, and then it was time to play hockey.

Bruge went to the face-off, but when the puck dropped, he ignored it, already dropping his gloves. The crowd went apeshit. Hands slapped against the partitions. Everyone stomped their feet Bruge went right for my brother, who met him. Both teams knew this would happen, and I knew the camera was going to look for me, so I stayed in the tunnel. Waiting.

Daniel had always lived for fighting. He loved the violence, and he used it to get in his opponents' heads. Bruge had zeroed in on him, but he was cold. Daniel was yapping, saying some shit. Bruge wasn't having it. He said nothing, his face impassive. Then he punched my brother in the head, without a word. He was out to pummel him as quickly as possible.

I saw Daniel falter, realizing this fight was different. Panic flared, briefly. His gaze cut to our bench, probably looking for me, but I wasn't there. I wanted him to flounder. If he had seen me, he might have remembered to be the asshole he'd always been, like he was fighting for our family's dynamics or something. But he was on his own with this. I caught the moment he decided to end the fight. He took Bruge to the ice. That's when the refs weighed in, stopping them. The rest of the players held back. This was business as usual.

The penalties were handed out, and both Bruge and Daniel went to the box.

Coach Hines did a line change, sending the first line out there, with Tyler taking the face-off. I moved out to the bench, standing in the back.

The game started, and it was rough. The checks were harder than normal, the skating faster.

Tyler scored while my brother was still in the penalty box, and he made sure to skate past Daniel, making eye contact with my brother with a smirk on his face. Daniel's nostrils flared. He shook his head, his mouth going, but Tyler had already passed.

I wondered what the announcers were saying, then I stopped thinking about it and took my own advice. No matter what, this was just another hockey game. Tyler's line came off, and second line went in with the third-line center filling in for Bruge until he got out of the box.

I felt Tyler's gaze on me a couple times, but I just watched the game, dissecting everything like I usually did. So far, the Grays were playing smoothly. After Bruge came out of the box, and my brother as well, the team kept strong. Sunny scored, with an assist from Tyler. They made sure to celebrate as close to the Montreal's bench as possible. And every single one of the Grays players looked over, finding my brother as they skated past.

I didn't go into the locker room during the period break. I usually didn't, preferring to let them keep to their routine. I stayed back and went over some notes. When it was time for the second period to start, the crowd was on their feet. Montreal hit the ice, and a chant rose up from the stands.

It took a second before I figured out the words.

"*Fuck you, Daniel. Fuck you! Fuck you, Daniel. Fuck you!*"

Javier, one of the assistant coaches, came over and showed me his tablet. He'd pulled up a clip from when Tyler and my brothers played in the state championship against each other. The crowd had chanted a similar jeer, "*Fuck you, Griffin. Fuck you!*"

These fans had turned it around.

"I think they went for your brother's first name because of you," Javier said. "We've got a Connors too."

I grinned. "It's perfect. Makes it more personal for Daniel." I was a little horrified that my nieces could hear this, but hockey fans were going to do what hockey fans were going to do. The chant wouldn't last long.

What I didn't say was that it wasn't likely to get in Daniel's head. If anything, my brother would thrive on the attention and the booing. He always liked it when the other team's fans hated him. That made him bigger and badder in their minds. And I saw it happening in real time. His chest puffed out and a cocky, shit-eating grin spread on his face. It was visible through his visor.

He skated past our bench, finding me, and I shook my head,

trying to convey that I knew what he was thinking. He was so fast that I don't know if it worked.

"He thinks he's such a legend."

I drew up short, surprised to find Meester had come up next to me. "What?"

"It's making it worse, isn't it?" He held up a glove toward the fans. "He's getting off on it."

I noted some of the fourth-line players paying attention to our conversation. I tapped one of them on the shoulder. "Take my brother out."

"Huh?" He gaped at me.

Their fourth-line winger's head snapped toward me, but he didn't say anything.

"He wants to fuck with our heads, but let's fuck with his instead," I told them. "My brother thinks this game is about him. It's not. He's not some hockey god among the mortals. He's just like you. Let's remind him of that. If a fourth-liner checks him, he'll feel disrespected."

One of the other guys leaned forward. "How about if only the fourth line goes after him?"

I fought back a smile. That would curdle my brother's blood. I met his eyes, keeping my voice neutral. "This is hockey, boys. Remember what I said in the locker room. Have fun." I paused. "However you deem that should be."

The matching grins on their faces sent a chill through me.

Javier whistled, moving aside. "This should be fun," he mumbled. He went over to Coach Hines, and their heads bent together for a moment. Coach glanced my way, a glimmer of amusement in his eyes before he barked out, "Fourth line, you're going to stay out a little longer for a few rounds."

He'd just given his approval. My brother was going to hate it.

For the rest of the second period, the fourth line as a whole went after my brother, but only the fourth line. It pissed my brother off, but he tried to rally. The crowd didn't understand what was going on. Their "fuck you, Daniel" chant had petered out, so now they just booed anytime he was on the ice.

Knowing Daniel, though, he didn't even hear their boos. He never had. He could tune them out. I knew because I'd been part of his training.

The second period ended right after Montreal scored. But they would still go into the third period down by one.

"You want to say anything?" Marken paused next to me as everyone headed down the tunnel. "Coach Hines wants to know."

"No. Just do what you normally do."

"Will do." He patted me on the shoulder. "Having him as a brother? People are watching. Fans are watching. And they all know. From my perspective, you're coming off like a smooth motherfucker. Fans are rallying around you too, if you pay attention."

He followed the team to the locker room.

I looked around the arena. I never paid attention to the fans. Football fans had no idea who I was, but hockey was different. I hadn't dared to look in the stands. I did now. Tentatively. A few girls near our bench noticed me looking and both immediately smiled. They nudged the guys they were with, and those guys each gave me a nod in respect.

"We got you, little Connors," one of them said.

I could read his lips.

A strange sensation went through me. Even as an adult, my expectation was that they would hate me. The fans. The players. Everyone. I forced myself to smile, trying to convey that I appreciated the respect before I moved down the tunnel.

I needed a moment and stepped into the bathroom.

Fans were fans. They could like me now and hate me within five minutes. I knew not to take anything personally. But having them show their support for me? Even for a moment? It shook me.

And I let it. I set a timer on my phone for one minute, and I let myself spiral—feeling, doubting, wondering, worrying. But when that alarm beeped, I stopped it. Full stop. Period. I was done indulging. I put everything away in my head. Locking it up, compartmentalizing every thought, doubt, and fear until it was all gone.

My mind was clear.

My emotions were steady.

I was ready for the third period.

73

TYLER

Third period was frustrating. It was back and forth the entire time. I got the puck. They took it back. Sunny got it, passed it, and they intercepted it. We checked each other hard into the boards. That was the game but tonight was especially rough. I wanted another goal. I wanted two more, and then we'd have some room to breathe. But Montreal was on our ass. When we got down to the two-minute mark, their goalie skated off and an extra shooter came on the ice.

When our line changed, I stayed, along with one of our defensemen. Daniel was on the ice, so I wasn't going anywhere. During the change, they took hold of the puck and tried to make a run for the net. They were passing, trying to draw us out, but we held them in place. They couldn't get near the goal, and they weren't getting a clear shot.

Then one of their guys swung to pass and missed.

I shot forward, nabbing the puck. And I was gone.

They were all behind me, and it was an empty net. I just needed to clear their last line. Two of their guys were closing in, so I tried tossing the puck into the air and over their heads. It went up as one of their guys hit me and the other tried to catch the puck in the air. He missed. It was too high, and I swung around, still with a clear line. Suddenly it was a race. The puck was sliding just to the side of the net. If I got control, I could tip it in.

Their fastest guy wasn't Connors. It was a guy named Estaban, and I assumed it was him coming after me. I reached the puck and glanced back. It *was* Estaban. He was closing in.

He expected me to tip the puck in, so he had his stick out, trying to block it. Instead I pulled to the side, and he couldn't stop. He tried to brake by grabbing the net, but it didn't matter. He sailed past me, and *then* I tipped the puck in.

The horn blasted. The red light flashed. Goal!

Throwing my arms in the air, I skated toward my bench to meet my teammates in a celly. We had won. 3-1.

"Fuck yeah, buddy!"

Just as I reached my first teammate, someone shoved me from behind.

"What?" I turned to look back, and my teammates were already in the scrum.

"Fuck off! Go fuck yourself."

"I don't think so," Bruge joined the fight.

It took me a second to realize what had happened. Jesse and Sunny had come off the bench to greet me and were now being held back by two Montreal players as Estaban tried to hold back Connors. He was spewing shit, trying to get to me.

"Fuck you, Griffin! You fucking piece of shit. You're pathetic."

I laughed, tipping my head back. "Whatever, Connors. Get over it." I gestured to the score. "You lost."

"Yeah? Well, go fuck my sister some more, then. You two deserve each other."

The game was over. The score was set. I was going to destroy him.

I shook my head, skating over to him, all nice and chill.

But as I went past Brick, he took my stick from me. Bruge took my glove. Sunny took my other glove and by that time, I was right in front of Daniel. I tipped my chin up. "You want to repeat that part about your sister again? I didn't quite catch that."

He snarled, lunging for me, but Estaban still held him back. "You fucking heard me. You were always obsessed with my family. What? You had to find the female version of me to fuc—"

I walloped him.

He didn't see it coming. Estaban didn't see it coming. And before either could recover, someone yanked Estaban out of the way and I hit Daniel again, hard enough that he tipped over into our bench. I followed, going for him again, except this time, he shook it off enough to start fighting back.

Finally. Fucking finally. I had my hands on him, and I could hit him all I wanted because of what he'd said. That was on tape. He'd come at me after the game was done. He'd shoved me from behind. I was due this fight, and I was going to deliver.

I kept hitting him, backing him all the way to the opening of our tunnel. Everyone had scattered. I felt hands trying to get between us and peel me away, but I wasn't budging. It felt *good* to hit him.

I wailed on him until finally someone got between us, managing to pull both of us away.

Daniel laughed, shaking his head and wiping a hand over his mouth. "What? You learn how to fight from my siste—"

I lunged for him again, but there were too many people between us. They held me back, but not him anymore. He straightened, unable to hold back a wince, and shook out his hand.

"You're done, Connors."

He laughed again. "Yeah?" He looked like he might chirp some more, but then his eyes went evil. *Shit*. He was going to hit me, and I couldn't defend myself. The people holding me back were holding my arms.

He reared back, and I prepared to take it, trying to maneuver my face so he would only get the side.

"Daniel!" Rain's voice came across the ice.

He faltered, turning to see her a few yards away, standing behind a couple of the assistant coaches. Her face was set in a fierce scowl, but she wasn't scared. She was pissed.

Daniel tipped his head back, more of that toxic laughter spilling from him. "Don't tell me you're on your back for all of the—"

BAM!

Daniel shut up and he fell down, because he'd just been laid out by Meester.

"Do us all a favor," Meester said calmly, standing over him. "*Please* shut the fuck up. Loser." He twisted in Rain's direction. "Think I got this assertive thing down now. Thanks, Rain."

He walked past her to the locker room.

She stared at her brother, blinking in shock.

The rest of the Montreal team swarmed in to help their teammate, and the assistant coaches motioned for us to get to the locker room. The crowd was going *insane*. We could hear them all the way down into the tunnel. It felt like the ceiling was going to cave in.

Coach Hines called us in. "We need our three stars. Bruge, you're third. Brick, you're second. Griffin, you're first. Toss your stuffed wolves to the fans and get your asses back in here."

74

RAIN

I was coming from my office when I saw Coach Hines in the hallway. He shook his head. "That was a shitshow."

I nodded. "Yes. It was."

He broke out in a grin. "But fuck if it wasn't satisfying to see Griffin let loose."

I laughed.

"Don't tell anyone I said that." He gestured toward the locker rooms. "Your boy's in with Hunter, getting his hands looked at. Again. And go home. Go celebrate the win tonight. It's still the holiday."

"Sounds good, Coach."

He waved and ducked into his office. I didn't understand the "again" part of what he'd said, but I headed for the trainer's room, where I saw him fussing over Tyler's hands.

"You can't keep doing this to your hands," Hunter said. "We need your hands. You need your hands. I shouldn't have to tell you that."

Tyler grimaced as he tried flexing his knuckles, but they were wrapped, with ice packs layered in the folds.

"You laid out my other brother, and I didn't know about it?" I asked.

Hunter shrieked, jumping and whirling around. "Oh! You scared me." Tyler grinned as Hunter stepped aside. "He's all yours."

Hunter went out, closing the door behind him. When I didn't move right away, Tyler made a grunting sound and widened his legs. "Get over here."

I lingered.

He made another exasperated sound and leaned forward, hooking a finger in my pants. He tugged me between his legs. Once I was there, he closed them behind me and pressed me against his chest. His arms went over my shoulders. "There," he said softly. His eyes traced my face, pausing on my lips. "Right where I will always want you."

My body heated. "I don't think you should say things like that when we're in the locker room."

"We're not in the locker room. We're in the trainer's room, which Hunter just turned over to us. He closed the door. Hunter never closes the door." Tyler tightened his legs around me and moved in to nuzzle my throat. "I missed you."

I closed my eyes, tingles shooting through me as he kissed my throat. We couldn't do this, but this one time I was going to give in. This *one* time. I melted into Tyler, brushing his neck with my lips as I murmured, "Did you hurt your hands before?"

He stiffened before raising his head.

I lifted my head to look back at him.

He cringed. "I...I might've lost it when you left the locker room, after you told everyone about your brothers."

My eyes widened with alarm. "What do you mean you lost it?"

He shrugged, looking away. "I might've tossed a bench."

"You tossed a bench?"

"Or two."

"*Or two?*" I could only gape at him. "What were you thinking?"

He pursed his lips together. "I wasn't. I thought they were going to let you walk out of here, away from the team, and I flipped out because I was worried I'd never see you again."

"So you lost your shit on your team?"

"Not my team. Just a few benches."

He didn't regret it. I could see that. He regretted having to tell me. I sighed. "Promise me something."

His eyes found mine. "Anything."

"Next time you're worried you're not going to see me, come after me. I'll never isolate like I did before, not from you. That's my promise to you. You'll always know where I am."

"Promise?"

"Promise."

He smirked. "That's probably a better idea."

I shook my head. "What did Coach say?"

He drew in a breath. "He gave me a lecture, similar to what you walked in on from Hunter. I had to apologize to the team and to Benny, and all the equipment staff. And of course I paid for the new ones. I got fined."

"You threw a manchild temper tantrum."

He scoffed but let his forehead fall to my shoulder. His hands curled around my hips, tugging me even closer. He'd taken a shower. His hair was still wet, and I reached up and tangled my fingers in it. He shivered at the touch, but when I let my hand drop, he shook his head, hugging me. "No. I like that."

I went back to running my hands through his hair.

"I freaked. I didn't handle it the best. That's also when I realized I loved you."

A shiver went down my spine, a good one.

Tyler lifted his head from my shoulder, a smug grin on his face. "You like hearing that, huh?"

"Shut up." I grinned, feeling my face heat. How was this

possible? The team knew about my relationship. They knew about me. And I was still here. I was standing in Tyler's arms just after a game where the entire team had gone to bat for me. I thought of all the things Coach Hines had said, his wife's concern, everything that Mal had done, stepping up and saving my job.

Finding out about Mal.

Tears rolled down my face before I knew it.

Tyler touched one of the tears. "Rain?"

I blew out an unsteady breath, trying to reel in the rest of my waterworks. "Just having a moment." My words were wobbly. "I'm realizing I've finally found my hockey family." I dug my head into Tyler's neck and shoulder as he held me.

He smoothed a hand down my back. "Get used to it, because I'm not letting you go anywhere anymore, and I highly doubt the team will either." He continued to rub my back. "I want to marry you, remember?"

"You meant that?"

He grinned at me, wickedly. "Fuck yeah, I did. Never said it before and don't intend to say it to anyone else." He gripped my hips and squeezed. "You're mine, Connors."

This man. The love I felt for him was everything. "Are you okay?" I asked. "After the game and everything?"

"Yeah. I won't get in trouble with the league. Your brother shoved me after the game was done. If anyone gets fined, it'll be him." He smiled. "I'm all good. Especially now with you here. You good?"

I nodded, resting my forehead against his. "I'm all good too."

"The guys want to celebrate again. They felt it's more appropriate tonight than any other night. You good with putting in an appearance?"

"Yep, I am." As I stepped back from him, he tugged on my shirt. "Hey."

I paused.

He wasn't looking at me. He seemed to be contemplating something. But when his eyes found mine again, they were crystal clear and filled with something vulnerable. "Want to check out apartments with me this weekend?"

I was suddenly dizzy and reached out to steady myself against his shoulder. "For you?"

"No." That vulnerable look doubled. "For us. I'm really sick of going to your hotel to see you, and this ain't ever changing. I want to get a place for us."

He'd already told me he loved me.

He'd said he wanted to marry me, twice.

I shouldn't be tearing up because he wanted to live with me, but I was. I totally was. "Yes." I could only whisper, but I smiled so widely it started to hurt.

"Yeah?" He grinned.

"Yeah." I kissed him.

He sealed his mouth to mine, and it was a long time before he let me go.

I was okay with that.

THE TEAM HAD DECIDED this celebration needed to be more personal, and it turned out Jesse had a house nearby. We all piled into his place, where he had a karaoke machine set up in the basement, complete with its own stage. Meester and Eric were the deejays.

Coaches Marken and Javier showed up. I didn't feel too awkward being here, though I pulled away from Tyler as they approached.

Both waved me off. "We're adults, Rain," Marken said. "If my wife had a night like you had tonight, I wouldn't let her out of my sight. I get it." Javier nodded beside him. "We get it."

I couldn't help my smile. One night. I would let Tyler and me be Tyler and me in front of the team for this night. Come tomorrow, it was back to business.

Later that night, I was telling Tyler that plan as we got back to my hotel. The doors slid open for us as we stepped inside. Tyler was just in front of me, but came to a complete stop. "What *the fuck* do you want?"

I moved around him, looked, and felt the floor fall from underneath me.

Dane was sitting in the lobby.

75

RAIN

"Dane." I stopped in my tracks, just inside the lobby doors.

He stood, his face hard. "I'd like to talk to my sister."

"Why the fuck now?" Tyler growled, taking a step toward him.

Dane's eyes flashed, but they settled on me again. If anything, he seemed... I didn't know. I couldn't place the emotion. I'd so rarely seen any emotion on Dane's face, so it wasn't natural. He'd always been impassive. A wall.

"I came to apologize," he said.

"Apologize for what?"

I touched Tyler's arm and moved around him, but I kept a hand on him. He drew in a shuddering breath, standing behind me, fitting himself against my back.

Dane's eyes followed our movements. His jaw clenched. "I should've said something. Stopped it. I should've..." He glanced away, then looked down at his hands, which were in fists at his sides. "I was a year older than you, Dylan."

Dylan.

I'd not been called that name in twelve years. I almost didn't realize that he was talking to me. "I go by Rain," I told him.

His eyes flared. "Because mom gave you that name?"

I nodded. "She said she'd always loved the name Rain Connors for me. He wanted the other name."

"You could've changed it." He cocked his head to the side, an unspoken question.

I shrugged, feeling my throat tighten. "It was the last thing I had from her, so I kept it."

"Do you even know mom's maiden name?"

I shook my head. "She never told me and… No one ever told me. I didn't search for it."

"I'm sorry for that."

I lifted a shoulder, wanting to shrug that off, but I couldn't. "Mom said she didn't have anyone. Was that a lie? Did she?"

He snorted. "Let's just say there's a reason Dad looked like a knight in shining armor to her. You're better off. I don't let my girls see them."

His girls.

"You named one of your daughters after me?"

He jerked his head to the side. I could tell that surprised him.

"I was in the bathroom at the arena and heard your wife talking to her. They mentioned Grandpa Keith. And his love for licorice…" I faltered, not knowing why I'd even brought her up. "I just assumed."

"They didn't see you?"

I shook my head. "I came out of the stall when they were leaving. She sounded happy."

His face clouded over and his shoulders slumped. "I was trying to survive too. Back then. Dad was—he was demanding and up our asses, and I'm sorry I didn't stop Daniel from being such an asshole to you."

I didn't know what to say or how to feel. I wasn't even sure what I was hearing.

"When you left, I never thought that'd actually be the last time I saw you," he continued after a moment. "I don't know what I thought. I was just—I was trying to survive. Look..." He stepped toward me before coming to an abrupt halt, his eyes lifting to meet Tyler's.

"There are a lot of things I'd like to say about how we grew up, but none of it's an excuse. None of it. I felt bad when you never came home, and I was shocked that you stayed away. I was hurt, but now, knowing things from your point of view, I had no reason to be hurt. I can't fix anything that happened, but I don't hate you. I never did. I want you to know that. I just—I was a shit brother and a shit person to you, and I'm sorry. I named Dylan after you because even if you don't want anything to do with me, you're still my sister. Daniel doesn't speak for me or my family, and if he doesn't change his fucking attitude about you, he's going to find that Dad is the only one talking to him. Lindy, my wife, she wants to meet you. She wants the girls to meet you. But that's not why I'm here. I...I'm sorry. I think all I can say is that I'm sorry."

I had no clue how to process any of this. None at all. It all spun around in my head, making me dizzy, and I leaned back on Tyler.

He held me up.

"What do you mean there are things you want to say about how we grew up? Things I don't know about?"

He shuddered. "No. Just that it was hard for me too. I missed Mom. Daniel turned into an asshole. And you were suddenly—it was just weird. Just things like that. I'm sorry." He studied Tyler. "You seem happy."

"We are." I could hear Tyler's smugness.

"Not talking to you, dipshit."

"We are. I am." I rested my head against Tyler's chest. I felt his arm curve tighter around me. "I love him."

Dane's eyes cooled at my words.

Tyler leaned forward, and I could hear his smirk. "You got something to say about that?"

"I'll always think you're a dipshit, but as long as you treat her right, maybe you're less of one than I thought."

My mind went back to exploding. Dane saying stuff like that? Somewhere I had stepped into an alternate world.

"*Anyway*, like I said, I wanted to come apologize. I owe you that. And if you want to meet Lindy or your nieces, they'd love that."

Fear spasmed in my chest.

"Just our family," he added. "And if you want to talk about growing up, we can do that too. It's... I've been to therapy. Dad fucked us all up. He's only in my life because of the girls. Trust me, I wish I had walked like you had."

"You always looked right through me," I rasped out. "As if I wasn't there."

He flinched, pain blazing bright over his face for a moment. "I know," he whispered. "I'm sorry."

"Why, though? Why was I invisible to you?"

He shook his head, starting to turn away.

I broke free from Tyler's arms and grabbed Dane. "Tell me."

"Because I wanted to be you," he snarled.

I gasped, my hand flying away from him.

"He ignored you. I was jealous as fuck, but..." New agony surged over his face. "I could see it was hurting you. And I was an asshole kid back then. I don't have anything to say to make any of it better except that I'm sorry I didn't come after you. I'm *really* sorry I didn't join you." His voice was thick with emotion, and he shook his head before whispering, "I'm just sorry, Dylan. And I needed to say that to you." He pressed something into my hand. "Here's my number if you want to talk again, but I gotta go." He brushed past us.

"Dane."

He stopped, but he didn't fully turn back. He glanced over his shoulder at me.

"I'm sorry too."

His head lowered, and the doors slid open and closed behind him.

76

RAIN

It was after we were leaving the rink on Saturday when Tyler got into his truck, but he didn't start it. He was staring straight ahead, pondering something.

After he didn't say anything for a beat, I asked, "What is it?"

His hands wrapped tight around the wheel before he loosened his grip and looked my way. He stated, "I want to take you out."

My eyebrows lifted. "You want to what?"

"Take you out. Like a date." He continued staring at me. Hard. "Everyone knows about us. There's no reason not to go out and I've done nothing to court you."

My eyebrows went all the way to my hairline. "Court me?"

"Yeah. I did ask you to marry me." His grin turned rueful.

I scoffed. "That's the conversation we're not talking about."

"*That's* the conversation? Of all of our conversations, it's that one that you want to avoid?" But he was grinning, and I relaxed.

I flicked my eyes up. "You're messing with me."

"I'm not." His tone was serious. So was his face. His stare was piercing. "I meant the marriage thing, but I can tell you're freaked out so I'll settle for bugging you about what kind of apartment you want to get."

I groaned. This had been a whole conversation when we were coming back from the bar last night. "Not this again. You know I don't care."

"We'll keep talking about it." He reached forward, starting the engine and I fell silent. When he pulled onto the interstate, he said, "Are you a romantic person?"

"No." My answer was automatic.

He cringed. "Ouch. Okay. Uh... Why not?"

I shrugged. "No one's done anything romantic like that for me. It'd probably just make me uncomfortable now."

He began chewing on his bottom lip as he drove to my hotel. He'd brought over a good amount of his clothes so we didn't have to go to his hotel as much. There'd be a conversation at one point if he should cancel his hotel, unofficially move into mine. That would depend on how long it took to look for a new place.

"Okay. I think I know what we can do. Some of it will be something we both like, outside of sex, and then the rest I'll see if you can start liking romantic gestures." He nodded to himself, his mind made up. "You go up to the room and dress—shit. I need to make sure I can do what I want to do. Uh... Dress comfortable, but cute. Outside clothes."

"Cute, but comfortable and outside? Those don't normally go together. Not here. We got snow this week."

"I know but be flexible. And grab your skates."

We were pulling into the parking lot and as he went to the front entrance, I studied him before exiting. The front door men were coming to the truck, but I waved them off before opening the door. "Skates?"

He flashed me a wicked grin, but I caught the delight in them. "We're doing something we both like first."

I sat with that and nodded because that sounded good to

me. Heading to the room, I went to the shower first. We'd be skating, but he said this was a date and after I cleaned up and was doing my hair, I couldn't deny that my stomach was in flutters. Nervousness, but also excitement. Going on a date with someone I knew that I'd have fun with was a whole different ordeal than a normal date. Plus, skating. There was nothing like feeling like I could fly and skating gave me that sensation.

I had pulled on some jeans when the door opened. Tyler came inside. "We're all set."

He ducked into the bathroom, but he had showered at the rink so I knew he wouldn't take long before he would be ready to go. When he was dressed and stepped into the living room where I was standing, he took one look at me. His mouth had opened, but he saw me and the words dried up. His eyes went hungry before he gave me the most wicked grin ever. "Fuck, Connors." He visibly swallowed, his gaze trailing down me again and *slowly* rising. "You want to actually leave this room, you shouldn't have let me see what you're wearing."

I wasn't wearing anything extravagant, but since this was a date and the public did know about us, I indulged. I was wearing a Grays sweatshirt. His Grays sweatshirt. His number. His name. It was in their "away" colors so most of it was a yellow/gold color, but I was also wearing some legging jeans and some cute white sneakers. My hair was pulled back in a loose French braid.

"I can take it off, if you'd like?"

His smirk was wolfish, sending tingles through me. "Yes, you will." His tone was dirty and suggestive. "Not until after we get back, but Jesus, if I can keep my hands off of you through the night, it'll be a damn miracle."

I began edging to the bedroom. Maybe this was too on-the-nose.

He blocked me. "Nope. No fucking way. I'm going to have a raging hard-on all night but now seeing you in this and there ain't anything else I want to see you in until I can peel this off of you tonight." He tugged me to him, bending his forehead to rest against mine lightly. "I love seeing you wear my number. My name. My woman. Fuck. I really fucking love you."

I was getting light-headed. "Yeah?"

"Yeah." He breathed against me, letting me feel him. "Ignore me tonight because I'm going to be having so many filthy thoughts. It's going to be torture, but I booked you—we need to go now if we're going to make it out of this hotel room." His tone was rough and urgent.

I had a fleeting reminder to grab my skates and then we were off for our date.

77

RAIN

I wasn't surprised when he took us to an indoor ice rink. He said he had booked something, but judging by the full parking lot, it wasn't this rink. As we went inside, the front entryway was full of people. Grandparents. Parents. Teenagers. Little kids were running around. Some were putting on skates. More than a few glanced our way and once they saw Tyler, they didn't look away. A small buzz started and I waited to see if people would approach Tyler. He didn't give them a chance. He took my hand and led me to the front desk where he paid for the general skate admission price. The attendant gave the price, looking and sounding bored.

Tyler paid in cash.

"Do you need skates?" the attendant asked, now actually looking at us.

Tyler shook his head. "Got our own." He had grabbed a pair he kept in his truck and led me to the rink, sitting on one of the side benches.

More than a few people followed us, watching. Phones were being lifted and aimed at Tyler. "You okay with the attention?"

Tyler had bent over to put his skates on but looked around

before shrugging. "A few of the younger skaters might come over for an autograph, but it'll be fine. You okay with it?"

I laughed. "After last night's game?" It was meant as a joke, but some of my chuckle faded because truth be told, I didn't think I'd ever get used to it. But this was Tyler and his world and I wasn't leaving. I reached over to squeeze is knee. "I'll be fine."

He was still studying me, serious, and straightened after he finished with his skates. "You sure?"

I nodded, bending to put mine on. "What's your plan?" I stood when I was done.

Tyler grinned, his eyebrows dipping a little as he observed me. "What do you mean?" He stood as well and I led the way.

"I mean..." Once my skate hit the ice, everything synced up inside of me.

It felt like home. Me. Tyler. Feeling the glide underneath me. A sudden rush hit me, making me dizzy. I quickly eyed who else was on the ice. Little kids that were pushing penguin and seal skate helpers. There were some teenagers. Moms and dads. A few older people as well, but in the rink, mostly everyone was paying attention to themselves.

My gut stirred. That was about to change.

I flashed Tyler a grin as I smacked his arm. "Tag. You're it." Then I was off.

I heard his laugh and knew he was skating behind me.

Neither of us could go as fast as we would've in an empty rink, but it was fun. Dodging people. Using the skate helpers to block him. People were watching us. I knew that. Caught more than a few phones pointed our way from the side, but I couldn't bring myself to worry about any of the attention.

It was a rush, almost matching Tyler in speed. He caught me, but he didn't catch me right away and I could tell that we were both surprised at how much he had to work to get me.

After the eighth time we just transferred who was "it," Tyler came up behind me and grabbed my hips. His chest warmed my back and he held me, as we both continued skating at a more leisurely pace. He dipped his head and I felt his breath against my neck. "I want this forever."

My insides exploded.

Twisting my neck, I looked up at him and found him watching me, his eyes were so dark, filled with a piercing somberness. His hands squeezed my hips. "Forever, Rain." He was slowing us down and he had drawn us over to the boards. At the moment, no one was around us so we had our own little section here. "I want this till I'm shitting my pants."

"Tyler." I half-laughed, half breathless too.

He moved around so he was facing me and pulled me against him again. "I mean it. If you don't want the same, you need to let me go. Do it now while I'll still shatter, but later... you'll absolutely destroy me."

I slid my hand up his chest, around his neck, and my fingers sank into his hair. Taking a good fistful before I looked him straight in the eyes. "You can shut up about that." I yanked on his hair. "It's forever for me too."

His eyes were smoldering. "Yeah?"

"Yeah," I said quietly.

He closed his eyes, his shoulders loosening, and he touched his head to mine. "Where have you been all my life?"

A twinge went up my spine, making me feel alive. Intoxicated.

My throat swelled up. "Lost."

His voice dropped to a whisper. "Not anymore and not ever again."

My heart was trying to pound its way out of my chest.

He dropped his forehead to my shoulder and sighed. "I booked us our own dine-in theater."

"You did what?"

He lifted his head, a primal glaze over his eyes and he

blinked it away before he could respond. "I thought after an hour of skating, we'd be hungry. I wanted it to be all date-like and what's more like a date than dinner and a movie? But I hate watching movies with strangers so I booked a whole theater. There's supposed to be wine and flowers waiting for you."

I was almost afraid to ask. "What movie?"

"Fuck if I know. It looked like killer zombie nuns or something."

He brushed a kiss to my forehead just as we heard a nervous, "Uh, Mr. Griffin? Could I get your autograph?" And our little moment was officially invaded, but by a boy who looked fourteen years old. Not killer zombie nuns.

I pulled away, giving Tyler some space as a few more people came over for autographs. Some wanted pictures with him. A few just wanted to ask who he was and to talk to him. Tyler was kind to each person until we were able to make our way out of there, heading for the theater.

He was right. The wine and flowers were romantic. There was a whole bouquet of lilacs and where he was able to order lilacs on such short notice, I had no idea. I was impressed. They smelled wonderfully.

The dinner was amazing.

The movie... The movie was actually romantic. They were fighting to live and they needed to sacrifice for the other a dozen times and in the end, there were tears. The dad chose to hold off the zombie nuns so his family could escape.

Tyler was sniffling next to me.

When the credits rolled across the screen and the theater lights turned on, I patted Tyler's hand. "You okay?"

"Yep." He cleared his throat, blinking as if there hadn't been any tears on his face at all. He stood. "All good. You? You good?"

I took the moment just to appreciate him. "I think you cried more when the family horse died."

"Oh, God." He had to turn away before he was composed again. He held up a finger. "She was their family member. She was good. All animals are good and don't tell me they aren't."

My chest filled with tenderness. Well, if I hadn't known before now, I knew for an absolute certainty now. We'd started for the door where some of the staff members were waiting to come in and clean.

I paused halfway there. "Tyler?" My voice was hoarse.

"Yeah?" He threw me a glance, but catching the expression on my face, he wheeled all the way around. "What is it?"

"Ask me again." Still hoarse.

"Ask you what..." But he stared at me before comprehension flared and his eyes got big. Real big. "Will you marry me?"

My heart was stuck in my throat but I was able to whisper, "Yes."

78

TYLER

April

The team's goal was to get into the playoffs when I joined, and tonight, we were going to cement those points to ensure our first place standing for the wild card spot. We were going against St. Louis for that spot. I wanted it. They were playing against Los Angeles tonight and we were playing against Boston, in Boston.

As we filed out on the ice and took up our spots on the line for the national anthem, I stared at the back of Dane's jersey. Maybe it was karmic that it was his team we were going against. In the months since we last saw him, he and Rain exchanged a few texts. His wife reached out and it was planned after the game to go to his house so Rain could meet her nieces for the first time, officially. I had mixed emotions centering around him. Daniel was a piece of shit. He was never going to change, but Dane was... I didn't know anymore. He was still an asshole, but he was trying. The jury would be out until after the meeting later tonight. It had to be tonight because we were flying back in the morning. Rain would be on the plane with the team. I floated the idea if she wanted to do the meeting in the morning, take her time, fly back herself or at the very least if Mal would wait and bring her back in his jet but she said no. She wanted me there and since we were so close to playoffs, I needed to be with the team as much as possible.

"You ready for this?" Sunny asked under his breath once the anthem was done and we were in our places.

I met his gaze and held up my glove. "Fuck yeah."

"We need more points than what St. Louis gets tonight."

"We'll get it."

"Damn right we will." He hit my glove and moved back for his spot as Dane glided to his spot. The referee moved in and held up the puck. He was looking between us. "You boys ready? No dirty shit, either of you."

Dane's cool eyes flicked to mine before bending forward. "Never, Dante."

The referee scoffed. "Right."

Whoever they had announcing to play hockey, sounded off and the puck was dropped.

Dane went for it, but I flicked my stick to block him and shot the puck behind me. Ray was there and he quickly sent it sailing to the other side of the ice where our defenseman was, who then sent it to Sunny.

I met him and we went across the blue line together, Sunny pushing the puck forward. We were met by their two defensemen. Sunny passed the puck ahead and around, hoping to sling shot it around the rink to me but I got there at the same time as Dane. We were battling for the puck against the boards now, shoving at each other.

"God. Fuck off," Dane rasped out, straining against me.

"You fuck off."

A normal game at this time, we'd be trading worse insults

except as I waited to see what else he'd say, I was surprised that was it.

"Is that all? You can't think of anything more intelligent against me?" I taunted, trying to wedge my skate in between him and the puck. His stick was there, stopping me.

He cursed. "You're such a pain in the ass. I don't know what my sister sees in you."

I laughed, abruptly. "Pretty sure your wife could answer that question."

"Hey!" He stopped trying for the puck and instead rounded on me. "You don't talk about my wife."

I got in his face. "And you can bring up your sister? I'm honestly sick and tired of you and your brother having your round at her."

"I—" He looked dumbfounded for a moment, but then Ray nabbed the puck from between us and he was off, rounding the goal.

A referee skated up. "We have a problem here?"

"No. Fuck." Dane shoved past me, checking my shoulder as he went and normally that would be something we could drop our gloves over, but when our defenseman glanced my way, I shook my head. Dane did look flustered when he left.

Ray was battling against the boards on the other side for the puck. I skated up behind them, snaked my stick in the middle, and then grunted as I hip-checked one of Boston's guys into the boards. The crowd was pounding against the partition, wanting for us to fight, but I had the puck.

I flicked it between my skates to Bruge who had come onto the ice. He was just past their blue line, in the middle of the ice and as he caught the pass, I slipped behind the goalie to the other side. He read my intention, pretended that he was going to pass to Ray and when everyone was looking that way, sent it to me without turning my way once. Their goalie caught on too late. I only had to raise my stick and the puck bounced off it, going just over their goalie's shoulders.

The red lights lit up. Goal!

That was one. We were going to keep going all night long.

Bruge hit me for the celly, along with the rest of our guys before my line skated off.

Sunny and Ray both met my glove with theirs on the bench.

Sunny was grinning widely. "I'm thinking of personal goals tonight since Doc Rain is all about that. We should all try to get hat tricks. Whoever gets theirs first, buys the others' drinks at our celebration."

Ray ducked his head, laughing. "If we all get hat tricks tonight, that would be *insane*."

I shook my head as we stood up and moved down the bench. "Not for drinks. Let's think of something else to celebrate. Rain and I have a family thing tonight."

"Oooh. Meeting the family..." Sunny trailed off as the implications hit him. "*Oh*. Do I console you?"

Ray barked out a laugh. "Nah, man. Just buy him a round at the bar when we get home. Let's keep thinking of a way to celebrate later."

A minute later and it was our turn again.

Dane scored.

I scored.

Sunny scored.

Boston scored.

I scored.

Ray scored.

Dane scored.

We won, five to two and we beat St. Louis for points. We

were the first in the wild card spot. And the guys no longer questioned how we were here. Looking around the locker room, they expected to win. There was no doubt or wide-eyes or wonderment. Just readiness and eagerness to whoever we were going to be playing against for the first rounds.

I was damn proud to be a Gray Wolf.

We were going to the playoffs.

79

RAIN

I came back from the rink after the players and found a cupcake wrapped in a cute package on the chair that I had sequestered as my own before the game. This one was chocolate with purple frosting on top. Two Oreo cookies stuck in the icing.

Glancing up, I caught a glimpse into the locker room. Tyler took the area by the goalies. They sat in the same spot no matter what locker room we were in. He requested to sit next to them. At first it caused an uproar. Any changes did that to a hockey locker room. Superstitions and all, but Bruge was the first to figure it out. From that position, Tyler usually had direct line of sight for wherever I ended up sitting. If we were able to use guest offices or not, he knew he could see me more in the hallway from his new spot.

I looked up now and saw him watching me. Everyone else was starting to change out. Not Tyler. He'd been waiting for me.

Giving him a shy smile, he blasted me back with a beaming one. My cheeks warmed and I fought from ducking my head because I still struggled with his direct attention. My brain liked to tell me it was a lie. That he didn't actually love me. He barely even liked me, but then he'd do something like this and my stomach was somersaulting.

Cupcakes.

I grinned before tucking it away in my bag. He'd been sneaking me these little treats since December at every away game. I didn't know if others were aware. I had to imagine they didn't because hockey players weren't known for being quiet. Someone would've said something.

Coach Hines stopped by my chair just as my hand came out of my bag. "St. Louis got three points tonight."

My mouth dried up. We got way more than three points tonight. "So, it's cemented."

He gave me a brief nod. "We would've been going anyway. I doubt that the Mustangs would've gotten enough points to usurp our standing, or St. Louis, but we're going to the playoffs."

"We're going to the playoffs." That'd been the goal since I came. My personal goal was to get them to the second round as well. "Do you know who we'll go up against?"

"Not sure. Probably Vegas."

"Vegas." Vegas was good. They were also liked by the NHL in general. "Refs could be biased."

"Yeah. We'll prepare the guys." My phone began buzzing and he glanced to the screen, seeing it was Dane calling. A frown pulled on his face. "You have that happening tonight."

"I do."

He glanced in the direction of where Tyler normally would be sitting. He had press surrounding him at the moment, and his head was down, listening to someone asking a question.

Coach Hines said, "Griff's going with you?"

"He is."

"Good." He dipped his head down in a firm nod. "You two should take off as soon as you're ready. I'll catch you up on the plane tomorrow with our debrief and you can run your notes by me as well." He began heading for the room he was using for a brief room, then paused. "We're doing a family dinner Saturday night to celebrate. You're invited."

Surprise hit me and I only had enough time to regurgitate, "I'm invited?"

"You and Griffin. Missy made sure to mention if you wanted to bring your man. It's not the first time I had a player become an unofficial part of the family. Won't be the last, but it's up to you. Missy would hang the moon if you came."

I found myself nodding. "We'll come."

"Great. I'll let her know. She'll cook double since we'll have a hockey player eating. If you need anything, reach out. Missy too. I've known that woman for most of my life and I've never heard her say something she doesn't mean."

"Thank you, Coach Hines. I mean it."

"Well. Good." His tone got gruff. "We'll see you on Saturday. You come empty handed and with an empty stomach. You hear me?"

"I hear you."

Tyler found me not long after, dressed and showered. His cheeks were flushed, no doubt from the shower. "Are you sure you want to do this?"

I began putting my things away before I stood, drawling, "What? Meet my niece who's named after me? You're totally right. We shouldn't go. Like, ever."

He rolled his eyes but was trying to hold back a smile. "You know what I mean. Meeting the nieces will be fun. I can start brainwashing them to believe how horrible their uncle is in hockey. I'll plant seeds tonight." He nudged my shoulder with his. "I meant going to his house. It's his turf. We can meet at the hotel. In the lobby. And maybe the rest of the team will just happen to also be there. It's more neutral territory."

My phone buzzed again and I checked it.

Dane: Not sure when you're heading over, but the girls are excited. Be warned. They've had sugar.

I showed Tyler the text, who whisked the phone from me and was typing back before I could register he was even doing it.

"Hey." I reached for the phone.

He stepped back and held it over my head, still typing. "And send." He was smug as he handed the phone back, then turned to head out the door. "Not sorry."

I groaned before I read what he'd sent to Dane.

Rain: Good. Give them more sugar and start preparing them for the awesomeness they're about to meet.

Rain: This is Tyler, by the way. I'm also pretty spectacular. Have you asked your wife yet? (Don't worry. I know she agrees.) I'm actually referring how fucking amazing their aunt is so I hope you've let them know.

Rain: Still Tyler. If there is even a hint at anyone in your household being rude to Rain, I have no problem dropping some truth bombs. The first being how truly much your entire family have sucked to Rain. You've been warned.

I sighed before typing out a quick text.

Rain: This is Rain. You already sent the address. I just ordered an Uber. Be there shortly.

I would not apologize for Tyler's texts. I goddamn loved that man *because* of his texts.

He was waiting for me in the hallway, his shoulder, hip, and the side of his head were leaning against the wall. He lifted his head up. "Are you mad at me?"

I frowned at him as I pulled the door shut. "For what?"

"For putting my nose where it doesn't belong." He motioned to the phone in my hand.

I checked both ways, but the hallway was empty before I stepped up to him. Tugging on his shirt, his head lowered and I went up on my tiptoes to brush my lips over his. I said once I was there, "Never. I'd do the same for you." My hand spread out against his chest and I felt his heart pound there. I lingered, savoring the feel of that heart.

As the kiss deepened, his hands splayed out over my hips. "Now I don't want to go for a whole different reason."

"Soon." I nipped at his lips one last time before leading the way to meet our ride. My hand slid to his and I laced our fingers, keeping my hand in his through the ride as well.

80

TYLER

Dane Connors's wife was nice. What the fuck. I wanted her to be stuck-up and to be a bitch. She was neither. Dane actually got a good one. I mean, I wouldn't date her, and she couldn't compare to Rain, but she was a catch. How the hell had Dane landed her?

Their girls were hellions.

They were cute hellions, but hellions. And they adored Rain right away, especially the one named after her. Dylan. I wanted to scoff when I met them all, even the little baby, but that little baby had the biggest set of cheeks on her face and the most adorable eyes. I'd only seen one other baby who was cuter, and that was my own niece. No one could match Zoey.

Except your own, a small voice told me, and I froze. My hand was lifting with a beer to take a sip and I couldn't breathe for a full second.

Children. Mine.

My eyes shot to Rain where she was sitting on the floor, playing hockey with a bunch of dolls and stuffed animals and yes. I wanted to have children with Rain.

Jesus Christ. I was finally growing up.

But I knew it with every inch of my body. When I had children, they would be with Rain. And we were going to get married, though that was still unofficial because we hadn't discussed any plans, like if we needed rings, or venues, or well—whatever Rain said she wanted. As of now, she said it was enough to know that we were unofficially engaged. I didn't altogether know what that meant, but it made her happy every time she said it so I was all for what made Rain the happiest.

Lindy sat down on the couch next to me after putting their youngest to bed, a glass of wine in her hand. "That is the look of a man very much smitten." Her gaze swept over her daughters before returning to me. "I don't take you as a 'I just melt for children' kind of guy so I'm guessing the head-over-heels look is for Dylan. The older one."

I gave her a shrewd look back. "She goes by Rain."

"Right." Her face cringed. "Sorry. Dane's always talked about her as Dylan. It'll take a little bit of time, but she'll only be Rain the next time we see you." Her head inclined toward me. "Which I'm hoping will be in the playoffs."

I gave her a death stare. "I do not need a reminder that Boston is also in the playoffs."

She laughed; the sound was free and loud. It drew attention from her little girls and also Rain, who was having a hard time from full-on beaming the whole night. Meeting her nieces, though I truly loathed their father, had been a great decision for Rain.

Lindy sighed. "I agree with you, by the way." She indicated Rain who had gone back to playing with the raccoon that didn't have a head, or a tail. He was trying to bat at the fake pancake that was the puck but kept missing because he didn't have a tail. "Dane's never wanted to share much about his childhood, but he would talk about Dy—Rain. He'd talk about Rain. After reading that article about you guys, I sat him down and had him tell me the parts he left out. Turns out, he left a lot out. Once I knew the whole story, I demanded he reach out."

I tensed. "He only reached out because you made him?"

She began laughing. "Good Lord, no. Dane's been wanting to reach out for years. He's just too scared. When I put my foot down, it gave him the excuse to finally do it."

Dane came into the room, a beer in hand with another he offered to me. He glared at me. "Congratulations."

When we first arrived, he'd been at the door for introductions, but a call took him away. He was just now entering the living room extravaganza with us.

I took the beer and gave him the biggest and most evil-looking smile I could muster. "Thanks." As he sat in the chair next to me, I added, "We have more points than you."

He paused right before he sat the whole way, giving me an unamused look. "We'll get to second round playoffs. Your team will be lucky to win even three of your games." His expression was like ice, and he clenched his jaw.

"Okay. Jeez. You two. Knock it off. This is family time." His wife leaned forward. "Family, honey. Remember?"

His jaw unclenched, but the iciness remained until he regarded the hockey game happening on the floor in front of us. A visible thawing came over him until the little girl playing with a Joker's doll waved at him. "Hi, Daddy! Look. This is Aunt Dylan."

Rain went still, but she was watching the little girl.

"I know," Dane said. "That's my sister. Just like you have your two sisters."

"I know! She's awesome." And it seemed she was done with Joker because she used him to bat the fake pancake in the air. It didn't work except the doll itself went flying across the living room. The other girl, who was older and quieter, and was playing the goalie, blinked in shock at the sudden appearance of Joker. Then burst out laughing.

Little Dylan shrieked, but it was okay. It was also in laughter.

"Not used to kids?" Dane had been watching me steadily. There was a smirk in that question.

"Kids? Kids, yes. I have a niece. Three little girls under the age of seven? No."

Lindy started laughing all over again. "He's funny." She motioned from Dane to me. "This is funny. Dane, you only had bad things to say about your high school rival."

His expression wasn't amused. "There are only bad things to say about him."

"Except for the fact he's going to be your brother-in-law," she chided him, a knowing grin on her face. "You might want to start changing your tune."

Dane didn't respond, but he also didn't tone down his glaring either.

"Daddy!" It was Little Dylan again. "Do you not like Aunt Dylan's boyfriend?"

"No. I hate him."

The oldest girl's head jerked up. She exclaimed, "Dad!"

Little Dylan admonished him, "That's a bad word. You can't say that word. You can't hate someone, Daddy. You said so yourself."

He only grimaced before he said grudgingly, "I severely don't like him. How about that?"

"But he's Aunt Dylan's boyfriend and she's family so that means you can't 'srrvly dislike' him."

Lindy said under her breath, "That's okay, sweetie."

"What's okay, Mommy?"

"Nothing. You're adorable. Did you know that?"

"Mom!"

"What?"

She was giggling, but she managed, "What did you mean when you said 'that's okay'?"

"It's nothing, but whatever it was, you get it from your father."

"What do I get from Daddy?"

"Nothing, because you get all your adorableness from me. But since we're talking about your dad, did you know that sometimes he struggles with this ability called communication. Do you know what that is?"

Little Dylan had migrated closer and she was serious as she took in their exchange. "Communeaon?"

"Yes. That."

"I don't know what that is."

The older one was also following the conversation. "That's what you do at church! That's how Angela said she's going to get drunk when she gets to eighth grade."

I had completely lost the train of thought in this conversation, but Lindy bit down on her lip to keep from full-out laughing. Once she was under control, she squeaked out, "Yes. Your dad struggles with that too."

"That's because he doesn't go to church," Little Dylan said, matter-of-factly, moving back to pick up a Penguin doll. It had been next to the Riddler and Two-Face. I was noting the theme of villain dolls in the room.

"How did this conversation turn around to me?" Dane asked.

Lindy finished her wine and stood from the couch. "Don't worry about it, honey. It's just called good battle tactic. And now that I've won this round, it's time you and your sister have a talk."

Rain had been silently listening to everything with a faint smile on her face.

Lindy said to her, "Want another glass of wine before my hubby takes you into the hockey dungeon?"

Rain looked alarmed before she scrambled to her feet. "Yes, please." I noted how she adverted her gaze so she wouldn't meet her brother's gaze as she passed him. Once they were in the kitchen, I studied Dane and saw he had his eyes closed.

"Preparing yourself?"

Dane opened his eyes, gave me a nasty look, but let it fade as he glanced at his girls. They were now in a shoot-out. The Batmobile was parked in front of the goal as Penguin was throwing things at it. Little Dylan was making exploding sounds so I was certain those were pretend bombs. So far, the Batmobile was winning because it hadn't exploded.

"You are such a pain in the ass. Did she have to fall for you?"

"Yes, because it's called karma. You're due."

He went back to glaring at me until Little Dylan called out, "If you keep looking at him like that then Mom is going to put you in a time-out, Dad."

Dane went from glaring to his eyes going wide and a bark of laughter ripped from him before he covered his mouth and stifled his laugh. "Jesus Christ," he said under his breath so they couldn't hear. "Their time-outs are where they have to go to bed. My girls hate going to bed."

Little Dylan was watching her dad, an avid intensity on her face because she was fully engrossed in what the adults were talking about. She began edging our way as if she could spy on us.

Dane shook his head and pointed at the game. "Finish up. Your dad and your aunt have to talk when you go to bed."

"But—" Her face puckered up. She was going to launch a counter attack except Dane shook his head, briskly. "Nope."

She glowered back at him, and that *was* hereditary, but she was no longer about to start crying. "Dad!"

"I mean it. Finish the game. Your sister looks like she's winning. The Batmobile seems to be impenetrable."

She harrumphed at him before going back to her shoot-out.

"Nice," I said under my breath.

He said under his, "Thanks. Years of experience."

I paused, side-eyeing him.

He paused, side-eying me.

We were both gripping our beers.

"For the record, this does not make us best friends."

He exhaled, "Thank God."

Then the older sister piped up, "Dad, you really need to start going to church."

I tipped my beer toward her. "Amen to that."

81

RAIN

Dane looked terrified when he took me to the dungeon, but immediately I relaxed when I saw he had a makeshift goalie set up in the back corner along with two hockey sticks. He picked one up and held it out to me. "You always had a killer slapshot."

He didn't use real pucks. I took the stick from him and bent down to assess what I was expected to hit. "Is that a wiffle puck?"

"Lindy made me buy those. She got tired of me trying to fix the wall all the time. I hit a pipe one time too."

I whistled. "Impressive."

He sent me a grin. "Thanks." He hooked one of the wiffle pucks and brought it over to where he was standing before lining up to take a shot. "So." He hit it and it sank behind the goalie, which looked taped together with pillows, duct-tape, and determination. "You want to talk about anything?"

I gave him an unimpressed look. "What a way to start. You should be a therapist. The skills you have at making people want to open up to you? Top *not*-notch."

He flashed me a grin as I wound up and sank another wiffle

puck in the net. "I see you've already picked up our ways in this Connors' household. We keep it together with dry wit and sarcasm. Lindy already fucking loves you. I can tell."

I began to swing on a second puck, but then I whiffed it before rounding to him. "What?"

He gave me a cool look, then sank his second puck in the net. "She gave me a look when I came into the living room just now. It was a whole conversation in one look, but she told me that I better make things right with you and insure you come around again and want to be a part of our family or I will be sleeping on that couch for a very long time." He indicated a ragged couch that looked as if it had been the net most of its life. It was more stuffing than couch at this point.

I remarked, "If we were in Minneapolis, I know a good couch person."

"What?"

"Nothing." I lined up for a third shot and didn't miss this time. "So. Yeah. This is our conversation, huh?"

"Seems like." His tone got serious.

So was mine. And I chanced a look at him again, seeing him watching me.

A burst of nerves exploded inside of me. "I don't know what to say here."

"You can say anything you want," he remarked, lightly. "I'd deserve it."

"Why?" I rounded to face him directly. Hockey, wiffle pucks, the net, all of it was forgotten.

His face shuddered, but I asked further, "Why didn't he love me?"

"He?"

"Keith."

He flinched. "I—I don't know, to be honest. He—" He glanced at me, uncertain.

"Don't hold back. I was there. I know how he treated me."

His mouth twisted before he swung, distractedly, at nothing on the floor. He was just swinging while he was thinking. "I don't know why he treated you the way he did. I think it was a mix that you were a girl. He wanted a boy. You weren't going to be in the NHL, though you could be in the women's professional league. And you were nice, Rain. You didn't demand his attention. I think that was part of it too."

"It was *my* fault."

"You didn't demand your space. You were owed it. Fuck. You were owed so much more than you were given, but you never cried about it or threw a fit. It was like you were nothing."

Now I flinched.

"I didn't mean—"

I waved that off. "Don't. I acted like nothing because that's how I was treated by you, by him, by Daniel."

"I'm sorry."

"I know." I averted my gaze to keep from breaking down. I hadn't expected our conversation to be like this, where I wanted to cry because Dane seemed to care. I had known he wanted to apologize. He already had, and I knew Lindy wanted to meet me, the girls too, but actually seeing he cared was a whole other experience.

"What did I do wrong?" I whispered the words to myself.

"Nothing."

I met Dane's gaze. He grimaced. "You did nothing wrong. You, just, were born into the wrong family."

Yeah. Maybe. I didn't know.

I decided then and there I wasn't going to tell him about Mal. I hadn't met my real father yet. That was planned for late in the summer. I needed time, which Mal understood and he gave it. I've been focused on the team and on my relationship. My connection to the Grays's owner hadn't been leaked. The press didn't know, and I hadn't been sure if I wanted to let Dane know or not.

I was going to keep some things to myself. It'd come out after this season was done, when I was no longer acting as their consultant. Or maybe it would never come out. I didn't care either way but I was okay with any of it, or all of it.

I was content.

I'd done my job. I helped get the team to the first round of playoffs, but I wanted them to get to the second round. My brother was standing in front of me, talking to me, apologizing to me, wanting me to be in his life and his family's life. And I had a man waiting for me upstairs that would tear the world apart for me if I asked.

Dane gave me an odd look. "You okay?"

"Yeah." It was the truth. "I'm okay. I'm going to be okay." I laughed. "I'm going to be better than okay, and for someone like me, that means the world." He was still giving me that weird look. I ignored it and stepped over to hug him.

Dane went rigid, his eyes widening.

I ignored that too and patted him on the back. "Thanks for making the first step, but I was already locked in the second I saw your little girls smiling at me."

I stepped back as he let out a harsh breath of air. "They tend to have that effect on people. It's their super power because I swear that my little girls are going to be criminal masterminds one day. Have you seen their dolls upstairs? Try to give them an angel doll and they throw a fit. Give them a devil doll and they're content as can be. I'm terrified. Lindy thinks it's awesome. She jokes they get it from me, but that's all her." By unspoken agreement we put away the hockey sticks and began for the stairs.

"She told Dad off."

I stopped just before starting up the stairs. "What?"

"Lindy. She invited him over for dinner, and before the girls came in, she informed him that he would never treat any of the females in this family how he treated you growing up. If he did, she would have no problem educating the girls on how he treated you and she'd let him try to explain it to them. Dad's usually reserved and on good behavior around Lindy, but for the first time he looked scared of her. I showed her the texts that Griff sent on your phone and she told me straight up to make sure you married that man. Consider yourself a part of our family again, whether you want to be or not." With that, he headed upstairs while I was rooted in place behind him.

But I was smiling.

I told Tyler how the conversation went once we got home and he laughed and laughed and said he couldn't wait to have Lindy meet Skylar.

I agreed.

EPILOGUE
RAIN

Going to Miriam's grave with Mal had become a tradition. We did it the first year after the Grays lost in the playoffs. And the regular season was done this year so Mal and I went to visit our cousin.

Our cousin.

I now thought of her as mine as well.

Mal bent down to fix some of the grass by her tombstone and when it was cleared, he held out his hand. I gave him the bouquet of flowers. Tyler was always giving me lilacs so I'd started bringing them for Miriam.

Mal placed them on the ground, in the middle and stood up to stand with me.

"Hey, sis." He took my hand, but he was speaking to Miriam. "I know you're over there. I know you're watching. I hope you're happy. We're doing the best we can on our side. I'll let Rain have her own time with you, but I'm doing well. Dad is doing well. Mom too. Grandpa passed, but I'm sure you know that. I miss you, little sister. Cousin." Mal had tears in his eyes. "I think of you every day. I met someone recently who filled my ear about signs so if you've got some pull on the other side, could you send me a pink balloon. I was told to be somewhat specific. Love you." He squeezed my hand before touching my shoulder and moving aside for me.

I knelt closer to the tombstone, sitting on the back of my heels. "I asked him to give us some privacy today, but you probably already know my surprise so I won't say it in words. I feel like I know you by now, but I always feel the same when I come here. I wished I had known about you earlier. Maybe I could've helped? Who knows. Your brother--our brother--he helped me a lot. He does well for others. He cares. I got to know Grandpa a bit too and I already miss him. Can you give him an extra hug for me? Tell him his new granddaughter misses him."

This was where she was buried, but I didn't believe that's only where she was. I believed she was around us all the time. Since knowing about her, I swear that I felt her at times too. Mal said the same, but he liked to shake off the thought.

I found comfort in it. Our loved ones were still with us. That meant my mom had never left my side. I liked that idea a whole lot.

After we were there a bit longer, Mal indicated he was ready to leave.

Once we were in his car, he asked as we pulled out of the cemetery, "Do you and Tyler have plans once the Grays are done?"

"Tyler will want to go on vacation and travel around. He mentioned taking Sky and Zoey to Europe. Probably swing into New York to see Nolan. You know. Travel around to see friends. Do you have plans?"

He shook his head. "I get to travel with my work. So..." He laughed to himself. "It's the same for me."

"Lindy wants to come to Minnesota and do a camping thing. She mentioned cabins. Would you be interested in joining us? You are my brother."

He softened. "I could probably be talked into an appearance. Bring Dad too."

Now I was the one softening. "Yeah. Bring Dad. That'd be nice. I don't think my nieces will have a problem having three grandpas."

"Certainly not. Especially when they go and see Grandpa Keith and tell him all about the toys you know Dad will insist on bringing."

Meeting my father had been life changing. It took a while until I was ready to meet him, and it took another year before I believed he actually wanted me in his life. I would always struggle with my stuff. It's how I was raised, but I was doing better.

"When do you start with your new client?"

"I'm taking all of June off for hockey and training camps start mid-July, but I'll check in with him and his team after the holiday. Touch base. We'll go from there."

"Are you excited to return to the NFL?"

My client had been in the first round pick for the NFL draft and he went to a team that was trying to do a rebuild. I finished my season with the Grays and agreed to help their minor league team the following year. A tier one Juniors team also asked for me to consult. I'd enjoyed going between the two. There was a different air to both levels of hockey. Freeing. Less pressure. It was contagious as soon as I walked into each arenas. But this year I got an offer to return to American football and I couldn't pass it up.

"I am, actually. It'll be a nice change, but I think I'll be going back and forth between the two sports for the foreseeable future."

"As long as it makes you happy."

"It does."

Mal dropped me off outside of the house I shared with Tyler. I walked in, he was yelling at the television. He'd been watching my brother's team in their round of the playoffs, but tonight I was grateful he hadn't invited half the team to watch with him.

They'd taken to just showing up as well, at all hours of the day and night.

"COME ON, YOU'RE FUCKING BLIND! These refs!" Tyler was on his feet, yelling at the screen as if the referees could hear him. "Connors completely high-sticked Nolan first. It was right in front of you. How did you not see it?"

I waited a beat, but the call stayed. New York took a penalty and my brother swept past the seats, hitting the partition where two fans quickly shoved their signs in his face.

One read, **You get your skating skills from your daughter. Not the other way around.**

I grinned at seeing Skylar make a face at Dane.

The second sign read, **Your wife plays better than you do.**

Eric was holding that one up.

The announcers were laughing and talking about the connection from Skylar, to Tyler, to me, to Dane and how it was full circle when the penalty call was against Tyler's best friend. What the announcers didn't know was that the whole reason Skylar was in New York for this game was because she and Nolan had started to see each other. That was full *full* circle, in my opinion.

Tyler was still ranting about the call so I commented, "Yelling at the television didn't work, huh?"

Tyler and Dane's relationship had gotten somewhat better. As had mine, but they still had a healthy dose of hatred for each other when it came to all things hockey. It was a work in progress that was at a standstill.

Tyler whipped around, a smile breaking out over his face. "You think your brother would invent some technology where we could make that happen. Your nice brother. Not your dickish brother who is not winning this game against New York."

"Is that how it works? You say it and therefore it happens."

He came over to me and wrapped his arms around me, lifting me up for a kiss. I was expecting a small lift, but Tyler had a different thought. He hoisted me all the way up so I wrapped my legs around his waist, and as he kissed me, he walked back to the couches. Sinking down, he kept me on his lap and patted my thigh. "You can stay right here. You will make watching this game bearable if you're within groping distance."

I wasn't about to argue so I settled against his chest and watched the rest of the game in his arms.

Boston won, and with that last win, they were going to the next round where the winner would get the championship trophy.

Tyler was grumbling about the game, but I moved to the side and tilted my head to see him better. "How are you feeling about that?"

He growled.

"Are you ready to go against Boston for the Cup? Funny how that worked out this year."

It was the first year they were going. I was doubtful it'd be their last.

"My old team couldn't do their job, so my new team will. It's everyone's job to beat your brothers. I will take pleasure in doing it myself this year."

I laughed but reached for him. Cupping his chin, I turned his head to fully look down at me. "I got a feeling the Grays are going to take it this year."

"You got a feeling?"

He was teasing, but I had a feeling the morning Dane and Lindy called last fall to tell us they were pregnant for a fourth time. I had a feeling the morning when Skylar called us crying because Zoey had a breakthrough in therapy. And it was just like the feeling I had the morning when the Grays won the seventh game in their last playoffs. The one that sent them for the championship trophy as well.

I moved my hand so it was covering my stomach.

He tracked my movement, his eyes going wide. His mouth fell open. "Wha—"

I whispered, "Yeah. I got a feeling."

"Are—" He was speechless. "Are you serious? Are you sure?" He grew alarmed. "Should you be sitting like this? We had sex last night. Like, hard sex. Can we do that? We shouldn't have done that. You're pregnant? Right? That's what you're saying?"

Happiness coursed through me. This was the ultimate happiness and I nodded, my voice breaking. "Yeah. We're going to have a baby."

"Really?"

"Really."

"Does this mean we can finally get married?"

I burst out laughing and shifted to straddle him. Wrapping my arms around his neck, I said, "Yes. We can finally get married."

"And that means we can tell people we've been engaged for two years now?"

"Yes."

"We can make it official?"

"Yes."

"Can we—"

"Can you shut up and kiss me?"

"I'll kiss you forever."

I tightened my arms around his neck and raised myself higher so I was face to face with him. "Promise?"

His eyes darkened. "Promise."

And he did.

Thank you for reading My Brother's Enemy!
If you enjoyed, please leave a review.
They *really* do help a lot.

Join my newsletter here to keep updated on more books coming, go to www.tijansbooks.com

RESOURCES

https://www.crisistextline.org/
Text 741741 from anywhere in the USA to text with a trained Crisis Counselor.

https://suicidepreventionlifeline.org
Call 1-800-273-8255 or if you go on their website, you can chat online.

For more facts about suicide prevention and warning signals, go to http://www.211bigbend.org/nationalsuicidepreventionlifeline
or call 1-800-273-TALK

RESOURCES

ACKNOWLEDGMENTS

I know someone who is/was/took on the lost child role in her family. She had no idea, but once she did, it was an eye opening experience for her. What Rain experienced when she found out the term for how she grew up was what this person experienced as well.

At the same time, I went to my first NHL hockey game last year and was blown away. I fell in love. And over the year, as I would go to the NHL games and experience the fun and how alive those games are and then have a front row seat to how this person was learning about what the lost child role was and how she *wasn't* alone, the entire experience stuck with me.

Rain and Tyler's story came out of it.

I'd like to thank the Minnesota Wild for giving me that joy and I'd like to honor anyone who might've grown up feeling as if they were also in the lost child role within their family.

There is help available. You are not alone. And, you matter.

Thank you, as well, to my readers. Your support is and has been immeasurable. I've said it before and I'll say it again: you guys help me to continue writing.

Thank you to my editor, beta readers, and proofreaders. Your hard work is appreciated so much.

Thank you to Debra and to Tami for both of your support and laughs.

And, as always, thank you to Bailey. I couldn't get through a day without my 11-year-old pup snuggles. Or, you know, just to generally devote my entire day to whatever Bailey needs to keep that smile on his face and his tail to wag.

I love you, Bailey.

ALSO BY TIJAN

Similar Sports Romances

The Not-Outcast (adult professional hockey)

Teardrop Shot (adult professional basketball)

Pine River (high school, MMA)

Ryan's Bed (high school, basketball)

Hockey With Benefits (college hockey)

Enemies (college, professional football)

Hate To Love You (college football)

Rich Prick (high school soccer)

Fallen Crest Series (high school to professional football)

Nate (adult ballet)

My Anti-Hero (adult professional football)

Fallen Crest Series

Books in this series:

Fallen Crest High

Fallen Crest Family

Fallen Crest Public

Fallen Fourth Down

Fallen Crest University

Logan Kade

Fallen Crest Home

Fallen Crest Forever

Kade

Mason

(Mason is a prequel novella and can be read at any point. For new readers, Fallen Crest High is intended to be the first book read.

For a complete list on extras and novellas, and also the reading order for all books set in the Fallen Crest/Roussou/Frisco world, go here.

Fallen Crest/Roussou Universe

Fallen Crest Series

Crew Series (Bren/Cross)

The Boy I Grew Up With (Heather/Channing standalone)

Rich Prick (Blaise/Aspen standalone)

Hockey With Benefits (Cruz/Mara standalone)

Nate (Nate/Quincey standalone)

Aveke (Zeke/Ava standalone)

A Kade Christmas

My Anti-Hero (Brett/Billie standalone)

Frisco (Shane/Kali standalone)

Kade

Motorcycle club romance:

Kess (short story)

Frisco (standalone)

Hot Biker Neighbor (novella)

If you wanted to read more about the Red Demon's history mentioned, check out:

The Boy I Grew Up With

Crew Princess

Always Crew

Series:

Broken and Screwed Series (YA/NA)

Jaded Series (YA/NA suspense)

Davy Harwood Series (paranormal)

Carter Reed Series (mafia)

The Insiders

The Kings Of New York Series (mafia)

Mafia Romance:

Cole

Bennett Mafia

Jonah Bennett

Canary

The Kings Of New York Series

Frisco

Paranormal Standalones and Series:

Evil

Micaela's Big Bad

The Tracker

Davy Harwood Series (paranormal)

Young Adult Standalones:

Ryan's Bed

A Whole New Crowd

Brady Remington Landed Me in Jail

Rich Prick

Pine River

College Standalones:

Antistepbrother

Kian

Enemies

Hockey With Benefits

Hate To Love You

Contemporary Romances:
Bad Boy Brody

Home Tears

Fighter

Rockstar Romance Standalone:

Sustain

Christmas novellas:

A Kade Christmas

A Christmas Song (Ryan's Bed holiday novella)

More books to come!

THE NOT-OUTCAST
CHAPTER 1

I was lit, weak, and horny.

That was not a good combination for me. Usually my willpower was strong, like industrial-strength super-latexed condom strong, but not tonight. Tonight, the combination of the booze and cocktails had melded together and taken down my last holdouts of willpower. I was gonzo and then I got this text.

Dean: Mustang party! Now! Where r u???

Dean was my colleague, but let's forget about why he would be texting me because we are not 'texting' colleagues. Kansas City Mustangs. That was the important part of that text, and it was getting all of my attention.

Dear God. I could hear the whistle of the impending bomb right before it hit.

That was the professional hockey team that *he* played on.

Party.

Did I mention the *he* that was him? He, as in the only rookie drafted for Kansas City's newer team? He signed his contract after he had one year at Silvard.

The *he* that the team's owners were hoping could be grown into one of the NHL's newest stars, but that'd been a three-year plan. Nope. *He* had different ideas because once he hit the ice in their first debut game, he scored a hat trick in the first period. First. Period. Playing against five to ten-year veterans, and that had not gone unnoticed. By everyone. After that *he* exploded into the NHL scene and in a big fucking way.

They started calling him Reaper Ryder after that.

It was the same *he* that I perved on during a brief stint in high school, and then again during that one year in college before he got whisked away to superstardom. Though, he didn't know any of that 411 about my perving habits.

The second text from Dean gave us the address where to go, and the whistle got louder, target hit...direct implosion.

It was two blocks away.

He was two blocks away, and there went my restraint because I'd kept away from him for the last four years when I moved to the same city he was living in—of course he didn't know that—but this city was totally amazeballs by the way.

I was doomed. I might as well start digging my own bunker at this rate because I was already downtown partaking in some celebratory boozetails, so here we were. Here I was, well *we* because I wasn't alone. My main girl since Silvard days, Sasha, was on my right, and Melanie on my left. Melanie came after Silvard, but that didn't matter. She was one of my girls. The three of us. We were awesomesauce, and we were walking into this building that looked like a downtown loft, one that was probably the humble abode to someone not so humble, but someone with old-money wealth who enjoyed partaking in their own boozetails as well.

I already felt a whole kemosabe camaraderie with whoever owned this joint.

"This place is *fucking* awesome."

That was Melanie. She enjoyed coffee, girls, and she was an amazing barista at Dino's Beans.

"Girl."

That was Sasha. She owned a strip club, told everyone she was an angry Russian, even though there wasn't one Russian strand of DNA in her body, and she enjoyed using one word for everything. That's not to say she didn't speak more than one-word answers, but those were her go-to for speaking.

"Whoa." That was me.

Melanie had jet-black hair. Sasha had ice-queen white hair, and me—I was the in between. My hair was usually a dusty blonde color, but today it looked a bit more lighter than dusty blonde. I still enjoyed it, and I also had super chill electric-blue eyes. The other two both had dark eyes so I figured I was still the 'in between' for the eyes, too.

When we entered that party, all eyes turned to us, and not one of us was fazed. We were used to it. Where we went, we got attention. Guys loved us (sometimes), girls hated us (usually), and we didn't care (ever). We weren't going to tone down our awesomeness because of their insecurities.

But we were all works in progress, or at least I was.

I was known to have entire conversations and whole other worlds and every version of apocalypses in my head. That was just me. You'll understand the more you get to know me, but trust me when I say that I'm a lot better than I used to be. Meds, therapy, and a dead junkie mother will do that to you.

But enough about me.

Melanie was the shit, and she really loved the word 'fuck.' A-*fucking*-lot.

Then there was Sasha, she'd been my roommate from college, and here we were, three years out of graduation (well, four for me since I graduated early, and don't ask me how that happened because it still shocked the hell out of me) and going strong. But we were on a mission.

That mission was more boozetails.

There were people everywhere. Stuffy people. One woman who had a tiara on her head. There were guys in suits, some in hella expensive suits, and tuxedos, too.

Whoa.

This wasn't just a party party. This was like a whole shindig party.

Fake Stanley Cups were placed all around with mucho dinero inside.

Crap.

I started to mentally shift through the emails—easier said than done when one was halfway to boozeopolis—that I liked to avoid and I was remembering some of the subject lines of those that I had skipped. There'd been a bunch from Dean lately, though, and one was about some 'Celebrity PR for Come Our Way' and I needed to double down on the crapattitude because I had a feeling we just waltzed into a fundraiser.

"Cheyenne!"

Dean rushed over to us, holding a boozetail in one hand, and his eyes glazed over. He was medium height with a more squat build that he easily could buff up more, but I didn't think Dean went to the gym. He was always at work and because of that, I usually saw him with his hair all messed up. That's how it was now, and his eyes glazed over.

My dude coworker was lit.

I started smiling, but then no. Not good. What corporate espionage was he up to by telling me to come here?

"Where's the bar, Deano?" Melanie.

I was impressed she hadn't used her favorite word.

"There." Directions from Sasha and like that, both my buds moved away.

I settled back, knowing they'd have my back. They'd be bringing the boozetails to me—even better—so I had the time to grin at Dean. "What's happening, hot stuff?"

He never got my quotes. Or jokes.

He didn't react and he grabbed my arm. "Have you read my emails?" Then he looked at me, his head moving back an inch. "What are you wearing?"

Nothing appropriate for a work event, that's for sure.

But I only upped my grin wattage. "I was going for a Daenerys theme. Felt like wanting to tame some dragons tonight." Except I took my own liberty with the outfit. Instead of her flowing robes and dresses, I was wearing a leather, almost corset-like top, one that wrapped around my neck and hung off one of my shoulders. The bottom was more Daenerys theme, a chiffon skirt with a slit up one thigh. And high heels strapped to my feet.

It shouldn't work, but it did. It so totally did, and I had woven colored threads in my hair so they were swinging free, free and lit.

He took another step back, looking me up and down again.

"You are," a pause, "something."

I scowled. "Dude. Insulting."

He had to blink a few times because he hadn't realized I spoke again, then he refocused. "Wait. You're downtown. There's no way you could've gotten here this fast, even if you were at the shelter, but I know you weren't at the shelter. And your place is an hour out."

Case in point, my outfit.

He was right.

Come Our Way. The name of our kitchen had been a marketing and genius ploy, one put in place by Deano himself, because while I wrote the grant that got us five million (not a common thing to happen for a start-up) and got us going, his job was actually to work on marketing and promotions to keep the money, spotlight, and volunteers streaming to our little kitchen. I maintained our grant, and I helped with literally everything else. I was the final say-so on all executive decisions, except for matters that we needed the board to oversee. We had another full-time staff member, but she liked to Netflix and chill (and really Netflix and chill with wine, not the other Netflix and chill) on her evenings. But all three of us manned our little kitchen that fed a lot of the downtown homeless in our corner in Kansas City.

And Dean knew I wasn't known for one to partake in alcoholic libations, but we were here, and I was thirsty.

It was my last day on my medication vacation. I was taking advantage of it.

It was a thing that happened to help cut down on build-up immunity. Sometimes I enjoyed it, but it was usually a whole struggle to get back on and make sure everything was smooth running.

But that wasn't something I was going to think about tonight, though my brain was already starting to go there. Tomorrow I'd go back to living almost like a saint.

Where were my girls with my drinkaloo?

Also, I was firmly not letting myself think of the *he* and that took mundo restraint because he had been a big major part of my daydreams since my junior year in high school through now—especially now since I've been living in the city where he was hockey royalty.

I didn't answer Dean, but spying another Stanley Cup filled with cash, I asked instead, "What's the funding for?"

"Oh!" He perked up, throwing his head back and finishing his drink. A waitress walked by with a tray loaded with fully filled champagne flutes. He snagged two, for himself. "That's why I'm here. I got the final acceptance that the Mustangs are going to dedicate an entire two days to Come Our Way. Two days, Cheyenne. Two days? Can you believe that?" He leaned in, excited, and I could smell how excited he was.

Booze breath. It's a thing.

I edged back a step. "Totally."

So not totally.

"That's awesome."

Really so not awesome.

It was a great PR day for the kitchen and for the team, I was sure that's why they agreed to do it. It wasn't uncommon for Come Our Way to have local celebrities pop in for a day or an hour to volunteer, but the media that followed them was always too much for me. I either stayed in the back kitchen, or I took a personal day. Media days were something *extra* extra. Flashing cameras. Razor-sharp reporters. Sometimes you got a good one who just wanted to spread good news about our mission, but sometimes you got the reporters who wanted to swing things to a more controversial article for the click-baits.

I wasn't down for that poundage.

Plus, the extra buzz in the entire building was like hay fever for my meds. I couldn't handle it, and therapy had taught me to avoid those types of situations, so hence why I usually disappeared—and if the entire team was coming for two days, it'd be insane. I was already not looking forward to it, and yes, I wasn't letting myself think of *him* being in my place of business. At all.

I thought he'd known me in high school, but that turned out to be a result of some slight delusions from my undiagnosed hyper disorder, so that was embarrassing, and then when college rolled around, I intentionally stayed in the background. But if he was going to be at my place for two days—forty-eight hours—there's no way he wouldn't see me, and that information was already bumbling through my head like an intoxicated bee hooked on coke and champagne. It just didn't know what to do or where to sting. Super painful.

Dean was still talking. "...and that's why I'm here. They reciprocated with an invite here, and by the way, it's so on-the-down-low that there's no security outside. Did you see that? To even get in here, you had to know about it."

That made no sense.

Dean didn't care. "And I've already met half the team. Oh!" His eyes were bouncing around just like my intoxicated inner bee. "I got tickets to their game on Sunday. They rocked preseason, did you see?" He kept edging closer and closer to me the more he talked, something that was so un-Dean-like that I was having a hard time processing all this newness of what was happening around me.

Dean was around the same age as me, a few years older. Coming straight from grad school with a masters in reinvigorating the world to give a fuck about homeless and runaways, he had an axe to grind and an agenda to save the world. He liked to cut loose. You had to in our profession because burnout had the highest success rate, but seeing him this tricked out had that bee flying sideways. He didn't know if he was in my bonnet or my hair braids.

Then I remembered; Dean was a hockey fan.

I was, too, but I kept my undying adoration on the downlow like a lot of things.

Not Dean. He was out of the closet and loud and proud about his love for the Kansas City Mustangs. He also turned traitor and was a Cans fan, as well as the Polars (boo, hiss), but both those teams weren't in this current building or city. So yeah, it made sense now. He was geeking out on the full freakout reader.

That, and I was wondering how much champagne he had already consumed because he just downed both those two flutes in front of me. He was so drunk that my own lit meter was heading down into the empty zone. Not cool. Not cool, indeed, and where were my girls?

Just then, I saw one of them.

And my lit meter skyrocketed right into the red zone.

The crowd parted. I had a clear view right smack to the bar, and there she was. And she wasn't alone.

Sasha had her sultry and seductive pose out, clearly liking what she saw, gazing up at *him*.

To keep reading click The Not-Outcast
or go to www.tijansbooks.com